A.C. 2084
A UTOPIAN NOVEL

Ismail Ersevim

A.C. 2084

Published by

MELROSE BOOKS

An Imprint of Melrose Press Limited
St Thomas Place, Ely
Cambridgeshire
CB7 4GG, UK
www.melrosebooks.com

FIRST EDITION

Copyright © Ismail Ersevim 2006

The Author asserts his moral right to
be identified as the author of this work

Cover designed by Amanda Barrett Creative Design

ISBN 1 905226 22 5

All rights reserved. No part of this publication may be reproduced,
stored in a retrieval system, or transmitted, in any form or by any means
electronic, mechanical, photocopying, recording or otherwise,
without the prior permission of the publishers.

This book is sold subject to the condition that it shall not,
by way of trade or otherwise, be lent, re-sold, hired out or
otherwise circulated without the publisher's prior consent
in any form of binding or cover other than that in which
it is published and without a similar condition including this
condition being imposed on the subsequent purchaser.

Printed and bound in Great Britain by:
CPI Bath, Lower Bristol Road,
Bath, BA2 3BL, UK

**Prof. Dr.
İSMAİL H. ERSEVİM LPIBA IOM**

A.C. 2084

A Utopian Novel

(THE NEW ATLANTIS REPUBLIC)

Salute to:
More's *Utopia (1516)*
Bacon's *New Atlantis (1626)*
Orwell's *1984 (1949)*

All personal and country names are fictional, except those which are registered in the history and the literature, as cited.

A.C. 2084

My special thanks to the publishers of:
"*Utopia*", Thomas More, Penguin Classics, N.Y. 1965, N.Y.
"*1984*", George Orwell, 1984 edition, Harcourt Brace Jovanovich, N.Y.

To enlighten and give the spirit and
courage to write this little book.

Dedicated to suffering humanity!

Contents

Chapter 1 1
Chapter 2 34
Chapter 3 46
Chapter 4 49
Chapter 5 52
Chapter 6 56
Chapter 7 64
Chapter 8 69
Chapter 9 76
Chapter 10 81
Chapter 11 92
Chapter 12 100
Chapter 13 110
Chapter 14 113
Chapter 15 119
Chapter 16 123
Chapter 17 131
Chapter 18 134
Chapter 19 159
Chapter 20 162
Chapter 21 169
Chapter 22 176
Chapter 23 193
Chapter 24 199
Chapter 25 215
Chapter 26 223
Chapter 27 234
Chapter 28 249
Chapter 29 263
Chapter 30 276
Chapter 31 283
Chapter 32 303

A.C. 2084

Chapter 1

A new beginning for many

HI! My name is Ismailov the 3rd. I am the President (namely the head) of New Atlantis. You very seldom see my picture on the giant screen. Not because I am too important or too busy; on the contrary, in our republic, no one is important, or rather, everyone is equally important or unimportant (*Animus aut velimus*). I welcome you to the ceremonies for the prospective new citizens' acceptance to our union. We very seldom appear this much in the public eye. At the present moment, not only I am appearing on our giant screens, namely those of our State of New Atlantis (N.A.), but also on the televisions of the other three best-known republics of the world; namely, South-Freedom Republics (S.F.R.), Muslim-Hindu-Buddhist-Arabian Republics (M.I.B.A.R.) and the New Oceanic Republics (N.O.R.). I shall mention a while later the details of the world's new political composition. Like any historian, I would love to leave these documents to the future.

Unfortunately, due to wars, bombings and natural disasters, many valuable documents and buildings were destroyed during the 20th and the first half of the 21st centuries. After the axis of the world shifted from 23.5 degrees to 23.55 degrees to the south-east, a new 'Ice Age' occurred in the northern hemisphere (in contrast, at the South Pole, the ice mountains loosened and floating around freely). Hence, a giant glacial flood covered most parts of the northern territories of the world, namely (with their old names) the northern parts of Merica, Nada, Ounland, Gland, Orway, Weden and Beria in A.C. 2024. Simultaneously, about 500,000 square miles of territory in the National Stone Park sank altogether and vanished instantly after a very serious earthquake at 9.9 level. In addition, the old mythical Atlantis, which we call New Atlantis, re-appeared as if nothing happened to it before. An unbelievable number of people, perhaps 150 million or more, moved to

A.C. 2084

different places, settled down on small islands, known and unknown territories. Most nations' outer boundaries are not well-defined, including ours. Several of them, which had been trying to get together under different names during the past century and a half, namely, N.E.T.O., Unified Nations, Ropean Unity and alike, lost their unique political roles and importance. We understand that in A.C.1984, exactly one hundred years ago, there were three most important blocks – East Asia, Eurasia and Oceania. That did not work well because human beings had not yet learned to control their aggression and passion to win and kill, and were continuing to control others through several means such as political parties, power, 'big brotherhood', money and petroleum. They let each other suffer inhumanely under the names of liberty, freedom and democracy. Then, we got wise, as I said above, after the A.C. 2024 disasters, taking these as the last 'signs' from the Lord of Universe that we should get together and establish the most eternal, the most respectable, unity of human beings as ever could be.

Now, from the Big Screen, I see the conference room in the guest house where about two hundred and forty eight candidates have arrived from three corners of the world to be considered our citizens. You, my citizens, now please follow my opening speech to our guests. Some of my sayings shall be a repetition for you but, I am sure, they shall strengthen your immortal ties with this land. Everyone seems to be sitting quietly and attentively, 'Trans-Care' earphones on, and are about to listen to me. I am not there, of course, but on the giant screen a sixty-year *young* gentleman's smiling face is ready to embrace everybody.

"Well, ladies and gentlemen, welcome to New Atlantis, utopian land of human kind. I am about to give you the opening speech of this mutual ecstasy. Before going any further, I want to be sure that your Trans-Cares, namely language translating earphones, are working properly. In A.C.1626, on a similar island, four languages were spoken: Hebrew, Latin, Greek and Spanish. Thanks to our ultra-modern scientific achievements, the earphones, which are tailored to your own native language of German, French, Italian or Spanish, will instantly translate the words into English and vice versa. In other words, as you speak one of these languages, everyone will perceive it back in his or her own language. Is there anyone whose machine is not working? Please raise your hand! I see no sign. Good, indeed, very good. Let us continue.

Chapter I   A new beginning for many

"The first and utmost important constitutional rights you shall have are 'freedom' and 'respect' as human beings. There is no class difference here, whatsoever. Everyone, after getting through some genetic, neurological and psychological tests, shall be assigned to a certain task or job. On this continent, there is always a job for everyone at his or her own performance level. This is the constitutional rule. Everyone has to work at least eight hours a day, six days a week. There is no monetary system whatsoever on this continent; yes, I underline once more, there is no monetary system. All needs are taken care of. No one has personal property. Everything is public property. Public buildings are built like pyramids and are therefore are earthquake-proof. The height is usually 33-storeys, which only one elevator goes up to. There are no taxes and no banks. No rich companies, expensive cars and jewellery, gold and alike. According to your personal abilities and performance, you shall be registered accordingly at the State Personnel Department, work division, and shall be provided with public utilities accordingly. Electrical public transportation systems, that is to say street cars and trains, covering whole territories like a spider's web, shall pass your doors every ten minutes. No fatal exhaust fumes, no gasoline, not even natural gas. Every kind of shop for either food or goods is wide open to everyone, for free. They are open twenty-four hours a day, seven days a week. They are, in general, self-service.

"General correspondence is conducted through the watches that are on your wrists and this can be projected onto the Big Screen in your home, if you wish. Push the button and read the message, that's all you have to do. Those private watches, carrying your citizenship numbers, tailored to you only, can transfer home screen material to you, should you be out for any reason or other as well as being the main communicator on this continent. Within a certain distance, when you speak to your closest ones, your personal pictures shall be projected and subsequently seen on the watches and Big Screens. So, it is advisable that every other thirty minutes or so, you push the automatic button on your wrist watch and read the message. Easy and comfortable.

"Your watch's battery is charged with an energy source that could be wind, water or organic based bio-energy. The batteries are good for 30 days only and at the end of this period, you have to exchange them at the 'Energy Supplies Exchange Stores' that are available throughout. All important telephone numbers can be registered from 01 to 99 through pushing the button. You may make calls automatically that way.

A.C. 2084

"When you have the message that you are assigned to a job, on the screen you'll receive the initial instructions and road map, timetable and the nature of the job. When you arrive at the job place, where you may or may not see the supervisor, sign in on the work-sheet. Information on where to find and how to use the necessary supplies in terms of working clothes, materials, tools and alike, is all indicated. At the end of the day, you just sign out. Your records go automatically to the State Personnel Department. If you want to work extra and gain more points to raise your collected points, simply do so. You don't have to ask anyone. If there is no extra job is available, you shall read the sign as such. Thus, we have eliminated every negative human factor that would affect your freedom and personal growth and happiness.

"As you may not have personal property, you also may not have personal books, records, astral-TV's, three-dimensional CDs, DVDs and alike. Whatever you need, you just go to one of those utility shops and get it. There, you only have to register your citizenship number and sign for it, that's all. You can keep the tools until they are broken or not working anymore, for some reason or other. Then you return them to the shops and leave them in some privately assigned 'deposit' places. No questions shall be asked. For portables like books, records, CDs etc, you may have from the shelves any 'reasonable' amount you want, and register what you take, but you can't keep them more than three months each. If you miss the returning time, you shall receive a friendly reminder from the State Personnel or Educational Department. That's all. But don't forget, these kind of reminders may, in the long run, reduce the achievement points that you collect life-long.

"As Adam's children suffered throughout centuries, here we call for peace and tranquillity. No firearms are permitted, not even bread knives can be carried. We have no Defence Ministry, soldiers, gendarmes or uniformed policemen. War is unconstitutional. In each house, attached to the dining table with a chain, there is a Magnum Directory in which you shall find the entire lists of doctors and hospitals, poison treatment centres and emergency services that serve you for free. (We keep these directories handy, just in case, since the children under 12 are not allowed to use screens and watch TV without parental consent.) The specialties and the names are registered in alphabetical order. Also, the structure of the State, functions and branches of the ministries are recorded in detail with appropriate telephone numbers. Should you need anything, push the attached button and on the screen you shall see the instructions, indicating that either you shall go to hospital or a doctor shall come to your home, or whoever his or her substitute might be. The same applies for other State services.

"Every citizen has to go through 12 years Lyceum education. This is provided at home. No school buildings, no school buses, no expensive after-school courses. Lectures are given through visual media, except for sports. There are sports arenas throughout the country where attendance is obligatory. Examinations are performed through 'Supreme-Externets', except again for sports.

"Here on this continent, due to our simple but extremely healthy life standards and style, we live long. We have an excellent healthcare network. No health insurance companies and all that jazz. When a baby is born, it gets the best care. Hospital care is mandatory. Needless to say, the care starts before the birth. Mothers are provided with free monthly check-ups prior to birth. Besides this pre-natal care, mothers are instructed at home through visual aids about the diet that they have to follow, the daily necessary physical exercises and any advice they may need. Right after the birth, the baby is checked thoroughly genetically. Through our very sensitive health policies, since I am myself a doctor, as a matter of fact a professor, almost all genetically determined and handicapped illnesses are cured through 'gen operations' at birth, even during pregnancy if and when possible. Mental sub-normalities, including all types of Mongolism, diabetes, manic-depressive illness, fragile-x-syndrome, spina bifida occulta and aperta, meningomyelocele, Arnold-Chiari malformation, malformations of Sylvian aqueduct, hydrocephalus, syringomyelia, hydromyelia, anencephaly, micrencephaly, porencephaly, microgyria, agyria, cortical heterotopia, cerebellar hypoplasia, cerebrocerebellar atrophy, cerebral cortical atrophy, subcortical and cystic encephalomalacia, Alzheimer's Disease, Huntington's Chorea and Tuberous Sclerosis are literally eradicated.

"When the child is one and a half years old, the mother goes to work. This is mandatory also. We have excellent baby day care centres throughout the continent. Care-givers are educated superbly at the child-mother care centres and associated pedagogy-child psychiatry clinics, in regard to babies' developmental levels and emotional needs.

"Here, on this continent, we don't have any import-export commerce systems. We cultivate all that we use. Clean air, green nature and stress-free life make us feel that we live in a paradise. As you may look around, you may easily see some 100, 120, even 130-year old peoples strolling about, upright. Life expectations are extended this far. Consequently, our government requires fifty active years' work in total for every citizen before he or she can obtain a right to retire. (Your earned extra achievement points may shorten this!) Once in a while, for any respectable reason, a worker may get vacation time of up to six months or so but this cannot be more than three times in a life time. When one retires, there are excellent 'Retirement Houses for Mature People' next to the sea-shore and in a three-storey dwelling. Again, No waiting list, no fees. Needless to say, there too, you are all provided with healthcare, walks, gymnasiums, exercise halls, swimming pools and tennis courts. Weekly dances, card games, family unions and do-it-yourself arts and crafts courses are also an inseparable part of daily living. Only in those retirement houses, chariots pulled by graceful horses replace the electrical systems of complex city life.

"We know well that all are still mortals. As Socrates said: 'The hour of departure has arrived and we go our ways – I to die and you to live. Which is better, God only knows.' Again, as A. Sachs had mentioned: 'Death is more universal than life; everyone dies but not everyone lives.' Anyway, if you look around, you will not see the accustomed cemeteries. Naturalised citizens may wish to send their beloved ones' bodies to their original countries; we permit this. From our beautiful port New Renfusa where you all arrived, we may sail to neighbouring or far away republics. But for those born here, when they die, and if willing, they follow our government's rules. As a principle, we utilise 'cremation grounds' to cremate the bodies and save the ashes. Cremations, of course, are the most sanitary system, definitely preventing many infectious and contagious diseases, though these are very rare. Nonetheless, the ashes are saved in private boxes, under the ground but in fully-lit rest-places where all the denominations sleep together. Yes, they rest eternally, altogether whether you are Jewish, Christian or Muslim. I advise you should visit there, just for meditation if you don't have any beloved ones there yet. At the entrance of the cremation grounds (Smasana), on one wall, you shall read one of the Sanskrit court poetries, discovered by a Buddhist scholar, Vidyakara, in A.C. 1100, and translated and published by Daniel Ingalls-Harvard Series, U.S.A., A.C. 1965, as follows:

> 'From my incarnation I infer that in a former birth,
> I surely gave you, Lord, no adoration
> From bowing to you in this birth I shall in future
> Be disincarnate and incapable of worship
> For these two sins, oh Lord, I beg forgiveness.'
> **Vidyakara**

Chapter 1 A new beginning for many

"And, on the opposing wall of the ossuary, great sayings from great Dante who, under the guidance of Beatrice and conducted by Virgilius, went to his journey through Paradise (Paradiso), Purgatory (Purgatorio) and Hell (Inferno). At the door of the latter appears:

'Per me si va nella citta dolante'
(The roads that go to the suffering city pass by from here),
'Per me si va nell'eterno dolore'
(The road that goes to the eternal suffering passes by from here),
'Per me si va tra la Perdua Gente'
(The road that exists between the lost humans passes by from here).
Dante Alighieri

"As to 'energy' issues in daily living, we favour a slogan in old America: 'No Nukes!' There is no reason to pollute the air, one of the most basic four elements of life, to destroy the nucleus of an atom that is the very essential, fundamental of human biology, make star wars and inhale the fumes either directly from such destruction or from leaking remnants of nuclear material at the bottom of the deserts or oceans, and eventually be a Hiroshima victim. No sir. Nature provided us with plenty of air that produces the wind, great oceans that provide water, and the eternal sun, ever and forever, the endless energy generator that provides light and heat. Ultra modern photo-cellular battery complexes give us enough energy to heat ourselves and use the energy for the rest of our needs.

"Now, before going any further, I would like to stop here and give you a chance to ask some questions to me, of course, if you like to. Anyone want to raise their hand?"

"Honourable Sir; my name is Raul, I am from Pain; what about after becoming a New Atlantis citizen, if I miss my home or change my mind, what chances do I have to return to my native land?"

"This is a good question. At the beginning of citizenship, there is a six-month trial period. Now, you are only a candidate. As you sign for your candidacy tomorrow, beginning the same morning, you shall receive an extensive physical and psychological evaluation – tests for skills, known and unknown to you. You shall also be given a series of vaccinations, like anti-AIDS, anti-SARS and anti-MARS. Recently, the other three world republics have been drawing attention to a new very virulent virus that seems to be brought from Mars by new travellers. Obviously it is passed not through only sexual contact but inhalation too. Here, we have to put in better controls against that. You also shall be given IQ and EQ tests. All these results shall be imprinted, along with cornea colour photos and finger prints, and a temporary citizenship number, on an I.D. card that shall allow you to enter many places. There are no locked doors on this continent and no police or security officers either. The card will enable you to enter shops, recreational places, drug stores, utility houses, etc., very readily when doors are closed."

"Sir, thank you for everything. My name is Amici, I am a Talian, and I love to travel a lot. In your constitution and governmental structure, is there any place for foreign countries' representation, like ambassadorship or commercial attaché positions, somewhere in the Terranean area? Thank you."

"My dear Amici, in sixty years of existence, we have not seen, and do not feel the need for, representation abroad. Not because we do not want to, but due to that monetary system, to cover the necessary expenses in those countries. Here we guest everyone free. Let us look at the map (*the map that is printed on the cover of the book is projected to the grand screen*) and see the spatial interrelations with the other republics.

(*A pointer, in the form of a light, follows the President's words.*) "Here is the map that is definitely known to us since the Neolithic period, presumably at the beginning of the time when settlement and civilisation, language and written systems came onto the scene. From temple stores, we began to find the conventionalised pictorial symbols which can be recognised as the prototypes of those signs which in later times stood for the names of the cities. This is how our civilisation began – with symbols and the start of the writing period.

"In short, this is the map of the last 12,000 years of human geographical history. Going along with Wegener (*pointing with the spot light to the corresponding continental boundaries of South Merica and Rica*), one day, these territories parted from each other – it was another big earthquake and the Merica continent, not being able to carry the entire north and south, plus, the glaciers covered most of the north, remained apart from Rica. That was next to the last. There was another blast on the outskirts of Gibraltar (the Mountain-of-Tarık, Ziyyad's son, named so after A.C. 711 as he passed through the strait for Spain and invaded there with only a fist-full of men 'after burning all ships behind'!) just at the beginning of the Oceanus, including Tarsessus from South Pain, Nary Islands, where a great civilization

Chapter I   A new beginning for many

existed, namely, the Nova Atlantis, this land where we are now standing on, plunged into the depth of the Oceanus. The year was A.C. 9,600. As some argue that Nova Atlantis is just the same of The New World or, old Ireland; South and North Merica, later on at the end of A.C. 1492 when the explorers landed in West Dies. If that was true, on those shores there should have seen some white-skinned ancestors and the savage explorers did not need to buy Hatton Island for 18 dollars from Redskins. Smoking and drinking should have floored the healthy owners of those virgin lands long before civilisation reached out and destroyed nature. If it were true, some archaeological remnants should have been found, somehow. So, forget it.

"I am not going to give you long detailed history of mankind, as you may already know most of that anyway. Let me give you a little bit more about the historical background of Nova Atlantis. Who told us that there was such a civilisation?

"First, Plato (A.C. 428 or 427–A.C. 348 or 347), mentioned in his first dialogue, *Timaios*, that taking famous Solon (B.C. 630–560) as a reliable source of such information, the existence of such a civilisation was present in nine-thousand-year-old Egyptian documents. The island republic was one of the most civilised ones, established just outside the Herakles Columns at Gibraltar.

"In his second dialogue, *Kritias*, Plato displays more elaborate knowledge of the mythical origins of Nova Atlantis. The island, a paradise of water and copper most probably was the extension of the famous Minos civilisation that dominated the entire Hellenistic world through myths and legends, throughout the centuries, supplying heroes and gods throughout. According to myth, an earthly woman, Kleito, Euenor's daughter, was married a god, Zeus' brother Poseidon, who was the god of all world seas. However, as time went by, general morals and life standards were so abused and had declined to such an extent due to increased immorality and lust, that Poseidon got mad (maybe he got jealous, what do you say?) and with the help of Zeus, within a night the civilisation had sunk into enraged waves of the Mediterranean Sea.

"In his first dialogue, *Timaio(s)*, Plato narrated somewhat derogatory comments about the Grecian way of life from an Egyptian priest who Stated that at the bifurcation point of the Niles, at the delta, there was a country named Saitikos that was reigned over by King Amasis. The biggest city, named Sais, where the king was born, was settled by a woman god, Neith. However, the Grecians called her Athena

A.C. 2084

(Zeus' daughter from Metis, the daughter of Oceanus and Tithys) to celebrate the victory over the Titans. She is the Goddess of Wisdom, Art, War and Peace; her symbols are a shield, spear, olive bough and owl. As she stamped her foot on the ground, the world's first olive tree sprang up. The Trojan Horse was dedicated to her. Solon frequently visited this city and during conversations observed that in comparison to those priests' deep knowledge of the universe, life and death and alike, the Grecians ashamedly knew almost nothing. Solon, to save face, spoke to them about the first human being God created: Phoroneus (Adam), of Flood, saver Deukalion and Pyrrha (Prophet Noah), several myths and the generations of his grand-children and alike. Then, one of the old priests had said to him with a gracious smile on his face: 'Aah, Solon, you Greeks are always child-like. In your land, there are no old people!' Solon asked in astonishment: 'What do you mean?' A priest replied: 'Your souls are too young. You don't have traditional ideas which ripen as times goes by. You don't have the means to survive, you are easily destroyed. The biggest disasters come through fire and water but there are other easy ways to destroy yourselves. For instance, in your home, people tell stories about a Phaeton, son of Helios (the God of Light, Son of Uranus and Mother Earth) who himself had died from the strike of a thunderbolt, when one day wanted to run the chariot of his father at the speed that he wished and couldn't, burnt everything down to dust. Yet, the truth is, there are thousands and thousands of celestial bodies in the sky and sometimes they fall to the earth and burn some parts of it. Here in Egypt, we don't have these fables and these kinds of disasters because the river of Niles, our eternal saver, through flooding saves us from them. Only a few shepherds on the tops of the mountains may die, whereas in your home, the city populations are swept away in thousands by the flood that comes from above. Here, the water spills from below, underground. Yes, Solon, the city State of Athens, to whom Athena's name was dedicated, was once one of the greatest city States before those floods – civilised and brave, a model existence with the most fair laws and civic life standards.'

"Solon, stunned, held fast to the arms of the old priest, his eyes filled with tears, and he begged him to tell him old stories about his own people, the whole truth. The priest grinned with grace and began to speak: 'OK, I shall reply your request. I do this for your sake as well as for the same goddess who had also established our own city, although one thousand years later than yours. Neith-Athena, that woman god, had set your town from a Greek hero Hephaistos who ran after HER who had laid his seeds to the earth while she was busy with building. According to the spiritual books, our city was established eight thousand years ago, yours was nine. To be honest, many of our laws, also the principles of the social structure, are borrowed from yours. First come the priests; then the other classes or categories formed among themselves, according to the jobs and skills that they were accustomed to do: shepherds, hunters, farmers and warriors. We used different war instruments, including the shield and spear, earlier than Asian nations. The laws that were passed provided the biggest harmony on earth, covering justice, style of life, sanitary precautions and medicine, sagacity and wisdom.'

"The old priest continued. 'The woman god established your city State in one of the most desirable places, with a temperate climate, believing that very intelligent men would be raised there, full of wisdom. She chose a land where knowledge and war would go hand in hand, as her personality dictated and demanded. You were so prosperous and just that we also borrowed from you a lot and here we hide that knowledge among our sacred and secret documents. In truth, old tablets indicate that one of your victories was greater than any others. Here is the story. There was a big State, beyond the Herakles Columns, in the shape of an island, named Atlantis, which filled a big part of the Oceanus, greater than the sum of Libya and Asia. Then, it was possible literally to walk through the big sea and pass through the other separate islands. Where the Columns stood, there seemed to be a small port at the entrance, but as you get out, there was a big sea. Around it, there were big lands. There was a very strong, indeed powerful, kingdom on that island. Their strong army used to assault to Europian and Asian countries, including Libya and almost part of Egypt, Tyrhenia (West of Italy). One day, the king wanted to attack your country too, to add one more glory to his achievements, maybe the greatest. However, your city State took the lead, fighting bravely against his armies and heroically saving the country heroically, before erecting a Column of Victory. Needless to say, from the Herakles Columns up to Egypt, the whole Mediterranean Sea was saved. Your king also saved a lot of slaves, giving them their freedom.'

"The priest added: 'However, after this big event, there came a big flood and a tremendously strong earthquake, and in one single night, all the big Atlantis island, including your brave fighters and beautiful lands, succumbed into the depth of the Oceanus. Muddy swamps covered many fertile fields and a part of Oceanus that even to day you can not pass through anymore.' Tears welled up in the eyes of the old priest.

"Well, what Socrates said in reality, namely beyond the legendary facts that were cited previously, in his own writings and/or Plato's 'dialogues', was: 'Every man must be his own ruler... a man should be temperate and master of himself, and ruler of his own pleasures and passions! The right order of the soul equates with temperance. Rhetoric and poetry should edify men, caring for the highest interests of the soul, other than delighting men, with giving pleasures. (One of his contemporaries, Alcimida, also said: 'All men are equal by nature. God left all men free, Nature has made no man a slave!')

"Socrates' mind raises these kind of arguments: Even a good and loyal soldier, when the time comes for self-defence or to protect the lives of his own citizens, may resort to firearms. The question is, besides the virtue of being a good soldier, should he never harm another man versus justifying and doing his job when deemed to be necessary? What makes self-defence or hurting 'enemies' – mostly fellow citizens anyway!- in wars 'just'? Does any revolution or uprising against a tyrant justify killing or harming him? Would it have been better just to have had Hitler assassinated during the Second World War, thus avoiding his killing of tens of millions of human beings?

"At about the same time, in A.C. 1943 to be exact, in the Warsaw ghetto revolt, was it 'just' to kill the wounded enemy forces? Would those men have been better if they merely suffered 'injustice' without mortaring back? Or, was this self-defence justifiable and how?

"By the same token, we can pose this question too: Is it 'just' for a law enforcement officer to find out and capture criminals via illegal means? Any 'unjust' is always absolutely in 'just'? When we let some particular criminals go un-apprehended and/or apprehended but unpunished, through wheeling and dealing or other means, political manoeuvres, being an informer himself, due to a general pardon or so solely that particular time and paricular types of crimes, how the harm done weighs? Don't we commit a crime (or perform an 'unjust') then against the people who committed the same type of crime or shall commit it at one time or another?

"So, this is why we try to block the occurrence of the precursors of crime: If you control and forbid the elements that are most likely to evoke a crime – for instance, money, the envy to possess real eState, firearms, the drinking of too much alcohol, seeing the neighbours'

Chapter 1   A new beginning for many

garden is greener than yours and alike – you reduce the chances of one being easily motivated and enslaved by insatiable envy, jealousy or greed.

"As I mentioned at the beginning of my speech, with the newest tectonic movements of the earth, at A.C. 29 February 2024, this island again surfaced in the ocean, however clean and untouched. In those years, namely the beginning of the A.C. 21st century, the civilised world, so-to-speak, was as usual just overcoming unbelievable aggression that had spread from the Mid-East territories. As you all may have read from the history books, some leaders of the Merica and Gland republics, with goodwill in their hearts, tried to bring *summum bonum* (the best) democracy and living standards to those areas. They were also willing to clean up the hidden, destructive weapons of nuclear origin. Ganistan, Rak and Ran suffered bloodshed. As we all know from psychology, aggression is contagious and invites more aggression. In those days, the world was crazy about football of every sort. The best defence is always offense, you cannot win a ball game unless you scream 'GOooooal!'. Tanks, rockets, mortars, bombs, suicide killings, promises of heaven, lust for petrol and power, grand, empty speeches for humanity and worldwide gatherings did not diminish the eternal fear, hatred and insatiable envy associated with the destruction of mankind. Mother Earth began to murmur too, producing unexpected hurricanes, cyclones, earthquakes, floods, forest fires and seasonal irregularities – unusually long rainy and hot days became an everyday story. An estrangement and not caring of others, feeling strange to even himself, insensitivities, extreme egoism, materialistic life style had become so prominent that, I am sure, one day, this time once more, Zeus, in spite of twenty some century that had brought gods down to only one -sometimes to none- bowed to the right towards the sun, moved the axis of half degree, and there we went: Glaciers moved down from the north, some five thousand acres in the National Stone Park collapsed and, most importantly, Nova Atlantis ascended to the surface. Then, please look up to the old map (pointing the new site of New Atlantis), little by little, the thinkers, the feelers, the campaigners against war and brutality, cloning, aggression, the hurting of animals, aggressive democracies and two-faced politicians, of their own free will chose to move from all over the world to this very promising land, starting with a blank page of human history since A.C. 2024. So, a new Anabasis, or a new pilgrimage, the most conscious ever, began and in ten years a new constitution had been declared here.

A.C. 2084

This was a real human victory over the weaknesses of man. I was a ten-year-old boy then and here I am now – and I love every single second of living here. (Applause! But this is too bad, it smells old world!)

"Now, if you look, here we are: New Atlantis (N.A.). This big territory is a human paradise, a self-governed, self-sufficient republic. Throughout the years, people from old Merica, Gland, Panya, Teguese, Uba, Nada, Talia, Rance, Dinavia, Lland, Gium, Enmark, Ibia, Nusia and alike, believing in our type of freedom and way of life, have got together here. Our population, as of today, namely A.C. May 31, 2084, is 16 million, 188 thousand and 767. We control birth and unnecessary over-growth; we live long and healthily; smoking and illicit drugs are forbidden.

"If we look at the other republics, on the old map you notice three other distinct conglomerations. After unsuccessful attempts by the Unified Nations and NETO, people began to make new moves and alliances, some of them to our surprise. Here, for instance (*pointing on the map with the spotlight*), Muslim-Hindu-Buddhist Allied Republics (M.H.B.A.R.), that includes Urkey – strangely enough until the unity with the prospective organisation was declined she was still on the waiting list to begin negotiations – Rak, Ran, Kistan, Ganistan, Udi Bia, Baycan, Menia, Jikistan, Menistan, Bekistan, Gyzistan, Ria, Banon, Rdan, Rabia, Gypt, Geria, Rocco, Yprus (Rael and Listin are still fighting for territorial and settlement boundaries and leadership like Alphonse Daudet's *La Chevre de Monsieur Séguin (Monsieur Séguin's Goat)*', not giving a humanly pass to pass through the strait, so far one side twenty million, the other seven and a half million dead declared. Perhaps only a new prophet could save them from that sado-masochism. Those hills are pregnant! Dia, Anka is a strange unity; but obviously they learned to overcome fighting, killing, uprising, praying and believing in a God who sent them to Heaven if they killed someone.

"Free South Republics (F.S.R.) (*pointing on the screen with the spotlight*), is a rather quiet union; we call them 'Glorious Penguins'. It covers a very large area, maybe the largest, coldest and quietest. It includes Razil, a part of Gentina, Kland Islands, Retinghausen-Scotia-Weddell seas and Tarctica; the South Rika countries, the South Rica Republics, Mali, Gascar, Central Rika Republics Ambia, Zania. They are peaceful but still in poverty. They have to struggle with corruption, money and power and lack of water and food. The powerful countries still offer them gunpowder instead of wheat. In general, they look like inactive volcanoes that erupt every thirty years or so.

"The last but not the least is New Oceanic Republics (N.O.R.), perhaps the most powerful and resourceful, including (***pointing out with the spotlight***) old nations like parts of Ina, Apan, Ivan, Rea (north and south unified in A.C. 2054), Golya, Lippines, Ailand, Os, Nam, Bodia, Mosa, Lasia; the Tralia continent, Acronesia, Asmania, Lynesia, Waiian Islands; and large seas, the South Cific Ocean, Asman Sea and a large part of Great Oceanus.

"Of course, between these, there are several small and large monarchies and republics, old and new, which try to live peacefully and respectfully, but still in an old fashion way, with commerce, money, illicit drugs, bribery, drug trafficking and every kind of mafia: Woman, land, politics -even the mafia mafia- and power sttrugle is still on the scene. Fortunately, these three big republics don't fight each other on a large scale because they know there would not be a winner and that it would be the end of mankind. As for the small republics, they still race cars, sell and exchange gold for firearms and celebrate their victories over their neighbours who have a bare existence. Of course, crocodiles laugh at them. But, life is a matter of choice, no one is superior to the other, we all are God's children, Amen.

"So, after this short briefing, to answer the gentleman who asked the original question whether a goodwill ambassador or political representative could be initiated in those friendly, brotherly countries, I am afraid not because, you may know by now, money, expenses, travel, parties and champagne that are unknowingly exchanged with the blood of poor and lonely people would mislead human beings again. When are we going to learn from the past? We, however, correspond with them through e-mails, exchange some permissible scientific data and goodwill anniversaries and alike, but that's all. Yes, you sir!

"Yes sir; could we bring our relatives, parents, to visit us once in a while? My name is Abdallah, I am from Ria."

"Good question. The answer is in principal 'yes' but just for a week after at least five years. We have an excellent guest house – where now you are residing – for the parents too. I would like to remind you again that we do not have any attractive gifts, goods, furs, cars, even postcards. Of course they would bring any personal belongings for themselves.

"Sir, what about sex? Oh, my name is Smith and I am from Many. I mean, I am a bachelor and over twenty five years of age. In your State how can a single man or woman satisfy that natural need?"

"Very good, indeed very good. Well, young people between the ages of 18 and 21, of both sexes, may attend parties, dances and go for dates or so under supervision. Over 21, however, if one is not in education and for some reason or other is not married, you automatically become eligible for membership of a 'bachelors without partners' group. Then, if everything goes alright, with the consent of a 'sexual relations team' composed of a nurse, a gynaecologist and a psychologist or psychiatrist, and taking the necessary precautions, you may have intimate relations if you want to. You have to report once in a while how things are going.

"As far as human rights are concerned, as I said before, males and females are equal to each other; nothing like as they say in old countries 'but sometimes some males are more equal than the females'. We do not endorse old Mormon practices in old Merica, nor some Lamik exercises which involve having more than one wife at the same time. Women need not be humiliated and deserve more respect than that."

"What about religious practices sir? My name is Mohammed and I am from Geria. Is there any governmental control over them?"

"For religious needs, incidentally, we are quite generous and in the neutral-positive corner. We, first of all, don't have any controls over anything, it is just a compulsive meticulousness on our part, just to take care of our citizens properly. Throughout the country, you may observe beautiful Christian churches standing solemnly side by side that could be of Catholic, Protestant, Presbyterian, Unitarian, Seven-Day Adventists or Born-again-Christian denominations, as well as Muslim mosques, Jewish temples, Buddhist or Taoist and Lamaian worship centres. After the age of 13, we urge everyone to attend to meditation classes and receive their mantras accordingly. This is a mandatory practice. As you well know, meditation is one of the best, maybe alone the best, vehicles to nurture yourself and develop a very reliable and trustable sense of self. It lowers all psychological and physical distresses and makes you a dignified, spotless person.

"As you might have learned so far, the 'talking screen' is our main communication vehicle. At the beginning, it may be bothersome to some of you to be seen and/or listened to all the time and seem somewhat embarrassing. There is noting to be embarrassed about, since if you are not doing wrong and anything different to that which a respectful citizen would and should do, why should any of us feel

Chapter I   A new beginning for many

so? There is a kind of protection after every limitation for your own good. When I was a small child, my father used to complain a lot, almost all the time, when in the old country we were at the bank and each time the bank clerk used to ask for I.D. He used to react badly, saying: 'How long I have been your customer? Don't you know me? Don't you ever trust me? Why I should assume to be someone else?' The clerk, with a nice smile, responded as usual: 'For your own protection my dear, your own good!' We say the same, 'for your own protection!', and are sure that there is no kind of maliciousness since everything is open and we are at your service. So, this is also for your good. You don't have to be self-conscious about it. Through 'just' listening, we are not taking any action against anyone, except if anything is unconstitutional, namely when there is a real danger of nullifying this union. Do the nude people feel embarrassed in the nudist camps since everyone is nude? No, never. Oh, I almost forgot, even though the religious ceremonies, too, are all 'screened', namely 'projected to the screens' for the benefit of the people who may not be able to attend to the temples, one exception is the meditation classes and/or practices since they belong only to you. There, you are refining yourself, whatever you think is yours. You share your thoughts and feelings with your Sanskrit supervisors anyway. Don't forget, all screen messages and recordings are automatically erased after ten years.

"I cordially invite you, as I very frequently do, to visit and participate in the Jewish Cabbala centres. These are a quiet treasure, giving you a chance to transit from an earthly life and way of thinking to a deep, mystical, ascending, lighted way of living and thinking. They started about 135 years ago in Hilie, in South Merica, and passed and spread through Gland and all other countries. Historian Gershom Scholem wrote a book, named *Major Trends in Jewish Mysticism* in A.C. 1946 as a first masterpiece in that. Anyway, it helps you to establish a direct contact with the creator rather than using some other spiritual leaders, rabbis or others. I shall give more details about this to you some other time. Of course, as many have asked me in the past, you also may ask 'If there is no money business in the country, what the hell are the Jewish people are doing here?' I really don't know, you have to ask this of them yourselves.

"Sir, my name is Dominic, and I am from Razil. What about if anyone commits a crime, for example stealing, lying, murdering and alike, how do you handle that should it occur? You have said you do not have policemen and jails, so I assume you do not have prisons either. How does your judiciary system work?"

"This is also a good question. Look, Dominic, envy, if abundant and out of control, is one of the most powerful means of directing human beings to be harmful to themselves and others. Where does envy come from?

"According to Melanie Klein, one of the foremost believers and practitioners of the Freudian concept of human psychology who lived at the beginning and during A.C. 20th Century, 'envy' is the most potent factor in undermining feelings of love and gratitude. She writes in her *Envy and Gratitude*, 'I consider that envy, is an oral-sadistic and anal-sadistic expression of destructive impulses, operative from the beginning of life, and that it has a constitutional basis'. According to Abraham – who was her analyst and mentor – a constitutional element in the strength of oral impulses is linked with the aetiology of manic-depressive illness. Envy is an angry feeling that another person possesses and enjoys something desirable. 'Jealousy' is based on envy but involves a relation to at least two people; it is mainly concerned with love that the subject feels (the love a baby feels for its mother, in fact for her breast!) is his due and has been taken away, or is in danger of being taken away, from him by his rival (usually, father or another sibling!). 'Greed' is an impetuous and insatiable craving, exceeding what the subject needs and what the object is able and willing to give. Jealousy involves a fear of losing what it has, envy is pain at seeing another have that which it wants for itself. 'Gratitude', therefore, is closely bound up with generosity.

"See what Shakespeare said in his *Othello*:

> 'But jealous souls will not be answer'd so;
> They are not were jealous for the cause,
> But jealous for they are jealous; 'tis a monster
> Begot upon himself, born on itself.'

"That indicates that the envious person is insatiable, he can never be satisfied. There are also close connections between jealousy, greed and envy. Shakespeare, however, does not differentiate:

> 'Oh beware my Lord of jealousy;
> It is the green-eyed monster which doth mock
> The meat it feeds on...'

"However, since we are away from any materialism and money,

jewellery, gambling, commerce, illicit drugs and trading women, and most importantly you citizens choose this way of living of your free will, the chances are, and have been, that our people do not commit crimes. You don't have to steal one loaf of bread to feed your hungry family as Hugo's Jean Valjean had done more than two hundred years ago. Under the rules, how can you get drunk, lose control and hurt some neighbours of yours? How you could bribe the people to commit a crime to get a higher job when all personal abilities and achievements, and public service records, are open and available for an easy inspection? You don't buy and sell for personal benefit and you are at the service of other brothers and sisters – how can you cheat people?

"As a last chapter, even though they are described in detail in your *Magnum Directory* at home, I would like to give the highlights of our governmental structure and how it works. As I said before, New Atlantis is a republic and has its own constitution, accepted and declared in A.C. 2034. It has one President and six ministers who are elected for ten-year terms. No political parties. What would the politics be about? The President, with no assistant, is the overall supervisor of the existing six departments: Dept. of Administration & Personnel; Dept. of Education & Research; Dept. of Health; Dept. of Agriculture & Industry; Dept. of Energy, Transportation & Communications; and Dept. of Engineering, Construction & Repair. The ministers and I are elected through computers, after a long and painful search and evaluation; that is to say, the sum of one's physical, psychological and social skills and public work and achievements throughout years, in a mathematical truth, are electronically compiled and calculated and the points are presented right in front of you. This way, you know who you are getting. These records are open to everyone and when the right time comes, the whole nation, in a genuine curiosity and respect, sits down in front of their Big Screens and happily watches what kind of elite people are coming to executive levels of management to serve them for the next ten years. No bright speeches, debates, empty promises, no false votes or alike. No one could be elected more than twice in a row. For example, next year there is going to be an election again. The Election Day is a national holiday, only one day, that's all we have. We don't have to have the glorifying ceremonies for the young people who, in essence for our own envies, wrong calculations and aggressive drives and selfishness, went into senseless wars, killed many and also in many cases got killed, and then talked

A.C. 2084

about Independence day and similar celebrations. For we did not save this country from anyone. God gave it to us as a gift and he ordered: Work, work and work. So we do.

"Now, is permit me to make a brief assessment of the previous systems that were offered, either on a fantasy and ideological or reality basis, and why they did not work completely as they should have done. Needless to say, my comments are just after-the-fact evaluations and not a criticism in the true sense for human beings would do what they could do. They did their best in the circumstances of those days, otherwise if the old-time emperors or conquerors, Hannibal or Attila the Hun, were armed with today's advances, the map of the world could have been quite different.

"Now, let us take that great man, a Statesman, a lawmaker and legislator, one-time House Speaker, a good human, Thomas More (A.C. 1478 – A.C. 1535). As you may know as well – if you don't, you may have the copy of his books from our libraries for free – he was the contemporary of great Erasmus, a good friend with whom he even shared a translated book from Latin, *Menoppus Goes to Hell*. Due to his hard and honest work, he was even elevated to be the private counsellor to Henry VIII, the famous king of England then. Seeing how human beings are treated and how they should be, especially being witness to the political illegalities and inhumanities in his high position, he created a 'Utopia Land' and a city of 'Amaurote', located at the side of the 'Anhydrus' river (A.C. 1516). Due to his position, he had to write it 'as if a very well-educated Portuguese sailor, a Raphael Hythlodaeus, who travelled all around the world and narrated to More what he had seen and what he himself lived through for five years as a citizen of such a land. He had to do it this way, just to protect himself, as if this was just a story. No question he was affected by religion; for instance, Raphael in Hebrew means 'God has healed', and Hythlodaeus, 'Nonsenso', a person who does not make any sense. He was famous then as a joker, making 'fun of everything'. By the same token, 'Anhydrus' means 'no water' and 'Utopia', 'no place'. He well knew then that it was impossible to create such a place for good human beings for in reality life was quite harsh for decent people like himself. What happened to him in his private life? Well, since he had refused to take an oath impinging the Pope's authority and upholding the King Henry VIII's divorce from his eighth wife, Catherine of Aragon, he was imprisoned and finally beheaded. It took only four hundred more years for Thomas More to be elevated to the sainthOod.

"Thus, regardless what his critics did say about him, whether he wanted to implant a Catholic soul in everyone, his work was one of the moral allegories or what he created was a political manifesto and/or to lay the seeds of communism far ahead of his time (Are you kidding, four hundred years ahead!), he had sensed that human beings could be treated better – by themselves – more honourably, use a greater sense of humour and still live in dignified ways.

"More's hero Nonsenso's imaginary travels that started from a port called Cape Frio had some basis in reality, too, as famous traveller Americo Vespucci had also departed from the same port in A.C. 1504 with twenty men. The number of accompanying explorers appears to be so small for such an expedition that it might seem unbelievable to some young people. Now, let us examine the basic living principals of More's Utopia and compare them with our system.

"Utopians have their own new alphabet and new tongue. That probably made reading more interesting and exciting as in our youth, in the old land, there was a current toward creating a new language, called Esperanto, meaning 'hope'. Secret things could be coded among lovers or friends to make the things private and unspoiled. However, in public life that did not work. Today, if a nation or union is defined as 'sharing the mutual history and fate as well as cultural values, using a language to communicate, living on a designated land with boundaries' and alike, it becomes necessary to utilise the already-known communication channels regardless of how much they might be modulated in different ways due to technical advances. As a scientist, I would also like to add a very important scientific point to this view. During human growth, namely in the early years of child development, say between the ages of nine months and two and a half years old, the human brain is constantly stimulated by the child's effort to converse, to internalise, to express, to symbolise the external stimuli in the shape of speech, behaviour and, later on, thoughts and creativities. Thus, adult speech that is utilised in an almost automatic fashion is the end result of a longstanding psycho-social and neurological growth and development in which the brain cells and communication neurons that are necessary to make connections amongst the various brain centres that register, develop and send different messages to form abstract thinking, thoughts and creativity. Thus, it is a very difficult phenomenon to communicate sensibly, using creative, highly technical pieces of words – that are developed late, without emotional connections at the beginnings – with emotional echoes, to develop an insight and create meaningful communication later in life. If such practices should have lasted at least three generations, newborns could be able to make some connections and emotional inner images that are common to everyone, nonetheless to the people in the same culture that could be brought out together as mutual language. Thus, after the individual has completed his growth and development, to create a meaningful communication through some artificial symbols that don't have any emotional implants within, it becomes just a burden, an artificial and most of the time useless vehicle with no real advance. Plus, it also may create a sense of split, estrangement to self and others as well.

"That's why we chose a very advanced scientific system to communicate. Through ear-phones (Trans-Care), one thinks and feels in your own native language in which the brain is trained – sayings are instantly translated into the other person's or his/her own language and thought-perceptual systems. Currently, we are able to deal with five languages but our language specialists are working on five more. Naturally, that's why we promote immigration, and with newcomers in the near future we shall then be able to help others too.

"Even though presently Sir Francis Bacon's 'Nova Atlantis' (A.C. 1626) is not in the scope of our study and criticism in depth, since it was the start, we would like to comment that in his utopian land, the Island of Bensalem, he had advocated 'difficult immigration procedures and formalities' that we do not impose. He had imposed upon those wanted to landed there, creating a tremendous amount of anxiety and bewilderment, keeping the people on starvation for a while, not allowing them to land, letting them to be acknowledged step-by-step cautiously; starting from the land up to visiting to listen to the Principle of The Local Institute for Scientific Research, and to present his audience with two thousand ducats as a gift for listening and attending which here we all DO NOT SUBSCRIBE. We welcome you here with open arms. You all are our honourable guests and prospective citizens of this very honourable country. Money is seduction and the tool that serves only to feed the flames of envy, greed, power and destruction.

"'New Atlantis' was written late, toward the end of Bacon's life, and published posthumously. It was an unfinished romance, we would say. Principally, it recounted the story of a Solomon House, built on the Island of Bensalem, with the aim, in secret ways, to teach and learn Christian culture, perhaps a kind of recreation and relief from the loads that were occupying his mind in those days. According to William Rawley, his literary representative and orator, that 'fable was designed to exhibit a college instituted for the interpretation of nature'. He wanted to compose an excellent machinery of an ideal human congregation. The investigations of Solomon's House were sought beneath the hills, in deep caverns, pools, lakes and mighty towers that were set at the top of the mountains. It also was a house of healing and was going to provide a chance for the deep study of medicine. There, in a secret religious place called 'in God's bosom', the experts studied the colours, the smells of the perfumes and alike. According to some reliable authors, that was an illusory extension of the work that the College of Emblematic Freemasonry – that Francis Bacon was an eminent member of – which was recommending study of the mysteries of nature and science.

"Let us continue with More. His people, in that story-land, appeared to be living at a slow pace, colourless motion, with moderate encouragement to work. There, people worked just six hours a day; even though food, clothing, housing, education and health services were provided to every citizen. To us, of course, in our times more than ever, more emphasis should have been put over working. We do prescribe a welfare State. We do not punish the people who don't work. Here in the New Atlantis if there are some people who don't work, it is not because either they do not wish to work or there is not enough work but because either they are retired or sick. There are always jobs available. There, every one was wearing the same clothes, for equality reasons I presume: We lived through 1984; equality should exist in your behaviour and social actions when 'justice' is the subject. As we said previously, you can wear anything you wish, provided that your status is plausible and respectable with the circumstances that you are in.

"As to sex matters, the prohibitions and punishments in the case of customs and laws being broken were very severe, however commensurate with Tudor English days' religious practices and social commitments. In this subject, 'pre-marital intercourse' was punished by compulsory celibacy for life; adultery was punished with slavery. Since our lifestyle is founded on the foundations of 'logical' – however controlled – provisions other than punitive systems, we do not give a chance for people to commit adultery. Repeating once more, many of you may not like 'wrist-watch' and 'screen' listening but declaring such wishes does not constitute proof of a crime – only doing it does that.

A.C. 2084

Thoughts and feelings are your personal properties; you may wish to express them anyway you want to provided you are not disturbing the public peace. You are only responsible for your actions. Needless to say, slavery is out of mode. If one cannot control his or her sexuality and creates fatherless or motherless parents, we do resort to surgical operation for the benefit of the rest of the free people.

"As to women's rights, as we shall point out later on, among other practices, once a month, all wives had to kneel down before their husband, confess all their sins and ask to be forgiven. (Women and children were men's property until A.C. 18th century) Here, we bow before our wives with love and devotion. And, no cloned babies, no rental mothers!

"So the things were for crime. Then, in England some 'selective' people were earning about £50,000 sterling a year while many starved on the roads and when they stole to fulfil their hunger and were caught, they were hung. This is a social injustice. Only God gives and takes.

"Now, let me give you some highlights of More's two books in this matter. In *Book One*, More is introduced to a reputable person, a Raphael Nonsenso, described as 'not a Polinesian type of sailor' by his close friend Peter Gilles, a priest, as a matter of fact, a cardinal. He is quite knowledgeable about Grecian and Latin languages (as was More himself!). He has left his property to his brother and gone on a sea voyage along with Americo Vespucci. His two favourite quotations were: 'The unburied dead covered by the sky', and, 'You can get to Heaven from anywhere!' He had travelled to Ceylon (Sri-Lanka), then to Calicut (India) and finally to the 'New Utopia World'.

"The reasons why the people had left England for this Utopia were: High prices for food that made poor people turn to thievery and become beggars; all classes of society were recklessly extravagant; farms were demolished; the rich had established monopolies in markets, robbing the poor, and no one stopped them. The people who did nothing increased tremendously in number and needed to be reduced. In brief, the very same social system which created the thieves in turn punished them for the crimes they committed. Death sentences should not have been applied due to the fact that 'God said, thou shall not kill!' Similarly, human beings were agreeing among themselves to legalise certain types of rape, adultery and perjury.

"Where was this 'Paradis'? In Persia, an autonomous, large community, named Tallstoria. Taxes were paid to the king for management expenditures. No military service, little contact with the outer world for fear of being invaded, living in the mountainous area, away from the sea, living in comfort if not in luxury, happily. If there was theft, the thief had to restore the damage with the owner of the house or business. No prison service, therefore if restitution had to be made, one had to publicly serve for the crime. (We whole-heartedly subscribe to that.) When for public use, money is necessary, volunteers do it. Convicts could also be hired for private enterprises and be whipped if they did not work hard enough. They all wore the same clothes which were easily distinguishable from others. He also carried a badge, indicating the district in which he lived. Food was provided at public expense, convicts served as servants. More had thought to apply the same system to England for it looked to be quite humane and working very well.

"Raphael, addressing the writer in a very sincere tone, commenced with: 'My Dear More' and continued with the particular stresses upon 'abolishing all private properties' and everything under the sun that 'is judged with money', thus maintaining 'fair distribution of goods among all!' If you push and create some turmoil in one part of politics, you can also cause disequilibrium in the other parts of the system. 'What is medicine for some people is poison for others – because, using a biblical saying, you can never pay Paul without robbing Peter!'

"Well, needless to say, I can applaud many parts of this system, particularly that of disowning money and public property. However, we still observe discrimination among the people with a special reference to the convicts. They are labelled with their dress and the carrying of a badge, being whipped and similar inhumane practices are still observed. There is also a discrepancy that if you don't circulate money or own any property, how and why can you pay the taxes to the king? As long as there is money circulating, you are asking for trouble. Where there are rich, that means that there are also poor. This is the social reality.

"In his *Book Two*, like *Sinbad the Sailor*, Raphael talks to More about a utopian island – in reality a crescent-like peninsula – about two hundred miles across in the middle, with a harbour which with its mouth forms a circle of five hundred miles, full of rocks and shoals. Without a utopian pilot, it is impossible to enter the harbour.

"There are 54 'splendid' big towns, called Aircastle, on the Island, 24 miles apart. Each of them is built on a gently sloping hillside, square shaped, leaning upon a River Nowater. There are stone-made, marvellous, arched bridges that connect two banks of the river to each other. There are also huge cisterns that hold extra water. Aircastles are surrounded – like in medieval times – by thick, high walls, fortified with observation towers and black houses, with frequent intervals. They are allocated to people every ten years. Attached to them, there are beautiful gardens in which one can cultivate fruit, grapes, flowers, wheat, vegetables and alike. Windows are glazed with protective linen fabrics. Here and there, the fields are ploughed by oxen, at public expense.

"An Aircastle consists of 30 houses, each containing forty adults who live under the supervision of the district controller who is also called 'styward'. Each year, twenty of those forty adults go out to the countries and new ones come in. Ten of these houses form a secondary unit that is under the supervision of the senior district controller or 'bencheater'. Each town may have at most 200 stywards and chooses its own mayor. There is a parliament, too, that is made up by mayors who are elected by public. Each town sends three representatives to the annual 'lietalk'.

"As to other details of everyday public life, they are as follows: Children are taken from the school and go into the fields, first to watch and then to work with the farmers for the benefit of the public. Other work includes that of stonemasons, blacksmiths, carpenters and that kind. There are no tailors or dressmakers for these things are done at home. They usually are of loose-fitting leather. The working day is six hours; three hours in the morning, then, a short lunch break and the other three hours in the afternoon. Since mothers also go to work, children are taken care of by foster mothers. Everyone goes to bed at 8 p.m. There is a mandatory school for children but for the grown-ups, there are public lectures in the mornings to attend.

"Gambling is regarded as a stupid, idiotic and undesirable activity, therefore is prohibited.

"Pleasures could be divided as "Mental" that comprises a philosophy of a well-spent life, full of spirits and good-will. One has to have a clear conscience and good behaviour.; and, "Physical" that consists of eating and drinking, satisfying the natural heat of the body, excretion, including sexual intercourse and rubbing and scratching to ease up the irritation and tension. Good readings, essentially from Old Greek Literature as Raphael himself thought them about the Old Greats, studying them from the original books especially about Plato,

Hippocrates' Notebooks and Galen's Handbook.

"So as far social life is concerned, the smallest unit is accepted as the 'household', consisting of the father-mother-children triangle. Each town consists of 6,000 households. Boys stay at home and as time goes by, whether he marries or not, the oldest boy is the boss at home. Girls, after getting married, move to their husbands' homes. The boys cannot marry under 21 and the girls under 18 years of age.

"An important marriage custom is this: The prospective bride, whether she is an unmarried woman or a widow, is exhibited stark naked to the prospective bridegroom by a recognised and respectable married woman and a suitable male chaperon who show the bridegroom naked to the bride. (Needless to say, to us, in our times, this is an out-of-mode unacceptable primitive exhibition, as in past centuries in some religious gatherings 'virginity control' was a big issue.) Most married couples are parted by death, except where one continuously exhibits bad behaviour and adultery. Adulterers are sentenced to the most unpleasant penal servitude. Attempted seduction is punished equally severely as actual seduction. Divorce is allowable by mutual consent, on the grounds of incompatibility, provided that both partners find new, suitable partners.

"Towns are divided in to four shopping centres where markets supply meat, bread, fruit and vegetables. There are special washing facilities that are run by the slaves. For health services, there are four hospitals located in the suburbs. Travel is permitted as groups, composed of six people. The permission is granted by the mayor. Sex is quite restricted. No ale-houses, brothels in the towns. 'Everyone has his eye on you!' Aircastles, after spending the entire products necessary for living for twelve months, that is to say corn, honey, wool, flax, timber, scarlet and purple roth, rawhide, wax, tallow, leather and livestock; after one seventh of these are given to the poor, the rest is exported.

"As to money affairs, silver and gold are rare materials here and iron is the most valuable. To prevent people of having 'funny' ideas, plates and drinking vessels are beautifully designed and simply made of glass and earthenware. On the island, there are pearls, diamonds, garnets, etc, in plenty but people don't even look upon them; however, they have the children wear them as ornaments.

"Each child receives a primary education. No one is allowed full-time education. Everyone is taught in his own language. Ethics have a tremendous meaning and worth in everyday life.

"Religion is highly respected; 'Every soul that is created by God, is immortal'.

There are several different religions on the island; also, sun-worshippers, moon-worshippers and worshippers of various planets. Most people accept the existence of a single divine power. That power is usually called 'The Parent!' Many Utopians, however, refuse to accept Christianity, but no one tries to discourage the spread of such beliefs either. When a person dies, people cherish this in a very cheerful and optimistic mood because the soul is commended to God where it belongs. After the funeral, the body is cremated. (Bravo! We do prescribe this here too, you know.) People are usually well-educated and pay no attention to omens, fortune-tellers or any of the common superstitious practices. (We, however, here, in New Atlantis do not interfere with tarot practices, Shamanistic studies and fortune-telling. Human beings had never been this much disillusioned, heartbroken and hopeless as far as the future is concerned. The 'Century of Anxiety and Hopelessness' had started right after the atomic bomb was thrown over old Japan territories, resulting in the end of hope for a decent, brotherly living, for good, A.C. 1945 on. That's why we offer a 'laissez-faire, laissez passer' policy in this respect, of course, under supervision. People have to believe in something of their own choice!

"Foreign tourists are accepted with open arms. They love to buy silver and other valuable stones but we only import iron.

"Slavery does still exist. More says: 'However we do not have any slaves by birth or buying them through slave markets or non-combat prisoners of life. They are Utopian convicts and condemned criminals who are acquired from foreign lands in large amounts.' (Well, as we mentioned above on many occasions, we don't subscribe to that. A convict or thief is always a convict or thief. Here in our State, we don't create an atmosphere where any type of crime would develop, we do not need 'bad seeds' that may potentially exist and spoil our soil.)

"Horses and oxen are our most valuable and usable animals. More States that there is a custom there. When one buys a horse with small amount of money, the horse is examined naked first but one may firmly refuse to buy it until he is firmly whipped and checked after the saddle and all the rest of harness is after taken off, to make sure that there are not any soars or wounds underneath.

"There is no formal military service. War is regarded as absolutely loathsome. It is a quite sub-human form of activity, although human beings are more addicted to that than any of the lower animals. (We also confirm this wholeheartedly and add to that 'any combination of all addictive substances'.) Even though both sexes are given military training at regular intervals, the Utopians were practically the only people on earth (by then, yes!) who appeared to fail to see 'anything glorious in war'. They do not initiate wars but do indulge in self-defence. They also feel ashamed of bloody victories. (We feel just the same here in New Atlantis. Killing justifies killing and aggression invites more aggression!)

"Well, our last study is that of Orwell's *1984*. What about it?

"Those years were indeed very tumultuous episodes of mankind. But the exact problem had started long ago. At the turn of the 20th century there began a kind of 'covert anxiety', as being demonstrated among the businessmen of New York who compulsively chose to work, work and work. Long before those times, Blaise Pascal (A.C.1623 – A.C. 1662) had described this search for diversion and steadily something to do and declared that the real reason for this social anxiety was not economical crisis and forthcoming A.C. 1929 depression, but the insecurity that humans began to feel toward the world and existence, in general. That building anxiety was turning to 'overt anxiety' from 'covert', as Auden and Camus had called it. 'What has been lost is the capacity to experience and have faith in one's self as a worthy and unique being.'

"Lynds, who had performed two studies in A.C. 1920'ies in Manhattan, N.Y. (famous Manhattan studies which described the New York executives changing lives, as outlined briefly above), States. 'Those people were afraid of something... probably of the insecurity in the face of a complicated world...' His observations were toward a retrenchment into more rigid and conservative economic and social ideologies.

"His contemporary, sociologist Robert Jay Lifton, who wrote a book about *Thought Reform and The Psychology of the Totalism* (A.C. 1961, N.Y.) had said: 'The contemporary personality is continually changing his identity. A process of numbing and an emotional withdrawal, stemming from the fear of an atomic-nuclear warfare is growing big.'

"One of the great psychiatrists of the 20th century, Rollo May, in his book *The Meaning of Anxiety*, historically, sociologically and analytically describes this phenomenon excellently (copyrighted in A.C. 1950 & 1975). A novel that was written by Wolfe and published in A.C. 1929, *You Can't Go Home Again!*, clearly illustrates this. Humans felt anxious and insecure towards the political totalitarianism and consequently began to slide and adhere to conservative ideologies. Long before Benedictus Spinosa (A.C. 1632 – A.C. 1677) had turned this escape into power. According to him, the State 'should protect its own citizens from any kind of harm'. As time went by, nations became crystallized as separate entities, first as monarchies and later on in more democratic forms that on the surface gave more liberty but deep inside, led humans to begin feeling unprotected and anxious. Thus, in the first half of the 20th century, as Paul Tillish pointed out, the cultural and religious beliefs and values began to loosen up if not get lost completely. Therefore, instead of living in fear and anxiety, it was much better to be a part of great power. Herbert Mathew had written: 'Fascism guarantees you a loaf of bread and somewhere to sleep. Even though it is a prison, it is nonetheless a safe prison. So, join in!' Is this a choice or a need? Maybe both. Just the same, as Martin Ebon had phrased: 'Communism is a product of a desperate wish to find a purpose in what seems to be confusion and emptiness'. How temporary could be, yet totalitarian regimes provided such 'sense of belonging' and a 'might'. Franklin D. ROosevelt, when chosen as President, in his acceptance speech had mentioned this in a classic 'The only thing we have to fear is fear itself!'

"The atomic bomb precipitated this anxiety as an irrecoverable, hopeless State of *eternal anxiety* that there is no hope for human beings. Hopelessness is far more effective than simple fear. Any moment something terrible can happen and you can't do anything about it. The problem then was 'how to use this fear in the development of new powers, alliances, cold wars' and alike. Thus, as Margaret Mead had indicated, man, who continually exhibits aggressive behaviour and ritualistic fighting, has constructed the cage in which he lives, through the meshes of which he views the world, has to have greater security than creatures in the wild because he is far more equipped to destroy others than those wild animals. As a matter of fact, man is the only animal who feels this helplessness and loss and the irreversible outcome of existence: death. So, humans have been creating at least two kinds of warfare that put the emphasis upon destruction/killing for its own sake: Head-hunting, cannibalism, blood feud and war games for the attainment of honours. In contrast, there is the kind of warfare which is primarily protective of the life of the group. Men killing on behalf of their women and children may be caught up in the lust of battle. The end result is that, modern leaders of States mobilise hatred as well as protection. So, we continually confuse these two essentially different types and in doing so, assume that the same set of motivations are involved in a world war.

"Sigmund Freud (A.C. 1856 – A.C. 1939) was perhaps correct in saying '... that the solution to the riddle of anxiety must cast a flood of light upon our whole mental existence ... since anxiety is the fundamental phenomenon and the central problem **of neurosis'**.

"Thus, when the world reached the year A.C. 1984, there were two giant blocks: one -so to speak – advocating a democratic way of existence, playing the role of world leadership; and the other, symbolised as a big bear, threatening a third world war, presenting more secret ways of brotherhood and utilising more rigid methods to provide safety and a sense of belonging, as Orwell had beautifully dramatised with the slogans that were lit throughout: 'WAR IS PEACE', 'FREEDOM IS SLAVERY' and 'IGNORANCE IS STRENGTH'. As if you know more, you learn more but pay the price for that. How insecure human beings are. One is listened and followed everywhere and all the time. Was it foolish? No, by no means. That was a natural evolution of mankind and a deliberate attempt to control and overcome the 'existence anxiety' that had come close to an annihilating point. In order not to suffer from that existentialistic anxiety, one has to justify aggressive drives in the way of expressing it, within and without society. Since the essential need was 'security and protection', there, there were established a series of institutions and ministries and forces, as the Ministry of Truth 'which concerned itself with news, entertainment, education and the fine arts; the Ministry of Peace 'which concerned itself with war'; and the Ministry of Love 'which maintained law and order'. That was the really frightening one. There were no windows in it at all. It was impossible to enter except on official business, and then only by penetrating a maze of barbed-wire entanglements, steel doors, and hidden machine-gun nests. The Ministry of Plenty, 'which was responsible for economic affairs' though quite often in cynical ways, demonstrated that dilemma, namely the complaining-suffering side on the one hand and the need side on the other. In Winston's personality and adventures, the wish and fear of freedom, at the expense of going through quite a series of sado-masochistic relations, ends with a compromise: To become an adjusted (?) citizen, who believes in 'two and two make five', may act as a total stranger to his most inner feelings that dominated and as a matter of fact, endangered, but also gave a meaning to his own existence. So, all values, wishes have to be justified, modulated in order just to live fearlessly. The past is considered 'dead', the future is 'unimaginable'. The sacred principles of everyday life are 'Newspeak, doubletalk and the mutability of the past'.

"Needless to say, the living standards were under any imaginable acceptable levels: stone buildings, no social interaction and plentiful mass insanity and aggression. The name of dwellings was 'Victory Mansions', in Winston's description, '...old flats, built in 1930 or whereabouts, and falling to pieces. The plaster flaked constantly from ceilings and walls, the pipes burst in every hard frost, the roof leaked whenever there was snow, the heating system was usually running at half steam when it was not closed down altogether for motives of economy...' Hear this casual excitement: 'In the far distance, a helicopter skimmed down between the roofs, hovered for an instant like a bluebottle, and darted away again with a curving flight. It was that Police Patrol, snooping into people's windows.' Some war goes on but no one knows exactly where and why, and some prisoners are hung. Usually there was rationing of many foods, chocolate was an extravagant piece of such celebrities. Winston has heard that 'the chocolate ration was to be reduced from thirty grams to twenty at the present week'. Right at that moment, 'telescreen was giving forth an ear-splitting whistle which continued on the same note for thirty seconds. It was sevenfifteen, getting-up time for office workers. Winston wrenched his body out of bed – naked, for a member of the Outer Party (working class, in contrast to Inner Party, ruling class) like him received only three thousand clothing coupons annually and a suit of pyjamas was six hundred – and seized a dingy singlet and a pair of shorts that were lying across a chair.'

"Winston, Orwell's hero, thought just for a while and wrote down: 'Down with Big Brother. Down with Big Brother,' filling half a page. 'He could not help feeling a twinge of panic. It was absurd, since the writing of those particular words was not more dangerous than the initial act of opening the diary; but for a moment he was tempted to tear out the spoiled pages and abandon the entire enterprise altogether. But he did not do so, however, because he knew that it was useless. Whether he wrote 'Down with Big Brother', or whether he refrained from writing it, made no difference. Whether he went on with the diary, or whether he did not go on with it, made no difference. The Thought Police would get him just the same.'

"Thus, by that date, there were three distinct States – Oceania, East Asia and Eurasia – whose boundaries were not too clear, and many small nations tried to survive on their own. Very little could be said about 'East Asia', beyond that it was run with oriental mysticism, beliefs and attitudes, had a tremendously cheap manpower economy orientation and a quite threatening manpower competitive resource yet to come and systematically became unified within itself."

"Well, ladies and gentlemen, my dear prospective citizens; I did not mean to give you a long lecture about the human history of the past two centuries, neither to sell or talk highly about our virtues, government style, living practices, human rights, restrictions and rules versus protection and human happiness. If it turned out to be that way, please forgive me. I wanted to lay all cards on the table before you endure long and painful evaluations from Monday morning on. Now, it is almost midnight, go to your guest rooms for a good night's sleep. Attached to your beds, you'll find small coolers that contain some vegetarian sandwiches and milk, fruit juices and alike for your midnight snacks. I wish you a very pleasant and prosperous future. See you again in six months, in finals. So long."

SUNDAY morning. I am opening my eyes with the yearning purr

Chapter 2

of our younger cat, Rocky, who is accustomed to visit our bedroom at exactly 8 a.m., of course at my wife Jada's side before the church bells strike. Since he was operated on quite early, say when he was about ten months old, even though he is six-and-a-half years old now, his voice is too thin and barely audible in spite of the fact that he is indeed a runner, jumper and chaser of his younger (she is not, but we say so anyways) twin, Cotton. He curves around my wife's covers and sidelines with her breasts which always evokes my Oedipal anxiety in spite of the fact that the king is long dead.

Nonetheless, it seems to be a sunny morning and a fresh breeze, like Rocky, snoops in from the window's *wasistas*, gently touching upon our cheeks.

"How are you my love, did you sleep well?"

"Fine," answered Jada, "I indeed feel well. How do you feel after a long and trying evening?"

"Good, indeed good."

"What is our programme to day?"

"Well, I guess after a shower and breakfast and Unitarian Church service as usual at Mega Town, I wonder would you also think about visiting the Animal World. I think it will be quite relaxing. What do you say?"

"I think it is an excellent idea. If you wish, we could visit the domestic animals part, leaving the wild animals to another time."

"I feel just the same. I don't feel wild enough to go there today and hustle, bustle with them. Let us start our morning meditation. Here I jump."

I did jump to the rug in the middle of the room while my wife

Chapter 2

remained in the bed, however sitting. As a routine we used to do some Yoga exercises, arm, leg, body movements, including lotus sitting. Then, we both sat on the bed, with our backs to the head-panel. We closed our eyes and began our daily trans-ascending meditation seance. It was a little bit hard for me since my mind was slipping easily to what kind address I had given last night. How did the newcomers take it? Any repercussions? If there were, what could they be? After several repetitions in my mind, I had to call my mantra at least three times to sweep them out. Then, the details of today's programme, then an empty but pleasant indefinable aloneness. After about 18 minutes we re-opened our eyes, feeling freshened and joyous. After exchanging kisses we rushed for washing, then my wife went to the kitchenette to prepare breakfast and I, to the door to pick up the daily news – *New Atlantis Times*.

The *New Atlantis Times*, the State's unique newspaper and a computer print-out, consists of four pages, coming out colourless and with virtually with no pictures on it. Page one summarises social and political – whatever it means – news, happenings and priorities; the second and third are on economic affairs and news on educational opportunities, research findings; and the fourth, daily Big Screen programmes. Even though one may see all these either on your watches if you use it properly and/or on your home screens. However, an old habit, genetically determined I guess, as a repetition of an historical morning habit that is coming from previous centuries, still goes on. Naturally no smoking or eating accompanies it, 'cause reading is done in your armchair and while eating your breakfast, you just eat your breakfast without burying your face into it, and, chat with your wife'.

Of course the first page was full of me. How I summarised the human psycho-social development throughout history, comparisons with previous models of living conditions and standards so on so forth. Well, obviously I have done a good job. But, I was still wondering, even though we have been doing these 'good jobs' throughout years, as a matter of fact twice a year, why had our population remained this small? Practically no one had left New Atlantis on the grounds of dissatisfaction or crime, with the added fact that life expectations were above world levels. Were we missing the ball and where? I should definitely discuss this matter with my ministers in near future.

"Honey, breakfast is ready!" shouted Jada.

We eat our meals at the kitchenette with the presence of the entire

A.C. 2084

family. So far you know me, my wife Jada and two out of three cats, the twins Rocky and Cotton. The real head of the family is a semi-Angora cat, Sweety, an eight-and-half years old white cat with classical black spots on the top of his head and almost the entirety of his tail, weighing also eight-and-a-half kilos, who might have been in search of 'between-meals' snacks long before he stood up in front of my wife and waited to be fed. He is eternally hungry and gives the impression that he has just come out of a famine. He will never drink from a still-cup but will come near a faucet and stand by in dignity until it is opened by you, then he licks it voraciously. That's why I said he is the real boss of the house. His greenish eyes are as deep as Oceanus and are so meaningful without words that when you gaze into them, it is impossible not to plunge into the depth of those labyrinths, reading a lot of myths, hearing a lot of music that is accompanied with old mythical lyres, never seen or heard before, perhaps the closest being Mendelssohn's *'Song without words'*. Rocky, is the 'most gentlemanly' of the three, guardian of the 'righteous cat behaviour' at home. That is to say, if either of the other two, particularly Sweety, does or is about to do something out of line, he will protest with a gentle jump and stern look. As if, in his previous life, he was commissioned as an officer in one of the old French palaces, may be Versailles? Cotton, who I call 'Gypsy Princess', eats whatever she finds with no objection whatsoever, for instance soya beans, cheese, olive, cake and a crust of bread that she always plays football with. When she is not paid enough attention, she scratches and scrubs the rug, like an angry goat. Rocky is also pointed with black spots on his top and towards the tail while Cotton is spotless white. So, here are they.

Well, it did not take too long to sit comfortably in the Atlantis Express that glided on the rails very smoothly, running along with the oak trees that are at least fifty years old aligning both sides of the road saluting us. I pushed the button on the side panel of the wagon: Music – Mozart and then Oboenkonzert KV 314 – and placed my earphones, hand in hand with Jada. She also selected Mendellssoon's Rondo Capriccioso, op.14 in E, and here we go. Nearly at the finish of the music, we stopped at the Mega Station, in mid-town, and walked to the Second Unitarian Church in Unitarian Street. People were taking their places silently, after picking up their hymn books. Here was the very Reverend Langdon. We all rose and began to sing the opening hymn:

Praise to the Lord,

> the Almighty, the King of creation;
> O my soul, praise him,
> For he is thy health and salvation;
> Come, ye who hear,
> Praise him in good adoration.

Then, there came, *Praise, My Soul, The King of Heaven*:

> Praise, my soul, the King of heaven;
> To his feet thy tribute bring,
> Ransomed, healed, restored,
> Forgiven,
> Who like thee his praise should
> Sing?
> Praise him! Praise Him!
> Praise the everlasting King.

And, finally, with everlasting melodies, *Amazing Grace*:

> Amazing grace! How sweet the sound
> that saved a wretch like me.
> I once was lost but now I am found;
> Was blind but now I see.
>
> The Lord has promised good to me,
> His word my hope secures;
> He will my shield and portion be
> As long as life endures.

The offering speech the reverend had chosen was a very illuminating one: What is human happiness, where are we coming from and where are we going to? What was the meaning of human existence and whom were we serving: God? Ourselves? What indeed had Jesus Christ told about human happiness? We listened to this sagacious and very learned man in almost ecstasy. Right after the service, at the parish hall, while serving some light drinks and sweets, people as usual began to group to plan how to spend the afternoon and evening meaningfully; some wanted to go to the shore and watch the dolphins; some, like us, wanted to go to the Animal World; some planned to gather in the evening for a mutual outing at the designated places of

A.C. 2084

Mega Forest.

I am, indeed, very fond of Reverend Langdon and this Unitarian Church for personal reasons. I had mentioned about my father previously, just once, that we had arrived here right at the 10th anniversary of the settlement here, on the island, and the exact year that the constitution had been signed. I was only ten years old then. As I had also mentioned somewhere, I am a physician, psychiatrist and child analyst, as my grand-father was. My father used to say I was 'exactly like him': I am a very hard-working person, honest, talkative and somewhat creative, a good administrator; constantly reading and sometimes writing. My grandfather was a real wizard however; besides medicine, he had finished two conservatories, was professor of psychology at three universities, had written several books about almost every subject, including poetry, religion and anthropology, Shamanism and alike; and had converted into Unitarianism while being in Rica. He had married and divorced many times, obviously seeking eternal peace and tranquillity through constant search. I dearly love him and adore him immensely; my late father, besides leaving his own ashes to me in his will, had also left to me his ash-box, personal notes and memoirs but, for some reason or other, in spite of the fact that they are just under my hands, in a safe, I still am in a kind of anxiety that I cannot detect why, I just cannot open it. Maybe one day, yes, maybe one day.

As to my father, he was a graduate of business administration in which he had a master's degree in Rica and was very much involved with computers whereas I am very limited in those skills and utilisation of them. He was a rather quiet type of person, however emanating a sense of security and easiness wherever he was present. When he was the head of the Department of Administration and Personnel, starting from A.C. 2034 until his death in A.C. 2053, he had helped Reverend Langdon who himself was a very young man, having been just come from Gland, to build up this church. He was also on the board of directors of it, as long as he lived. So, he had given one of my grandfather's poems to the reverend who was kind enough to hang it in a gilded wooden frame that is still hung in the parish hall where we are having our snacks and drinks now. It goes like this:

GOD IS IN ME!

Chapter 2

God is in me,
I am Unitarian.

Sometimes I wonder,
How God looks like?
I would like to touch Him,
sit on His lap, hold His hands,
play with His beard, and
listen to Creation stories
of the World;
the wisdom that He gave to coyote
to create me, you and all.

When I feel Him in me,
I am warm and free,
As free as
a Rainbow Gypsy;
Reading palms, telling fortunes,
singing and dancing.
My heart then
is full of cobalt blue.

When I don't feel Him in me,
I am cold and distant,
as many as millions of eon years.
Then I am scared of Evil
who may take over my soul.

I, humble human me,
hence offer a reconciliation
to God and to the Evil
for an eternal peace
for me, for you, for all.

God is in me,
God is Unitarian.

Ismailov
My dad had worked very hard for many years to realise European

unity. However, he did not have too much success. He used to worry for 'humanity' constantly, tears in his eyes most of the time. He used to say: "It may sound a Utopian dream but one day, yes one day, it will come true. We will get together as one nation in the whole world, hand in hand." Carrying the same feelings, although in much more settled ways, my granddad had written a poem on the subject and handed it over to my dad. My father, due respect to him, always carried that poem in his briefcase, hoping that one day their mutual dream would come true. Here is how it goes:

UNITED STATES OF EUROPE

I had a dream the other night,
in which
I was sailing "dans la mouche"
with my French cousin
all along Seine, in Paris.
Then, in Hamburg
eating at McDonald's
with my German brother-in-law.

I visited my grandparents' graveyards,
in Tessaloniki, Greece;
also Gevgili, Yugoslavia
at my step-mother's beloved homeland.

My blue-eyed nieces, distant cousins,
of Swedish, Norwegian beauties;
Polish peasants, Hungarian barons and gypsies,
red-cheeked Irish girls who still rhyme
McCormack songs;
Blue-jeaned Russian comrades,
strolling along Blue Danube or Volga,
all "Hello!" to you;
"Hasta Manana" to the widows,
of the bull-fighters of Seville, and,
"Amore" to "Tutti ragazze della Roma".

Thus, time seems to arrive

Chapter 2

> to sing along, hand-in-hand;
> "Allons, enfants de L'Europe
> "Le jour de l'union est arrivé!"
> **Ismailov**

We left the church with inner feelings closer to the sky and to ourselves at the same time.

The train took another 23 minutes to reach the Animal World. There were carriages for retired elderly people readily available to take them inside the Animal World rides while we chose to walk along in the shadows amid mildly bitter odours of pines. There were signs on the screens, throughout: WELCOME TO PETS' WORLD, WELCOME TO OURSELVES / IF YOU LOVE PETS, YOU LOVE YOURSELVES AND GOD LOVES YOU TOO/ DID YOU KISS YOUR PET TO DAY? Even some poetry:

> Come my beautiful cat,
> onto my loving heart!
> Guy de Maupassant and alike.

About ten acres of territory is devoted to cats, dogs, horses, little pets like gerbils, rats and turtles; there is also a very special bird house.

Just before entering the dog houses, here is the world masterpiece, *Epitaph to a Dog*, by Lord Byron:

> Near this spot
> Are deposited the Remains
> Of one
> Who possessed Beauty
> Without Vanity,
> Strength without Insolence,
> Courage without Ferocity,
> And all the Virtues of Man
> Without his Vices.
>
> This praise, which would be unmeaning flattery
> If inscribed over Human Ashes,
> Is but a just tribute to the Memory of
> "Boatswain," a Dog
> Who was born at Newfoundland,

A.C. 2084

May, 1803,
And died at Newstead Abbey
Nov. 18, 1808.

While walking around, we met a family, obviously one of the newcomers, a young mother and father holding a five-to-six year old girl by the hand, who has no ear-phones and looking around in astonishment. When she told her family,
"Zot gan!" (this: the zoo), I jumped:
"Brukhim ha-baim!" (You are welcome!). She opened her eyes more, was surprised.
"Ma shimka?" (What is your name?). A little bit embarrassed, she murmured:
"Sarah!" I got encouraged, presenting my wife to her and her family, I said:
"Shimi Ismailov, zooi ishti Jada. Toda, shalom!" (My name is Ismailov, here is my wife Jada. Thank you, good day!). We left them behind, smiling. What a good feeling it was to surprise and welcome that little innocent Jewish girl.

Even though we appreciate the others too, our love is with cats primarily, as you already may have guessed. Here the cats live in groups in wooden two-storey houses, a large garden at the front, side-by-side. On each house, right at the entrance, there is a sign indicating the race and origin of that group of cats, like 'Longhair Breeds' and 'Shorthair Breeds', as two big sorts. Then, a particular floor or the entire house may be allocated to Himalayan, Birman, Turkish Angora or Van, Norwegian Forest, Javanese, Persian, Tiffany cats for longhaired ones, and British Short Hair, American Short Hair, Maine Coon, Egyptian Mau, Siamese, Scottish Fold, for shorthaired ones. The State's pet is the Abyssinian-Utopia Cat. Room corners are decorated with thin mattresses, crossed with colourful blue, yellow, white and red ribbons; meal plates and water cups are placed beside their beds. Each of them has his or her own sand box. In their sleeping time, there is always light music. Strangely enough, according to pet care givers, the most liked melodies among cats had been found to be that of Edward Grieg's *Lyric Pieces, Op.43*, and *Heart Wounds, Op.14 – The Last Fall*. Many love Vivaldi's concertos and go right to sleep, regardless of how upset they might have been previously.

There are three full-time veterinarians who live in the grounds and enough care-givers. Each of them is vaccinated regularly, yearly, against Feline Rhinotracheitis Calici, Feline Panleukopenia and rabies, regardless. This is State law. When you come to visit here, the care-takers tell you which ones have to be "just watched, observed", which ones to play with. No feeding is allowed since this is already well taken care of.

When I used to teach at the Mega University, in the Geriatric Psychiatry Department, I used to get some volunteers to take cats (and sometimes dogs and caged birds too) to the sick elderly people to calm them down and sometimes remind them of old good days, at least twice a week, one and a half hours each, as 'pet therapy' hours. That was good for both the children who brought them to the aged and for the aged who, through loving them, appreciated their own happy childhoods.

Freud was the first one to indicate the relation of the child to animals that had its roots in the earliest existence of man: the primitive man. He admires them as free-willed creatures, free to their bones to do whatever they want to do – as he himself wishes to – and through taking care of a pet, a child is repeating his own personal developmental stages (ontogenesis), repeating his own being taken care of. A pet gives the child an insensitive, sometimes, unrealistic delusion: One day he shall teach the pet how to talk and they shall share the secrets of life. Several research studies also indicated that if small children hurt animals, they cannot establish positive relations with human beings too. This early sign, along with bed-wetting and fire-setting (those are passive and active types of aggressions) may strongly suggest a forthcoming anti-social personality.

Many healthy children dream of aggression towards the animal figures in their dreams, indicating the fear that they naturally experience in their developmental years that the growing aggression inside may break through, indicating the animal side of human beings. Consequently, if he can tame a dog, he can control his own 'barking' aggression too.

Anthropologists, too, had written about how the primitive people have been 'buddies' with wild animals, like alligators which they swam with. They were 'brothers in souls'. In the Jungian psychology, that means that the animals are symbols of the embodiment of the 'shadow', the semi-demon part of our 'persona' (the mask that we have to carry through life socially); that only after that integration can we control the animal wild parts of self.

Well, let us walk about two hundred yards to the east, and see how

A.C. 2084

beautiful dog-houses are made here. Whether one likes it or not, the dogs' place is a smelly one, quite different to that of cats, however a masterpiece that was said by Coleridge a long time ago, is hung right at the entrance of Dog Country (Don't mention the Bird House yet!) to prepare you for inside.

> In Köln, a town of monks and bones,
> And pavements fanged with murderous stones
> And rags, and hags, and hideous wenches
> I counted two and seventy stenches.
> All well defined, and several stinks.

Of course, these are said to illuminate how smells, odours or scents do offer a paradise to a dog for not only does it smell them but it also tastes them through saliva where they dissolve. A dog, different to a horse, when given extra gifts of food – titbits – can appreciate these as a reward for either a coming event or one it has already achieved. A horse, when given some sugar cubes and its head caressed, can also perceive this as an appreciation but cannot connect with a performance. A horse does not mind being approached when it is fed while a dog, even a good-tempered one, does get bothered when approached during feeding. By the same token, a dog is quite nervous and difficult when he is hungry or starving. As to sleep patterns, dogs are 'intermediate polyphasic', meaning that they sleep all day along and night, if given the chance, with intervals. Cats (and also night birds) are 'polyphasic': namely, they sleep about 16 hours a day with some intervals of activity, mainly preferring to sleep. Men and birds are alike. Dogs, like birds, hear very well even from far distances and are also able to determine the direction of the sounds.

That's why, as you know well, dogs are the best company for the blind and the hunter. Here, in New Atlantis, we have a few kinds of dogs but not so many, for hunting is forbidden and since we do not need to protect the sheep and cattle, we preserve a few kinds just for friendship and the beauty of them. We cultivate Huskies, Pyrenean Mountain Dogs, Elkhounds and Toy Spaniels.

We breed the animals here but just to keep their races going. Therefore, both for the cats and dogs, we just maintain a certain balance as far as the total number is concerned. Our surgical procedures, which are of course performed by the qualified veterinarians are quite in order and are also at the service of our citizens, at different places as Pet Care Centres throughout the island. Even though we are one of the least travelling republics on earth, just in case, if a family is willing to visit their parents in old countries and they possess some animals at home, their animals are well taken care of – as guests – in those pet shelters. Needless to say, as far as home animals are concerned, besides free medical check-ups, all food and nourishment materials are supplied free by the government. No private enterprise. No pet selling and buying, like slaves!

On returning, we were a little bit tired, but what pleasant tiredness it was. Obviously, the sun was also tired of shining and greeting all of us. After another peaceful meditating period we were in our beds, sleeping comfortably. So were the cats.
TODAY is Monday. As we have been saying from the very beginning,

Chapter 3

today is the beginning of the evaluation of the newcomers. They are going first to gather at the Personnel Department, then, as groups, shall be forwarded to the hospitals for physical check-ups, lab studies, blood and urinalysis and alike; then, personality and performance tests to determine what their aptitudes could be. Needless to say, our social workers shall lead them wherever they are supposed to go and do.

So, I myself too am going to be with Mr. Keith Gleem for a while. Mr. Gleem is the Minister of Administration and Personnel. With the shining morning sun, I got up and after performing clean-up routines, with my portable Mega-Jasper under my arm, here we go. After a few minutes walk, here I am at the 18th floor of Pyramid A, the first of the Atlantis Mega Pyramids.

"Good morning Keith!"

"Good morning Mr. President!"

"I am sure you have all statistics of these 248 newcomers. I would like to study them with you and make some temporary plans."

"Naturally. Please open your Mega-Jasper, and connect to our Knowledge Bank. Please push the buttons KN-BK-IMMIG-com. Good. Now, let us follow them together.

First, as usual, we organised them according to the sexes: 148 males, 120 females who have 84 children – 44 males and 40 females, ages ranging from 8 to 15. All young families. That leaves 32 bachelors, of whom 25 are males and 7, females. In general this trend seems to be good, because more families are arriving with children than single adventurers, fortune hunters. This is a 43percent higher ratio than for the last immigration. However, this situation obliges us more with child care. The oldest couple are 63 and 61 years of age respectively.

Chapter 3

The average age is 31.5, that is also very, very good.

"As to original countries where they came from, the statistics are as follows: Gland: 44, Rica: 34, Nada: 25, Veden: 20, Way: 20, Taly: 20, Pain: 18, Guese: 17, Rance: 14, Gium: 11, Razil: 10, Rael: 8 and Key: 7. That is a good mixed group. Quite international.

"According to religions: Christian: 202, Muslim: 7, Jewish: 27, Mormon: 12. No Atheists, no Buddhists this time."

"Special needs and requests: Nothing very special beyond the usual questions about child rearing, living standards, working conditions, and so on. In your speech, you already outlined almost all of them perfectly clearly. They shall find the answers on their screens. Oh, I almost forgot. A small group of five would like to establish a Masonic Lodge. As far as I know, this the first time in our history."

"A Masonic Lodge request? Indeed, interesting. We could speak about it in our Mega Cabinet meeting, maybe tomorrow, maybe later on. Well, how goes the housing?"

"Very well. We, as usual, are routinely placing them according to the family size. Singles in one-bedroom units; family with no children and with one child in two-bedroom units; family with two children in three-bedroom units, and so on so forth. From this afternoon, they shall be moving to the Mega-Pyramids 3 and 4 and card-keys will be given. At the weekend, all rooms shall be cleaned, hot running water and electricity will all be set and mega waste lines be controlled. Needless to say, starting from tomorrow morning, all the statistics cited above, plus the full names and prospective citizenship numbers of the people, that is to say starting from 16,188,768, and, ending with 16,189,015, shall be printed in our *New Atlantis Times* journal. So, you see, everything is under control, Sir."

"What are the chances for prospective job assignments?"

"Well, Mr. President, we have some openings, of course as flexible as possible, at certain numbers of general stores, two or three in animal houses, two at the crematory, twenty five for supervisorship, one at the engineering department, eight at the secretarial filing department, sixty at farms and one hundred and twenty in agricultural areas and so on. According to test results and physical examinations, we shall make a good distribution of the people according to the needs. Well, as you know this may take a few weeks. Naturally I shall report to you as soon as the results are finalised."

"Well, Keith, you are doing a superb job, as usual. You are a good person, a good man, and a good Samaritan. Naturally, we shall also publish the final classifications, assignments, everything in *Atlantis Times* too. Incidentally, your credential points are piling up and I am proud of you."

"Thank you sir. Your wonderful leadership is highly appreciated deep in our hearts."

NOW, it is Monday evening. As I worked all day and am having

Chapter 4

supper with my wife, it is time to 'review' some meetings that happen regularly on Monday evenings, as had been scheduled throughout the years. What meetings are those? Well, they are usually secular and non-secular, social organisations like community meetings to reply to any complaint or wish, Mormons, Yogists gatherings, both for practice and administrative meetings.

Before, I had mentioned that 'screens' (meaning also recordings of sights and sounds) are not done during those private sessions but for the sake of national security, we do record those at Presidential level. I, as a President, am residing at the 32nd floor of the Pyramid I. 33rd floor is designated as 'Information Gathering Lab', our famous, secretive 'I.G.L.', like old 'S.I.A.', where whatever goes on in the State boundaries are constantly recorded and continually filed. Some evenings, while my wife watches BBS Special's Home Repair Teams in old Land, I review these recordings. In fact they do not reveal too much because everything seems to be going alright. Private talks, appearances do not even touch me. In brief, in spite of the fact that the sights are not recorded but the sounds are through mega-microchips placed in the machines of their wrist watches. Everyone has to wear those watches.

Mormons' meetings had always interested me. My grandfather, who also was a professor of psychiatry, had been in old Rica for more than thirty-three years. Amongst many marriages that he indulged in, once he was married to a Mormon girl, however it lasted very briefly. My late father mentioned very little about it and, as a matter of fact, my grandfather's ashes, along with some 'very personal material' kept in a steel case, looking like a briefcase and even travelling across the

A.C. 2084

ocean, passing through generations, had come to my custody that I had mentioned before. I never bothered to open and look what they are. My impression had been that my grandfather's faith, in a very strange way, had followed certain strange lines, decisions that he had made, moves and a lot of unhappiness besides tremendous successes and alike, were in very vague ways connected with the divorce from one Mormon girl. Anyway, maybe just through some curiosity but nothing else, my interest in Mormons remained at a mediocre level, although always live.

Here on the island, the Mormon community had impressed me as hard-working, serious and responsible people, strictly following rules and regulations, as in old Merica, but in some strange ways, giving the psychologist part of me a vibe as if 'waiting the day to come!'. Strangely enough, their church's name is, as you may know, The Church of Jesus Christ of The Latter-day Saints. They are very obedient to their elders in a quite patriarchal style, they never miss Sunday masses and lunches at their fathers' houses with their families.

Anyways, after entering their temple, the screen shuts off. Now let us listen to the sounds.

"Hi George, how are you?"

"Thank you, your parents, children?"

"They are fine too. Thank you."

"Well, as I hear, there are twelve newcomers from our 'old land' (They sounded very secretive!) Could we meet them immediately and give our love and support? We need them badly" (Need badly, what does it mean?)

"Sure, Excellency, you bet!" (Excellency? What did he mean by that?)

(Some mixed-up, indistinguishable sounds, walking, steps, laughter and then):

"Well, you are welcome to our land of opportunity, togetherness, love and respect."

"Thank you honourable sir. I bring you all the warmth, greetings and good wishes of our celestial prophet. They eagerly and proudly follow your endeavours here to stay in a unity and lightful leadership of the Church of The Latter-day Saints. (Some words are not heard well.) ... sure day is coming close.... tinuing the search and chance to recover ..... whatever hand we can give you."

"There seems to be six or seven people from the meditation group who also would like to come our meetings, they say, is it permissible

Chapter 4

Your majesty? because...(nothing more is heard!) Meditation group in Mormons? What is cooking there, or am I getting paranoid as I am getting older, but of course wiser too. And, most importantly, what is this 'Excellency' business?

"Thank you, and Jesus Christ bless all of you! See all of you Monday evenings at 8.p.m."

I got goose pimples, if not a little bit startled. What did those words mean: "We badly need them...The day is coming close!" Is this the resurrection of Christ or something else? What "to continue (I guess!) the search and recover"? What is missing and what shall be recovered? Are they after anybody in particular? Again, "Excellency"? Strange but somewhat thrilling. In spite of the fact that we don't see faces, the voices recorded can later on easily be compared with live recordings and the identities of the personalities could be elicited instantly. That is not the problem; the problem is, in our very prosperous and peaceful country, why should there be a problem? What is the secret or code that they are talking about?

I turned the screen on. Newcomers, after a long and tiring examination day, appeared to be cheerfully gathering at the Mega Citizenship Hall and chatting about what went on during the day. All smiling, shaking hands and getting acquainted. Obviously, the procedures go as scheduled; they ate their supper in some place or other, and with some light music in the background, Chopin's *Polonaises* and Brahms' *Hungarian Dances 1 through 5*. People drink some fruit juices accompanied with some freshly-made cookies. Life there appears to be just in order, perhaps the best for some.

THIS morning I wanted to visit our Education Department, headed

Chapter 5

by Prof. Dr. Edith Plump. I gave her a ring, after breakfast at an appropriate time.

"Hi Edith! I am Ismailov, how are you my dear professor?"

"Oh, good morning Mr. President. I am doing very well. You know, we just finished the educational year and we are compiling the year-end test results in regard to pupils' achievement tests. What can I do for you Sir?"

"Well, if you are not that much busy, I would like to visit you within an hour or so, and would like to take your views about the children's performance and generally about the education in our republic. Your wishes and plans for the next year or so, you know."

"You are more than welcome. See you in an hour!"

"See you!"

Since we are on a relatively small island and a lowly populated State, the management of educational matters, beside the others, appears to be well under control. Also, the State boundaries are so firm and limited so that like a human ego, it becomes 'visible and viable' to manage.

As I had mentioned earlier too, since our education system works basically through supreme externet and Big Screen systems, we don't need elaborate school buildings, extra management personnel, heating, lighting and building repairs, while equally important, quite burdensome transportation problems that we nullified. Still for occasional gatherings, competitions, family-child relations, library, children's final evaluation scores and school health reports, etc., some buildings are designed that also are used as a museum where children's pictures and their art works are hung on the walls. For visual arts and

Chapter 5

stage work, auditoriums with 500 seats are available.

Therefore, for the primary and secondary education, we have three main buildings located exactly where they stand: North, Central and South Primary (and Secondary) School Centres. They are maintained with minimum up-keep personnel. Primary education is mandatory, starting at the age of six and ending at the age of eighteen. Human history, geography, physics, mathematics, languages, music, citizenship, health, gymnastics, arts and crafts and electronics constitute the curriculum. Then there are two-year craft schools and above them, university education. The dress is informal and at the choice of the children and their families.

When I visited her, Edith was on her two feet, running from one electronic machine to another. Quite contrary to her surname, she is as tiny as a little herb, of short stature, a smart brunette with large eye-glasses, always on the run. A workaholic and a chronic bachelor. We shook hands in a friendly way and sat on comfortable leather armchairs and sipped our coffees.

"Edith, shoot!"

"Well, Mr. President, really nothing new. My general complaint, rather wishful thinking, as you know well, had always been to give our students more international experience which they badly lack. I know the circumstances, of course, that if we would like to send some students of ours abroad, we would have to pay some money which we can't because we don't have it. Some time ago you touched too on seriously thinking about some 'exchange programmes', hosting and educating some, say ten, foreign students and exchanging the same? That would be perfect free propaganda for our country too, what about that?"

"Edith, very well, I am whole-heartedly behind that. Who is the chief for international affairs?"

"Brian. Brian Ahern, young, smart and a very ambitious man. He had already gotten in touch with some places in Gland and Way, but with no definite results obtained yet!"

"Let us make this project a number one priority for the coming year. I think Merica, Rance, Many, still should be under the consideration, plus S.F.R. or M.I. B.A.R., whichever could be possible. Make him prepare a colourful brochure of our land, natural and scientific works that we have accomplished, our unmatched hospitality, say ten to twenty students in sociology, international communication and alike. What else have you got on your mind?"

A.C. 2084

"Well, Sir, even though our basic principle in education is home study, except applied sciences like medicine, electronics, engineering and alike, children, particularly in their growing years, may still be in need of larger contacts with their classmates since, as you know better, they are spending too much time at home and are therefore too mechanically-orientated. Yes we do have gymnasiums, field trips, children's sport camps and alike, but they still are in need of more continuous inter-relatedness, exchange and sharing."

"Yes, Edith, we have discussed this before too. I know very well but if we increase togetherness too much, to become too close and intimate, this may lead to the children forming gangs and developing extreme and bright ideas about, say, the type of government, ambitious political games and unlimited entertainment at will. Don't you think so? Just the same concern goes for the 'student exchange programmes' too. Imagine, our clever, however innocent, children go abroad and see racing cars, yachts, private helicopters, night clubs and night adventures, drugs, the earning of money, the ownership of chateaus in Zerland, gambling casinos – with that kind of envy, we should just be the same as the rest of the world. That scares me. But, we cannot live in extreme isolation either, since one can suppress basic human ambitions, like fighting, supremacy, being at the top other than comfortably living at the same level, to a certain degree but we have to open some safety windows to breathe. The skill, of course, is how to do that!"

"You are quite right, Mr. President, we should carefully prepare more challenges and keep our statistics alive as to achievement scores on the one hand, and some anti-social activities, divorce rate or a fall in the work performance and alike, on the other. Sporting activities go well, as intellectual-mind expanding activities. Meanwhile, almost everyone is in more than two or three social-intellectual-moral-mind expanding groups, besides religious obligations and meditation, Yoga, Kabalah centres and alike. Maybe they should be more with nature and some activities like mountain climbing, scuba diving, miniature golf, horse races..."

"And, ... horse betting. Don't get that serious Edith, I am just kidding. Maybe my over-protectiveness speaks again. I don't know, I appreciate that kind of expansions but we should be quite careful and go step-by-step. What about our summer literary festival?"

"Next week I shall meet with Michael Deem, our co-ordinator and supervisor for the summer festival. On what branches we should set that up?"

"My dear Edith, you know we have not yet developed our own national style of architecture and design, a sculpting school, a well-established culture that has its own opera and music style. As you know well, these things may take up to a few hundred years to develop and mould into some kind of international integration and recognition. I suggest we again should concentrate upon poetry and short stories and advertising for stage theatrical manuscripts for the next year. After your initial meeting with Michael, please have him call me. I have particular thoughts and ideas on how we can enrich this year's programme to make it one of the best. Oh, if we can have any positive reply to our student exchange programme, we can invite them too to this festival just to give an idea of who we are and what we are. OK?"

"OK dear Ismailov. You are number one: a good leader, a good fellow and a good scholar. Oh, the newly-arrived eighty four children's evaluation studies are under way. I am sure we shall find the right place for them. God bless you. Say hello to your lovely wife Jada."

"Thanks Edith. Continue your good work. God bless you too."

This afternoon, I would like to look up my notes and in the evening give

Chapter 6

the introductory classes to the newcomers in reference to meditation, although I needed to spend some time with a research paper relating to the copper minerals on the island. We most need iron, since buildings all over are built to be earthquake-proof. However, copper, both as an element and as an amalgamation with others, has tremendous value for our future economy.

So, I went to the conference room at the guest house, this time, however, to make an opening speech on that subject. There, there were almost two hundred newcomers having crackers and refreshments in the attached small service room. They applauded me whole-heartedly. Now it was their turn to stage their ingenuity, as an appreciation for my Saturday night welcoming speech.

In our republic, meditation courses are headed by a Dr. Akhbar, formerly an internist from Akistan who has indeed devoted his life to that. He has written several books about this very fine art of the human soul, scientifically proving the existence of a close interrelatedness between meditation and a good health, life longevity, a blissful life with no sick periods. He is also associate professor in the Faculty of Internal Medicine, so we are close friends too. With his warm welcome and a brief introduction, he gave me the floor. So, I started to talk.

"Meditation, in a way, had been a way of living to me, perhaps like that of a Zens. It had been running among my family members for the last three generations and I am quite an advocate of it. True learning and practise in this celestial field require some serious studies in Social Psychiatry, Shamanism and the Analytical Psychology of Carl Gustave Jung, as well as the works of great anthropologists like Mircea Eliade and Joseph Campbell. I had also studied Sanksrit to go deeper in these personal pilgrimages. So, every other six months, when newcomers like you are in, I give the opening lessons about it and some other teachers and practitioners follow it through. Even in the mornings, when we start school classes, of course reflected on the Big Screen, we start with a meditation that is a kind of silent prayer. I never get tired of speaking about it. If you have, or you shall have children registered in classes, and, if it fits into your time, you can meditate with your kids. Believe me, it is a thrilling experience.

"Well, some schools declare that, 'Meditation, is a science of creative intelligence of mankind'. Even though we do not know whether the animals, at least the mammalians, do meditate or not, human beings do so. On the other hand, since 'science' means 'an objective system of things that if applied according to certain methodology and principals, its results could be proven everywhere just the same', in the simplest sense, such 'internal bliss' could not be put on the same measuring scale to any other abstract things, like happiness, sorrow or any quality of feeling. Therefore, it is a little bit unfair to absolute concrete sciences like mathematics, physics and chemistry to call 'meditation' just the same as 'science' as they are. Nonetheless, if applied properly, the positive results of such indulgence affect human beings so delightfully and have them ascend to the skies to eternity, so to speak, that we can be sure about its nearly scientific outcome in the service of mankind.

"A generally asked question is: 'What does meditation provide?'

"If we can look up to the nature and dynamics of life, we see one of the most essential elements of them being fulfilment. So, first, it does 'fulfil'.

"Secondly, as human beings, during everyday life struggles, due to our weaknesses, under some circumstances, we may suffer. Meditation, through using the creative intelligence, lessens the burden of suffering to a bearable degree. From another angle, meditation eases problem-solving, forcing you to locate your thoughts right in the heart of the problems.

"Through practicing it twice daily, one can enrich the reservoir of thinking, hope and problem-solving abilities, thus our creativity is constantly functioning, rewarding and ascending. Our sensory organs, also being motivated with our 'will-to learn', 'will-to experience', following the pathways of natural evolution of life, sharpen our motor-perceptual abilities, bringing us close to superior degree of performances. You can recall better, too. Through elevated self-confidence and feeling happier, one learns how to hinder the number one enemy of modern times: stress. You manipulate the environment in the service of bettering your interpersonal relationships, comradeships and sharing. You have a better knowledge of yourself and the universe around you.

"Through practising meditation, we also are entering in dialectic teaching, as Plato first described it, a technique that indicates mind reaching the idea of 'good'. It also reaches the point of studying human consciousness and having him take more and more responsibility in its management, consequently being a better human being and a better citizen.

"Of course, we are practicing 'trans-ascending meditation', coming right from the Brahmins, as described in 'Upanishads'. It refers to an 'absolute' part of **being** that is an un-manifested part of the **existence** and the basis for thought energy; also the ultimate reality of creation, the eternal truth, and what there was, what it is and what shall be. **Being** does manifest itself, primarily in the form of 'prana' (breathing) – which is the absolute of power and nature of **being,** and later on in the form of 'mind' (thinking): this is the duality of existence. **Being** is the basis for **'thinking'** and thinking is the basis for **'doing'**.

"There is no question that during meditation seances, the whole body rests up and a tremendous amount of energy is compiled. That's why, in old countries where this type is meditation is exercised, the teachers used to advise 'not to drive cars on the street right after the meditation'. Again, during the seances, the pulse, breathing, blood pressure and lactate level in the blood all fall below the normal values; in contrast, the skin's resistance is raised, which is also good.

"According to some Indian and Chinese Yogis, to inhale and exhale involves the negative and positive energy levels in the universe at any given time; thus, 'taking in' (yang) and 'taking out' (yin) are the two most essential movements that help to regulate your body electricity and have you relaxed. By the same token, according to some Indian Yogis, in the universe there is a cosmic energy (prana). When this very concentrated energy is taken in and out regularly, added with meditation, it can heal soul and body from many illnesses. At least those energies are transferred to the personal psychic energy for better use.

"Of course, there are various types of meditations since it is known from the old Roman Emperor Marcus Aurelius Antoninus (A.C. 121 – A.C. 180), who was also a poet and is very famous for his book *The Meditations* – the first on the subject which principally emphasises

Chapter 6

the Stoistic philosophy of Epictetus, and many others, including some religious currents which encourage people 'to think deeper in thought and praying', and alike are also considered as 'meditation'. What we mean here, 'just meditation in the form of meditation'; no prior ideas or anything to focus on, to clarify, to enlighten nothing at all. Your qualified teachers here, all trained and educated in Sanskrit philosophy and Eastern religions, shall meet you in small groups, giving you some instruction and knowledge of 'what to do', in fact, 'what not to do', and at the end, your 'mantras' will be given to you after small personal ceremonies held before fireplaces in old Sanskrit style.

"In addition to these, I think it will be proper to give you a little bit of knowledge about Yoga exercises and Zen Buddhism, in spite of the fact that I am neither a Yogist nor a Zen-Buddhist!

"I know very little about Zen and Zen Buddhism. What I know is through my interest in meditation and consequent reading of some related books like *How Zen Thinks?*. It is already a very quiet, personal, rather passive and self-contained occupation that does not offer too much challenge it seems to me, at least to my personality patterns which are more externalised, shared and used collectively with the people who I believe I am under obligation and to be of service. On the other hand, I confess it could be one of the most graceful methods of improving oneself if one needs it and wants to find out. I, wherever I am, try not to change anymore perhaps, but to refine more whatever I have in my hands, if I can. Nonetheless, since I am the President of New Atlantis Republic, I have an obligation to my people for what we offer here and what our thinking process and philosophy are about the philosophical, social, psychological existences and activities we offer to the people in this land.

"Zen crystallises all of the philosophy of the East. However, it is not an ordinary philosophical system, founded upon logic and analysis.

"Zen, in the sense of intellectual analysis, has nothing to teach us. One would say it is quite chaotic. It does not have any secret books or dramatic tenets. In a way, while practicing Zen, we teach ourselves and Zen merely points the way.

"Zen claims to be Buddhism. Having no philosophy and all doctrinal authority is denied; however, it is not a nihilistic, self-destructive discipline; on the contrary, it is eternally affirmative, however of what?

"Zen does not deny the existence of God but 'No God in Zen' that is neither denied nor insisted upon, as it is in the Jewish, Christian and Muslim faiths. Thus, in a strict sense, Zen is neither a religion nor a philosophy. The principles of it are rather a kind of bunch of flowers, some precious metallic or wooden pieces here and there, in a garden (of Eden?).

"Zen is the spirit of a man, Zen proponents say. He believes in the inner beauty, goodness and purity (So do all the other systems and religions). The legend says when Sakyamuni was born, he lifted one hand toward the heavens and pointed out the earth with the other, and exclaimed: 'Above the heavens and below the heavens, I alone the honoured one!' Don't you think he had referred to the uniqueness and God-like values of human existence and spirit in spite of the fact that he is mortal? To me, it carries an existentialistic value: be aware of your existence, don't question, cherish it, honour it, do whatever you can while existing!

"Zen is not confounded with a form of meditation either. Zen proposes to discipline the mind itself which he may pursue in a form of meditative style. In classical 'meditation', a man has to 'fix' his mind on something: God, infinite love; or, concentrating on any subject at all, to study deeper, to analyse, to solve whatever it might be. A Zen does not do so. To me, his practise style comes pretty close to the Maharishi's Transcendental Meditation (T.M.). However, to my knowledge, Zen does not posses a 'mantra'. Zen defies any kind of concept formation or the experiencing of any concrete feelings.

T.M. is a spontaneous process of direct perception, being a vertical action; it opens awareness little by little to deeper levels of the human mind (transcend means 'to go beyond'). The Maharishi defined mantra as a sound; however, its effects are not known. It must be suited to the individual and properly applied after a lengthy period of individual instruction and group practise, step by step.

"As we know, Buddhism means 'enlightenment', as its root word 'Budh' means 'to wake'; Buddha was a personalist and urged his followers to 'value their personal experience, above everything, of emancipating self from the bondage of birth and death', as human beings long for immortality, eternal life, liberation and absolute freedom.

"As for Zen, he seeks 'reality' and this can not be found in 'conformity'. He goes beyond formality to reality and says: 'Be the living truth itself' or, simply, 'Be!'.

"Now, just a little bit of Yoga.

"Yoga is considered by many to be a method of re-integration.

Chapter 6

No doubt, sensory impulses are thoroughly mastered. This mastery protects vital functions from dangerous interference. This is achieved by a Yogi, through going straight to the root of the most powerful instincts, controlling his vital functions through a deep knowledge of those particular processes and emotive regions of the body and the mind. On the other hand, Yoga keeps itself aloof from emotional and sentimental impulses. It abides in cold logic.

"No doubt, it is a mastery over your own 'physical' weaknesses, therefore how one would like to ascend his (or her) psychic abilities and turn to different methods of doing it, like meditation, psychotherapy, analysis and alike, one could do the same for the physical aspect of his 'being-ness'. Nonetheless, I feel strongly that Yoga and like mastery works, besides being a little bit overly used, if not abused, commercially, go beyond medical logic; care and 'repair beyond maintenance' is a little bit of a luxury for me. However, while having meditation classes, our teachers taught us some basic poses of our bodies. They were no doubt were quite useful but that's all.

"Thus, being a responsible President when it comes to my peoples' physical and mental health, I strongly suggest and endorse every legitimate endeavour to become a better person and citizen of this country. Natural human aggression that springs from our inner sources has to be controlled in artistic and aesthetic ways, particularly here in the New Atlantis State since we do not prescribe the other ways for letting out aggression first, then feeling sorry and trying to remedy it. That is a vicious cycle anyway. The importance of sports – that cannot bring any commercial benefit to anyone under our circumstances in our State – and human controlling devices, like Yoga, deserve a lot of respect.

"Thus, let me tell you a few words about the Yogi's world views and Yoga itself. The Yogi looks at daily life as a 'crisis' situation, an 'unbalanced State', originating from our ancestral unconscious, with fears and obsessions collected and transmitted from generation to generation (Jung's collective unconscious). In order to bring our planet back into 'balance', it is necessary to regain our personal balances through a nearly perfect control of the body and the mind with proper self-discipline.

"The Yogi sees life as a triangle. 'Birth' is the first corner, the starting point of this triangle; then there is a 'growth-anabolic' phase going upward, reaching the second point of the triangle; and then there is the 'decline-catabolic' phase, down to death which would not be the final point, indicating the 'life after' which deals with birth again.

"The ancient wisdom of Yoga incorporates five basic principles: proper movements (exercises), proper breathing, proper rest (relaxation), proper diet (nutrition) and deep thinking (meditation). The most modern classification of meditation poses comprises eight basic elements, including those previously mentioned:

1) Yama: The ethics.
2) Niyama: Religious observances.
3) Asana: Body postures.
4) Pranayama: Breathing exercises.
5) Prathayara: Withdrawal of senses from objects.
6) Darana: Concentration.
7) Dhyana: Meditation.
8) Samadri: Super consciousness.

"The old Chinese had a saying: 'Truly a flexible back makes a long life!'. As a medical man, I subscribe to that and also add '...brings a lot of children too!'

"Therefore, as an extension of the brain, to keep the spine well-maintained, meaning 'strong and flexible', is the most single important goal and expectation of Yoga exercises.

External massages and Prana-acupuncture that is given to the body to keep the flow of nerve energy also can keep one going quite smoothly.

"Considering the body-soul twinship, the spiritual aspect of Yoga exercises is also of prime importance since the Yogis believe the science of Yoga also gives a practical and scientifically well-prepared method of finding truth in religion (or life!).

"Thus, the Yoga exercises, step-by-step, carry through, besides their physical implications, the spiritual principals too, paralyzing -so to speak- in and outsides; via practicing Bandhas (application methods of muscular locks) and Mudras (application of Hatha Yogic postures, to maintain the nervous systems' electric currency to provide a "Serpent Power"- Kundalini Shakti); doing right breathing, modulating the sense perceptions if and when necessary, concentrating and meditating intensely; thus, reaching a better mental balance, and, at the final analysis, realising the "Supreme-Super consciousness", having the "Personal I, Ego", to merge with "God", who is undeniably a Supreme Ego.

"There are three kinds of bandhas:

1) Chin: Jalandhara bandha.
2) Anal: Moola bandha.
3) Abdominal: Uddiyana bandha.

"Only through Yogic breathing, concentrating and mudras (that latter comprises the stimulation of chakra centres located in the astral body) can one achieve 'bliss' (*ananda*). The six most important centres are:

1) Muladhara (four petals), located at the lower end of the spine.
2) Swadhisthana (six petals), located at the genital organs.
3) Manipura (ten petals), located at the navel.
4) Anahata (twelve petals), located at the heart.
5) Vishudha (sixteen petals), located at the throat.
6) Ajna (two petals), between the two eyebrows.

"A seventh one, with one thousand petals, Sahasrara, is at the centre of the brain. Needless to say, each one of these centres, from a scientific point of view, is a nerve plexus.

"Lastly, as technical information, I would like to cite 'body poses'. We were taught first, Padmasan (Lotus pose). You sit legs crossed, soles touching the opposite sides of the abdomen, knees also touching the ground, hands on the chest, as if praying.

"The others are of different combinations of the extremities. In Siddhasan, legs crossed, one is buckled under the body, right foot above and touching the body. In Mukthasan, the heels close to the pubic bone, body erect. In Vajrasan, one keeps practically the kneeling situation. Swastikasan is the ankle-lock pose; one leg is forward, the other touches the inguinal.

"There are twelve Soorya Namaskar exercises which include erecting straight up, bending to various poses, extending your limbs, being on one or both of them, completely buckling down to the earth while putting your palms adhered to it. Of course these movements include inhalation and exhalation exercises and indeed stage a nearly perfect human gymnastic show: Healthy and mighty.

"So, I tell all of you: Pratinandati Nirvanam (Welcome Bliss!)

Chapter 7

AS I have been elected, electronically, 'President' of the New Atlantis Republic, naturally I have taken leave of absence from the Mega University of New Atlantis. Consequently, except for a few occasions when I give some guest lectures in my specialty of child and adult psychiatry, I usually satisfy my professional needs through the Health Department of the republic that is headed by Prof. Dr. Debra Thin. So, today, Wednesday morning, I am going to make a visit to her which has always been a pleasure. Even though I am expected, I gave a ring to this delightful lady, one of the easiest going persons on the earth. Full of joy, a voice replied:

"Hello? Oh, your picture just appeared on my watch. Yes my dear President, how are you? I am waiting for you with coffee and *millefeuille* pastry. Exactly at 10 a.m. *Au-revoir!*"

Debra, who for some reason or other does not like to be called Debbie, is tall, robust, quite the contrary to what her surname may suggest, a talkative, creative, joyous person. She has one weakness: sweets. Wherever she goes or whoever she invites, one should be on a sugar-restricted regime two days prior to that visit, otherwise you may go into diabetic coma. She herself makes cookies, decorates them, and joyfully shares them with you. She is so warm and insistent that no one can refuse her. Her husband, who was a microbiology professor, had died about ten years ago due to an unknown infection while working at the research lab and national mourning was declared for him. Having no child, she seems to give herself completely to work, day and night, however without losing her rich sociability.

Here we are. Debra also is at the Pyramid A Apartments, 18th floor, however at the east side, opposite the Personnel Department that occupies the west side. So, in two minutes, I was in her office. This

Chapter 7

is the advanced civilization. You do not need a car being driven by a private chauffeur who is gossiping behind you anyway and at nights takes the car for bar adventures, gasoline expense, a parking place, air pollution – you name it. You walk if you can, if the place is far, then you take an electrical streetcar. No tickets, no turnstiles, no sleepy workers complaining and expecting a wage increase every other three months. Anyway, there I am.

Before going into future plans about our republic's health programme, let me give you a brief sketch about how our health system works. First of all, there is no private enterprise, rich middle men who only care about money, drug firms and intriguing pharmaceutical biddings. There are two systems that provide health care: university and the State. On the island we have only one university, New Atlantis University, which was founded about twenty five years ago. Its major divisions are Faculty of Medicine, Faculty of Law, Faculty of Economy, Faculty of Engineering and Electronics, Faculty of Literature and Languages, Faculty of Education, Faculty of Agriculture and Mining.

The Faculty of Medicine gives a six-year education, both in theory and practice, and then three to four years specialty training. The only difference from other places on the earth is that if anyone is choosing to go further to become a specialist, the first year has to be spent in the 'Research' department of the faculty, with special training in electronics (that naturally covers the computer) and communication, statistics, languages, music and philosophy. We have one teaching hospital where we accept the patients too. Each faculty has one professor and chairman, one associate professor, two specialist head assistants and enough assistants. They are assigned to the medical apartments close by the hospital building, in the same block, within walking distance. Needless to say, the hospital gives twenty-four-hour service, around the clock. The waiting list is unheard of. There are constantly two doctors on duty in each branch, with proper supervisors being on 'second call'. There are out-patient departments that are run six days a week.

The State has one seventeen-storey high, again Pyramid-like, general hospital, covering all specialties. There are four fully-designed operating rooms with well-trained staff. Service is continually provided. On the first floor, there is one State pharmacy that gives necessary drugs for free to the patients who may come from private doctors, university or State hospitals or health centres. The first floor is occupied by administration, education, conference room, doctors'

65

offices, laboratories, etc. The second floor is entirely devoted to geriatrics that we will mention about it a while later. The third floor is for children. The paediatrics unit contains everything imaginable in it. The fourth floor is the psychiatric unit. Child psychiatry occupies a special section downstairs on the third floor with the other children in paediatrics. So it goes up, covering all specialty fields. Private physicians give free services, eight hours a day, six days a week, in their assigned parts of the State.

There are two fully-staffed health centres at the two corners of the island. They take care of emergencies as well as hospitalisations of short duration. Seriously ill patients and the ones who require more sophisticated care are transferred immediately to the centre.

"Well, Debra, what's up?

"Mr. President, you know we have been working seriously on the aging process and doing quite exploratory research on it. In the fall, I would like to make a two-day symposium on aging and reveal all our findings on it. But if I can summarise now in a few sentences. The primary stage of the research is almost completed. As you know, we were applying the internationally-known approaches to see where we are standing. Classically, in any research, as far as the methodology is concerned, the first approach is the 'biological' one. So, we did what everyone had done before. Namely, we also used non-vertebrates like Cephaloids, examining their eyes, and comparing them with mammalians and noting the differences through aging. Senescence increases death rates, we already know that, but with what intervals and with what differences and sequences?

"The second one is the 'physiologic' approach. In that we continue to work on rats and guinea pigs. Between, sometimes you find interesting things like snakes in which the fertility increases as age advances, in contrast to birds, fowl for example, in which it decreases, as expected. The third method is, as is well-known and is perhaps the most important, to 'study of the aging of the cells' themselves. For Protozoas' lives, we theoretically may say they are eternal, because when a cell is divided and as a result is rejuvenated, it never dies, it keeps multiplying, bringing out new and young generations. (She laughed) I don't know whether one can do this in human beings, because we are not only the composition of cell systems but also of the ability to synthesise the enzymes and hormones, connective tissue fibres; Incidentally, our 'basic-cell proliferation methods', too, are in advance. That relies upon the replacement embryonic healthy cells to replace the deadly carcinogous

Chapter 7

cells that are already destroyed by chemotherapy.

"In the arena of prevention, we do measure the vibration of capillary networks in the body through our mega-magnetic vibrators that reflect the results instantly on the screen. Any vibration that is higher than 200 vibrations/per second, draws the attention to those capillaries for further electronic tomographic studies to detect infections, extreme congestions, beginning of hyperplasic movements, who knows.

"In leukaemia and alike blood cancers, the 'implantation of bone marrow' is amongst the routines. Intravenous 'basal-cell transformation' has within the last eight years or so been replaced by the direct 'intrathecal injections' that don't produce shocks, resulting in considerable advances and recoveries.

"Poly-flu vaccinations have within the last twenty years or so virtually annihilated deaths from grippe in the old age population "Debra my dear, what about the 'sensory studies' that you were making of the elderly?

"Well, one of my chief assistants is still working on that. According to the length of life in old times, they used to say 'all sensory abilities diminish as senescence starts at the age of 65'. Since our lives now go to 100, 110 or even 120 years, our initial findings indicate that the first sign of senescence – that is the decrease of eyesight – is above international levels here, say at about the ages of 79, even 83. The electroencephalic changes that also occur, even by the age of 55, do not become obvious by the age of 79 or 80. Strangely enough, the hearing impairment is on the increase in spite of the fact that here we are living in a less noisy and less stressful situation. The reason might be a relative social isolation and less (negative) stimuli in the social life of the elderly, near isolation. If and when we shall be coming close to be affirmative as far as the results are concerned, then perhaps, in elderly or retirement homes, we could create more stimulation and consequently more of an invitation to life. That could be music, choral work, nature studies and trips, etc. We do quite a bit of Audubon travelling and bird-watching, however it may not be enough.

"Excellent Debra, excellent!"

"Well, you are our leader. You taught all these to us."

"What about old Raymond Pearl's TIAL (Total Immediate Ancestral Longevity) Index? Since it is obtained through the addition of the ages of the person's ancestors, adding about four to five grandparents' ages and so on, and obviously we do not live long enough in this land, do you think to make some changes in this system, like using other scales?"

"Well, Professor Ismailov, we are just compiling the basic information about the individuals and their parents who are coming close to being grandparents. We measure bone length, the developmental scales as to when the child starts to teethe, to walk, to talk, to function in a physically superior way, if that is the case, in what areas and alike, and then compare and evaluate those with psycho-social abilities and performances, plus life style. We are far from the final results but we are working on it."

"What about cancer research and new advances?"

"Working hand in hand with the Research Department of the University, Prof. Dr. Timurov, we found that we are having nearly excellent results with the 'freezing' technique in soft tissue cancer operations since it does minimise the bleeding and spread of the cancer tissue particles; and the 'modified robot laser technique' in more solid cancers, like those of the proState and lung. With 'modified-AIDS TIII' virus extracts that we had injected into proState cancers we have had 99percent success so far. Very good results are also obtained in colon cancers. That relies upon the 'self-destruction' theory, you know."

"Since we do not smoke in this land, we are at the top, rather than the bottom, of lung cancer distribution and rates in the world due to smoking and toxic substances. But, as you always say, we do not forget that 'the older person is the product of the culture', so, we are focusing heavily on the dynamics and ingredients of those psycho-social factors. One day we expect to win an Obel prize for our gerentologic studies, I believe."

"Excellent, Debra. I am sure we shall have gigantic progress with the preventive part of serious illnesses but death, at least for now, is still inescapable. Future studies should be focused upon 'mutations in chromosomes and major genes' and 'cellular aging' in which discovering some chemical mysteries, our prevention may come to a maximum level. Well, thanks a lot for this scientific feast."

"But you know, a feast can not be completed without some fresh pastry and juice, *n'est-ce pas?*"

"*Oui madame, avec plaisure.*"

You see, how sweet it is to work with Prof. Debra Thin.

THIS evening – that is Wednesday evening – after spending all my

Chapter 8

afternoon in the Mega Sports Centre where I did some gymnastics, that is to say, a short walk of one and a half kilometres, and then had a ping-pong match with one of the youngsters that was a delightful experience, I took my bath, or rather had my sauna, had a medium-sized vegetable sandwich and super de-caffeinated coffee, sweetened with herbal chocolate, lay on a chaise-long under a chestnut tree in the backyard and lounged into thoughts. How life was beautiful if one knows how to manage it properly and not misuse it. The order in nature is so high and perfect, consequently how difficult it is to displace, disarrange and molest it? How can one disarrange these beautiful trees, acacias, linden trees, myrtles and chestnuts, the serenity, green grass and chirping birds? Who can match their melodies? Just watch and enjoy this harmony and bliss. You don't need to analyse and make some idiotic comments, pseudo-philosophies about life and all the other matters; don't be a fool, just lay down, look up to the skies, then close your eyes and just meditate. Don't talk and disturb nature's eternal symphony!

This evening, I am going to the Shamanistic Study Centre in downtown headed by Ibn-ul Kadeem, who has been a real devotee on this very sublime subject. He is about fifty years old, always dressed in his Indian shawls and special cap, wrapped with a turban's sash, lined up with turquoise blue bids around it. A round, well-kept black beard with greyish touches that rightly gives him a sage-virtuous man appearance, always smiling and sincere. One of his grandparents had come from Raq, the other from Ran, before emigrating to Akistan, then studying Shamanism in Mongolia, Kırghyzistan and Tajikistan, then finally settling down with us. He knows my ancestral education and interest, as well as mine in this field, and as happens in some other fields, he leaves the opening lectures up to me. He always salutes me with a polite bow and addresses me as 'your honourable Excellency!' So, there I go.

As I arrived at the centre a few minutes before 8 p.m. I received a very warm welcome. About one hundred and fifty newcomers and another two hundred to two hundred fifty participants had filled the auditorium ahead of the scheduled time, that is to say 8 p.m. After introducing me briefly, as usual as "My Honourable Excellency, Professor Dr. Ismailov!" and so on and so forth, a flood of applause caressed my ego, to tell the truth. Being a humble man, instead of standing behind the desk, I sat on the edge of the stage, swinging my legs freely. From there, I started to talk.

"I personally had very little interest in Shamanism other than some anthropological courses that I had taken when I was studying the symbolism, stealth and belief systems in primitive societies, and of course under the influence of Freudian and Jungian write-ups about the origins and development of religions. But in my family, again my celebrated grandfather Prof. Dr. Sailor, while being trained abroad, had had some years studying Shamanism in Ale University, and later on upon returning to his native land, he had given some courses and demonstrations at the Municipal Theatre and even published a book about it. Since in this land I am the only experienced and knowledgeable psychiatric professor and no one else had shown any real interest in this subject since I am sure the others who are living on other continents and islands were too busy with money making. So I would like to initiate some classes here and in due time, I am sure we shall find more chances to have some exchange students trained more in old continents and may train us here. Meantime, I am utilising my grandfather's notes and experiences and our mega-internet library.

"At any rate, for all practical purposes we could say, Shamanism is the original religion of Siberian people, primarily of Yakuts, Mongols, Tatars, Buryats and alike, mostly Turkish clans, before Mohammedinism. The Shaman, the person who represented this religion, was a kind of medicine man, a magician, a curer, a priest and an adviser to the chief of the tribe. However, I would like to underline from the very beginning that one could look at the Shamanistic stage as the beginnings of the settlement of clan life in the society that could be found in the world almost everywhere then, in North and South Merica continents, Indonesia, Oceania and elsewhere in spite of the fact that there was no direct communication and acknowledgement of these existences between them.

"The Shaman may also have an epileptic crisis, an ecstatic State during which he believes his soul leaves his body and ascends to the sky or descends to the underworld. As we know, these experiences are not restricted to the Shamans, some prophets and persons, as reported, had also had similar experiences. He also has 'helping spirits'. He is in touch with dead souls and spirits but he never becomes controlled by them. He can mediate the individual's private gods, celestial or infernal, bring the person's soul back which was angry or put out by him, consequently leaving him and having him feel sick. The Shaman's main tools are his mask and, most importantly, his drum. He travels abroad, through the clouds, beneath the earth visiting Hades, the king of dead souls, with the help of his drum. Even though he is the key man of the tribe, the Shaman may take off to live in the wilderness all by himself for long periods. He can talk to the animals, plants and the rocks.

"Let us elaborate just a little bit about talking to rocks. Usually a rock has four faces: The top that you are facing, the bottom that you face if you turn it around, the side that looks inwards and the side that looks outwards.

"You receive the rock, 'as it is', and you do not twirl it around. You should not encourage the change. Now, as a Shamanic experiment, I make you take such a rock and put it in front of you. Now, look at it carefully.

Q – What do you see?
A – Profile of a face, listening.
Q – Good. Now, you (to someone else), 'turn the rock!' (She comes and turns the rock around.) Look and say: What do you see?
A – A bird in flight... wing-like.
Q – Now, you (to someone else), turn the rock! Come and look and say: What do you see?
A –. Looks like a seal... Seal in the bowl.
Q – (To someone else): You come and tell me, what do you see?
A – (He comes slowly!) A fish with a tail.
Q – How did you arrive at those images?
A – Looks peaceful.
Q – Do you want to listen, or let it go?
A – This is a bird of flight. Let the wing span. (He lets her go!)
"If you are running the show, repeat all the original questions, as

simplified above, then repeat all the answers. If anyone does not remember, the Shaman helps to remind them. 'Images' usually give some symbol messages, like:

Face: Quieten down and listen!
Bird: Freedom – let go!
Seal: Be playful. Communicate this to the original question.
Fish. To move with insurance. Flow!

"In Shamanistic studies, one has to be able to read 'the signs' too: circles; openings and holes in the rocks and trees, i.e. getting old, repetitions, mythical, secret caverns, underworld dead souls, sorrow and alike. Do always remember what Arioli said: 'The difference between the history and myth: the myth is always right!'

"Shamanic power is said to have been inherited from ancestors, so it runs in families and is considered a family profession. Before being recognised and selected, however, a Shaman candidate has to have two kinds of teaching; one, ecstatic experiences, like dream interpretation, trance, clairvoyance; and, two, traditional Shamanistic techniques, the functions, nature and names of the spirits, secret language, speaking tongues, good enough knowledge about the mythology and genealogy of the clan which he lives in. A candidate, therefore, has to pass through some 'initiation' that is generally is public and a kind of challenge, full of rituals. These ecstatic and didactic performances make the tribe choose or not its own Shaman.

"As many ethnologists and anthropologists have studied the 'personality of the Shaman', besides possible hereditary maintenance of the post, it is clear that many tribes, clans and islanders choose their own Shaman, according to their wish and preference. First of all, many scientists looked at Siberian and Arctic Shamanism as a neurotic phenomenon, very specifically as 'Arctic Hysteria'. There, there is a cosmic milieu, polar irritation, long dark nights, lack of sun, restrictions in vitamins and green vegetables, and the expectation of the people that someone show an extraordinary performance and/or miracles. Cataleptic (frozen-like, motionless) States are very convenient to justify souls quitting bodies, going for a long voyage, journeying into the sky or underworld. Indonesian Shamanism was discovered to be a real mental sickness. The 'Niue' Shaman is an epileptic or extremely nervous person.

"Samoa Shamans are diviners. The Batak of Sumatra and

other Indonesian people choose sickly and weak individuals. In the Andaman Islands, epileptics are considered great magicians. Candidates for Shamanship among the Araucanians of Chile are always sickly, morbidly sensitive people, also having some physical diseases like cardiac and digestive system disorders and especially suffering from vertigo. Yamana of Tierra del Fuego Shamans were of hysteroid, epileptoid and ascetic people, having almost the same psychic structure as those of priests and sorcerers who preferred to study the supernatural. Many of them sang, jumped in the air for hours even days, travelled tremendous distances without feeling any tiredness that is quite specific to maniacs.

"As history recorded, Arctic and mid-Asia Shamans had risen to the clouds with their horses and created wonders. They call this tremendous power Utcha; this springs from 'celestial spirits' and is given to some Shamans as 'the divine rights'.

"Naturally, we do not mean that the Shaman is a solely sick man, but he is all above the sicknesses who had been able to survive a hostile environment full of danger and inconveniences, at the midst of natural and human-made problems, has succeeded in curing himself. In general, Siberian Shamans are considered to have good memory, good nervous controls, showing no mental disintegration and be absolutely superior to average clan people. The Talupang (of Venezuela) and Amozonian Shamans, too, are considered to be highly intelligent and in good control.

"Initiation ecstasies, visions and alike experiences are very important for a Shaman's acceptance. In the Yakuts' Shamanic system, the evil spirits may carry the future Shaman's soul to the underworld where it is supposed to stay somewhere between one and three years. The Shaman himself has to observe that the evil spirits cut his head off, torture him, dismember him and alike. He waits there for the maturation process. Sometimes a mythical bird makes the transportation back and forth, twice the life time of it. The same bird may sit in one of the gigantic trees' branches where there are some nests and the Shaman's soul stays in an incubation State for again, one-to-three years until maturation. Visions and dreams also are abundantly exercised: While playing his drum, the Shaman candidate can see himself being divided into bits and pieces, laying unconscious for seven days and nights.

"Many candidates visit some mysterious islands, cornered with seas where the Life Tree (Tree of the Lord) is erected. Next to it there are nine herbs, representatives of all the plants on the earth. He also may go for a long journey, going over high mountains, challenging wild beasts and big wild birds, representing the evil spirits from who they are dug, the head is chopped off, hands and legs are mutilated. When they bleed, they feel better, his face and hands remaining blue. Sometimes, while travelling through the underworld, the Shaman's own ancestors eat his flesh and drink his blood from his belly. Again, an anthropological marvel, in spite of the existence of a big ocean between, Siberian and Australian Shamans show a lot of likeness in these experiences and rituals.

"One of the requirements to become a Shaman is that of entering into a 'secret society'. This entrance also presupposes some rites to be performed. The mutual happening at the end is that of 'death and resurrection of the candidate'. However, before this end, the candidate has to go through a series of symbolic happenings such as a seclusion period, somewhere like a wood, bush and alike, imitating the embryo period of mankind; then masking, powdering the face with the ashes, imitating the pallid appearance of ghosts; symbolic burial ceremonies either in the temples or fetish houses; symbolic descent to the underworld – the land of the dead – while he has to be put in hypnotic sleep, fortified by some calming drinks and a series of challenges like being beaten, eaten, exposed to the fire, air suspension, amputation of the extremities and alike. If the Shamanic candidate is considered to be solely a medicine man, then he is exposed to another initiation in which the candidate is given much higher powers since this is going to be a vocation that may last through generations. So, those ceremonies are performed with unusual ecstatic experiences. Needless to say, these Shamanic powers were inherited from the first Shamans who really did fly through the clouds while being on their horses and performed miracles with their drums which their present-day parents and grandparents could not perform.

"In a way, the Shaman is a mythological hero: he rises every morning from the 'ordinary world' of the others, using – if necessary – the helping spirits, starts a kind of travelling and returns back. During this affair, his most important tool is his drum. Next time, I shall tell you quite interesting stories about the Shaman's drum and I shall play it for you while performing a very private healing affair.

"Thus, we observe that, Shamans and Shamanism are not simply a religious thread, an occupation or a primitive kind of religious practice but also a nation's representatives of cultural patterns. Namely, a Shaman is also a cultural ambassador. What is a nation? Ernest Renan had asked this question in A.C. 1882: *'Que'est-ce qu'une nation?'* and given the answer as: 'A nation is a psychic principle; there are two basic stones on which to build this. One, to have traditional rich cultural values that the people experience and live through together. Two, the people who made these values as ways of daily living a natural inheritance and agreed to carry them along and protect them, live with them of their own free will.' This is a holistic approach and is functional. Thus, a nation is qualified and identified with its cultural values and inheritance. The principals that design living patterns and value judgments also provide the stability, the continuity and protection of that nation.

"Well, this is the end of our lesson, part I. Next Wednesday, at the same time, I shall continue with the subject, giving more group practice samples with Shamanism as the second and last part of my Shamanism classes. Be good and so long!"

Even though I repeat these lectures every other six months, commensurate with the arrival of newcomers, each time I feel a very special pleasure that thrills me to my bones.

GOOD morning. Now, it is Thursday morning. And it is time to visit

Chapter 9

our Agriculture, Industry and Mining Department. I seem to be having you follow me wherever I go, as if we are reading a sea captain's open daily diary. Let me tell you a secret. If in this short life you really do want to be happy, keep working, preferably for other people; since they shall do the same for you. This shall really be a truly giving, sharing life and thirty-three prophets in the old and new testaments said just the same: 'Work as if you shall never die, pray as if you shall die tomorrow; and work is the best prayer!'

The head of this department is Mr. Timothy (who enjoys being called 'Tim') Allstar, an ex-baseball player, by profession a mechanical engineer. His office is on the 17th floor of Pyramid A. You shall be really surprised as you enter into his department which covers almost the entire 400-meter square of the floor. Here is exactly the duplicate of our lovely State. In the largest room, the entire island is reconstructed with live trees, forests, mines, beeches, factories, windmills, energy accumulation centres from wind, sun and water and waterfalls, all are represented as live as possible, of course in miniature forms. Tim always repeats 'I believe what I see!' Therefore, all present and future projects, with drawings and actual numbers, are marked and placed in proper forms, in proper places. That is why the other department heads, namely, Atilla Weakball, another chief engineer and the Minister of Energy, Transportation and Communication Department, and Mr. Jack Depare, chief engineer and the head of the Department of Engineering, Construction and Repair, frequently meet here, exchange information and plan together. Needless to say, from their offices too, through large screens, information that is not secret knowledge can be shared too. But these guys, who were nearly card-a-holics before coming to this country, namely ex-poker players, enjoy being, talking

Chapter 9

and working together. Their new (pre)occupation was golf. That's why, winter or summer, dry or wet, you can see these three hard-working, serious men trying to beat each other on the green in very child-like competition, bringing out sounds like 'Ah, oh, Oh, God, I just missed it.' 'Ooo, a birdy!' jumping in the air to the other two's dismay. That is what our lives are all about on this island. Their families, wives and children, too, are quite close and visit each other, frequently picnicking, hula-hooping and alike. That is why they are also called the Three Old Musketeers of New Atlantis.

So, when I called Tim, I requested the other two chiefs to be there too, if they were not there anyway, for the reason that this week for me was extremely busy, due to the newcomers, and as is well known, the fact that I had to make several 'opening' speeches and appearances and so on and so forth. In five minutes, Tim, Atilla, Jack and I were in this amazing little scale model of New Atlantis, in comfortable cane chairs – that was Tim's choice and we had to respect that – sipping our fresh pineapple juices.

"Yes, Tim, you shoot first. Anything new in your department, especially, as we were talking about your last endeavours to base the entire agriculture on organic farming?"

"Yes, Sir, our endeavours in using the seed and vegetative propagating material in organic farming is indeed increasing. The utilised agricultural area in our State is about 60 percent of the entire land. This ratio is quite high and desirable in comparison with other nations of the world. Even though life standards increasingly rely on a high degree of industry, the increased population still needs to be fed. This of course requires large, well-cultivated lands. Natural difficulties are, one, since we do not import these seeds, we just cultivate here, it takes some time to develop chemical work-up, set up machinery and educate the farmers, some of whom are newcomers in general, that is problem number two. They love the business but are used to do farming in the old style. We keep them involved with rather small farmhouse projects, close to large agricultural areas (*getting up, and showing on the maquette the designated places*) as designed by Atilla and his co-workers, imitating their old lives, namely living with farm animals near by, not in multi-storey skyscrapers, still having the fringe benefits of living in this very modern world and utilising the other facilities of New Atlantis. I understand that in this new group, there are at least 30 to 35 people who are eligible for my department; if I can place them before Fall after initial training, working with computers,

77

we can select a few people who can work at a higher level of teaching and planning. So, I am sure, potatoes, tomatoes, cauliflowers, salad, egg-plants, more than our yearly supply of wheat and corn, in a year or so, shall be entirely under this system."

"What about re-cycling, returning the remaining nutrients and waste products to the soil?"

"That is going very well too. This is also a matter of education. You know, working closely with Atilla and Jack, in central town and secondary towns, we have developed new collector systems, mounted in skyscrapers in separate lines to the other paper, glass and metallic products. From now on, unused organic materials or remnants shall be collected and used in much higher percentages."

"How goes the programme of abolition and destruction of synthetic chemicals, fertilisers, herbicides, growth hormones, antibiotics and so on?"

"We have succeeded in that nearly by 95 percent, Sir. People still may use them but not deliberately, without knowing and/or needing them. Since we do not import them either but used to manufacture them ourselves, sometimes people just do it, seeing no harm in it. We constantly search and educate. I am sure in a couple years' time, everything shall be under control."

"Tim, anything else?"

"Sir, not really, but as you know last summer and early this spring we nearly suffered a drought. We have to create some artificial rain I guess. Jack, Atilla and I were talking about it the other day. We may resort to that in due time."

"If you need any help from my Yogis, meditators or Shamans, just let me know."

Three gentlemen's gracious smiles were my reply.

"OK, Atilla, how are your gigantic energy resources? Is mother nature still good to you? Needless to say, our needs are steadily getting bigger and bigger every day. Any energy shortage on the horizon, old, new projects, what do you say?"

"Sir, it is true that as (with a nice smile on his face!) the number of even the simplest, wrist watches is increasing and new educational activities, new means of compiling the waste products as we just talked about and giving more opportunities to people to have recreation, naturally requires more energy. But this is the challenge to us; in this scientific age, without resorting to very dangerous nuclear devices, we have to utilise what we can. We all are happy with our train-street car

Chapter 9

system that works excellently. Three of us were thinking of developing an aerial – teleferic – telesiege system all around our island. We began to make some local inspections, measuring up the distances and necessary stations between (*he, too, getting up and pointing to the possible entourage on the maquette!*), how we can utilise our principal metal resources of iron and copper, the manpower, etc. Naturally, besides what this project will bring to us, we equally shall require tremendous amounts of energy. That is why we were also working on a new 're-collecting energy' project, for instance. What I mean by that is if we climb up to the hill with whatever energy we're using, how can we reverse and re-use it while coming down in the next instance? A sort of a discharging-recharging complex."

"Amazing, really amazing. Now I understand better why you are playing that much golf! Any chance of recovering your energies when you hit the ball? (And I smiled.)"

"Well," Jack entered in, "the way that we miss the ball indeed is a great waste, but seriously speaking, we are thinking about it for every single moving object."

"A few chemists suggested," continued Atilla, "we perhaps could use some old chemical reactions and formulations, like the Methan gas that inevitably comes out from our mines, instead of being neutralised and being made harmless, should be burnt with the waste products. The results could be quite satisfactory as far as the electricity as a final product is concerned but I do not know how we can prevent any explosion. Beside my due respect for the chemists, I do not feel safe playing with potentially dangerous materials. Just the same, ordinary coal, when burnt, brings out carbon dioxide and some calories. On the island, there are some unused coal mines that are out of mode. Could they be rejuvenated just to get some energy? I don't know."

"Some people ask me, Mr. President, when are we going to use some robots in our house or in mien pits where there is always the danger of explosion? These are families with children, partly for the sake of fun, but partly due to modernisation, so to speak. Yes, in our modern houses, heating, dust clearing, cooling are automatic, transportation is just in front of your door, but it is hard for me to justify bringing some machines in to do some jobs in place of humans, like cooking that we used to enjoy, or some other ordinary things. I don't know, what do you think gentlemen?"

"Well," said Atilla, "I guess there is no harm but in my life style I like what we are, how we are. In due time, if the people want, we can make a general inquiry and study that seriously. But I doubt I shall say yes for a long time to come."

"So do I," said Jack and Tim.

"What about our wind-centrals? How much power have we now?"

"As of this year, they are able to produce 20205 megawatts, Mr. President," replied Atilla. "We do expect this year a 7 to 8 percent increase."

"OK gentlemen, thank you very much. Soon you may hear from me about an emergency administrative meeting in reference to establishment of a Masonic Lodge?"

"What, a Masonic Lodge?" the three of them sighed together.

"Yes, a Masonic Lodge. Brotherhood is brotherhood. I will let you know soon. So long. Give my regards to your graceful wives."

On their way out I heard their murmurs: "Hmm. What we needed – a Masonic Lodge! Good! Good! Good!"

TODAY is Friday, it is a holy day for the Muslim community. As many of you may know, at Friday noon, going to a mosque to perform a

Chapter 10

'namaz' is mandatory for all Muslims.

As I mentioned before, we also have several small 'djamis' (small ones called 'mesdgits') around the island but the biggest mosque is at the Mega Central Square, downtown, a few hundred yards away from the Christian churches. As you may already know, the Islamic religion demands people pray five times a day. It is not necessary to go to a mosque each time but all the sacred, as the Prophet and his Kahlifs used to do, go to a mosque at nOon on Friday. (Quite a paradox I believe, among four follower Kahlifs [Halifa, Khalife] of Mohammed after his ascent to heaven – Ebubekir, Ali, Omar and Osman. Three of them were assassinated on Fridays while praying. Ye still it is the most sacred praying time!) As the first step, a 'muezzin', the religious person who gives the call to prayer, climbs from inside onto the minaret's balcony, a round structure in the middle of the minaret, and sings in a very private way. (In modern times, however, many used to utilise microphones instead.) Here on the island, I of course permit whatever rituals demand, except for the usage of microphones. I asked the muezzins to utilise their godly, normal, beautiful voices as naturally as possible. (I doubt whether in his time, Mohammed would have given permission to utilise metallic devices!). Any rate, these are a few clues for the people to know about Muslim principals, paying love and respect for the creator.

Being both a President (so I do almost at all openings) and in the past coming from the same faith, today I am going to go to the mosque to welcome new Muslims there. Imam Hodja is the religious leader of the faith. He usually wears a black robe, as do many other priests, and there is a very special turban on his head. He is in the foremost line.

A.C. 2084

Women and men classically cannot pray side by side as Christians do; they are segregated. Classically, if there is a balcony, women go up there; if there isn't, they line up at the back of the mosque. Before entering, either at the hall or at home, you have to have some special cleaning of the appearing parts of the body, namely hands, feet, face, top of your head and alike with water: 'abdest', otherwise your 'namaz' (total praying session at that time) is not acceptable. You have to take your shoes off at the door, leave them there and walk on beautiful rugs bare-footed. Or some may prefer to wear sandals, or rather slippers, which are available to the public if they choose. There, you read some prayers, silently murmuring while following the leader Imam-Hodja, and doing exactly the same up and down kneeling movements with the other participants (djamaat community), in a synchronised way. Namaz, according to the time of the day, that is to say, before sunrise, noon, afternoon, right after sunset and mid-evening, has different lengths – each part is called 'rekat'. If you forget, don't worry, keep praying silently and follow the leader or 'mumin-religious' person next to you...

At any rate, I took my 'abdest', just in case, and went downtown to the unique mosque there, at the centre of the city. Head Imam Abdullah Hodja greeted me and shook hands with a great affection, keeping them vigorously for a while between his two hands, and said how happy he was at seeing me there. I mentioned to him that, with his permission, I would like to attend some classes he usually gave to beginners when they come to the State, 'Recognising Islam' or 'Principles of Islam'. I said, as usual, I would give some additional speeches about historical and ethnological aspects of this great religion too. He thanked me again whole-heartedly for my close interest and the help and support I was trying to give when and if necessary.

Imam Abdullah very gracefully introduced me to the community, citing that I, as the President, would like to give some historical, ethnic and philosophical aspects of this great religion, each Friday, after the namaz for perhaps a few weeks in a row, then leaving things up to him. The name of this short course was going to be *'Recognising Islam, Koran and Mohammed, Historical Facts'*.

We djamaat altogether, under the leadership of Imam Abdullah, executing the Friday noon namaz in almost ecstasy. Then I started to address the people in the previously mentioned subjects. My fear was that I am an academic person and almost always too documentative. I feared that some people might have been bored. On the other hand, my

Chapter 10

performing namaz with them might have given them some confidence and closeness. We will see.

Part 1

(Of the Arabs before Mohammed; In the time of Ignorance; Geography, History, Religion, Learning and Customs)

"The Arabs, and the country they inhabit, which themselves call Jezirat al Arab, or 'the Peninsula of the Arabians', but Arabia were so named from Arabs, a small territory in the province of Tebama to which Yarab, the son of Kahtan, the father of ancient Arabs, gave the name and where, some ages after dwelt Ismael, the son of Abraham by Hagar. The name of Arabia used in a more extensive sense sometimes covers all that large tract of land bounded by the river Eufrates, the Persian Gulf, The Sindian, Indian and Red Seas, and part of the Mediterranean: more than two-thirds of which country is properly called Arabia. Arabs have possessed most of the land from the flood and made themselves masters of the rest, either by settlements, or continual incursions; for which reason the Turks and Persians to this day call the whole Arabistan, or the country of Arabs.

"But the limits of Arabia, in its more usual and proper sense, are much narrower, reaching no farther northwards than the Isthmus, which runs from Ailaa to the head of the Persian Gulf, and the borders of the territory of Cufa; which track of land the Greeks nearly comprehended under the name 'Arabia the Happy'.

"Proper Arabia according to the oriental writers was generally divided into five provinces: Yaman, Hejaz, Tehama, Najd and Yamama, to which some add Bahrein, as a sixth. Some authors reduce them all to two: Yaman and Hejaz. Most modern atlases demonstrate it as Saudi Arabia, Jordan, Lebanon, Syria, Yaman (Yemen) Arab Republic, People's Democratic Republic of Yaman (Yemen) and Kuwait.

"This country has been famous from all antiquity for the happiness of the climate, the fertility and the riches, which induced Alexander the Great, after his return from his Indian expedition, to form a design of conquering it and fixing there his royal seat. But his death, which happened soon afterwards, prevented the execution of this project. Aegyptians shutting their ports off to the external world on one side and the deserts that are impassable to strangers on the other were the reason why Arabia was so little known to the Greeks and Rome.

A.C. 2084

Yemen, lying along the Red Sea, is a dry, barren desert, bounded by mountains, well watered, yielding great plenty and a variety of fruit, in particular excellent corn, grapes and spices.

"The Province of Hejaz is bounded on the south by Yemen, on the west by the Red Sea, on the north by the deserts of Syria and on the east by the province of Najd. This province is famous for its two chief cities, Mecca and Medina, one of which is celebrated for its temple and having giving birth to Mohammed and the other for being the place of his residence for the last ten years of his life and of his interment.

"Mecca is sometimes called Becca – the words are synonymous and signify a place of great concourse – and is certainly one of the most ancient cities in the world. It is thought by some to be the 'Mesa of the Scripture', a name not unknown to the Arabians, and supposed to have been taken from one of Ismael's sons. It is seated in a stony and barren valley, surrounded on all sides by mountains. An old Koran, printed in A.C. 1850, describes: 'The length of Mecca, from south to north, is about two miles, and its breadth, from the fOot of the mountains Ajyad to the top of another, called Konikaan, about a mile. In the midst of this space stands the city, built in stone cut from the neighbouring mountains. There being no springs in Mecca, the water is unfit and bitter to drink except for that from the well Zemzem which offers water for eternity. The pilgrims who return from the Hadj – pilgrimage visits – who call themselves Hadji bring zemzem to their countrymen in small pots, allegedly good for all kinds of illnesses and for those who wish for an eternal life. The Sharif (or Prince) of the province has a well-planted garden at his castle of Marbaa, about three miles west from the city. The temple of Mecca is the reputed holiness of this territory.' Now Mecca, after the national capital of Riyadh, is the most populous city of Saudi Arabia, with a population easily passing 300,000 spread over 10 square miles (26 square kilometres). During the pilgrimage, however, the city expands with more than a million worshippers who come from the four corners of the world. Then, the central courtyard of al-Haram Mosque is honoured by the crowd as the holiest shrine of Islam.

"Mecca, throughout history, had almost remained independent, although it accepted for a while the power of Damascus-Syria and later of the Abbusid caliphate of Baghdad-Iraq. In A.C. 1269 it began to be controlled by Egyptian Mamluk sultans. In A.C. 1517, the expanding Ottoman Empire headed by Sultan Selim II conquered the city and took over the duties of their caliph. After the World War I in A.C.

Chapter 10

1918, the control of Mecca was divided between the Mohammedan descendant Sharifs and the Wahhakis of Central Arabia. The latest, the Wahhabi King Ibn Sa'üd, entered the city in A.C. 1925 and it then became an inseparable part of the Kingdom of Saudi Arabia.

"Since the World War II, A.C. 1945, Mecca has expanded the roads through the mountain gaps, constructed beautiful modern new streets in the old city and transformed itself into a modern existence. The Square Mosque is magnificent in its size and architecture, enlarged from 313,520 to 1,724,032 square feet now (that corresponds from 29,127 to 160,168 square metres) to accommodate more than 300,000 worshippers at one time. To meet the demands, more and more comfortable hotels and guest houses are being constructed.

"Medina, Arabic Al-Madinah, formally Al Madinha Al-Mudawwaran (The most Glorious City) – one of the two most sacred cities of Islam – which until Mohammed's retreat (A.C. 622) was called Yathreb, is a walled city about half as big as Mecca. It is built on a plain, with salt in many places, yet it is tolerably fruitful, particularly in dates, but more especially near the mountains, two of which are Ohod in the north and Air on the south. Here lies Mohammed, interred in a magnificent building, covered with a cupola, and adjoining the east side of the great temple which is built in the midst of the city.

"The oasis was settled by Jews expelled from Palestine. After the hijrah-hegira, control passed to Arabs. That was maintained until A.C. 661 when Damascus took control. The city was sacked in A.C. 683 by caliphs and native amirs and the friction lasted for a long time. After Ottoman Empire's rigid rule which started in A.C. 1517, control eventually entered Wahhabis domination. Even though the Turks built up the Hejaz railroad between A.C. 1904 – A.C. 1908, the control by them was diminished. During the World War I, A.C. 1914-18, the mutual work of Husayn Ibn'Ali, the sharif of Mecca and the British officer T. E. Lawrence (Lawrence of Arabia) almost brought independence. Then, Ibn Sa'ud, starting in A.C. 1925, established his own dynasty.

"In Medina, among the historic monuments, one could cite, besides the tomb of Mohammed in the Prophet's Mosque, The Mosque of Quba, the Mosque of Two Qiblahs, the tomb of Hamza, and the Islamic University that was founded in A.C. 1961.

"Turning back to the developmental stages of the Islamic Empire, still in the tribes' period, the most famous tribes amongst those ancient Arabians were Ad, Thamud, Tasm, Jadis, the former Jorham and Amalek.

A.C. 2084

"The tribe of Ad were descended from Ad, son of Aws, the son of Aram, the son of Sem, the son of Noah. His posterity was greatly multiplied in the province of Hadramut, the Winding Sands. Their first king was Shedad, the son of Ad, who had built a magnificent city, a fine palace adorned with delicious gardens wit the purpose of creating in his subjects a superstitious veneration of himself as a god. This garden or paradise was called the 'Garden of Irem' and is mentioned in the Koran. It is said to stand in the desert of Aden, invisible except very rarely when God permits it to be seen.

"The descendents of Ad, in the process of time, fell from the worship of true God into idolatry; God sent the prophet Hud to preach to and reclaim them. But they refused to acknowledge his mission, or obey him. So God sent a hot and suffocating wind, which blew seven nights and eight days together, entering their nostrils and passing through their bodies, destroying them all except for a very few who had believed in Hud and retired with him to another place. That prophet afterwards returned into Hadramut and was buried near Hasec, where there a small town, called Kabr Hud, now stands. Before the Adites were so severely punished, God, to humble them and incline them to hearken to the preaching of his prophet, afflicted them with drought for years. So, upon it, they sent Lokman – a different name from one who lived in David's time – with sixty others to Mecca to beg for rain; but since they did not obtain it, Lokman with some of his company stayed in Mecca and therefore escaped destruction. According to the Koran, Lokman gave rise to another tribe called 'the latter Ad'. However, since his descendants continued with idolatry, as witnessed by the Koran, they were returned to monkeys.

"The tribe of Thamud were the posterity of Thamud, the son of Gather, the son of Aram, who as they fell into idolatry, the prophet Saleh was sent to bring them back to the worship of the true God. This prophet lived between the time of Hud and of Abraham. A small number of the people of Thamud hearkened to the remonstrating of Saleh but the rest required, as a proof of his mission, that he should cause a she-camel big and young to come out of a rock in their presence. He accordingly obtained it of God and the camel was immediately delivered of a young one ready weaned. But they, instead of believing, cut the hamstrings of the camel and killed her – at which act of impiety, God, being highly displeased, three days afterwards struck them dead in their houses through an earthquake and a terrible noise from heaven, which some say was the voice of Gabriel the archangel crying aloud, 'Die all of you!' Saleh and those who were reformed by him were saved from his destruction, the prophet going into Palestine and from thence to Mecca, where he ended his days.

"The tragic destructions of these two potent tribes are often insisted on in the Koran as instances of God's judgment on obstinate unbelievers.

"The tribe of Tasm were the posterity of Lud, the son of Sem and Jadis of the descendants of Jether. These two tribes dwelt promiscuously together under the government of Tasm, till a certain tyrant made a law that no maid of the tribe of Jadis should marry, unless they deflowered by him. The Jadisians would not endure this and formed a conspiracy. They invited the king and chiefs of Tasm to an entertainment, privately hid their swords in the sand, and in the midst of their mirth fell on them and slew them all, and extirpated the greatest part of the tribe. However, the few who escaped obtained the aid of the king of Yaman, then, as it is said, Dhu Habshan Ebn Akran, assaulted the Jadis and utterly destroyed them, there being scarcely any mention made at that time of either of those tribes.

"The former tribe of Jorham (whose ancestor some pretend was one of the eighty persons saved in the ark with Noah, according to Mohammedan tradition) was contemporary with Ad and utterly perished.

"The tribe of Amelek were descended from Amelek, the son of Eliphaz the son of Esau, though some of the oriental authors say Amelek was the son of Ham, the son of Noah, and others the son of Azd, the son of Sem. The posterity of this person made themselves very powerful and before the time of Joseph, conquered lower Egypt under their king Walid, the first who took the name of Pharaoo, as the eastern writers tell us, seeming by these Amelejites to mean the same people which the Egyptian historians call Phoenician shepherds. But after they had possessed the throne of Egypt for some generations, they were expelled by the natives and at length totally destroyed by the Israelites.

"The present Arabians, according to their own historians, are sprung from two stocks: Kahtan, the same with Joctan the son of Eber, and Adnan, descended in a direct line from Ismael, the son of Abraham and Hagar; the posterity of the former they call al Arab al Ariba, meaning the 'genuine' or 'pure Arabs' or 'institious Arabs', although some reckon the ancient lost tribes to have been the only pure Arabians, therefore the posterity of Kahran are also Mostareba, which word likewise signifies 'institious Arabs', though in a nearer degree than Mostareba: The descendants of Ismael being the more distant graff.

"Besides these tribes of Arabs, who were all descended from the race of Sem, others of them were the posterity of Ham by his son Cuch which name is in the scripture constantly given to the Arabs and their country; though according to reliable resources they are rendered in Utopia; but strictly speaking, the Cushites did not inhabit so-called proper Arabia but the banks of the Euphrates and the Persian Gulf, whether they came from Chuzestan or Sussiana, the original settlement of their father. They might probably mix themselves in the process of time with Arabs of the other race.

"The Arabians were for some centuries under the government of the descendants of Kahtan; Yarab, one of his sons founding the kingdom of Yaman, and Jorham, another of them that of Hejaz.

"The province of Yamian, or the better part of it, particularly the provinces of Saba and Hadramaut, was governed by the princes of the tribe of Hamyar. Though at length the kingdom was passed to the descendants of Cahlan, his brother, who still retained the title of king of Hamyar, and had all of them the general title off Tobbsa which signifies successor, and was affected to this race of princess, as that of Caesar was to the Roman emperors, and Khalif to the successor of Mohammed. There were several lesser princes who reigned in other parts of Yaman and were mostly, if not altogether, subject to the king of Hamyar, whom they called the 'great king', but of these history has recorded nothing remarkable or anything that may be depended upon.

"The first great calamity that befell the tribes in Yaman was the inundation of Aram, which happened soon after the time of Alexander the Great, and is famous in Arabian history. No less than eight tribes were forced to abandon their dwellings upon this occasion, some of which gave rise to the two kingdoms of Ghassan and Hira. And this was probably the time of the migration of those tribes or colonies which were which were led into Mesopotamia by three chiefs – Becr, Modar and Rabla – from whom the three provinces of that country are still named, Diyar Becr, Diyar Modar and Diyar Rabla. Abdshems, surnamed Saba, having built the city from called Saba and afterwards Mareb, made a vast mound of dam to serve as a basin or reservoir to receive the water which came down from the mountains, not only for the use of the inhabitants and the watering of their lands but also to keep the country they had subjected in greater awe by being masters of the water. This building stood like a mountain above their city and was by them esteemed so strong that they were in no apprehension of it ever failing. The water rose to the height of almost twenty fathoms (1 fathom =1.83 m.) and was kept in on every side by work so solid that many of the inhabitants had their houses built upon it. Every family had a certain portion of this water which was distributed by aqueducts. But at length, God being highly displeased at their great pride and insolence, and resolving to humble and disperse them, sent a mighty flood, which broke down the mound at night while the inhabitants were asleep and carried away the whole city with the neighbouring towns and people.

"The tribes which remained in Yaman after this terrible devastation still continued under the obedience of the former princes till about 70 years before Mohammed, when the king of Ethiopia sent over forces to assist the Christians of Taman against the cruel persecution of their king Dhu Novas, a bigoted Jew. They drove him to a point where he forced his horse into the sea and so lost his life and crown, after which the country was governed by four Ethiopian princes successively, till Seif the son of Dhu Yazan of the tribe Hamyar, obtaining succour from Khosru Anushirwan, king of Persia, which had been denied him by the emperor Heraclius, recovered the throne and drove out the Ethiopians. However, he himself was slain by some of those who were left behind. The Persians appointed the succeeding princes till Yaman fell into the hands of Mohammed, to whom Bazan, or rather Badhan, the last of them, submitted and embraced his new religion.

"This kingdom of the Hamyarites is said to have lasted 2,020 years, or as others say above 3,000, the length of the reign of each prince being very uncertain.

"It has been already observed that two kingdoms were founded by those who had left their country on occasion of the inundation of Aram; they were both out of the proper limits of Arabia. One of them was the Kingdom of Ghassan. The founders of this kingdom were of the tribe of Azd, who settling in Syria Damascena near a water called Ghassan, thence took their name and drove out the Dejaamian Arabs of the tribe of Salih, who before possessed the country, where they maintained the kingdom for 400 years (others say 600 and Abulfeda more exactly counts 616). Five of these princes were named Hareth, which the Greeks write as Aretas, and one of them it was whose governor ordered the gates of Damascus to be watched to take St.

A.C. 2084

Paul. This tribe were Christians, their last king being Jabalas the son of al Ayham, who on the Arabs' successes in Syria professed Mohammedism under Kahlif Omar; but receiving disgust from him, returned to his former faith and retired to Constantinople.

"The other kingdom was that of Hira, which was founded by Malec of the descendants of Cahlan in Chaldea or Irak; but after three descendants, the throne came by marriage to the Lakhmians, called also the Mondars (the general name of those princes), who preserved their dominion, notwithstanding some small interruption by the Persians, till the Khalifat of Abubeer, when the Mondar al Maghrur, the last of them, lost his life and crown to Khaled Ebu al Walid. This kingdom lasted 622 years, eight months. Its princes were under the protection of the kings of Persia, whose lieutenants they were over the Arabs of Iraq, as the kings of Ghassan were for the Roman emperors over those of Syria.

"Jorham, the son of Kahtan, reigned in Hejaz, where his posterity kept the throne till the time of Ismael, but on his marrying the daughter of Modad, by whom he had twelve sons, Kidar, one of them, had the crown resigned to him by his uncles the Jorhamites, though others may be descendants of Ismael expelled that tribe, who retiring to Jooainah, were various fortune, at last all destroyed by an inundation.

"After the expulsion of the Jorhamites, the government of Hejaz seems not to have continued for many centuries in the hands of one prince but to have been divided among the heads of tribes; almost in the same manner as the Arabs of the desert are governed at this day. At Mecca, an aristocracy prevailed, where the chief management of affairs till the time of Mohammed was in the tribe of Koreish, especially after they had got the custody of the Caaba from the tribe of Khozaah.

"After the time of Mohammed, Arabia was about three centuries under the Khalifs, his successors. But in the year A.C. 325 of the Hejra, a great part of that country was in the hands of the Karmatians, a new sect who has committed great outrages and disorders even in Mecca, and to whom the Khalifs were obliged to pay tribute so that the pilgrimage thither might be performed. Afterwards, Yaman was governed by the house of Thabateba, descended from Ali, the son-in-law of Mohammed, whose sovereignty in Arabia some place so high as the time of Charlemagne. However, it was the posterity of Ali, or pretenders to be such, who reigned in Yaman and Egypt so early as the tenth century. The crown of Yaman descends not regularly from father to son but generally to the prince of the blood royal who is

Chapter 10

most in favour with the great ones, or has the strongest interest.

"The governors of Mecca and Medina, who have always been of the race of Mohammed, also threw off their subjection to the Khalifs, since which time four principal families, all descended from Hasan the son of Ali, have reigned there under the title of Sharif which signifies noble, as they reckon themselves to be on account of their descent. These are Banu Kader, Banu Musa Thani, Banu Hashem and Banu Kitada – all were on the throne of Mecca where they have reigned above 500 years.

"The kings of Yaman, as well as the princes of Mecca and Medina, had always been absolutely independent and not at all subject even in Ottoman Empire times. These princes often made cruel wars among themselves, giving Ottoman emperor Selim I and son (Magnificent) Soliman an opportunity to make themselves masters of the coasts of Arabia and the Red Sea, and a part of Yaman, by means of a fleet built at Sues; but their successors have not been able to maintain their conquests except for the port of Jadda, where they have a Basha (Pasha-General) whose authority was very small.

"In summary, Arabians preserved their liberty and had very little interruption from outside forces. The Assyrian or Median empires never got a footing among them. The Persian monarchs, though they were their friends, never make them tributary and were so far from being their masters that Cambyses, on his expedition against Egypt, was obliged to ask their leave to pass through their territories; and, when Alexander (the Great) had subdued that mighty empire, the Arabians had so little apprehension of him that they alone, of all neighbouring nations, sent no ambassadors to him, either the first or last. The Romans never conquered any part of Arabia proper so called; the most they did was make some tribes in Syria tributary to them. The best was done by Augustus Caesar as far as invasion, or penetration is concerned. Yet he too was so far from subduing it that he soon was obliged to return without effecting anything considerable, having lost the best part of his army to sickness and other accidents.

"Well gentlemen and very holy Imam Abdullah, thank you very much for listening to me. We will continue at next week's Friday 'namaz'. God bless all of you." And I left there in a hurry.
YES, I left there in a hurry, because I was going to serve (I hope he will be satisfied too!) another prophet's establishment of another

Chapter 11

great religion, as a matter of fact, the number one to start with at the Monotheistic episode of mankind, the Jewish faith. I was rushing to the Jewish synagogue to meet (Chief) Rabbi David and Rabbi Braun, the head of the Kabalahh Centre, this Friday afternoon at the opening ceremonies there for 'Week Day Afternoon Ceremonies' and I was just a little bit late.

Though I was tired, I was content with what I was doing. Here at the Jewish Centre, thank God, I was not going to talk for now, just be a listener and participant. All religions of course are respectable and dignified but Jewish celebrations appear to be having much more 'live ethical' components to me. Stories are alive, colourful and meaningful, and rituals are executed cheerfully with a lot of show, so to speak. Children run around – in others they are not that free – with their caps and attire that they have and are the source of cheer. You feel the family sincerity more. So, there seems to be just a little bit more motility and fun in Jewish celebrations.

Both rabbis, who also are my sincere friends for many years, greeted me respectfully. Besides newcomers, there were plenty of old 'customers', the people from other denominations like me. Soon after I arrived and took my place, Head Rabbi David started to his opening speech with his deep, strong voice.

"This Friday afternoon, I do welcome all of you to our services. Today, I would like to give some glimpses of the all-pervading and radiant optimism of the prayers that are irradiated by a glorious universalism with an unfailing vision of hope and betterment for all men. We will exercise weekday afternoon services in Judaism, also preparing for tomorrow's great Sabbath services. From time to time,

Chapter 11

I shall remind you of the ceremonial attitudes here in the synagogue, for the newcomers of course.

"Every day in the year, there exist three services of prayer: Shahrit – morning service; Minhah – afternoon service, and Arvith – evening service. For Sabbaths and festivals, a Musaf (additional service) is added to the morning service.

"As one enters the synagogue, one bows reverently toward the Torah in the Ark, joining the *Psalmist (5:8)* in worshipful obeisance to where the temple of old stood in the holy city.

"In the Minhah (afternoon service), as in the Shahrith (morning service), prayers are brought as an offering to God every day as was done in the temple in Jerusalem of old. The name Minhah, which means 'gift' or 'tribute', was given especially to the grain offering that was brought to both morning and afternoon services in the temple. It is also associated with 'menubath hashemesh', the sunset, which begins half an hour after midday when the reading of the afternoon service may start. Traditional Jewish thought ascribes the origin of the Minhah prayer to Isaac, of whom we are told (*Genesis 24:63*) that 'he went out to meditate in the field toward eventide'.

* **ASHREI**:

"The afternoon service is opened with biblical verses, *Psalms 84:5* and *144:15*, proclaiming the happiness of those who dwell in God's sanctuary. The ecstatic universal vision and sublime praise of *Psalm 145* are climaxed by the verse *Psalm 115:18* expressing our wish to bless the God to whom we would sing praise – Halelujah. Now we start and let us sing and perform together."

(On entering the synagogue say)

Lo, though Thine abundant love I enter Thy house;
In reverence for Thee I bow toward Thy holy temple.

* **ASHREI**:

Happy are they who dwell in Thy house,
Forever shall they praise Thee, Selah.
Happy the people whose lot is thus,
Happy the people whose God is the Lord.

(A Psalm of Praise. Of David. *Psalm 145*)
I extol Thee, my God, the King,
And evermore would bless Thy name.

A.C. 2084

Every day I shall bless Thee,
And I would praise Thy name forever and ever.

Lord, Thou are great and highly extolled,
Yet inscrutable is Thy greatness.
One generation to another shall praise Thy works,
And recount Thy mighty acts.

Let me speak of brilliant glory of Thy majesty,
And of Thy wondrous works,
And I will declare Thy greatness.
Men shall speak of the night of Thine awesome acts,
They shall recount Thy goodness abundant,
And joyously sing of Thy righteousness.

The Lord is gracious and compassionate,
Long forbearing and of great mercy.
The Lord is good to all,
And His tenderness is over all His works.

All Thy works shall praise Thee, O Lord,
And Thy devoted servants shall bless Thee.
They shall speak of the glory of Thy kingdom,
And talk of Thy power.

To make known to the sons of men Thy mighty acts,
And the glorious splendour of Thy kingdom.
The kingdom is an everlasting kingdom,
And Thy dominion is through all generations.

Lord, Thou upholdest all the falling,
And raisest up all who are bowed down.
The eyes of all wait on Thee,
And Thou givest them their food in its season.

Thou openest Thy hand
And satisfiest all living with favour.
The Lord is righteous in all His ways,
And merciful in all His works.
The Lord is near to all who call on Him,
The all who call on Him in truth.
He fulfils the desire of those who revere Him,
He hears their cry and saves them.
The Lord preserves all who love Him,
But all the wicked He will destroy.

My mouth shall speak the praise of the Lord,
Yes, all flesh bless His holy name forever and ever.

And we, we will bless the Lord
Henceforth and forever, Hallelujah – Praise the Lord.

* READER'S KADDISH:
86
"For the recitation of the devout prayer of glorification of God's name there is required the presence of at least a minyan, the religious quorum of ten men of the Jewish people. This short Kaddish marks the end of the preceding biblical readings."

(Recited by the Reader in public worship)

Exalted and hallowed be God's great name
In this world of His creation.
May His will be fulfilled
And His sovereignty revealed
In the days of your lifetime
And the life of the whole house of Israel
Speedily and soon,
And say, Amen.

(Congregation and Reader respond)

Be His great name blessed forever,
Yea, to all eternity.

Be the name of the most Holy One blessed,
Praised and honoured, extolled and glorified,
Adored and exalted Supremely.

(Congregation and Reader respond):

Blessed (*) be He,

Beyond all blessings and hymns, praises and consolations
That may be uttered in this world,
And say, Amen. (**)

* THE SHEMONEH ESREH (Eighteen Blessings):

(*) Between Rash Hashana and Yom Kippur say instead: Far beyond
(**) For the order of the afternoon service on the Fast of the tenth, the Reader continues with the reading of Shemoneh Esreh. (see following!)

A.C. 2084

"The central prayer around which the daily morning service, afternoon and evening services are built is the Shemoneh Esreh (Eighteen Blessings). This prayer had been offered for more than two thousand years by the worshipper while standing feet together and facing the Holy Land. It is prayed individually and silently; in a congregation it is repeated aloud by the Hazzan (*) in the morning and afternoon sessions. Originally twelve and thirteen prayers of petition were offered between the three opening blessings praising God and three final blessings of thanksgiving."

(The congregation rises to read the Shemoneh Esreh in silent devotion. The Reader repeats the Shemoneh Esreh at the conclusion of silent prayer)

As I proclaim the name of the Lord, ascribe greatness to our God. Lord, open my lips, that my mouth may declare Thy praise.

Blessed (**) art Thou, Lord our God and God of our fathers, God of Abraham, God of Isaac and God of Jacob, the God who is great, mighty and awesome, God sublime who lavishes tender goodness. Master of all, Thou art mindful of the loving piety of our fathers, and for Thine own sake Thou wilt lovingly bring a Redeemer to their children's children.

(Between Rosh Hashanah (***) and Yom Kippur (****) add)

Remember us for life, divine King who delights in life. Inscribe us in the book of life to fulfil Thy purpose, God of life.

King who dost succour, save, and shield, blessed (**) art Thou, Lord, shield of Abraham.
Lord who art mighty for all eternity, Thou revivest the dead. Thou art is great in saving the living.

(*) HAZZAN: Hebrew name for the 'Cantor', the official in the synagogue who is the leading person to lead worshippers in prayer.
(**) BLESSED: Before invoking the name of God one bows here.
(***) ROSH HASHANAH: Meaning 'the head of the year', terming the Jewish New Year observance. It is celebrated on the first and second days of the month of Tishre, that is also the first month of the Jewish calendar, namely September-October, and indicates the Ten Days of Penitence.
(****) YOM KIPPUR: Hebrew for the Day of Atonement and the most solemn day in the Jewish religion. It is observed on the tenth day of Tishre. In the Bible it is described as a 'Sabbath of Solemn Rest'. Work, as well as the taking of food and drink, are strictly forbidden and there is constant prayer in the synagogue.

Chapter 11

(From Shemini Hag Atsereth (*) until Pesah (**) add)

By making the wind to blow and the rain to fall.

Sustaining them in love. Thou upholdest the falling. Thou healest the sick, Thou freest the bound. In Thy great love Thou revivest the dead, keeping faith with those who sleep in the dust. Who is like Thee, Lord of power! Who can be compared with Thee, King who sends death, and who in the flowering of Thy saving power gives life!

(Between Rash Hashanah and Yom Kippur add)

Who is like Thee, merciful Father, in Thy compassion remembering for first

Thou hast created!

Thou wilt keep faith in reviving the dead. Blessed art Thou, Lord who revives the dead.

* **KEDUSHAH** (Holiness):

"In the Hazzan's repetition of their blessing in the Shemoneh Esreh, the Kedushah (Holiness) is included. Then all stand and join in the sanctification of God's name by echoing from prophetic visions the words of the angels proclaiming that the divine holiness fills all the earth (*Isiah 6:3*) as other angels respond that his glory fills all (*Ezekiel 3:12*), and the Jewish people affirm with the *Psalms (146:10)* that Zion's God will be supreme forever."

(In the repetition, The Kedushah is recited while standing)

(Congregation and Reader respond)

Let us hallow Thy name in this world below, own as in the prophet's vision

The Seraphim hallowing it in the heavenly heights calls to one another.

(*) SHEMINI HAG ATSERETH (Sukkot): Hebrew name of the Feast of Tabernacles, the fall festival that begins on the 15th day of Tishre. According to the Bible, the eighth day shall be observed as a Feast of Conclusion (Shemini Atzeret).
(**) PESAH (Passover): The Jewish festival commemorating the deliverance of the Israelites from Egypt. The first day of the festival falls upon the 15th of April (corresponding to March-April months in the Jewish claendar) and lasts for eight days.

(Congregation and Reader respond)

Holy, holy, holy is the Lord of hosts,

A.C. 2084

The fullness of all the earth is His glory.

(Congregation with the Reader responding)

Responding in blessing, they say:

(Congregation and Reader respond)

Blessed and glorified is the Lord from His abode.

(Congregation with the Reader responding)

And in His Holy Words is written.

(Congregation and Reader respond)

The Lord shall reign forever,
Your God, O Zion, through all generations.
Hallelujah – Praise the Lord.

(Reader)

To all generations we would proclaim Thy greatness, and to all eternity declare Thy holiness, and may the praise of Thee, our God, never leave our mouth, for Thou art God and King, great and holy; * blessed art Thou, Lord, the holy God.

** AL HANNISSISM:

"During the eight days of Hanukkah, there is added to the Shemoneh Esreh in every service a special thanksgiving introduced by cumulative words of praise. It recalls the divine deliverance from the terrible Syrian tyranny in the days of the Maccabees. On PURIM (*) there is added a similar paragraph that is also introduced by Al Hannissim. This recalls the deliverance which came to the Jews in Persia in the days of Mordecai, as recorded in the Biblical Book of Esther. 'For all this, divine King, be Thou blessed and exalted ever more.'"

(*) Between Rash Hashanah and Yom Kippur, conclude this blessing thus: "blessed art Thou, Lord, the holy King".
(**) PURIM: Jewish festival observed annually on the 14th day of the Hebrew month of Adare (February-March), commemorating the miracle of survival from Haman's plot to kill all the Jews in Persia.)

* AL HANNISSISM:

Chapter 11

(On Hanukkah add the following Al Hannissism)

We thank Thee also for the wonders, the deliverance, and the triumphant victory and liberation which Thou hast wrought for our fathers in days of old at this season. It happened in the days of Mattathias son of Johanan, and his sons the Hasmonean high priests. Then the cruel Hellenist power rose up to force Thy people Israel to forget Thy Torah and transgress the commands of Thy will. In that hour of their trial, Thou in Thy great mercy didst rise to take up their cause and defend their rights. Meting out retribution Thou hast delivered the strong into the hand of the weak, many into the hand of the few, the impure into the hand of the righteous, and tyrants into the hands of devotees of Thy teaching. By Thy great and saving deliverance of Thy people Israel Thou hast made for Thyself unto this very day a great and holy name in Thy world. Then Thy children came to the profaned shrine of Thy house, cleared Thy Temple, cleansed Thy sanctuary, kindled lights in its holy courts, and instituted these eight days of dedication to sing thanksgiving praise to Thy great name.

(On Purim add the following Al Hannissism)

We thank Thee also for the wonders, the deliverance, and the triumphant victory and liberation which Thou hast wrought for our fathers in days of old at this season. It happened in Shushan, the Persian capital, in the time of Mordecai and Esther. Then the wicked Haman rose up and sought to slay and utterly annihilate all the Jews, young and old, women and babes, in one day, the thirteenth day of the twelfth month, Adar. In Thy great mercy Thou hast frustrated his counsel and subverted his designs, causing them to recoil on his own head until he and his sons were hanged on the gallows.

After the last 'Amen', I left the synagogue, with mythical sounds and prayers still vibrating in the air. Naturally, I am planning to attend Kabalah classes, next week. Tomorrow is the greatest day of the Jewish faith, the Sabbath. We shall observe it together.

To day is Saturday. This is the first Saturday after our newcomers honoured us, last weekend. Today is the famous Jewish holiday

Chapter 12

Sabbath.

So, I had my breakfast with my lovely wife and three cats, at least two of them lying on the dinner table, having been first fed by my wife. What beautiful scenery that is! What say those beautiful ocean deep, ocean blue eyes? Then, I had just a look in the new *Atlantis News* where there was nothing other than usual daily happenings, weekend screening programmes and alike. Then, I rang Rabbi David:

"Hello Rabbi David."

"Oh, hello honourable President."

"Well, it was very nice of you to illuminate us yesterday, as usual. I assume, today, you shall continue particularly about the Sabbath, will you?"

"Yes, principally yes, but I would like to give some knowledge about our people's origins, connected with it."

"Superb. You don't have any objection, then, to my being there too?"

"You just give us honour. See you at 10 a.m."

"See you. God bless you!"

"God bless you too."

And, there I was again at the beautiful synagogue, downtown, after about a 12-minute train ride. Rabbi David in front, in his official rabbi's robe with his helpers behind, greeted me respectfully and I, also respectfully bowing toward the Torah in the Arc, took my seat, in the first row in this magnificent Solomon's Hall. The whole synagogue was full and there was an obvious joy and sincerity easily inspired in the air for this first holy togetherness among newcomers. Soon after my arrival, Rabbi David took his place and began to dis-

Chapter 12

course:

"I am Rabbi David and the head rabbi and President of this New Atlantis synagogue. I assume I met many of you yesterday. I wholeheartedly welcome all of you, for a joint togetherness – children and the aged, old and new, children of Abraham, in this beautiful temple, in this beautiful land of New Atlantis.

"I assume almost all of you are of Jewish faith and see that twenty-seven newcomers are here, plus, I see some new faces too. Our doors are open to all God-lovers and believers, regardless of your religious background. Consequently, first I would like to make an introductory speech, about the Jewish faith and values; later on we shall enter in our regular Sabbath ceremonies. You shall find your '*Siddur*' on your desks that are written both in Hebrew and English. During the week, I would like to get together with the heads of the families and structure some programmes for both grown-ups and children in reference to our regular ceremonies and Kabalah readings. For your acknowledgement, I would like to say, our practice and teachings all are under the auspices of The Rabbinical Council.

"Well, as you may very well know, *Siddur* is the *Jewish Prayer Book* that carries the depths of not only the Jewish faith but also the history of all humanity. It constantly and continually radiates optimism. It greets every single new-born day with the cascading assertion that God has endowed men with a pure soul. In the human soul, there is undeniable basic goodness. The book prescribes the Law and the way of salvation for all mankind.

"The exiled, wandering Jew has tirelessly passed forward leaden-winged centuries joyously ever, to regenerate his own people again and re-build Zion. In his divine destiny, the *Prayer Book* has been a 'must' instrument to survive. It has been confirmed repetitiously that it shall remain forever to comfort the Jewish people in their sorrows.

The ideals of a 'golden age' are set not in the past but in and for the future; blessings and prayers in this book are addressed to God not only as our and our fathers' God, but also to Him, as Avinu shebashamayim, our father who art in heaven; Meleh haolam, the King of the whole universe; and Ribbono shel glam, the Universal Lord. The daily worship echoes the biblical ideals of daily living and the brotherhood that all men should live together, under the sovereignty and dignity of one father, the father of all mankind.

"The *Prayer Book* also reflects the Jewish social idealism. It aims to reach out to a noble, spiritual society. Communal praying and worship bring a lot of strength and through devotion, the congregation reads in the psalmist's words 'Let my prayer come to Three, O Lord, in an acceptable time', is destined for God's kingdom on earth.

"The *Siddur* also contains ecstatic praises of God as man's infinite ideal. The springing biblical psalms praise God's love and compassion and his mercy that tempers justice for all. Meah Berahoth (hundred blessings) link everyone to his blessings through a spiritualising transformation right into the souls.

"Judaism demands that every single Jew should study Torah (*The Book of Proverbs*), in order to be the victor of his quest of to conquer the knowledge and truth that leads to 'right'. As you may know, the meaning of the word Torah is 'teaching'. It responds to the demands and questions of the soul, particularly those of mystical longings. Judaism insists upon the celestial marriage of faith and reason.

"Now, I would like to talk about Israel, our homeland's historical background, a little bit.

"As the bible says, the patriarch Joseph was named 'Israel' by the angel of God, with whom he had wrestled. Thereafter, the descendants of Israel were called 'Bene Israel' (the children of Israel).

"After the death of King Solomon, ten Israelite tribes that were living in Northern Palestine revolted against the 'House of David' and under the leadership of Jeroboam, son of Nebat, the Kingdom of Israel was established in B.C. 933. That kingdom lasted for 211 years, ending in the year B.C. 722. The capital was Shechem, then King Omri moved it to Samaria. There were no outside invaders for a while; however inside, there were constant struggles and continuing changes. The tribes, under kings, used idol worship and then prophet Elijah opened a war against idolatry. The last king was Hoseha who reigned B.C. 734 – B.C.722 – the kingdom was destroyed by Assyrians that year. Naturally, some exile had begun. Some 150 years later the people of the southern kingdom of Judah also suffered exile, almost a fate for the Jewish people until they finally established a State, after World War II, on A.C. May 14th 1948, when Palestine was divided into a Jewish and an Arab State.

"As far as origins are concerned, according to the *Bible*, first the semitic tribes of Hebrews emigrated from Mesopotamia about B.C. 2,000 and settled in Canaan. Jacob and his family later on moved to Egypt to search for a better life and established themselves in the Goshen area. There, through several centuries, the descendants of the patriarchs Abraham, Isaac and Jacob, multiplying greatly, developed

Chapter 12

into twelve Israelite tribes – the Children of Israel. However, the pharaohs of Egypt put them into slavery, before the Israelites were freed by the prophet Moses and returned again to Canaan under the leadership of Joshua.

"After a long struggle, they finally united under the kingship of Saul, followed by Samuel, David and Solomon, and were able to establish the 'Kingdom of Israel'. After Solomon's death, the Israeli country was divided into a northern kingdom (Israel) that comprised ten tribes and a southern kingdom (Judah). After 200 years of existence, Israel was destroyed by Assyrians. Judah survived and thus represented the Jews alone, as a nation. However, in B.C. 586, Judah, too, was destroyed and taken over by the Babylonians and most of the people had to move into Babylon. After this event, for hundreds of years, Judans lived under Persian, Egyptian and Syrian submissions. Then, in the year B.C. 168, as a result of a Maccabean uprising, Judah became re-established until Roman rule which occurred in the year B.C. 63. Then, until A.C. 1948, spreading around the world, they had remained 'wandering Jews'. As history notices, in A.C. 16th century, the King of Spain called them out of the country, then the Emperor Great Soleman of the Ottoman Empire invited them to settle in the territories of the said empire. The faithful Jewish people have never forgotten that Turkish hospitality.

"No doubt, the *Prayer Book* is an outgrowth of the scriptures. Even though its language is that of the biblical Hebrew, it is also mixed with that of Aramaic which also is seen here and there in the *Bible*. In it, there are very valuable phrases, thoughts and inspirations, also important information about the synagogue services, more than fifty psalms from the scripture's *Rupt Hymn Book,* reflecting the Jewish spiritual vision two thousand years ago when biblical prophets had spoken.

"The services today are reminiscent of the organised Israeli Children's worship, in the tabernacle of Moses and Aaron, in the wilds and the shrine at Shiloh, as well as in King Solomon's Temple and later on, in the temple that was erected in Zion. The psalms that we are chanting today were all chanted gloriously in the temple of old.

"Now, let us observe the Sabbath.

"It had been said that 'the more the Jews preserved the Sabbath, the more the Sabbath preserved the Jews!' How true that is. From old times on, the faithful Jewish people, before the sunset that was going to give birth to the Sabbath, had prepared themselves for that glorious event. As we read from Talmud, Rabbi Hanina used to put his best

A.C. 2084

clothing on, saying: 'Come, let us go forth and greet the Sabbath queen.' In this spirit, now we are reading *'The Biblical Song of Songs'* in praise of the Israel bride that had already come. Please be aware of the fact that, beginning next week, we shall read parts 2 and 3 next Friday afternoon and there on."

Chapter One – *The Song of Songs,* which is Solomon's.

> He would kiss me with the kisses on his lips; thy wooing is sweeter than wine. Sweet art thou as fragrant perfume, as scent poured forth art thou; maidens needs must love thee. O take me with thee, that we may run away; for the king has brought me to his chambers, saying, 'We shall be glad and rejoice in thee, and chant the praises'. But thy coming is sweeter than wine. Maidens needs must love thee.

Dark am I, but comely, ye daughters of Jerusalem, dark as the tents of Kedar, comely as the curtains of Solomon. Stare not at me because I am swarthy, for it s the sun has scorched me. My own mother's sons dealt harshly with me; They made me keeper of the wineyards. My own wineyard – my fairness – I have not kept.

Tell me, O thou whom my soul loves, where art thou pasturing they flocks? Where now dost thou let them rest at noon? Lest I wander astray by the flocks of thy companions.
As if thou knows not, thou loveliest of women! Roam forth in the tracks of the flock and pasture thy kids beside the tents of the shepherds.

I liken thee, my dear one, to my steeds in Pharaoh's chariots. How comely would be thy cheeks bedight with jewelled wreaths! How comely thy neck arrayed with chains of jewels! We will make thee wreaths of gold for thy cheeks and for thy neck pendants of silver.

So long as thou, O king, wast in thy divan, (and in my wineyard,) my spikenard gave forth its scent. My beloved is to me a cluster of myrrh which rests all night on my heart. My beloved is to me a spray of henna in the wineyards of Engedi.

Lo, thou, my dear, lo, thou art fair. Thine eyes are dovelike.
Lo, thou, my beloved, art fair and very sweet, and our couch is a simple green bower. Our house beams are of cedar, our rafters of cypress.

Chapter 12

"Now, we are proceeding with Lehu Nerannenah: 'Come, let us sing praises to the Lord' is the opening call of *Psalms* 95 to 100 and *Psalm* 29; six psalms symbolise the six working days of the week. In the sixth, seven times repetition of the phrase 'the voice of the Lord' is also reminiscent of the seventh day Sabbath and is associated with the seven benedictions of the Sabbath Amidah. 'The Lord will bless His people with peace' is a very suitable introduction to the Sabbath that brings the blessing of peace.

(Psalm 85)

Come, let us sing praises to the Lord,
Let us chant in joy to the Rock (*) of our salvation.
Let us come before His presence with thanksgiving.
With joyous songs we shall chant to Him.

For above all gods.
The Lord is a great God and a great King,
In whose hands are the depths of the earth,
And the heights of the mountains are His.

His is the sea, it is He who made it,
And His hands formed the dry land.
Come, let us know bow down and kneel,
Let us bend the knee before the Lord our Maker.

For He is our God,
And we are the people of His pasture,
The flock guided by His hand.
O that you would this day hearken to My voice!
Harden not your heart as at Meribah,

(*) Rock of Ages = Maos Tzur: Opening words of the Hebrew hymn for Hanukkah (one of the biggest feasts of the Jewish religion; it starts on the 25th day of the month Kislev, the third month of the Jewish calendar, corresponding to November-December, of 30 or 31-day duration, and lasts for eight days. It means 'Lights of Dedication' or 'Feast of Dedication', sung after the lighting of the Hannukah candles. In English literature it is known as 'The Rock of the Ages' and signifies the Maccabean victory (a dynasty started by Jadah Maccabeus in the second century B.C., fighting against the despotic ruler of Syria, Antiochus. It lasted for 120 years and in the end bowed to Persian rule) and compares it to the deliverance of Israel from Egypt.

A.C. 2084

As on the day at Massah in the wilderness.

When your fathers tried Me;
They tested Me, though they had seen My work.
Forty years was I wearied with that generation
And I said they are a people who err in their heart;
So that I swore in My anger
That they should not come to the resting place I had appointed.

(*Psalm 96*)

Sing to the Lord a new song,
Sing to the Lord, all the earth.
Sing to the Lord, bless His name;
Day by day proclaim His saving power.

Declare His glory among the nations,
His wonders among all the peoples,
For great is the Lord and exalted in praise;
Awesome is He Above all gods.

For all the gods of the heathens are idols,
But the Lord made the heavens.
Grandeur and majesty are in His presence,
Strength and beauty are in His Temple.

Ascribe to the Lord, you families of nations,
Ascribe to the Lord glory and might.
Ascribe to the Lord in the beauty of holiness;
Bring an offering and come to His courts.

Worship the Lord in the beauty of holiness;
Tremble before Him, all the earth,
Though the world is fixed that it he not moved......
Declare among the nations, "The Lord reigns;
He will judge the peoples with equity."

Let the heavens be glad and the earth rejoice,
Let the ocean roar and the fullness thereof,

Chapter 12

> Let the field rejoice and all that is therein,
> Let all trees of the forest then sing for joy before the Lord.
>
> For He comes, yes, He comes to judge the earth;
> He will judge the world with righteousness,
> And peoples with His undeviating law.

"A Sabbath cannot be a Sabbath without 'The Sabbath's Psalm'. This is the 92nd Psalm. This was chanted by the Levites (members of the tribe Levi; third son of Jacob, and the father of the tribe Levi.) on the Sabbath day in the temple of Jerusalem. Then comes the *93rd Psalm* that acclaims the God of Creation which was completed in the sixth day, before the Sabbath."

A PSALM. A SONG. FOR THE SABBATH DAY

(Psalm 92)

> It is good to give thanks to the Lord,
> And sing praise to Thy name, O Most High,
> To declare Thy loving kindness in the morning.
> And Thy faithfulness at night,
>
> With a ten-stringed harp and with psaltery,
> With solemn song upon the lyre.
> For Thou, O Lord, hast made me rejoice through Thy work,
> I sing praise of the works of Thy hands.
>
> Lord, how great are Thy works,
> How exceeding deep Thy thoughts!
> The dullard observes not,
> Nor does a knave understand this,
>
> That when evil men spring up as grass,
> And those who do only iniquity flourish,
> It is for their utter destruction.
>
> But Thou art supreme forever, O Lord,
> For lo, Thine enemies, O Lord,

A.C. 2084

> For lo, Thine enemies shall perish;
> They who do only iniquity shall be dispersed.
>
> But my horn of strength Thou hast raised up
> Like that of the wild ox;
> I am anointed with fresh oil.
> My eye has looked on those who lie in wait for me,
> My ears hear when the wicked rise against me.
>
> The righteous shall flourish as the palm tree,
> Growing strong as a cedar in Lebanon.
> Planted in the House of the Lord,
> They flourish in the courts of our God.
> They shall bear fruit still in old age,
> Vigorous with the sap of life shall they be.
> To proclaim that the Lord is just,
> My Rock, in whom is no unrighteousness.

(*Psalm 93*)

> The Lord reigns, robed in majesty,
> The Lord is robed and girt with power
> So that the world is set firm
> That it cannot be moved.
>
> Thy throne is established from of old,
> From everlasting art Thou.
> The floods have lifted up, O Lord,
> The floods have lifted up their voice,
> The floods have lifted up their roaring.
>
> But above the thunder of many waters,
> Mighty waters, breakers of the sea,
> Mighty art Thou, Lord on high.
> The testimonies are exceeding sure;
> Holiness beseems Thy House,
> O Lord, for evermore.

So, that was the end of today's Sabbath services at the New Atlantis Synagogue, in downtown. It was so serene and blissful. God bless all

Chapter 12

the people who attend and also who do not attend services. It is time to go home and be with my family.

Before taking off at the street-car station nearby, I wanted to extend my journey and have a tour around. Pushing the music button again at the side of window, choosing Vivaldi's *Double Concerto Per Eco* for violins and string orchestra, I leant back and plunged into deep thoughts for the 65 minutes duration of that magnificent music and silently absorbed the miracle of being alive and a part of a living, seeing and feeling world. This land was 'a chosen land' years ago when our ancestors, including mine, who chose this territory were in a dreaming stage, wondering whether they were going to find eternal happiness through living like 'just human beings', away from all kind of indecencies, mockery, envy and bloodshed. Their dream had come true, thank God, and here we were and how happy I was simply being a worldly President of these lovely people, young and old. I returned home completely refreshed and rested, hugged my beloved ones at home, sipped my lemonade in front of the Big Screen and watched some sporting events. It was a quite loaded week, full of events, and everything seemed to be in good control.

"What your plans are for tomorrow, my dear?" whispered my wife.

"Oh, let me think, I guess it will be good idea to visit the French Catholic Church for their Sunday services tomorrow morning. In the afternoon, I am afraid I shall have to spare some time to make some preparation for the evening's cabinet meeting. You know, some new people want to establish a Masonic Lodge. We have to interview them too. Now, I should make some calls for those. I am glad you alerted me."

"My pleasure. When you meet upstairs for the cabinet meeting, we wives could get together for a cup of tea and cake, that shall be lovely," cheered Jada.

I got up and called Keith so that he should call the other ministers for a cabinet meeting here, tomorrow, Sunday evening at 8 p.m., as well as the applicants for a possible Masonic Lodge establishment meeting at 9 p.m. at the Presidential Rectangular Office, on the 33rd floor as well. These arrangements were confirmed in ten minutes time. I succumbed into my comfortable armchair again. A youngster was screaming at the top of his voice: "Goal.... goal, goal, goal.."

The French Catholic Church is a relatively small but very charming, gracious building, situated at the corners of Mega Station and Venus

Chapter 13

Avenues. Its President, Pere Pierre Durand, is originally from Negal of Rika, a retired medical man and a sage religious person. As he was getting older, like all of us, his eyesight had begun to diminish and that had upset him terribly due to the fact that he was an avid reader. But, he, solemnly had said then: "As old Greeks say, when humans' eyesight weakens, the wisdom eyes shine!" So, he chose the pious occupation. His great personality, in spite of the fact of his being black, had spread and conquered everybody's hearts. His lovely and devoted wife Lola had always been his 'eyes and ears', directing him everywhere, wherever they went.

So, as we arrived at this graceful church, Pere Pierre and Lola were just getting out of their quarters. We met halfway and hugged each other with love and compassion. Then Jada and I took our 'pre-assigned seats' for government cabinet members, of course in the first row, as usual. Needless to say, before taking our seats, we did not neglect to burn candles and to kneel down before the altar. The beautiful odours of the scents had already filled the entire air. And, right on the dot at eleven o'clock, as the organ began to vibrate its celestial melodies, Pere Pierre and his assistants, also altar boys in a line, entered the ceremonial area. The church was completely full of worshippers, very few of them with the earphones (Trans-Cares) in their ears, who all rose. The small reading books in our palms, along with the priest we began to read:

PETIT JESUS, NOUS OFFRONS AVEC VOUS LA PATENE A DIEU, NOTRE PERE DU CIEL, PAR LES MAINS DE NOTRE BONNE MERE LA SAINT EGLISE, C'EST A DIRE EN UNION AVEC LE PAPE, AVEC NOTRE EVEQUE ET AVEC NOS PRETRES.

(Jesus child, we are offering the sacred bowl to God with you, our

Chapter 13

Father in Heaven, by the hands of our church's servant angel, namely with the unity of the Pope with our Bishop and Priests.)

Then, we sat down solemnly and Pere Pierre read the morning prayer, while we listened carefully and wholeheartedly.

Au nom du Pere, et du Fils, et du Saint-Spirit.
(In the name of Father, and of the Son and of the Holy Spirit)

Mon Dieu, je crois fermement que vous etes partout et particulierement en ce lieu. Je vous adore comme mon Créateur et mon souverain Maitre, et je me soumets entirement a Vous.
(I believe firmly that You are everywhere and particularly in this place. I adore You as my Creator and frequenter Master, and I submit myself entirely to You.)

Je vour remercie, o mon Dieu, de m'avoir crété, de m'avoir racheté et fait chrétien, comme aussi de toutes les autres graces que j'ai reçues de vous, et particulierement de m'avoir conservé durant cette nuit.
(O my God, I am grateful to you for you created me, you redeemed me and made me Christian; and all the other graces that I receive from You and particularly of conserving me during to night." And so on.

After the communion was performed for the ones who desired, with the accompaniment of org, the prayers sang a hymn: 'Marchons, chrétiens' (Christians, let us walk).

Marchons, chrétiens au combat, a glorie,
Marchons, chrétiens, sur les pas de Jésus.
Nous remporterons la victoire,
Et la couronne des élus.
(Christians, let us walk to the glory,
Christians, let us walk on the feet of Jesus.
We are winning the victory,
And, the crown of the élite)

The ceremonies ended with Schubert's *'Gloria'*:

A.C. 2084

> Gloire, gloire au Seigneur, à Lui gloire,
> Diront sans fin les esprits bien heureux
> Gloire, gloire au Seigneur, à Lui gloire,
> Paix au coeur droit ne cherchant que les Cieux
> (Glory, glory to God, glory to Him,
> Let us say endlessly happy spirits
> Glory, glory to God, glory to Him,
> Peace to the right soul that searches nothing but skies!)

How serene all of these were. Indescribable and unforgettable.

For tonight's cabinet meeting we gathered at the Rectangular Office, as I had cited before. The reason for that office name was very simple.

Chapter 14

In this room, at the top of the 33rd floor of Pyramid I, everything is shaped in the form of a rectangle. Was there a 'secret' freemason amongst our founding fathers? I don't know. The windows, tables, chairs, the library material, electrical systems and decorative material were all in a rectangular shape. From the windows, it was possible to see far away distances, the four corners of the republic island. Also the IGL (Information Gathering Laboratory) and an observatory occupying the top space. Even though all precautions were taken against possible fire, and just in case of a power failure, an iron spiral staircase, protected with unbreakable glass 10 cm thick, descends from here down to the bottom on the outside of the building, passing every single storey, to evacuate the people if and when needed. Next to the lightning rod at the utmost point, there was a waving flag – the flag of New Atlantis, a white base and a rainbow at the middle: 'Hope of all mankind'.

Needless to say, all my ministers were right on time in the Rectangular Office, taking their seats all around me at the Rectangular Table. I touched the 'registration' at the beginning of the Conference. There is no need for mini-skirted female secretaries to accompany us in our meetings late on Sunday nights. At the end, we compile our printed material by hand, each receives one, one extra copy is left on the table so that the following morning a regular clerk, when they come to work, by the direction of the Personnel Department head, shall file the minutes of the meeting, using whatever forms are proper.

"OK gentlemen, the prospects shall be here within an hour or so. We shall interview the applicants and if everything is OK, naturally we will give the green light. Keith, you have given me the list of the five men and some characteristics, as such:

George K., 33, bachelor, country came from: Reece;
Smith L., 39, married, from: Gland;
Clarke M., 28, single, from: Rance;
Gregor S., 34, married, from: Merica, and
Yani Z., 30, single, from: Alta Island.

"Keith, would you be kind enough make photocopies of this list for the other ministers? Thank you!" As Keith went to the next room to the copying centre for that purpose, I continued:

"Needless to say, Keith is going to check tomorrow morning on the International Information Centre through 'double-pink lines' whether these men have any undesirable record or not. Suppose they don't have any, how we should proceed?

"Where are they going to function?" asked Jack, "namely where they are going to meet? Do they need any permanent housing, any supplies? Or, are they going to use one of the temples that already exist?"

"Since they are supposed to go to their own secret meetings, continuous ceremonies and rituals, they need a separate, independent place. Where do you think such a place could exist? Atilla, what do you think; as I visited the French Church this morning, there I saw the unused chapel, at the other corner of the garden, under chestnut trees. (I addressed that minute to Keith who was just returning from the copying room and was distributing the list of names) Keith, is that building suitable and available for them or do you think or we have to provide some other place?"

"Mr. President, I think it is available. We last used that gracious building for three elderly French nuns as special dormitories as well as for some private prayer sessions, but when they needed more supervised medical care, we took them to the Retirement House. Since then it has been free. Jack, tomorrow morning, why don't send me one of your building supervisors to my office so that we can visit the French Church together and see what we can do."

"You bet I shall do Keith."

"I myself, too, in the morning shall call Pere Pierre and request permission from him for such a possibility," I said. "I want to be sure that he should not have any other respectable projects in mind. OK?"

"OK."

"Furthermore, for any other cleaning, repair, personnel, kitchen or

Chapter 14

service material needs, you Jack and Keith, between you, I am sure will arrange things, won't you?"

"Yes Sir, by all means!"

"Jack, I have a very special request for you. The other night, as usual, I was screening the entire halls, especially the sacred meetings, of course with no picture on but the sound appeared to be somewhat disappearing, coming and going, weak or interrupted, noisy. Particularly that of the Mormon's church. Would you be kind enough to check there, of course in as natural a manner as possible, and let me know whether there is anything wrong with the communication lines? For this prospective building too, in the grounds of St. Ethienne Church?"

"Sure, Mr. President. Now already is the beginning of the summer and we are about to start making a general surveillance of all. I shall pay particular attention to the buildings that you mentioned. And, I will report back to you."

"Thank you Jack. And, thanks to your gracious ladies, Edith and Debra – I hope I did not over-use you that much tonight. Besides the subjects that we spoke about personally at the beginning of the week, is there anything that you would like to contribute tonight?"

Both ladies with velvety smiles, said: "Thank you, Mr. President. You are quite busy tonight. Nothing special. If there shall be, you know, we are quick to lay eggs!" (Everyone laughed!)

At this point the group of five, in their clean attire and with polite mannerisms, appeared at the open door and, after the customary formal introductions, that is to say name exchanges between all, we all sat down on the chairs around the Rectangular Table.

"Well, gentlemen, first of all I hope you feel very comfortable here in our land, that is also going to be your land. There has been a complete week since your arrival. Is everything in order? Settlement in the houses, the routine evaluations?"

"Yes, Mr. President, everything is in order, nearly perfect," responded Smith L. "We are from Gland, have two children, Alec 5, and Heather 7, who immensely love the clean and orderly way of life over here. Plenty of room to run. Big Screen to watch everything really big, you know kids. I am sure. Mr. Gleem's office received the total evaluations. I guess, in a short while, we shall be provided with some jobs that I am quite anxious to start."

"What was your job or training in your home?"

"I am a mechanic; I worked as a master mechanic in the auto-repair business, then in some industrial machinery, the milk industry and alike. My wife used to work in nursing homes for the elderly."

"You gentlemen, let us start from George K. Would you like to summarise with a few sentences who are you and what you were doing before coming here?"

"Well, I am from Reece, a bachelor. I worked in the sailing business and, in the production and repair of sailcloth I also worked in a winehouse as a taster for years."

"I am sure we shall use your first qualification at large. Well, Mr. Clarke M., what about you?"

"Sir, I am from Rance; also single. I am principally an auto-mechanic. I was one of the private chauffeurs for a motor company vice-President for years."

"Mr. Gregor S., you Sir?"

"Well, I am from Merica, Sir. I worked on a news stand for years, then I had my own. I am married, having one son of 7, Gary. He is quite a boy. My wife worked at the Education Department as teacher's helper with the pre-schoolers."

"And you, Mr.Yani Z, the last but not the least, what about your whereabouts?"

"Well, I'm from Alta Island and am a graduate of a junior college, specialising in public relations, also doing a lot of work guiding tourists. I am a bachelor too."

"Very fine gentlemen, I thank you for this briefing. Now, would you tell me how did you get the idea of establishing a Freemasonry Lodge in this New Atlantis Republic? Did you know each other before and most importantly, what are your credentials in freemasonry, if you would like to be the founders of this brotherhood?"

"No, Mr. President, we did not know each other until we came here to the island by boat," replied Mr. Smith L. "We all belong to certain nominations, as usual, and the least has a third, namely a 'Masters', degree in freemasonry in our original homes, registered officially in the Lodges that are internationally registered and recognised. I, for the past two years, was The Right Worshipful Senior Grand Warden at the Battleborough, Lodge No:176 in Land, having finished my 33rd degree two years ago. Junior Grand Warden then, I was. You should not have any doubts about it, otherwise, how could we initiate this very responsible and respectful project here? On the way, before reaching New Renfusa, we met by chance – as you may have heard, masons recognise each other by their general mannerisms and the way

Chapter 14

that they walk, talk, etc.- and talked about whether any Lodge was present in our new land; naturally none of us knew what facilities were present here and what we could practice."

"This is much more than I expected Mr. Smith L., truthfully. The rest of you, also are registered in an internationally acceptable free and accepted masons Lodges?"

"Yes Sir, surely we are!"

I plunged into thoughts and then looking to the faces of my cabinet members to see whether things were satisfactory or not for them too to start with. After reading a green light in their looks, I started to talk slowly.

"Gentlemen. Based upon your words, I, as President of this Republic of New Atlantis, also taking into account of my cabinet members 'silent' OKs, initially give you a start for your noble project. Starting tomorrow morning, through Mr. Gleem's office, the Minister of Administration and Personnel, your names will be forwarded to your original Lodges where you are registered for an official check. Again by tomorrow, our Administrative Department officials will start a search for your worshipping place. Initially, we thought the old chapel at the St. Ethienne French Catholic Church grounds, if Pere Pierre has no objection."

Clarke joyously interrupted my words. "Oh, Mr. President, I hope it will come true. It is a beautiful place. Incidentally, I saw you there this morning with your wife. It was my first visit, but I loved it."

"Oh, good, I am glad you liked it. And, as I know somehow about freemasonry, I advise you to start working within yourselves. First of all:

1) Addressed to me, write up your project and apply and register at the Department of Administration.
2) For the offices to be held, divide the possible titles and duties among yourself. To start with, since you are just five people now, I advise the following offices and officers should be decided and nominated by you: The Most Worshipful of Grand Master, The Right Worshipful of Junior Grand Warden, The Very Worshipful of Grand Secretary, The Very Worshipful of Junior Grand Deacon, and The Worshipful Grand Sword Bearer. Forward those names immediately to me.
3) I shall forward these nominations and my approval and endorsements, of course temporarily, to the Lodges that you are

registered with, and with their final advice, either directly or through them, I shall endeavour to register you with International Free and Accepted Masons.

4) At the first opportunity, that is to say within a few days, or a week or so, I would like to present you to the entire nation first on the Big Screen and give some introduction. I am sure that some people know something about this organisation. I personally don't want anything hidden or secretive. Everything should be as open as a clean heart, all your activities and sharing shall be open. As the old Greeks used to say: 'A real honest person could act when he is alone, as if he is in the presence of Zeus!'

"D'accord gentlemen?"

"D'accord Mr. President. Thanks a million."

Then, they shook hands, one-by-one, and left us. The general consensus among us about the meeting had been a very favourable one. And, our ministers extended their congratulations and thanks to me for a brief but efficient, fruitful and informative meeting. I said: "This is my duty. This is why I am here for."

"OK three musketeers, pick up your wives and kids, and go home. Ladies, thanks for your graceful existence too. I have to meditate now and read some books as usual. Pleasant dreams!"

This is Monday morning. Another 'not that much routine week' is just about to start. The major difference, of course, is the newcomers to

Chapter 15

the State. For every six months or so, they bring new flesh and blood, the city State is in a State of liveliness and joy. So, I requested Edith to accompany me. She very graciously agreed to a train ride city tour, at times getting off at the very streets and restaurants where people were shopping, eating and taking new things to their new homes in joy. This is quite an education for us and I am sure for them too.

So, at about 10 a.m., we got on the train right in front of Pyramid I and circled around, as I call it 'newcomers' follies'. Old timers used to say in French: *'Bon observeur, bon médécin!'* (A good observer is a good medical man!) Trains of course were presently much fuller than in previous weeks. People who had almost completed all medical and personal achievement tests and evaluations were now throwing themselves into the streets, ice-cream parlours, restaurants and shopping plazas in free, dreamland gratification. We were witnessing first the wishful shopping chit-chat like "Mom, I really want to have a nice, pink nightgown. Maybe two. The other day I saw such beautiful gym shoes. All white and blue, red stripes around. Wow!" "Dad, I saw blue jeans I used to dream of. Is it true, as they say, that they are all for free? Then, I would like to go to ice-cream parlour too, I haven't eaten a banana split for a long, long time!" "Mom, do you remember, you promised me an Angora cat. This weekend shall we go to the Animal World and get one?" "Of course my dear." "I hope it is not that expensive." "It is for free for the citizens, we don't have to pay anything!" "Mom, how come? Why should things be for free? Who pays the money?" "The government. Money is not circulating in the market but I and daddy shall be working every day somewhere. So, everyone helps everyone even without knowing each other and every person is equal. Isn't it nice? On our way back, we can buy some toys too." "Good, mom, but what we shall do when Santa Claus comes to town in Christmas?" "Here Christmas is every day. Santa Claus, as you have just started to understand and discover last holiday season, is just a symbol of goodness, kindness and giving. If human beings would, and really could, be a Santa Claus, here is our chance. That's why we left your grandparents and the other beloved friends behind, not just for an adventure but for a dream that can come true, not through statesmen, politicians and armed soldiers but through the very essence of our own existence: God-loving, human-loving, unselfish, hardworking, non-envious, giving, sharing individuals. Let's get off. We came to downtown!"

There, we got off too. We entered one of the largest department stores in downtown, Jacey's! There, too, you can easily track the eager-beaver new customers who, in spite of their best will and dignity, nearly attack whatever is offered or on the scene. But within the next six months or so, for the next newcomers, they will just smile, remembering how they themselves had behaved six months ago.

My old habit is to visit book stores, not of course the sort where people look for 'Do-it-yourself, 'How you can be more successful in business or sex? or 'The name of the game is money' kind of books – we don't display those that much because people's wants are different and indeed there is no need for them. Teenagers, of course, are too busy chatting through intercontinental viewers – talkers who do not have time to read anything. Some adults, going back to past centuries in a time-tunnel to re-experience past romances, may prefer *Anna Carenina, Doctor Jivago* or existentialistic and post-existentialistic novels. *Stranger, Now?, Return of Hamlet, Would King Lear Live in the 21st Century?, Don Quijote, Welcome Home!, Celestial Melody, Shaman's Loves, Dimensions of Sky Life, The Fate of the Universe, Physiology and Histology of Thinking and Love, Art of Praying and Dying, Angel Follies, The Anatomy of the Religion, Frequencies in Thinking and Feeling For Each Other, Stories from Previous Lives, The Poetry of Non-Being, Phobias in Flowers* and *The Invisible Bridge Between Sun and MOon* are best-sellers now, of course just by definition, although as with anything else, all books are free too.

Though human beings continue to eat popcorn, cheese burgers, mushroom burgers, burger burgers, chocolates, candies, cheesoronies, macoronies, roni-ronies, fried potatoes, fried bananas, pickled melons and watermelons; drink mineral waters, sherbets and fruit juices; and eat every kind of meat including frogs, crocodiles, fish, sheep and

Chapter 15

chicken, fresh or cooked, baked or fried, we rather encourage the eating of green vegetables and fruit -cauliflowers, spinach, squashes and beans, salads, broccoli, carrots, mushrooms, apples, peaches, melon, grapes and figs, fresh or desiccated. So, nothing is new in this old world.

Toy stores are really booming. The younger the age, the more ambitious and insatiable the children are. "Hey, look at that, mom, I want that electric train. I want that flying helicopter too. Oh, look at those puzzles and colouring sets. Mom, are there any guns, machine guns here? No? Oh, too bad?" The attending clerk advises one type of toy from each department; so one has to chose either an electric train or a helicopter; crayons or a water colour set; if you choose a three-wheel bicycle, you cannot have a two-wheeler at the same time. Notebooks, unless a very special type is required for school, should be one at a time. You can eat chocolate, or chocolate cake, even chocolate cake with ice-cream on it, but you cannot eat chocolate cake and *mille-feuille* pastry too. It is a health principle. Too much is too much, and being over-weight is a medical sickness. Besides, from an early age, children have to learn to control their eating habits. We respect the old saying 'One is what he eats!'

Dress and clothing departments are much the same in essence but operate at a much slower pace and with less ambition displayed. "I love these skirts, can I have two of them? No? OK, I can have only one, this straw yellow one. Thank you." "Can I have this shawl? OK, Thank you. This pair of gloves. I need underclothes too. How many? One pair each? OK. Measure 36 please. Handkerchiefs? One? OK. This pair of moccasins? No.8.5 for my feet? Perfect! Thank you. Let me try, oh, fits perfectly. Let me see, what else? Can I go to the parfumery department too? Today? Oh, thank you."

Edith and I sat at the cafeteria for a light luncheon. Here, the service is either self-service for ready things or you may order something cooked, like an omelette, which we both did. With an additional fruit salad and a glass of milk, we were quite satisfied. The people who were serving were very pleasant, doing their shift work very diligently and willingly. Three-shift cafeterias and restaurants are restricted only to highly-populated areas, like hospitals, factories and alike, otherwise two-shift services are generally good enough to serve the entire population around the clock, seven days a week. Drug stores also work only two shifts, and in case of any need, hospitals and health centres throughout the island could supply the emergency medicine. As we said before, transportation, namely railcar service, is available every ten minutes and that is also on twenty-four-hour a day basis, although between 10 p.m. and 1 a.m. they come down to every twenty minutes, and from 1 a.m. until 7 a.m. they are available every half an hour. Should there be any accident or mishap of any kind and someone needs any help, with transportation or any health issue, you could push a red button that is placed on a special small concrete construction at one hundred metre intervals on both sides of the streets and in a few minutes an emergency vehicle from a nearby hospital, a male helper and a registered nurse with a first-aid kit in hand, will rush to your area immediately, for those concrete blocks are all numbered, coded and mapped. On the same block, protected with a thick glass, there is also a red phone that you can pick up and use to speak to someone who can help you twenty hours a day, regardless of who you are and where you are. We love our citizens and care about them.

Well, this kind of life might be boring to some people because of the non-existence of gangsters, car races, police chases, bullet firing and drunk people shouting loudly and alike. When I was a young boy on our arrival here, there was still no police force; instead some night-watchmen were making rounds. They were not carrying guns but mops. They were dressed in dark blue coats with the same colour caskets on their heads. Their communication system was that of whistles. On each street there was one and through a special whistling they let each other know their whereabouts. They were ready to help people if needed, say if someone was assaulted or a house was about to be broken into, like two hundred years ago some third world countries used to experience. They were very friendly fellows. They would chat with the young girls who were coming from late movies and would accompany them if needed, help an elderly lady cross the street or assist someone searching for a pharmacy and alike. Now, everything is more efficient, fast and formal. After relaying this to Edith, who did not have this experience as a youngster, I thanked her for her lovely company and wished a nice time for the rest of the day.

Well, this is Monday evening again, and after having my supper with my wife, I am in my home and at the special work desk. As I

Chapter 16

experienced something strange last Monday evening, I am dying to hear what is going on in the Mormon church!

I touch the 'sound' button and am awaiting anxiously. At last something begins to be heard.

"Sarvan abhivadaye vah! (Meaning: I greet you all!). Oh, they speak in Sanskrit. A few unclear voices.

"Ciram adarsanem aryasya vayam udvignah!" (We have been distressed at not seeing your honour for a long time!)

Cirasya kalasya praptah asi." (You have arrived after a long time.)
"Anyah kuh agacchati?" (Who else is coming?)
"George ca Kevork!" (George and Kevork!)
"Sadhu." (Good.)
"Bhhagavant." (Your reverence.)
"Mitranam eva priyam etat. (To friends, this is a welcome night.)
Arya, api satror uyasenam upalah-dham?" (Have you discovered a weakness of your enemy, sir?)
"Na tatha!" (Not yet!)
"Jnayatam punah kim etad iti!" (Find out again what it is!)
"Api khalu svapna esa syat?" (Could this indeed be a dream?)
"Kim uktavan asi?" (What did you say?)
"Api khalu svapna esa syat, aryah?" (Could it be indeed a dream, your Excellency?)
"Khalu!.. punar, drsya." (Certainly! but, to be seen..)
"Akarnayati!" (Listen to!) ... then, something incomprehensible..
"Ni ayam katha-vibhago ismabhir anyena va sruta:parvah." (This part of the story has not been heard before by us or anyone else), a few sounds, then:

"Tat kim ity asankase?" (Why then are you afraid?)
"Avagacchami te tesmin sauhardam." (I understand your fondness for him.)
"Kim tu 'katham asmahbir upagantavya' iti sampadharayami!" (But I am wondering how we should approach him!)
"Icchathı aivı aitan, na va?" (Do you want this or not?)
"Dehi me prativacanam." (Give me an answer.)
"Asmi!" (I am).
"Distya dharma. Sadhu! Su:yanah. N'edam vismarisyami!" (Congratulations!
Bravo! Good man! I will not forget this!)
"Sru! Apnuhi prathama... anyutha, hata! Asti mant Moroni Plates. Band ca pariraksyantam asya pranah. Aduna!" (Listen! Obtain first... otherwise, kill! He is the possessor of Moroni Plates. Enter into his friendship and spare his life! Now!)

I turned the knob off. I had heard enough. This was really and truly astonishing for me, and was occurring for the first time at Presidential level. From time to time, we hear some loose talk, threat or some uprising-like moves but they never come alive in spite of the fact that we do not have any armed police force. People come here of their own choosing but knowing a little bit of personal and social psychology, when the basic needs are not satisfied, then oppressed, repressed envies, desires and feelings may come close to the surface. But, I sincerely believe that the system *in toto* does not permit for grandiosity or foul play. If you don't have a monetary system, in spite of the fact that this may partially curtail a healthy challenge in commerce and maybe in national growth and advance in some areas, we are advanced enough as far as civilisation is concerned; we people who came from old worlds, know better what "we should not do" rather than "what we should do". At the moment, the republic is going through the second generation – like me – who is in power and everything (except this last mystery, to be truthful!) seems to be under good control. But, I sincerely believe that after the third generation's dominance, the nation shall really level off.

Anyway, let us come to the puzzle. There are a lot of serious questions which need to be answered. First of all, why do people speak Sanskrit? I am the only one in this nation, due to my social psychiatry education, who knows that dead language, as I had mentioned earlier somewhere. It is well possible they don't want anybody to hear and

Chapter 16

know what they are up to. Perhaps, perhaps not. Secondly, who is this "your majesty?" Since we are not a political empire or an emirate, or a "safe" place for escapees from genocide, this could well be a religious or sacred chevaliers group adventures or ambitions or something like that. The request for the establishment of a Freemasonry Lodge which came contemporary with this mystery now gains a special importance; is it a complete coincidence or is there any interrelatedness between? What are those "Moroni Plates"? Never heard of them. The person I gather supposedly has them is who? One of the State greats? Or me? Oh my gosh, I am really thrilled, since they talked of a "killing" that had never occurred in this State's history over the past sixty years, not even once. I know I do not have such a thing in my possession. I don't have any ambition of any sort, any unsatisfied envy, an eye on anything, God knows that and my people here know that. I do not have any hidden property or steel safes or... Wait a minute, let me think. When I said "steel safe", that brought to my mind my grandfather's belongings that were passed from him to the third generation, namely to me, for safe-keeping; but for God's sake, even I don't know what they are? Anyway, this is one important point to search for. But before anything else, I am going up to the Presidential Library to do a little bit of research in ancient books and encyclopaedias, and see what they write about Mormons and those Moroni Plates. As I started to move, I felt better. If there is an unrevealed mystery somewhere, I know I am the person to solve that. Oh, I already feel better now.

Our library may not be comparable to those of Atican's or ancient nations' national galleries, but for research it is incomparably better and much more practical than most of them, in a way, quite unique. As I had been elected President of the New Atlantis Republic, I donated my ten thousand Latin, French, German, English, Italian, Sanskrit, Spanish, Turkish and Arabic volumes to this very special library. Secondly, from my childhood onwards, I myself kept writing "the contents" and "idioms" in crayon at the tops of the pages of the books that I read and later on, those notes were classified and entered into our supreme mega computers. Throughout the years, either at the university while teaching or in general education programmes, I advocated this system to the entire nation. Now, almost anyone who reads a book does the same and, whether they donate the book or just bring it in temporarily, they let it be borrowed by our master librarians for a while and all these titles are compiled in huge volumes. For instance, if you touch the word "love", in a split second, the compilation of all idioms, sayings, verses from poems or a few sentences from all write-ups come on to your screen, like from the Bible or Koran, from Aristo's *State*, or Aristoteles' *Greek Theatre* or Solon's *Sayings*, Homer's *Iliada*, Shakespeare's *King Lear* or *Hamlet*, V. Hugo's *Miserables*, S. Zweig's *The History of Yesteryears*" Chechov's *Three Sisters*, etc. This system, of course permits valuable research projects in depth. In any case, for this personal contribution of mine, I am really proud of myself. Once more, whatever I have learned in this world, is not mine, it is the product of this culture and shall remain so consciously, and will be renewed, rejuvenated and re-appearing in the subconscious of the forthcoming generations as "collective unconscious". Incidentally, for old-timers like me, the best gift to give a friend is a book, especially old prints. The rest are published by the State and free exchange is already the mode. We share everything openly in this land.

There were relatively a few books and limited information about Mormons and Moroni Plates but the good old *Encyclopaedia Ritannica*, Panati's book about *"Sacred Things and Customs"*, directly gave me the initial information and knowledge that I badly needed. I could not find an original *"Book of Mormons"* that I should request from the leader of the church right tomorrow morning. That could also give me a chance to visit the church tomorrow evening anyway. (Let me see whether I shall be able to identify those voices that I heard from the system. Shame, shame on me!) As you also shall learn with me, the relatively short resources about this subject are due to Mormonism's quite late presentation to the world, say for the last couple of centuries or so, thus not being a well-studied subject to the thinkers and philosophers of the world, as the other great religions might have been.

Well, here it is what the books say about this religion.

Old Testament informs us that God assigned three archangels to different duties: Michael, 'like God' (Hebrew), was the national guardian angel for Israel. He is imagined as the warrior leader of the heavenly hosts against the forces of evil. During early and medieval Christianity, he is regarded as the helper of the Christian forces against the heathen. He is the heavenly high priest who keeps the keys of heaven. In Islam, called 'Mika(i)l', he is recognised as the controller of the forces of the nature, with his 1,000 assistants called 'karüibiyün' (cerubim) providing men with food and knowledge. He was the one who delivered Moses the Ten Commandments which tuned to a much deeper piety. His feast day is on September 20th. Along with Gabriel, they did herald the birth of monotheistic Judaism, Christian-based

Christianity, and the Koran inspired Islam.

Gabriel is conceived as 'God's man' (Hebrew), 'God's messenger', who announced to the Virgin Mary she was to bear Son of God as well as announcing the coming birth of Joon the Baptist. In Islam, he is recognised as 'Gibril' (Gebreal), 'faithful spirit', also revealed the Koran to Mohammed. In Christian art, Gabriel is depicted as a human figure with long hair and multi-coloured wings, holding a sceptre or a lily. His feast day is on March 24th.

Raphael, 'God heals' (Hebrew), is known as the healer of the Tobit's blindness (The apocryphal book of Tobit) and the conqueror of the demon Asmodeus. Also 'patron of travellers', He is 'the angel of the spirits of men'. His feast day is on October 24th.

In the A.C. 1820s, in the U.S.A., in Palmyra, N.Y. to be exact, the Mormon archangel Moroni inspired a teenager named Joseph Smith to establish the 'Church of Jesus Christ of Latter-day Saints'.

As Mormon doctrine dictates, God, who was a man once upon a time, had married a 'heavenly mother' and therefore had been a father of 'spirit children' who had assumed outwardly bodily shapes and populated the world. Marriage is a very sacred thing for Mormons and they are expected to marry at a Mormon temple in two styles in their own choice: 'for time', and 'for eternity'. First through 'baptism, then 'marriage through a Mormon temple', a Mormon himself becomes God-like.

Consequently, Mormons are very deeply attached to the church and labour, even endlessly one would say. One of the most prominent beliefs is that they are "able to convert the souls of deceased non-believers" through a ceremonial staging called 'baptism of the dead'. In A.C. 1995, Jews had asked Mormons "to stop converting dead Jewish Holocaust victims" of the World War Two (A.C. 1938-45) into the Mormon faith. Upon this request, Mormon church Administration Headquarters in Salt Lake City, Utah, had agreed to remove more than 380,000 Jewish people's names – that were registered at the International Genealogical Index – from such baptism. However, it is known that the church still practices the conversion of dead souls – at the moment about 20 million are registered.

Mormon life, in reality, heavily depends upon the family, however male-oriented. The wife achieves exaltation, a kind of ecstasy, through participating in her husband's eternal priesthood. The husband, who is a man, is a kind of priest and even God, or his representative. Their belief extends to the point that the glorified-exalted couples spend eternity in painless and pleasurable procreations; they must continue their existence in all other planets too where they may be worshipping the original heavenly father and mother.

Mormons believe that, they did live in Christ's time. We already know that Christianity had itself figured out from the Jewish Sacred Scriptures, beyond any doubt. Similarly, according to the Islamic belief, Jewish prophet Abraham was the first Muslim. Thus, if this is true, Islam antedates Judaism. According to the Latter-day Saints' theology, during his lifetime, Jesus Christ himself had established here, on earth, particularly at Jerusalem, the original 'The Church of Jesus Christ', and 'the Saints' were its members. After his resurrection, Jesus had visited the New World (America) and there, before ascending to heaven, he had established a church that was the beginning of the official re-starting of Mormons in the modern world.

In the year A.C. 1820, a fifteen-year old young man Joseph Smith (A.C. 1805 – A.C.1844) received his first divine vision. Jesus Christ, through his (Mormon) archangel Moroni, had warned him "not to go to any other church, since until then, a true church did not exist!" Following that, in the forthcoming ten years or so, he inspired a series of revelations that had claimed him as a reverend, then the first prophet of the new church, namely the 'The Church of Jesus Christ of Latter-day Saints'. Then, the previously established 'The Earlier-day Saints Church' was made extinct. Reverend Smith, however, had to be involved in several bloody battles, like Mohammed. He moved around a lot with his followers and died at the very early age of 39 during one of those battles.

Since Mormons also believed in polygamy and practiced so – including the founder prophet), in A.C. 1856, a Republican Presidential platform enacted a law against that. Until A.C. 1890, more than one thousand men were convicted on 'polygamy' charges. On the same date, the U.S. Supreme Court gave its final decision on this issue: "The polygamy is illegal!" By coincidence, a Wilford Woodruff, the head of the Mormon church in Utah then, said he had "received a divine command on the issue that the multiple wives practice should be stopped!" Therefore, it did stop.

The history of the religions teaches us that all religions and/or sacred belief systems had their own books of inspiration: For Judaism, Tanak-*Old Testament*; for Christianity, *New Testament*-Apocrypha (Hidden things); for Islam, The *Koran*-The Recitation; for Confucianism, *Analects*-Selected Sayings of Confucius; for Hinduism, The *Vedas*-the wisdom; for Buddhism, The *Tipitaka*-three baskets; and for Mormonism, the

Chapter 16

Book of Mormon.

Joseph Smith, the founder prophet, had received from the angel Moroni the 'golden Moroni plates', a kind of 'tablets' that were the proof of the old Israeli registration of Mormons, sacred history and beliefs, which due to wars and constant moves during the settling of the mid-west provinces of the USA in A.C. 1850's completely disappeared and until nowadays, their whereabouts were not known. Supposedly, Reverend Smith translated that knowledge into English and turned it into the Mormonic Bible. The *Book of Mormons* accepts God as a real person with a visible body of flesh and bones; that is originally registered in papyric writings, collected and saved at the Metropolitan Museum of Art in New York City.

The other very interesting claim in the *Book of Mormon* – reportedly, I have not read it yet! – according to the writings of those who supposedly read them, is that the virtuous, industrious, fair-skinned Nephites were later on exterminated by the sinful, red-skinned Lamanites. There follows the life philosophy of Mormons: God's good people are first very prosperous and prideful, then decadent; finally, they are punished and they repent. This moral cycle is very well known and recorded in the sacred literature.

The *Book of Mormons* denies the existence of the 'original sin' and the family relationships could be eternal. This view is more anthropometric than that of theocentric.

One of Joseph Smith's revealed scriptures was *The Book of Abraham*. Similar writings, as said above, on papyrus exist in the Metropolitan Museum of Art. In Smith's translation, people with 'black skins' were cursed and, pertaining to the priesthood, black Afro-Americans were excluded from any office in the Mormon church.

Very interesting material, tiring to the eyes and mind, but it taught me several things and fired me forwards to search more. It is quite late at night; tomorrow morning I shall make arrangements to attend the Mormon church, perhaps to start with a private visit tomorrow evening; then, yes, open my grandpa's memoirs and start to read. I believe it contains very important information, maybe the keys to this puzzle that possibly, or probably, maybe threatening somebody's life, including my own. Anyway. For tonight, at least our *Idioms' Encyclopaedia* gained some new 'key words' and corresponding entries, like: Mormons, Joseph Smith, *The Book of Mormons*, *The Book of Abraham*, Nephites, Lamanites, Moroni Plates, Wilford Woodruff and enriched the World War II Holocausts, archangel Michael, archangel Raphael, archangel Gabriel, Mohammed,

A.C. 2084

polygamy, Islam, Judaism and Christianity.

I am going to bed. Goodnight everybody!

As I sat at my desk, naturally the first thing came to my mind was to call Mormon church headquarters downtown and request an

Chapter 17

appointment for this evening, if it were possible, with Reverend Arthur, the President of the church. It did not take too long to accomplish that; Reverend Arthur, in his very calm and settled, sure tone of voice, greeted me with his usual gentlemanly and charmingly attitude:
"Good morning Mr. President!"
"Good morning Reverend Arthur."
"It is indeed a pleasure to hear from you. I know how busy you might be that we have not seen you in our church for a while. What can I do for your Excellency?"
"My dear friend, I would like to make a visit with you, if possible this evening. Are you too busy?"
"Yes and no, but for you naturally no. From these newcomers there seems to be a very interesting small group that would like to join our church, so they are coming to visit us again this evening. You may meet them if you wish but that is not absolutely necessarily. We could meet in the Parish Hall or in my office. We can invite a few others, commensurate with the intent of your visit, by all means."
"OK, thank you, I shall be there; say at 7.30 p.m., alright?"
"Alright sir, perfect. See you then."
I took a deep breath. My heart was slightly pounding in my chest cage, but this had to be done. As they used to say in the old country: "You have to hold the bull by the horns, otherwise he can nail you down!" Also, as the French say: "Anything that starts, has to finish!" Soon after that I received a message from Edith, Minister of Education – you also know her by now – who would like to send her assistant, Michael Deem, if I wished, for the Summer Literary Festival. Naturally I said yes; at this point and time in my life, I needed a little bit of

festival-like activities. Even the thought of it should relax my mind a little bit – that, as you know well, had recently been under some tension.

Michael Deem, a slim, tall, serious looking gentleman with an Education Degree (Ed.D.), soon appeared in my office. He greeted me very gently and shook hands warmly. He was holding a rather thick bunch under his arm.

"Sit down, please. Last week when we were talking about the festival with Dr. Plump, even though we did not fix a proximate date for the event, we both had the impression that, particularly being quite busy with prospective citizens, the festival would be staged towards the end of the summer. Is there any change in planning?"

"Yes, Sir. You were right, we were already busy with the evaluations anyway. But they are finished astonishingly early and, during our contacts with people, they showed a tremendous interest in the musical and theatrical festivals, staging their original countries' dress, music, dances and alike, various cultural activities too. Consequently, Dr. Plump and I thought we should consult with you, and if you wish, either we should replace the Literary Festival with that type of more elaborate, cultural festival towards the end of the summer or, do the Literary Festival soon, say in a few weeks, and then, towards the end of the summer, stage the other. What do you think, Sir?"

"Thank you for asking me. Well, I still favour doing the Literary Festival for the fact that for the past twenty-five years, it has almost been a traditional event; we should not skip this year. Is there any other obstacle or reason we should not make it soon?"

"Oh, no, we could do it anytime. If you wish."

"I shall call the communication department right away and give necessary directives for Big Screen appearances and advertising. You also may get in touch with Mr. Clarke who is the chief of that division for further details. I think the general plan should be this way: People should be informed that the festival will be of two days duration, at one weekend, say two or three weeks from now, depending upon your readiness. The subjects for competition for this year are again 'Poems' and 'Short Stories'. Everyone shall participate with only one entry, and shall read it himself or herself. As a place, I still recommend the Torpedo Fish Beach Green Field, the picnic field next to the Animal World, so that while people compete with each other, they may also have a chance to go and visit animals and also to swim. Between the competitors, celebrity literary men and women should read some

Chapter 17

poems and literary pieces before the competitions and between, just to decorate the event. What do you say, Mr. Deem?"

"Sounds very good, Sir."

"Naturally, Dr. Plump and you make the final decision. I am sure you will not forget to select a jury, under Edith's chairpersonship, of course including you too. So, by Friday let us get in touch with each other and see where we are. OK young man?"

"Thank you Sir, much obliged!"

It took another two minutes to make a call to Mr. Clarke and give him highlights of our plan. As usual, in our State everyone is in 'alesta', ready to sail at any minute, anywhere. I was rushing, on the other hand, to run and get out of the diary of my grandfather's sealed bag that had been in dust for almost half a century. How exciting it is uncovering some mysteries and hidden material, as we used to enjoy in our mid-childhood, playing hide-and-seek in the closets.

Even though I know whole-heartedly that the time has come to open past history and read my grandfather's diary – I had avoided this

Chapter 18

for a long time – it was as if there was a hidden hand pulling me back. My grandfather, who was also a physician, as you know, an analyst, the first man in the family tree who had crossed the family and country boundaries, extended himself to the other challenges of the world. A man with a legendary reputation in his own life style, with the adventures, accomplishments, glories and defeats which he went through. My father, Ismailov the 2nd, or with his first name Souhi, used to talk about him all the time. Frankly, I appreciated that very much but I am a person who, as a principle, lives in the present and the future while still being respectful, non-judgmental and silent about the past, because I believe human beings do whatever they can under those circumstances, nothing else. However, in spite of the fact that my attitude is "the past is past, let it rest there!", I wanted to remember my grandfather as he was in my memories. When I came to New Atlantis with my dad, as I said before, I was only ten-years-old, and had left grandfather in Old Country. He died 18 years later and my dad went to his funeral and brought back his ashes that are right here, in a steel briefcase, right in front of me now. My father had told me that, since my grandfather had not died in this country, that we did not need to store his ashes in the common crematory here, though if one day I wanted to do it, I could do so. I should keep this case that contains "the body ashes" and "very important material, diary, etc". That might involve me one way or the other and, one day, the situation was going to speak for itself and in a way obliging me to open it and reveal the secrets, if it had any. To me, the right time now seemed to be ringing its invisible bells. The opening code of the lock of the steel briefcase was 177, my primary school number that was most sacred to grandfather, my father had said. So, here we are,

Chapter 17

without any ceremony other than my heavily-pounding heartbeats, I said "Open Sesame!" and opened the lock.

At the left side of the briefcase there is a wooden box, obviously hand-made and looking very special. It is covered with very delicate flowery figures all around. A small wooden key is in its hole. Obviously this is the ash-box. Under it, there lays a "Glorious *Koran*", as I was told, given to him by the most beloved person in his life, his aunt, with the promise "to be buried with it!" The rest of the case is full of several beautifully and compulsively arranged cartoon files. Each of them is carefully marked for its content: 'My Childhood', 'School Years', 'University Years', 'Military Service', 'First Marriage', 'Across the Ocean', 'My Children', 'Second Marriage', 'Glorious, Achievement Years', 'Decline and Return!'

I am a very patient person and I wished I could read all of them, line by line and in order, from the beginning up to the end. Maybe one day. Now, I have to be away from all sensitivities and emotions, I would like to find some facts that most probably caused my grandfather's constant moving around, unexpected decline and the rest of the circumstances. What was the mystery? What was the inside story of those recordings that I have not been able to connect? Since I was the grandson and carrying "the remains of my ancestors", hopefully reading and decoding, if necessary, these documents, would bring an end to the unrest just described.

I already remember the highlights of his beginnings, medical school years in old country and then crossing the ocean with a boat for a "new start" somewhere, as we all have done, and the trials and tribulations connected with those. But I am so impatient and would like to start from the second marriage, of which even my father who himself lived it through was not very knowledgeable, not knowing the tiny details of inside stories – as a matter of fact, he had a half-brother who he had never seen in his life-time. So, I think for many good reasons, I should start from the second marriage on.

DR. ISMAILOV, Sr
(Diary – The Second Marriage)

A.C. 2084

July 19, 1968
Code Island

I am very excited today. My son Ismailov Jr., whose nickname is Souhi, has begun to take piano lessons. This could be a simple event for anyone, I assume, but it is quite important for me. As I had detailed my youthhood events, during my educational years, I was mesmerised by the piano melodies that used to spring from our next neighbour's walls. Schuberts, Schumans and Beethovens were my dream fathers. In spite of my begging, my father and step-mother refused to do anything about it because "it was unnecessary", in spite of the fact that my father was the owner of a small grocery store, also a three-storey apartment in mid-town, and my step-mother's six-year-old son was going to a private school; and she had a sizeable income herself as a dress-maker.

Then, I went to an Oriental Music School and learned Eastern Music, all by myself, but had promised to myself that "one day, yes, one day, I would grow up, earn some money, and buy a piano". As I also gave some information in the chapters on the inconveniences and mishaps in the 'first marriage' diary, the day that my son was born, I had bought a piano for him, a 'Stark', upright piano. My ex-(first) wife then had shouted, yelled at me, saying that I had not bought that gift for her but for myself, since that was an old wish of mine (forgetting the mink fur that I had bought for her after the delivery). After she left us, my son was too small to play yet and due to work in the hospital and preparing myself for medical examinations, I really had not had a chance. But now, after having passed the medical examinations and being appointed as Commissioner in the State, and my beloved son has reached the age of eight, the time was right to start.

So, I asked around. They recommended a Mrs. K., a young mother in her late twenties, a private music teacher. I arranged the tuition first in a way that I should come at the beginning of the lesson, go to my work and come back again at the end, which I did. A pleasant, blonde lady reported that my son was of above mediocre talent, had a "good ear", and we would start, if I wish. After getting my son's consent, we started. In my son's honour, I had already brought a chocolate cake that we shared together. I believed my son's start was also going to give me an initiation, an incentive in the same subject. Due to my age, business and so on I would not start like a small child, but perhaps do a correspondence course with a local supervising teacher doing the job, since I knew the notes and the tones, musicality and the rest quite a bit, in general. Anyway, this is how did we start this thing.

Chapter 18

August 17, 1968
Code Island

Piano lessons with my son go very well. In the evening, after having our supper, he plays some melodies. Now he is fingering 'The Jingle bells, Jingle bells'. I bet he will be playing the Christmas melodies at the Holy Season. Last year in school he had done very well too, being at the top. The only thing worrying me is that since he is the only child in this small family, with no mother, plus the fact that his father is a workaholic who has virtually no time for anything else, he has very few friends. He goes to the sporting activities, baseball practices that I seldom visit during those times. I don't want to bring him up in complete isolation from the outside world. He has very good manners and is well-accepted among his friends. I sometimes invite them to play in our small backyard and he goes with his friends, but they have to come back at sun-down. We don't have anyone to take care of our house on a permanent basis, as I myself decided to do so. On Saturdays, the two of us vacuum the one-and-a half storey ranch where the floors are covered with wall-to-wall carpets, pile up the garbage together and then go for a ride, to the restaurants, bowling, basketball or baseball games. A good and clean life but it needs a little bit more colour.

This Sunday morning, while my son was studying piano and I, in my pyjamas, was sweeping and vacuuming the basement, where also my home office was located, the dOor-bell rang. Since I was not dressed properly yet, I hesitated a little bit; then, with the automatic sweeper in my hands, opened the door. There, a young lady in about her twenties was standing, thin and polite, also holding a book in her hand. With a gracious smile on her face, she asked:

"Is there a lady in the house?"

A little bit angry perhaps, but polite, I answered: "No young lady, there is no lady in this house, here I am, and there, my son is playing piano. What can I do for you?"

"Do you believe in God?"

"Of course I believe but why you are asking these questions to me right at the dOor. Obviously I cannot invite you inside because you came unannounced and visibly I am not in good shape to accept a guest, particularly a lady!"

"Well, we are Seventh-Day Adventists (she was alone but at the cross of the street, a young man was standing by and perhaps considering him she referred to 'we') and would give you a chance to know the Lord better that could help you in case off....."

A.C. 2084

"Look lady," I roared, "what I need now is neither the Lord nor, what did you say, seventh day..."

"Seventh-Day Adventists!"

"Yes, Seventh-Day Adventists... but a lady who shall make my bed also share it and sweep the floors for me!" and perhaps being a little bit rude, I closed the door roughly.

Well, this type of behaviour was somewhat strange for me, being such a well-tempered man, but I did not think that I had done terribly wrong. Perhaps He was sending me messages that there was really something lacking in the household.

September 1, 1968
Code Island

My lack of a new marriage is giving me signals but in strange ways.

Today is Sunday again and the picture in the house is just the same. Some light housework and my son studying piano or playing with Atari and Nintendo.

The doorbell rang again. Strange. I do not have many friends and if I have, they are mostly professionals. People very rarely contact me and if they do, they call me first, as a rule. Anyway, at least I am relatively better dressed than during the previous episode. I opened the door. There stood a relatively older looking couple, of Oriental features, probably Chinese, and a relatively young looking girl, all cleanly dressed up, who bowed politely.

"Hello, I am Dr. Ismailov, Sr. Are you sure you are at the right place? Who are you looking for?"

"Oh, no. We are at right place!" replied the fatherly gentleman. "You don't know me but we know you. Yes you are Dr. Ismailov. Can we come in?"

A little bit surprised I was, but since the cleaning was almost over, and I had nothing else to do particularly at that time, I invited them in. Indeed, they were exactly similar to the visits in my old home. You visit someone anytime you want to, as if they are ready for you since they may not have anything else to do other than just waiting for the guests that God sends you. If you don't find anyone home at the time of your visit, it does not matter, you can come again until you succeed. A little bit hesitantly I opened the door wide. "Please, come in!"

We climbed five to six stone steps to go upstairs. Up there, there is a saloon/day room and next to it a kitchen, one facing the street and the other the backyard. To the left, there are three bedrooms of medium sizes are located side by side. For me and my son, these are comfortable enough. After I got rid of what I had in my hands, we sat together in day room

Chapter 18

and a few minutes later my son, who did not know what was going on, also came in and greeted them silently and went right back to his room. For a while we exchanged smiles with no words. Of course I asked them whether they would like to drink some tea or coffee. With a similar smile on all their faces, a "tea!" sound 'with accent' came out.

"With sugar?"

"Yes, please!"

It took just a few minutes for me to prepare the teacups and tea bags to offer them.

"Any biscuits, salteens or cookies with it?"

"No, thank you!"

A while later we were all sitting together, sipping from our teacups and still smiling at each other. This time I decided not to ask any questions and go along with the pantomime. The gentleman finally broke the silence and very politely started his speech:

"Sir, you don't know us, we are very honourable people; we do know you, as we sought you out, you are a very honourable person too. We know you are also a wise, learned man from Orient; a doctor and a professor, single, taking care of his child, alone. (After cleaning his throat and looking at his wife and his young companion) My daughter is here, now a student at the University of Code Island. We all are citizens and living very comfortably here. We thought …. that… you may need… to have a wife, in your accustomed style, but you are not a citizen and soon, after completing your permissible time here, your visa shall expire and you shall have to leave this country. Correct?"

"Yes, correct, so far."

"Well, what my wife and I thought, since it is very hard to find an eligible man of good character, if you wish to, we would like to offer our daughter to you as wife. You would then automatically become a citizen and live happily after. Do you understand?"

"Well, I not only understood well but I am also greatly bewildered by the boldness of the offer." I raised my eyes to the ceiling and sent a silent message to the Creator. "How quick you got the message. Seventh-Day Adventists may have a direct red line with you!" Then, I succumbed into thoughts. Yes, I have heard a lot about these 'arranged marriages' leading to citizenships and it could have been, or would have been, possible. I asked a question to the father:

"How old is the young lady?"

"Twenty, but she is very skilled in home affairs and child-rearing. She took care of our other five children until recently."

A.C. 2084

I looked at the girl; she was smiling with a grace. A negotiation has been going on concerning her entire life and she was quite submissive, accepting the deal even before the start.

"Well," I responded, "as you may appreciate well, in spite of the fact that I am 39 years old, however healthy and relatively young, yes, I do contemplate marriage at times, especially in a foreign country like here. But this offer came to me rather suddenly and as a surprise, to tell the truth. Please leave your business card, with your names and telephone numbers and allow me a certain time to think and share this important subject with my son. Either you shall hear positively or, ... you won't hear anything. Thank you very much for this honour."

We bowed in two lines, facing each other, and they left quietly, as they had come in. Was this a dream? This book, needless to say, was closed even before it was opened.

September 15, 1968
Code Island

I had been appointed chief consultant to the Child Psychiatric Service, which was quite a surprise to me. This was actually a residential care centre for children aged six to eighteen, providing one to three years in-patient treatment to children with psychiatric disturbances, principally behaviour disorders. It is a kind of hospital where all medical and neurological studies are done but which also contains an educational unit where with some specially trained people, called residential care centre workers and special teachers" children are able to attend to school, hand-in-hand with the private psychiatric care. That was great. So, it was possible to sit with children in classes where their disturbances were observed directly and then, in the afternoon, we were able to offer the children group and occupational therapies along with sports and activities. That also gave a chance for everyone involved to work closely together as a working team, gathering with the families in order to train them also, thus giving altogether better service to the children. A night time, they slept there and we and young residents were also on duty. Besides being consultant to the unit, I was also assigned to be the Chief of Autistic Unit, a brand new, mysterious field that had been very recently under the scope of research and treatment. As to my State job, since I was literally 'timeless' there, I would also have worked up to two days somewhere else too, they said. Very good indeed.

In that unit, there was a young teacher, just out of college, having been trained as "counsellor" to these kind of children, however with no clinical experience. These children do not speak, they do not relate to people;

Chapter 18

when they look at you, they 'look through you'. They are much more in an inanimate world than an animate one. Anyway, of course they need more intimate care, like being held by the hand, singing together in circles, spelling every single letter and syllable of the things to have them register in their minds. When they cried, they cried with an unearthly voice and we all had to squeeze them to our chests to give them an inner sense of love and security. This tedious work, of course brought me too close to the young lady too and vice versa, who, indeed, most of the time felt helpless and incompetent before these children who don't even smile or give any human emotional response to your most inner driven hugs. At times she came close to tears, saying "In church, I pray to God for these helpless children, at nights they enter in my dreams. What injustice is this, as if these are from Mars? So, God help me!", most of the time, ending in my arms.

Since I was getting – I guess – some messages from the same God about another union, I began to think about this young girl, maybe? She was 21, I myself almost 40. Mary -that was the worker's name – I have been respectfully treating in the service, as well as giving her some rides some late afternoons to her home since she did not have a car yet. One day she invited me in to meet her mother. Naturally I accepted. They were living in a mediocrely-furnished two-storey house on the other side of the city. Her older sister was already married and living on the other side of the ocean. Her mother was a chemist-pharmacist and divorced from her husband who owned an antique furniture store near-by, seldom visited the house and always slept in his shop. They were Catholics. I newly heard the inside story about Catholicism that since they were married in the church, if they were permitted to get a divorce, that was on the condition they did not marry again since in the church they had already made a commitment to God 'for good'.

I never met her father during this relationship but her mother who, in general stood between Mary and I, all the time giving her frank opinion as "friendship is OK, marriage is No".

I had them meet my son too and some Sundays, almost two out of three, I brought him into their house in the morning, then we went to the Catholic church altogether and there I began to take some catechism classes. According to the priest, those classes were not a guarantee that the Catholic Church was going to give me an OK for a possible marriage. I, as a divorced Muslim, may not marry a single, unmarried Catholic girl in the church, in spite of the fact that since I was not baptised before, my previous marriage may not have been counted anyway; but in order to make a final decision, the whole case may go to the bishop's office and then perhaps up

A.C. 2084

to Rome.

Well, these days are light on one side and dark on the other. I am the victim of the battle among two religious principles who are suppose to make we poor human beings loving, good and happy citizens in this world and prepare us for the other side: God's eternal residence. How many times in my dreams have I observed Mohammed playing swords with Jesus Christ. God, help me!

September 30, 1978
Code Island

Everything is going alright, since I see Mary in the centre, go to my State job, then have consultations in the other clinics around and come home and cook hamburger, rice pilave and make salads for both my son and myself. The relationship with Mary, from closeness seems to be turning to love and affection, although sometimes that is spoiled by her mother's spellbound attempts. Meanwhile, some of Mary's young student friends come to visit her home, thus giving her mother a chance to strike us, stating to her daughter: "Look, here are some young Christians, you are just wasting your time with an old goat! If you shall really be getting serious about marriage, I may put my head in the oven, like old Jewish mothers used to do over their unfaithful daughters!" When I heard this, I of course worried a lot but I offered my 'help' to her mother, namely should she wish to put her head in the oven, could I help her then? She banged the telephone in my face.

The cathechism classes are going really good. To my surprise, I have rediscovered a lot of religious material that was similar to my native religion, obviously coming out of the Old Testament.

If we shall have time, we'll come back to the *Old Testament*. For now, since our time is limited for six months, I would like to start "to study the *Bible*, according to Mathew," said father Protano, my sponsor. So, we started. First we studied *The Book of the Origin of Jesus Christ – The Coming of the Saviour*. 'Now when Jesus was born in Bethlehem of Judea, in the days of King Herod, behold, Magi came from the East to Jerusalem, saying: "Where is he that is born king of Jews? For we have seen his star in the East and have come to worship him."' But when King Herod heard this, he was troubled, and so was all Jerusalem with him. And gathering together all the chief priests and scribes of the people, he inquired of them where the Christ was to be born. And they said to him "in Bethlehem of Judea"; and thou Bethlehem, of the land of Juda, art by no means least among the princes of Juda; for from thee shall come forth a leader who shall rule my people Israel....... "And when they saw the star they rejoiced exceedingly. And

Chapter 18

entering the house, they found the child with Mary, his mother, and falling down they worshipped him. And opening their treasures they offered him gifts of gold, frankincense and myrrh.......But when they had departed, behold, an angel of the Lord appeared in a dream to Joseph, saying, 'Arise, and take the child and mother, and flee into Egypt, and remain there until I tell thee. For Herod will seek the child to destroy him'. So he arose, and took the child and his mother by night, and withdrew into Egypt and remained there until the death of Herod." Then, the baptism of Jesus: "Then Jesus came from Galilee to John, at the Jordan, to be baptised by him. And John was for hindering him, and said: 'It is I who ought to be baptised by thee, and dost thou come to me?' But Jesus answered and said to him. 'Let it be so now, for so it becomes to us fulfil all justice.' Then he permitted him. And when Jesus had been baptised, he immediately came up from the water. And behold, the heavens were opened to him, and he saw the spirit of God descending as a dove and coming upon him. And behold, a voice from the heavens said 'This is my beloved son, in whom I am well pleased'."

Naturally, at times I asked some stupid questions of my mentor, like "Why didn't God help little Jesus and his mother Mary right in his native town to protect them from the wrath of King Herod? How come a God and son of God — that itself is very hard to accept for a foreigner, at least in the beginning — had to be baptised by a mortal being, John, even though he was also great and closest to Jesus? I cannot write here my priest's answers to those and like questions that I asked throughout, but he principally told me that in belief systems, either you believe or you don't; you cannot question the scriptures, miracles, revelations or any of the divine inspirations. They are celestial and immortal, they are as they are, what they are, that's all!

Then, the journeys of Jesus everywhere to preach. He was at Capharnaum. The people who sat in darkness saw a great light; and upon those who sat in the region and shadow of death, a light arose. From that time Jesus began to preach, and to say, "Repent, for the kingdom of heaven is at hand".

Then Jesus, while walking by the sea of Galilee, saw two brothers, Simon, who is called Peter, and his brother Andrew, casting a net into the sea (for they were fishermen). And he said to them: "Come, follow me, and I will make you fishers of men." And at once they left the nets and followed him. And going further on, he saw two other brothers, James the son of Zebedee, and his brother John, in a boat with Zebedee their father, mending their nets; and he called them. And immediately they left their nets and their father and followed him.

Thus, Jesus started his mission of preaching and showing miracles in the synagogues, preaching the gospel of the kingdom, and healing every disease and every sickness among the people. And his fame spread into all Syria; and they brought to him all the sick suffering from various diseases and torments, those possessed, and lunatics, and paralytics; and he cured them.

Needless to say I am deeply grateful to Father Protano who dictated all of these word by word, line by line from his notes and different bibles to me since no book was allowed to be brought out of the church. This way, that valuable information was becoming more valuable to me too. I did write all of them in my own handwriting and shall keep them the rest of my life.

October 7, 1968
Code Island

Today's cathechism was the best of all. Father Protano, in almost ecstasy, read to me the highlights of Jesus' *Sermon on the Mountain*.

"Blessed are the poor in spirit, since theirs is the kingdom of heaven. Blessed are the meek, for they shall possess the earth. Blessed are they who mourn, for they shall be comforted. Blessed are they who hunger and thirst for justice, for they shall be satisfied. Blessed are the merciful for they shall obtain mercy. Blessed are the clean of heart, for they shall see God. Blessed are the peacemakers, for they shall be called children of God. Blessed are they who suffer persecution for justice' sake, for theirs is the kingdom of heaven. Blessed are you when men reproach you, and persecute you, and, speaking falsely, say all manner of evil against you, for my sake. Rejoice and exult, because your reward is great in heaven; for so did they persecute the prophets who were before you."

After hearing all these great sayings, my eyes, chest and heart were all full of bliss. "My dear Father," I said to Father Protano, "I don't know whether there is or there shall be a heaven after death; but why don't we all emphasise the importance of man himself, whether he is the representative of God that could be – or not; and, apply all the principles that Jesus brings spring-water clear to the world: Love and justice, caring and sharing, empathy for each other. Don't forget that I, you, he or she, even it, we, you and they, all are blessed with the same stuff that Jesus prescribes; and, the importance of existence and truly exercising to live a truly good life, as we already have a chance of just being on the Earth". The father's eyes grew big, he took a deep breath and said: "I can frankly say, you are a far more advanced Catholic than any of my original ones. God bless you. You are learning and advancing tremendously." Since I had found a chance to be a

Chapter 18

little bit personal, without thinking of taking any advantages of this closeness I posed a question to the father:

"Father, what do you think my chances are to be with Mary? We are two good, innocent people; we are both free and not interested in someone else; we attend the same church and embrace the same moral values; then, why not?"

Father, though sincere, took a rather serious position, telling me that as long as a divorce case and a child existed, the church had to put forward certain stiff religious principles to abide with.

"But, father, if someone commits a crime and ask for forgiveness, even in one confession session God forgives one for a moral sin committed, let me ask for forgiveness from him not just once but thousands of times. But what kind of immorality am I charged with? Is it a sin being born into another religion that might be another great prophet's way of explaining the same routes of everyday living to reach the same God? I feel persecuted and how does this persecution fits into Jesus' sayings, as above, 'Blessed are you when you are reproached and persecuted!'?"

"Son, your lesson is finished today. See you next Sunday, after the mass."

Well, I returned home, but divided within myself, as a believer or not a believer of anything at all. I called Mary and explained to her what had happened this noon time. She also had mixed feelings. "My dear Ismailov," she said, "I have been to church all my life and as long as go by the books, everything appears to be beautiful. I still am not doing anything wrong, I believe. The church's dogmas can appear to us beyond logic or any reasonable comprehension, but they are put and they shall be going as such, till eternity. Look my dear, what I have been thinking... Hey, are you there, do you listen to me?" "Yes, my love, of course I am here, I am not in love with Father Protano but you!" "OK honey, look. I don't know whether you know, but there is a Presbyterian Church that is the closest to the Catholic Church amongst all others. That church, though somewhat tough on principles, does not care too much about divorce. So, it may be possible to get married there; I, in all white. But I guess, first, I have to convince my mother in that matter; second, we have to find a priest that may sympathise with us." "OK, until she gives a positive answer, I am going to put the oven off for a while then (we both laughed!). Well, that's it now. Let me prepare my son to go out and perhaps have a nice Chinese dinner and play miniature golf at the nearby play area after that. Love you, bye!" "Bye, love you too!"

October 11, 1968
Code Island

Tonight, we are invited to Mary's home for my birthday. (Strange, I never knew that my grandfather's birth date was October 11 too. What a coincidence! Very striking!) Souhi and I dressed quite formally, bought a cake for four and a bouquet of flowers for Virgina, Mary's mother – she looks like Virginia Woolf, except in her genie and ingenuity in creativity, personal grace... and sometimes I wish her Woolf's fate.

Both Mary and mother were also dressed nicely and I did not sense any hostile feelings to start with. It was nice to be with a family, at least at certain times of the year, like Thanksgiving and Christmas. Virginia asked my son how the piano lessons were going. She did not need to ask me how the business was going since I was most of the time with Mary, she might have obtained the daily news from her. Besides, indeed there is not too much fun, or rather something to report in my business. What can you say about human misery, suffering, strange and unacceptable attitudes, feelings, etc. Just to be polite, I asked Virginia how things were going in her work. With a cool look, she said "As it is, always. No change!" I was dying to hear from mom anything at all about our situation but she maintained an absolute silence. She indeed was a good Catholic, except for the divorce that she had exercised like me – however, according to her religion, that action was permissible provided that the subjects who divorced were not permitted to marry in church again. On the the hand, my divorce that was permissible in my faith was not acceptable to hers. I am getting confused.

After a brief celebration and the exchange of personal gifts, Mary wanted to murmur some news to my ears as we found a quiet corner for a while. She, in a warm and sincere voice, said that her mother had last Monday gone to see the head priest, Father Pagan, in the Catholic church and asked seriously the probabilities of our prospective marriage. Fathers Pagan and Pratono had given me a clean, respectable and passable note regarding my personality, character, attendance of classes and sincerity in the will to unify with Mary; but the "Catholic church can not be managed with Cannon rule; love is love, people can do anything what they would like to do; even we, could have married outside of church but considering new trends, namely newly mortifying attacks on the Catholic church, the validity of the Trinity Principle and the death and resurrection of the Jesus Christ and alike, subjects were pushing the church to be quite rigid and stand firm on basic principles of it".

So, they decided that I should apply to the bishop's local office for such permission. Should it not be granted then, that is quite possible, I shall have to write to Rome, to His Holiness' Ecumenical Council, for consideration.

Chapter 18

Mary was smiling: "Isn't it good? At least they are showing a way and perhaps testing iusout, but nevertheless it is the only way." "Rome may take at least two years to respond my dear, and, what will it respond if it responds? That blows my head off and tomorrow I am going right into those priests' office and ask them very, very important questions. I am fed up and have decided to become a musketeer, a sword in my hand. That is enough idiocy!" Then, I pulled my son as fast as possible and left there. Mary was thoughtful and worried and her witch mother was triumphantly smiling from the window and waving her fingers.

I am not going to write the details of what happened the next day at the church office. Whatever I had been suffering from the minute that I stepped in, in this Continent,

seems to create enough hell in me that is going to break loose. Well, I am sure, you shall read in a few months, or next year probably in a book form what and how I had suffered in this Dante's Hell. I already decided about the name of the book: *Wheelwright*. First I thought of *Challenge of Believing versus Non-believing*, or *Wars among Gods* that was going to be a Grecian style write-up that would sound like a drama. However, I wanted to make it a human comedy where there was no winner but everybody was going to have fun, so, I insisted on the name *Wheelwright*. Read it and remember me. For the time being, I am closing this book with the intention of not ever opening it again. "So long and see you in Heaven, Mary, if I go there; see you in Hell, Virginia, if I go there."

October 25, 1968
Code Island

Mrs. K., my son's music teacher, for the first time complained, rather gently pointing out my son Ismailov 2nd's relatively poor performance as far as the piano is concerned. She claimed: "I see a kind of disinterest, an unwillingness to commit himself. He does not seem to have the joy he used to possess. Naturally, as a young, growing boy, he may have some transitory issues to cope with, approaching the pre-teens. But regardless of how little I know about you, I feel and breathe a nearly perfect, comfortable air whenever I come to your house. I know I cannot put my nose into your private family affairs... but my empathy and respect for the little guy is quite deep. Is there anything I could do?"

I outlined to her that he had lost his mother at the age of two years and nine months old and had never seen her again. Recently, I was in a serious relationship with a young lady that might have ended up with a matrimony;

however, due to some technical factors, that possibility was nullified. We did not talk to him yet about the details of it, we both, in a rather quiet, passive way, are trying to absorb the outcome of it, I guess. Since this was a reality, we had to deal with it as it came out. That was all. I thanked her for her interest and requested that she should not probe anything, please. She did not need to be any kinder than before, just keep going with an understanding of the situation, that was all I wanted at this moment. She thanked me for my frankness and wished better days to come.

Well, I guess we grown-ups all behave the same way. "The child is a child, he could be seen but not heard." We do not know how to approach them properly. There is no school for it. To lose his mother was not my son's choice, rather it was mine due to incompatibility in the marriage and, for heaven's sake, in the long run, it was going to be far more deleterious for my child than whatever could happen from now on. Of course this is my fantasy, and since there is no way of measuring it up, we have to live and learn, if we can. Even though I am a prominent child psychiatrist, that does not help me too much, other than perhaps preventing myself from doing something wrong with goodwill, like being overly indulgent with him, feeling sorry for him and treating him accordingly, buying useless toys or making some pleasant offers, as if nothing bad happened. I never forget the famous French proverb, *'L'enfer est pavé de bons intentions!'* (The hell is paved with good intentions!) Yes, I am holding tight nowadays, but when I am ready, I am sure, I shall speak to my son about our mutual fate, at least I'll thank him for his understanding and not complaining about what he has been through and alike. Kant, I am losing my respect for you; where existed those individuals that were determining their own fates? Uufff. I am tired, I am going to bed!

November 24, 1968
Code Island

I have not been writing for a long time. I guess, I had not had enough energy. I was quite busy too. I had resigned from that Private Child Psychiatric Hospital and indulged rather keenly and deeply in community mental health affairs. Since it was in my power and duty, I was in touch with clergymen, firemen and teachers to make meetings with them and discuss the community mental health protective services, child neglect, unnecessary punishments, early detection of behavioural difficulties, parent-child interaction, i.e. how we can detect the tendency to suicide and avoid succumbing into drug habits and alike. I was arranging State-wide symposiums, conferences and T.V. talks. I indeed felt quite good and energetic. Between, whenever possible, I was

Chapter 18

able to talk with my junior too, referring to our mutual loss, his durability and capacity to endure this sort of things and finally telling him how much I was proud of him.

Yesterday was Thanksgiving Day and we were invited to our piano teacher's home, as guests. That was our first visit to their home and also a chance to meet her husband and nine-year-old daughter. The atmosphere was very good, simple and sincere, filled with the natural ingredients of a natural home. No doubt I felt I missed Mary and the related home atmosphere. We watched plenty of college football follies too. After a while, when her husband and two children were watching T.V. and looking at the family album, Mrs. K., with a very sincere voice and friendly manner, talked to me about my possible loneliness, plus the fact that the child needs a female touch and so on and so forth, so, if I am willing to meet an unmarried young lady, a nurse, with a strong sense of family and integrity, no smoking, no drinking, no premarital adventures, she would do whatever she could. Of course my heart was empty. I could not put myself in my son's shoes to see whether he needs a mother or not; my need for a faithful wife was obvious.

I told her I would think about it; at my age and experience of life perhaps a 'logical marriage' was, or could be, a much more logical preference than a 'love story.' I asked more about that young lady. She said she was a Mormon girl, age 26, living with her father and mother who were very dignified people; the mother of course was a housewife, the older sister had already been married for the past three years and had a small baby girl. The father, an engineer, also held a very high, important position in the church administration, "Councillor or something like that". The family lived in their own house, in a small village called Lake Laman, right at the border of the other neighbouring State. She worked as a registered nurse at the surgical unit of a local district hospital.

I told Mrs. K. that I tentatively and hesitantly said "yes, let me meet her," although I did not know anything about Mormons. While she could make an arrangement for such a brief togetherness, I would search, perhaps through encyclopaedias, about the religious principles and customs of that church. Needless to say, I was not going to go through another 'divorce story' experience. So, I think I felt a little bit anxious about the possibility of this new adventure but it was getting a little bit strange to sit at governmental dinners all alone, at one head of the table all by myself, with an unmarried priest at the other end, while all the others, including the governor and the ministers, were with their delightful wives. For sure, I was missing something and this adventure, that probably was going to be the last, maybe was worth a try. Needless to say, last night it took too long to fall asleep and in my dreams, Father Protano with a devilish smile, kept looking at me, without saying a word.

December 1, 1968
Code Island

During the week I had a chance to go to the library and seek out some information about Mormons from various books. Again, the best results came from *Encyclopedia Tannica* (Gosh, one hundred years later, what a coincidence!). It may be of public knowledge for an ordinary citizen but for a foreigner, it is a brand new history and quite interesting to read. I had to rush because Mrs. K. had already arranged with the Lady Francis (that was the name of the lady, my prospective date!) to go to a movie. However three of us altogether going alone with a strange man socially was also not permissible in Mormonism, so someone had to chaperon us. Good so far. This shall take place tomorrow evening.

In my previously-dated memoirs, I provided some headlines about the Book of Mormon, Lamanites, Moroni Plates and the foundation of this religion by a prophet – Reverend James Smith of New York. Therefore, I do not need to repeat what I said before. The only small bit of knowledge I gathered from new resources that I would like to add is this: Moroni Plate, as a proof of the glorious Israeli and Gentile backgrounds of Mormons, was delivered to Prophet Smith by a male angel, Moroni himself in Kirkland, in front of two witnesses: David Whitmer and Martin Harris. That plate was saved and protected at the Mormon headquarters for eternity.

> The essential principals of Mormonism could be summarised, as follows;
> God has evolved from man.
> Men might evolve into gods
> The Persons of Trinity are of distinct beings.
> Human souls pre-existed. Christ came to the earth so that 'all might be saved and raised from the dead', but, 'a person's future is determined by his-hers own action.'
> Justification is by faith and obedience.
> Obedience to be ordinances of the church.
> Repentance and baptism are performed through immersion.
> Laying on the hands for spirit gifts, including prophecy, revelation, speaking in tongues (I had met some people in one of the 'born-again Christian churches who were speaking in tongues, meaning without knowing about anyone, they were able to speak, communicate with each other, not only with persons but with their ancestors too which was quite an experience for me!)

Chapter 18

Faithful members of the church would inherit eternal life as gods.
When Christ returns, then shall be 'the temple work', principally 'baptism on behalf of dead' shall be in order;
Proselytism, polygamy were set by Smith himself but legally declined in 1890.

As I understand it, Prophet Smith and his followers had quite a lot of opposition to their existence and celestial claims that they are from Israel long before Jesus Christ, that their priesthood and rituals are "true representatives of true church", the American Indians are their descendents, and the prophet is ordained as such by an angel, Moroni, to settle this discipline throughout the U.S.A., spreading to Ohio and Missouri, even using force when necessary. That had them involved in actual battles with the government and a lot of blood was shed, for example during the Mountain Meadows massacre, A.C. 1857. (Mohammed, too, indulged in several wars while trying to spread Islam.) Reverend Smith himself was killed in one of these battles as early as in 1844, at the age of 39, right after building a new city, Nauvoo, in A.C.1839. However, his disciples, Lieut. Gen. Brigham Young, who later went on became governor in A.C. 1852, and his son, Joseph Smith III, in Iowa and Illinois set the church (A.C. 1852-60) on very strong foundations for worship in Utah thereafter, later extending themselves to England and Scandinavia. Prophet Smith was once in touch with a Masonic Lodge and was present at their meetings quite frequently, it was reported.

As far as the administrative structure is concerned, each church has a President who is one of the descendants of the prophet and is appointed by revelation. In every church there are two councillors who possess very powerful political power, a council of twelve apostles, The First Council of Seventy.

Mormon people live close by their churches and attend them very regularly and religiously. 4,000 to 5,000 people live in 'stakes'; a few hundred stakes are managed by a President and the bishop.

Well, it seems to be interesting; it sounds to me like a Middle Age chivalry kind of institution with some mystery course. I felt a kind of chill too. Anyway, now at least I feel half-ready to meet young lady Francis, my prospective bride, I guess. An untouched girl, late sixties in Merica, non-smoker, non-drinker and at the service of man obediently? Hard to believe, but we will see.

December 2, 1968
Code Island

A.C. 2084

It is slightly after midnight. We just returned from *Camelot*. Its music had mesmerised me. Needless to say, Mrs. K., I and Lady Francis were altogether at the Central Cinema, on the first balcony. Having a third person between had really facilitated this important 'first get together' event, especially when it was amalgamated with a historical and mythical masterpiece.

Lady Francis is of medium height, somewhat plump but not necessarily fat, with curvy blondish hair and large green frog-eyes. She talks nearly in an alto voice, however giving a sense of purity and serenity. On a few occasions when our fingers touched each other I felt a kind of cold and sweaty trembling but definitely not oestrogen-driven and ridden body extensions. One immediately felt a kind of security and trust. After the movies, too, not much was said. We shook hands and said goodbye to each other.

About half-an-hour later Mrs. K. called me up and in a curious-sounding voice asked my opinion of Lady Francis. Of course I could not completely know a person in such a relatively short time, neither could she, but my first impression was positive. Love could have developed later on, at this age and moment in my life, a logical marriage was perhaps much wiser than an immediate fall in love, I guess. Mrs. K. said Lady Francis had liked me a lot; I was serious, mature but witty too, and, trustworthy. "What shall be our next step?" I asked Mrs. K.; she said that, if it was alright with me, next Sunday I am invited for a Sunday dinner in their home with the family. This jet speed, while somewhat scaring me, was giving me some sense of 'right' since, if things were not this much in order, the succession of the events could not have been this smooth. So, I keep my fingers crossed, and shall wait for next Sunday. Meanwhile I'd better to read a little bit more about Mormons.

December 10, 1968
Sea-Chief, Chussett

Today at noon, I and my junior were present at Lady Francis' home, one of the small private properties in the assigned locality in one of the Mormon stakes, in a small town called Sea-Chief, in our neighbouring State Chussett. All names around here are old American Indian tribes' names. As Mormons State that Indians come from Mormon blood, they may feel very secure and comfortable with their choice of settlement.

All family members greeted us right at the door, including the father – that really impressed me. That was the custom that I am used to observing. The family really impressed me as a very honourable one. Father was in his fifties with slightly greyish hair and eye-glasses, a serious but sincere man,

Chapter 18

an engineer, as I said before; a healthy, strong man and obviously the true head of the house. Mother, who looked exactly like her daughter, somewhat plump, emotional but sincere, thanked me many times for the bouquet of flowers that my son presented to her. The older sister was not present at the beginning; she was going to visit later on with her husband and baby. Without talking too much, we silently and solemnly sat at the pre-designated seats at the dinner table. Lady Francis and I were facing each other, husband and wife also, and my son somewhere between. Father, before the start, raised his hands in the air halfway through and said his prayers:

"I pray to the Father in the name of Christ; O God, the Eternal Father, we ask thee in the name of thy Son, Jesus Christ, to bless and sanctify this bread to the souls of all those who partake of it; that they may eat in remembrance of the body of thy Son, and witness unto thee. O god, the Eternal Father, that they are willing to take upon them the name of thy Son, and always remember him, and keep his commandments which he hath given them, that they may always have his Spirit to be with them. Amen." And after he took his first bite of bread, we were allowed to take our own.

Lunch went on in a quiet but superficial atmosphere, with random talks about my and father's jobs, my son's school, Lady Francis' hospital work and alike. As dessert, cold fruit juice was served. All were fine with me. I was dying to be alone with my bride-to-be and talk about various facts of life, her feelings about marriage and sharing life with someone who had come from abroad, with a son in hand, whether she had any thoughts about having more children, our future home, namely where to live, finances and alike. However, there did not occur any chance for these kinds of things for we were never left alone long enough. These things were obviously taken for granted, mature grown-ups could have made their own decisions later on or any time; obviously the most important thing at the present time was my suitability to the Mormon congregation.

Thus, early in the afternoon, while the rest of the family was busy with getting acquainted with each other, the father and I sat aside and he drew the conclusions. He said, openly, he had liked me; he already has heard about my reputation, righteousness, decency, hard and humanitarian work that I had been doing, and specially taking care of my child, all alone. It was not fair for a man with my qualities to carry on this kind of lonely life. God himself could not stand to be alone and had created man thereof. "Here we are," he said. "We are opening our arms to you. If you don't have any objection, next Sunday morning, please come to church, be our guest and observe the ceremonies. There, the President of the church shall explain to you the basic rules of the church and what to do for a church wedding that is absolutely required." Then, if everything was going to be alright, by Christmas time, at the holy season that was just a few weeks ahead anyway, we would marry. I wholeheartedly accepted the programme, for especially the day before Christmas was my son's birthday; why could we not meet the dates?

Early in the afternoon, Lady Francis' older sister, husband and their nearly two-year-old baby girl arrived. They, too, were open, sincere and joyous people. They wished us luck and we, waving hands, took off, going for a ride in the beautiful surroundings and wilderness of nature, in spite of the winter season. Everywhere was white but the roads were clean the and sun was shining all over. I asked my son's opinion how he was feeling about this forthcoming marriage; he, with a very clever smile, answered: "Dad, this is your business, it does not make any difference to me as long I am with you." This boy should have been a prophet himself. May be he is, time will show.

December 17, 1968
Code Island

I woke up early this wintry Sunday morning. I took my bath and put my best suit on. I don't need to impress anyone but I do not wish any technical matter should be a subject to spoil my image. I left my son with my next neighbour, a doctor's family from Uba. I am not rich but I always had good cars to run since before I even knew how to change the tyres. Anyway, my blue Mercedes shines and slides over the crisp icy, snowy roads and here I come.

The Church of Jesus Christ of Latter-day Saints is one of the newly-set, well-built churches in Code Island, close to the Sea-Chief, Chussett, town line. Mr. Normand, my prospective father-in-law who was the senior councillor and deacon in the church hierarchy, personally met me at the door alongside the President of the Church. After shaking hands, we quickly entered one of the small administrative offices. The office was furnished very neatly and simply. On the walls, Reverend Smith's pictures were faced by that of Jesus Christ.

Reverend Harold, in a very nice voice, asked about my original religion, marital status, and the degree of the knowledge about Mormonism. I summarised briefly my status and mentioned about my willingness to marry Mr. Normand's daughter Francis.

He informed me that in the Mormon church, there are two kinds of marriages; one, 'marriage for time', and the other, 'marriage for eternity', or 'celestial marriage'. The marriage for time loses its validity after death. It is believed that some 'not that much responsible people who neither are not out of the world, nor are supposed to give in marriage' may prefer that type. That way, they do not abide by the church's law completely but they are not outcasts. They are saved, too, but without enlarging themselves; they remain singly and without exaltation. In short, some people may prefer this lower form of marriage or the person's civic condition may not be suitable for more than this.

'Celestial marriage' is only performed in the holy temples, like here, and the participants eventually shall be rewarded with a celestial or higher grade of exaltation to come. The other name for this type of marriage is 'sealing'. Indeed, two good people are sealed to each other until eternity and even thereafter. The President, who also is 'chief priest', said: "By a revelation by Prophet Smith, in A.C. 1843, polygamy was permitted. Then the prophet spoke of women "given unto him to multiply and replenish the earth... and for their exaltation in the eternal worlds, that they may bear the souls of men," namely, says a note, "the souls or spirits of men to be born in heaven". But, with another revelation in A.C. 1890, conforming with federal regulations, polygamy was abolished. President Wilford Woodruff, on A.C. November 1, 1890, addressing to the saints at Logan, Utah, said: "I want to say this: I should have let all the temples go out our hands; I should have gone to prison myself, and let every man go there, had not the God of heaven commanded me to do what I did do; and when the hour came that I was commanded to do that, it was all clear to me." (Published in *Deseret News*, A.C. November 7, 1891.)

"Therefore, my son Ismailov, if you marry Francis, as long as you remain married to her, you may not marry another person at the same time.

"Knowing Francis and now you, and considering Mr. Normand's position in this church, you owe it to marry in celestial form, only that fits you. That means you shall have some ceremonies prior to the declaration and sanction of the wedding which is an inseparable part of our rituals. You shall never tell anyone in your lifetime about the details of those rituals, maybe just of the highlights, or your personal feelings if and when deemed to be necessary, in goodwill and not serving any evil souls, that's all. Otherwise, the results may be unthinkable. We recognise one year's time as adjustment to the church and its principles. So, God forbid if anything happens within the next twelve months, even separation may be possible; but after a year, your said and unsaid commitments to church seals you to them until eternity.

"I repeat, my son, again, that just as the relationship between husband and wife who are married only 'for time' does not carry over into the spirit world, so also is the bond of parents and children broken by death, unless they are sealed by the proper temple rite. It is a part of the celestial marriage rite to seal the children to the parents for eternity. But for a son (of who you have one!) whose parents were not so sealed till eternity, a way is provided whereby a family connection in the future world may be continued. He can, by proxy, marry his parents for eternity and be sealed unto them through these proxies. This is frequently done today by new converts to the faith. But here, too, the 'sealing' is not accepted unless it is freely accepted and all the conditions met by those who are sealed. Do you understand all what I am saying?"

"I believe so, Sir!"

"Well, then, what date you choose? Mr. Normand mentioned one day before Christmas. Even though the church is exceedingly busy those days, as you may already know, if you wish we could arrange it. D' accord?"

"D' accord!"

"See you on December 23, 2 p.m., for your celestial marriage. Good luck to you for now."

"Yes Sir, on December 23, 2 p.m., for celestial marriage. Thank you."

We all shook hands and I left the church, however in a kind of half-daze. They first appeared to be very plausible, acceptable and honourable principles, perhaps paving a road to a clean life. I am sure they still are but what created a kind of chill in me was those commitments. I am a man of belief and commitment but I had never plunged into this deep chain of commitments. I felt I was a small drop in an ocean, fresh and enticing, but frightening too. Well, "*Courage mon ami, courage!*" (Courage my friend, courage!), I consoled myself. I don't think I shall be able to sleep tonight, and considering my son's age, that is almost nine, I am not going to give any details about these church commitments – more than half of them are obscure events even to me – at least, at this point.

December 24, 1968
Two Thousand Islands

Well, you can congratulate me for my gigantic courage in what I achieved yesterday noon at the Mormon church. Francis was all in white and I was all in black: the eternal challenge of contrasts. All guests were ready on time, including my own little son, who was dressed up nicely with a black bow-tie, solemnly standing, gathered at the Ceremonial Hall.

As we had practiced before, Reverend Harold invited Francis and me to stand before him, and began to read some paragraphs from *The Book of Mormon*:

Chapter 18

"Here, Ismailov and Francis are standing before me, also meaning before Jesus Christ, the eternal God, to perform a celestial marriage in this holy church. However, according to our covenant principles this sort, Ismailov has to be 'ordained' by an elder in the Melchizedek priesthood (this was not told to me before and don't know what is all about!) and also receive the other blessings pertaining to the house of the Lord, all of which the Lord has indicated shall be administered in his holy temple. As these blessings are made available for the living, they are also made available for their worthy dead. Now, we are taking our groom to be ordained and go through some ritualistic, spiritual experiences before the Council of Twelve Apostles in our celestial ceremony chamber."

He began to walk and I followed him. After two or three minutes walk, in the eastern part of the church, we entered in an incense-filled 'holy room,' before the said members of the church. There, they blindfolded me, turned the electricity off and pushed me forward. (I cannot say what experiences I had thereafter, what kind of questions were asked and what kind of suggestions were made due to high secrecy. I was not bewildered or scared whatsoever because I had had similar experiences at the initiation of my third degree of 'master' freemasonry, just two years ago.) Obviously I had passed the necessary trials and tribulations. Then, I was un-blindfolded and returned, with my hand held by Reverend Harold, to the Ceremonial Hall.

There, again Reverend Harold, before the crowd, began to read some passages from the *Book of Moroni*:

"And again, I exhort you, my brethren, that ye deny not the 'gifts of God', for they are many; and they come from the same God. And there are different ways that these gifts are administered; but it is the same God who worketh all in all; and they are given by the same manifestations of the Spirit of God unto men, to prophet them (10:8).

"For behold, to one is given by the Spirit of God, that he may teach the word of 'wisdom' (10:9);

"And to another, that he may teach the word 'knowledge' by the same spirit (10:10);

"Wherefore, there must be 'faith', and if there must be faith there must also be hope; and if there must be hope there must also be charity (10:20);

"And again I would exhort you that ye would 'come unto Christ, and lay hold upon every good 'gift' and not the evil gift, nor the unclean thing. (10:30)."

Then, Reverend Harold addressed me: "The rings, please!"

I handed them to him, with somewhat trembling fingers. The holy man

A.C. 2084

took both of them and after examining them for a very short while, put them on the ring fingers of me and my fiancé Francis and finished his blessings:

"Francis and Ismailov; as both of you came unto Christ, king of heaven, our creator, to conjugate in the form of celestial marriage in this holy church, The Church of Jesus Christ of Latter-day Saints, having passed successfully all the necessary qualification tests to be a member of this congregation before the President, councils, The Council of Twelve Apostles, deacon, all priests, in order to share the gifts of Jesus Christ on this earth and in death thereafter, I declare you husband and wife. God bless you too. Amen. Now, you can embrace each other."

That was it and I am now a junior member of the Mormon church. I am sure I shall abide with all rules and regulations of it. There is no reason why I may not do so. I am coming to a close in my writings, because my bride is just awakening. So long.

* * *

I read those written parts of my grandfather's life story without raising my head from the top of my desk; and, when I raised it up, I was in a kind of daze. I sure was mesmerised by the fluidity of the events, all intertwined with each other though appearing to occur independently, displaying a faith. Were they personal choices or pre-destined? I wouldn't know. Oh my God, the time is almost 6 p.m., I should rush to my lovely wife to share dinner; then of course, you know where I am going. Now, at least I feel much more confident and sure of myself that I could control the situation better than before, whatever the circumstances would bring. Because I am much more acknowledged and equipped than before. We shall see.

I had previously mentioned about the architectural designs of our houses that mainly depended heavily on earthquake-proof principles

Chapter 19

and were built accordingly – as many storeys high as possible but almost pyramid shaped, looking like old Assurian ziggurats. Old people's homes were built much closer to the earth, nonetheless they looked similar. However, we permitted worship centres to be constructed as they were, or might have been, in their original features in old times. Thus, their looks, besides being very distinguished and serene, offer to the eyes beautiful panoramic scenes of different worlds. Classical Christian churches, Muslim mosques and Jewish temples are already known to many people but a Mormon church, due to its rarity, presents a different kind of construction. One would say, "Oh, how beautiful a Gothic chateau it is. Look at that cathedral from the Middle Ages!" It is rich, big and grandiose from outside but warm and friendly from inside. However, wherever you go, you feel as if you are in Salt Lake City, Utah.

Anyway, I was at the Church of Jesus Christ of the Latter-day Saints just on time, for a visit, as previously cited. Needless to say, with a small group of assistants behind, Reverend Arthur Brenner, President, shook hands with me in quite lively fashion, shaking a few times successively, and presented me to his company: "Here is Mr. George Kwell." When I shook hands with him, I immediately recognised him: He was the person who had come with a group of five to ask about the possibility of establishing the Masonic Lodge. He, too, was very much emotional at being with me again. "Here is Kevork Papazian, one of our most precious servants of the church, councillor." "How do you do Mr. Papazian!" Reverend Arthur continued to present. "Here is the one of the utmost respectable persons, the last treasure who just joined us; his Excellency Reverend Pudowski!" A deep, bass baritone voice said "My pleasure, Sir!", shaking me because that was the exact voice, however speaking in Sanskrit then, who last night was giving out the orders. I looked into his eyes, they were as large as and as deep as oceans, and appeared to be spotlessly clean. Nonetheless I

A.C. 2084

felt myself encircled and squeezed by a fiery-red iron. "The other councillor and the deacon shall join us later on. They are getting ready for tonight's grand assembly. Let us go into my office, if you wish," and we walked.

Still under the influence of my readings from my granddad, I and others followed him into his private office which I had never been before. I sat down in a comfortable easy chair, right at the entrance. The others also sat silently, after me. I looked around and make a polite comment about the beautiful internal design and delightful furnishings. The President calmly and quietly responded with a few polite words, but behind them, I felt there was going to come a strong wind, playing innocent perhaps, silently but strongly pushing me into a rather difficult situation "OK, please tell us, why you are here?", knowing that, as we used to say in poker games in the old home, "having the ace of spades in your palm!", he did not need to worry about anything. "The card is in my hands!"

Of course he did not ask the above question, but kept looking – as a matter of fact, they were all doing the same – into my eyes. After an initial anxiety State that I experienced for certain seconds, I said:

"Mr. President. I have some questions and puzzles on my mind, perhaps related to the Mormon church and Mormonism. However, I do not feel competent enough to find some plausible answers and to be fair to myself and to all the people in this republic, including you Mormons, who have been very respectable citizens throughout. I don't want to go in circles and repeat things that I myself am not clear on."

"I appreciate your frankness and sincerity," replied Reverend Arthur. "Your nobility and fairness is well known to everybody in the State. We do know your values and goodwill but still we do not know the essence or matrix of the problem. How can we help you, Sir?"

"As time goes by, I am sure, I will be more specific. At the present time, I enriched my knowledge just a little bit more about the Mormon church through reading but of course it is not good enough. I went over the known encyclopaedias and some religious books, naturally not good enough. (After pausing for a while) I very specifically want to know more about the Moroni Angel and Moroni Plates. (As soon as I mentioned these, their eyes circled around and gave some sparks to each other – maybe so, maybe my paranoia) I don't know whether you permit *The Book of Mormon* to circulate outside of the church, do you?"

Chapter 19

"Under normal circumstances 'no', but for your Excellency that isn't the case (looking at the others and then getting up and going to one of the cabinets, bringing out a rather small book with a dark blue jacket). Here it is your honour, this should be our gift to you, keep it as long as you wish. And, after reading, if you need some interpretations, needless to say, we are all at your service."

I was really grateful to them in a way, maybe connecting inner thoughts and feelings via subconscious avenues, but they were outwardly nonetheless polite and helpful. I was just at the beginning of the mystery but my conscious was clear from the very beginnings that there was unfinished business somewhere, and that was touching, if not threatening, somebody's – perhaps my – existence and only someone like me with a State power and goodwill for humanity and the fairness of 'Khalifa Omar' could make some people happy and, at the same time, fulfil some justice long awaited. In other words, in a civilised way, we had exchanged some messages for everybody's benefit. I believe human beings could resolve all man-made problems, provided they keep their goodwill and intentions wild open, addressing the very hearts of the other brethren. Well, once again, here is the greatness of the New Atlantis Republic: One is for all, all is for one! Although I am all worked up for *The Book of Mormon*, tonight, I have to fulfil my previous commitment to the Shamanistic Centre. If you

Chapter 20

have some free time and would like to listen to me on this subject, please come and be my guests, follow me to the centre and come up to the performance on the stage to one of the most remarkable practices of Shamanism, since we do not show those worship activities on the Big Screen.

It is a rainy day today. As an island State, the rain usually comes as a storm since the island is wide open from four sides. With tremendous noise and high speed, the wind comes and sweeps everything, whatever it can. It is as if there is another flood. Birds restlessly fly around with wild screams, the sun is also hidden behind angry clouds, nature takes its cold shower and then, suddenly, everything stops, the sun smiles, the clouds get whiter, thinner and fluffy, then the nature symphony starts from *adaggio* again.

So I watched the rain drops playing their last dances from my window and succumbed into thoughts again. Yes, where I was? The other nights' hearing bells ring in my ears, repeating, "Sru! Apnuhi prathama... Anyutha, hata! Asti mant Moroni Plates. Band ca pariraksyantam asya pranah. Aduna!" "Listen! Obtain first... otherwise, kill! He is the possessor of Moroni Plates. Enter into his friendship and spare his life! Now!") George and Kevork ha! How friendly they were in the church. Wouldn't they know I am innocent if there is some secret in it? Yes, I am innocent. Do they know I am innocent? Yes, they know. **What** they are after is somewhat known to me but **why** is not known. Shall they give me enough chance to resolve this problem? Yes, it appears so. If I couldn't resolve it, could they harm me? I don't know, yes or no. I am anxious to finish my grandfather's diary and

Chapter 20

read a little bit more from *The Book of Mormon*. But now, I am on my way to the Shamanistic Centre and here I am in a place with different air.

The Shamanism Centre's leader, Ibn-ul Kadeem, greeted me warmly, and jokingly asked: "Are you ready to be on the stage, Excellency?" "By all means, I always feel young when I come here. Are people ready? I brought my hat and mask that are in my handbag; did you prepare a Shaman's drum and a small rug at the stage for my use?" "Yes, all are ready, your Excellency!" "Six of your students too?" "Yes, your Excellency!"

"Good evening ladies and gentlemen.

"Last week, we talked about some principles or components of the 'culture' and seeing the Shaman as a cultural ambassador of any given, particularly those of primitive or developing, masses of human societies. We talked about the 'initiation exercises of the Shaman' and related experiences, and as anyone of you could be a Shaman candidate, we looked over the small personal experiences that could happen, for instance having 'underworld' and 'sky trips' and other visits. As you may recall, during these trips, the Shaman generally takes his drum, may use his mask and may resort to his 'sacred animal' if he needs too.

"As you may imagine, all the details of these performances are cultural patterns of the people whoever they represent. Culture, of course, is closely related to some symbols that are transmitted from generations to generations. Though these symbols may change from time to time, (the swastika was originally a mid-Asia sign to show the four corners of the roads and was used for the same purpose in South America too; it also means 'fortune', 'luck' well-being' in Sanskrit; the Nazis used them in A.C. 1930s for a different cause), they have to give some service to the nation which they belong to. Some of those practices may not seem to be acceptable to general views, such as in Old India when women were burnt after their husbands' death. On the other hand, today, in Enga, the same is observed; however the woman is strangled. Blood-related people through the father are not permitted to marry but if a child is born from such a relation, there is permission for infanticide.

"Mircea Eliade (A.C. 1907 Bukarest, Romania – A.C. 1986 Chicago, U.S.A.), who is the dean of modern anthropology, taught us first how the Shaman is charged with doing something almost impossible looking, a kind of clearance of dirty jobs. In Borneo, for instance, it is believed that a devil psyche (though it might be her next neighbour) enters in a woman's body (Incubus) and the Shaman (Bungai) is called to take that devil out her body through some black magic and rituals. There, for every 200 people there is one Shaman. If someone is sick, that means his or her healthy soul is angry at that person, leaves and goes somewhere else. The Shaman, in general with his drum, has to travel, find it and bring it back.

"Here, as a practicum let me show how this is done. Suppose we have a sick person, a young woman. (I call a woman, from the crowd who is listening to this lecture.) She has tremendous abdominal pain and is suffering. (I lay a small rug in the middle of the stage and let the woman actually lay on the rug! I also take out Shaman's hat out of my bag, that is a round, cane or wicker, hat with several feathers around and a Shaman's mask, looking like it has been taken from old African Tarzan movies, and wear both of them In addition, I take the drum that I am provided with by the centre, and start to beat it with regular strokes, of medium height for number of minutes. Then, with a series of three quick strokes, I stop drumming, put the drum aside and lay on the floor, next to the sick lady.)

(Then, addressing the audience while laying down) "So far, through opening ceremonies, we have given the signal to the 'sick soul' of the lady 'here we are coming to look for you!'. Now, I am going to examine the lady's body to see whether her soul is there or not!" I put my ear on her abdomen. After searching through for a while, I tell her: "Your soul left you. She might have been angry with you, and hostile to you. Now, my duty is to find it and bring it back to you!"

Then, I straightened myself up and clapped my hands, six students of Ibn-ul Kadeem, run to the middle of the stage, form a 'canoe' around the patient, kneeling down with some distance between, namely two at each side, one in front and one at the back; I tell everyone: "This is the spiritual canoe and we are all going to search for this woman's soul who left her!". I also sit at the middle in the canoe, next to the patient, and drum slowly and regularly, with simple beats, with regular intervals. During this drumming, six youths, using just their arms, imitate rowing forward, also synchronising their bodies accordingly. This scene gives the false impression that it as if the ship is going forward after the lost, rather escaped, soul. Anyway, after six or seven minutes' beating, I suddenly beat the drum vigorously, three times with three sharp beats, and stop. All arm and body movements stop too. That means we have come to a cave where the escaped soul might be hidden somewhere. I got up alone, get out of the boat, and

Chapter 20

go to the audience one by one, asking:

"Do you have an extra soul on you? Ha? Any extra guest?" (Also checking with my finger tips their immediately reachable pockets, their hair on the head, even touching their stomach. Finally, like a magician, I find the soul somewhere – generally in an innocent child's pocket. I pretend to hold something very delicate in my fingers, carry it very carefully in the air, show the audience turning one hundred and eighty degrees around and then put it in my pocket. Then I re-enter the canoe, sit down, then lie down slowly, and take the soul out of my pocket).

"Now, I put the soul in my mouth, and breathe it to the patient's abdomen!" (I do this a few times, with deep breathing.) Then I ask the sick woman:

"How do you feel now?" She, somewhat stunned, thinks and moves her eyelashes anxiously, checks herself how she feels, and finally murmurs:

"Oo, indeed, I feel very well!"

"OK, your soul is back; you are reconciled. From now on, you give good care to it!". Then, I took my drum in my hands again, started to the same beats as before, the six youths start again to move their arms, hands and bodies move in reverse; meaning we are going home. Again, after a few minutes of striking, I give three strong beats then stop. We all get out of the boat and greet the audience. Plenty of applause, deservedly so!)

Not only in primitive societies, but also in highly-cultured populations and nations too, Shamans are charged with important duties. In old Hungary, Shamans are called 'taltos' and their principal duties are to cure, to find out witches, to limit the devil's misdeeds and alike. In order to achieve these, a Shaman can transmute himself into a horse or a bull; do his job in reality or in his dreams. According to their beliefs, a Shaman is created in his mother's womb; thus he is sacred; if there is a war on the earth, he flies in the skies to save his country. He has a very strong sense of 'finding the things out', particularly those of treasures. Here it is, a very well known Hungarian myth, regarding a Shaman's endeavour to recover a treasure, and the games that he played even to his own people.

Once upon a time there was a very famous Shaman (taltos), a Francis Csuba, (1721 A.C.), in Csökmö. To the people's belief, there was a hidden treasure in a nearby swamp, however under the control of a monstrous dragon. Csuba promised his people he would recover this treasure and give it to them, as they deserved. So, he took a long and thick rope, tied one end to the entire people's hand and then promises to tie the other to the dragon's hand. But he cheats them and ties the other end to a tree. In addition, he makes his helper sit on a nearby tree, with nude buttocks facing the peasants, having him blow a trumpet. Then, he addresses the people: "Who is in sexual relation with his neighbour's wife has to let go the rope due to the reason that the dragon will eat him first!" Everybody in a panic left the rope and escaped as far as he could go. Some other version of the story is that the taltos, who is a very good-willed person, scares the dragon off and the people gain their treasure.

* * *

"In more than one way, we said, the Shaman is a mythological hero. He rises from everybody's ordinary life style, when necessary utilising 'the helping spirits', and goes on his journey, which could involve travelling the world, underworld or skies. One of the most useful tools that accompanies him on almost every trip is his drum. One of the grand masters of anthropology, Joseph Campbell, in A.C. 1980, cites these notes about that famous drum of the Shaman:

'Once upon a time, there was a famous Shaman, Morgan Kara, in the tribe of Barade of Siberia, who had the custody of a double-faced drum through which, it had been said, the Shaman was able to call dead souls. On the other hand, the head of his clan, Örlin Khan, believed that it was also in his rights to call the dead souls and even to protect them. Heartbroken, Örlin Khan complains about Shaman Kara to Tengri, the head of gods, and asks him to correct the situation. The god Tengri wanted to challenge the young, demanding Shaman in a competition, as follows. He puts a dead man's soul in an empty bottle and hides it somewhere. Morgan Kara goes on an 'under-world' journey to search for that soul with his famous double-faced drum but cannot find it anywhere. Then he tries the 'upper-world', sky-land, and there observes that the soul is resting in an empty bottle but Tengri's finger is blocking the open end. Shaman Kara immediately transmutes himself into a hornet and bites Tengri on his forehead. Naturally, the god Tengri takes his hand off the bottle and holds his forehead; then, Shaman Kara picks up the soul and runs to the 'middle-world'. Tengri, being mad, instantaneously creates a thunderbolt that strikes Kara's drum and from that day on, a Shaman can never have a double-faced drum again.'

If we can sum up the Shaman's daily responsibilities and functions, they are:

1) Divination: To answer directed questions, for example "to search for a teacher in the universe".
2) Clairvoyance: Foretell the events that presently are not in sight but shall : occur in the near future;
3) Finding, searching: Of/for lost souls, valuable belongings and alike.
4) Healing, curing: To do whatever can possibly be done, was demonstrated previously, searching through the spiritual 'canoe'.

The Shaman, travels at three levels (Shamanic Format):

1) In the Lower World: The world of the dead, the ancestors' resting place. You can do an exercise for this too. Lay down for about ten minutes. A drum, played by someone else, can accompany this trip. The Shaman candidate closes his eyes and lets himself go to the under world. Since this could be somewhat scary, you can call on 'spirit helpers' – those are invisible souls – to accompany your body or your own 'power animal' (that you usually carry in your heart, as an image, even as a bracelet, necklace or ring, primarily a symbolic docile animal like cat, dog or cow and it cannot be a serpent, bird or any kind of reptile). The candidate, during the trip, may ask whoever he is seeking – dead ancestors, an old friend, even his own power animal – how people are feeling there and then about in ten minutes, return back under the provisions of his power animal. The trip ends when the drum beats fast and loud on four successive occasions.
2) In the Middle World: The world which we live in. Thus, he again travels under the leadership of his power animal, or all alone, primarily in nature – rocks, plains, plants, forests, country. Solitude, therefore, is one of the most fundamental principles of Shaman-hood. However this is not a passive but rather an active experience. A Shaman candidate, during this 'nature trip', searches and finds out 'power spots' in nature and sings 'power songs'.

Thus, to strengthening your 'survival skills', utilising this kind of trip, you should do these kinds of exercises:

Exer. 1: Just before sundown, sit in your seat, close your eyes, shake your 'bell'-which is another tool you must carry on you as a Shaman candidate – and invite all (living) souls, try to sing joyously. That should take about 15-20 minutes.

Exer. 2: Do your 'devination' job. Close your eyes, go for a trip to the places that you already know; a friend's, grand-mother's house, school, foreign countries, and come back.

Exer. 3: Travel and search places that you have never been in.10 minutes.

Exer. 4: One evening, right after sundown, go alone for an outside ride; lift your head, look up to the skies, choose a star; enter into that star, travel together with that star in the sky; come back after 10 minutes.

Exer. 5: Visit your close friends, relatives for 10 minutes.

Exer. 6: Quartz crystal, which you also must carry on you as the symbol of power, is one of your important helpers. With him, travel in this physical world with pride and strength, go to unknown places, meet the unknown people, and come back within ten minutes.

3) In the Upper World: The ultimate place where gods live.

Exer. 1: Lie down, and close your eyes. Think of the top of a mountain or the flames. Climb step by step, look around and admire the beauty and majesty of the universe; in order to achieve the ascendance, you have to pierce through a 'membrane' that could be scary, so use your power animal or helping spirits. You must turn back within 10-12 minutes.

Exer. 2: You may repeat the above mentioned exercise through using 'quartz crystal' as your power animal.

Thus end the exercises.

Sipping my coffee, looking into complex possibility and probability issues about current unsolved problems, I am trying to programme

Chapter 21

the day. Let us see whether everything seems to be under control or not. All starting and ongoing programmes are on track. First, I should check with the Administration and Personnel Department whether Keith was able to do something about the chapel for a probable freemasonry house site.

"Keith, good morning!"

"Good morning Sir!"

"Did anything come out with Pere Pierre in reference to our prospective plans at the chapel?"

"Yes Sir, yesterday afternoon I have been able to finalise with Pere Pierre who gladly gave his consent. This morning the cleaning team is going to wash and dust the entire place. I am sure, electricity, heat and other services will be ready by this afternoon too. Then, of course, I shall wait to hear from you and the groups the specific requests and changes which have to be made."

"Very good. Would you be kind enough to get in touch with, let me see, which one could be considered as leader? Smith L. I guess, the oldest, wisest and most advanced in degree. Anyhow, would you tell him, or whoever you can catch from the group, that I would like to meet them to night at 8 p.m. at the chapel so we should do some planning? Any results yet about the personal backgrounds from Ternational Biography Centre?"

"Not yet Sir, I shall get in touch with Mr. Smith right away. Incidentally, if you permit, I also would like to be at the chapel myself to see things first hand."

"Thank you Keith, be good!"

"Thank you, Sir, much obliged!"

A.C. 2084

Good, that was OK. Now what? Even though it was just on Tuesday, the day before yesterday, with Michael Deem, the supervisor of the Summer Literary Festival, I wondered whether they had come to a conclusion about the date of the festival?

Then, I gave a ring to Edith.

"Hi, Edith, gracious lady. What's up?"

"Everything is in order, Sir. The other day, you obviously had a very fruitful meeting with Michael. As usual, you are one step ahead of me, I was going to give you a call that we should put the festival in the air one week from this coming weekend."

"Very good Edith. Make your final plans and start to advertise right away. The beginning of next week we should get together and review the things that are already done. Oh, you know my neurosis, if you put me too among the celebrities who would read some 'decoration' poems between, I would appreciate that very much."

"I already put you in Sir, without your Olympic torch, we are lightless. You know that."

"You are a jewel. God bless you! So long!

"So long, Sir!"

With a comfort that I felt inside me, I am reviewing my speeches, classes and attendance for the rest of the week. Let us have a look at them.

This afternoon, I could read perhaps my grandfather's diary, which is thrilling, or *The Book of Mormon*, or can review the other notes, let me decide what to read after lunch.

This evening, that is to say, Thursday afternoon, as you know, I am going to the French church chapel to meet the founders of the prospective Masonic Lodge applicants. To see Mr. George K., who also is among the Mormon church celebrities and gives me a little bit of vertigo. Any misconnections, misdeeds? I do not know yet but I have to keep a close eye on him.

Tomorrow noon, I have to continue at the Muslim mosque with the lecture about 'recognising Islam!' Since it involves a lot of historical names, dates and data, whether it comes rather heavy to some people, I don't know. Since I am the President, the people even though they know better, don't dare to criticise me one way or the other.

Saturday, I cannot miss the Jewish temple. This year I don't want to interrupt the series of beginning classes that are quite educational.

For Sunday, I have to consult with my wife too. We will wait and

Chapter 21

see, whatever comes up.

Thus, even without waiting for lunch, with an inner impulse of curiosity I immersed myself in *The Book of Mormon*.

In the 'Introduction' section of the book, it simply cites, "*The Book of Mormon* is a volume of holy scripture comparable to the *Bible*. It is a record of God's dealings with the ancient inhabitants of The Americas and contains, as does the *Bible*, the fullness of the everlasting gospel".

The Testimony of the Prophet Joseph Smith is the most striking part of the beginning of the book:

"On the evening of the ... twenty-first of September (1823) ... I betook myself to prayer and supplication of Almighty God...

"While I was thus in the act of calling upon God, I discovered a light appearing in my room, which continued to increase until the room was lighter than at noonday, when immediately a personage appeared at my bedside, standing in the air, for his feet did not touch the floor.

"He had on a loose robe of most exquisite whiteness. It was a whiteness beyond anything earthly I had ever seen; nor do I believe that any earthly thing could be made to appear so exceedingly white and brilliant. His hands were naked, as were his legs, a little above the ankles. His head and neck were also bare. I could discover that he had no other clothing on but this robe, as it was open, so that I could see into his bosom.

"Not only was his robe exceedingly white, but his whole person was glorious beyond description, and his countenance truly like lightning. The room was exceedingly light, but not so very bright as immediately around his person. When I first looked upon him, I was afraid; but the fear soon left me.

"He called me by name, and said unto me that he was a messenger sent from the presence of God to me, and that his name was Moroni; that God had had a work for me to do; and that my name should be had for good and evil among all nations, kindreds, and tongues, or that it should be both good and evil spoken all people.

"He said there was a book deposited, written upon gold plates, giving an account of the former inhabitants of this continent, and the source from whence they sprang. He also said that the fullness of the everlasting gospel was contained in it, as delivered by the saviour to the ancient inhabitants.

"Also, that there were two stones in silver bows – fastened to a breastplate that is called the Urim and Thummim – deposited with the

A.C. 2084

plates; and the possession and use of these stones were what constituted 'seers' in ancient or former times; and that God had prepared them for the purpose of translating the book.

"Again, he told me, that when I got those plates of which he had spoken – for the time that they should be obtained was not yet fulfilled – I should not show them to any person; neither the breastplate with the Urim and Thummim; only to those to whom I should be commanded to show them; if I did I should be destroyed. While he was conversing with me about the plates, the vision was opened to my mind that I could see the place where they were deposited, and that so clearly and distinctly that I knew the place again when I visited it."

The other important chapters of the book are spread all over. It seems to be indeed a kind of testament we know, but decorated with different references. In deep notes, they corresponded with their classical biblical versions. If I can take a few, for instance:

The First Book of Nephi, in 'Chapter 1', cites: "Nephi begins the record of his people. *Lehi* (Younger son of Helaman) sees in a vision a pillar of fire and reads a book of prophecy. He praises God, foretells the coming of the Messiah and prophesies the destruction of Jerusalem."

'Chapter 2': "Lehi takes the family into the wilderness by the Red Sea. They leave their property. Lehi offers a sacrifice to the Lord and teaches his sons to keep the commandments..."

'Chapter 3': "Lehi's sons return to Jerusalem to obtain the plates of brass. Laban refuses to give them up."

'Chapter 5': "Sarah complains against Lehi. Both rejoice over the return of their sons. They offer sacrifices. The plates of brass contain writings of Moses and the prophets......"

'Chapter 6': "Nephri writes of the things of God. His purpose is to persuade men to come into the God of Abraham and be saved."

'Chapter 7': "Lehi's sons return to Jerusalem and enlist Ishmael and his household in their cause."

'Chapter 8': "Lehi sees a vision of the tree of life."

'Chapter 9': "Nephi makes two sets of records. Each is called the plates of Nephi. The larger plates contain a secular history; the smaller ones deal primarily with sacred things."

'Chapter 10': "Lehi predicts the Babylonian captivity. He tells of the coming among the Jews of a Messiah, a saviour, a redeemer. He tells also of a coming of the one who should baptise the Lamb of God. Lehi tells of the death and resurrection of the Messiah."

'Chapter 15': "Lehi's seed are to receive the gospel from the gentiles

Chapter 21

in the latter days. The gathering of Israel is likened unto an olive tree whose natural branches shall be grafted on again."

'Chapter 16': "The wicked take the truth to be hard. Lehi's sons marry the daughters of Ismael . The Liahona guides their course in the wilderness. Messages from Lord are written on the Liahona from time to time. Ishmael dies."

'Chapter 17': "Nephi is commanded to build a ship. His brethren oppose him."

'Chapter 18', "The ship is finished. The births of Jacob and Joseph are mentioned. The company embarks for the promised land. The sons of Ishmael and their wives join in revelry and rebellion. Nephi is bound and the ship is driven back by a terrible tempest. Nephi is freed and by his prayer the storm ceases. They arrive in the promised land."

'Chapter 19': "Nephi makes plates of ore and records the history of his people. The God of Israel will come six hundred years from the time Lehi left Jerusalem. Nephi tells of his sufferings and crucifixion. The Jews shall be despised and scattered until the latter days, when they shall return onto the Lord."

'Chapter 20': "The Lord reveals His purposes to Israel. They have been chosen in the furnace of affliction and are to go forth from Babylon."

'Chapter 21': "Messiah shall be a light to the gentiles and shall free the prisoners. Israel shall be gathered with power in the last days."

'Chapter 22': "Israel shall be scattered upon all the face of the earth. The gentiles shall nurse and nourish Israel with the gospel in the last days. Israel shall be gathered and saved, and the wicked shall burn as stubble. The kingdom of the devil shall be destroyed and Satan shall be bound."

And, these are some excerpts from the *Second Book of Nephi*:

"An account of the death of Lehi, Nephi's brethren rebel against him. The Lord warns Nephi to depart into the wilderness and he journeys there."

'Chapter 1': "And now my son, Laman, and also Lemuel and Sam, and also my sons who are the sons of Ishmael, behold, if ye will hearken unto the voice of Nephi ye shall not perish. And if ye will hearken unto him I leave unto you a blessing, ye, even my first blessing."

'Chapter 2': "Redemption cometh through the Holy Messiah. Freedom of choice (agency) is essential existence and progression."

A.C. 2084

'Chapter 3': "Joseph in Egypt saw the Nephites in vision. He prophesied of Joseph Smith, the latter-day seer; of Moses, who would deliver Israel; and of the coming forth of *The Book of Mormon*."

'Chapter 5': "The Nephites separate themselves from the Lamanites, keep the law of Moses and build a temple. Because of their unbelief, the Lamanites are cursed, receive a skin of blackness, and become a scourge unto the Nephites."

'Chapter 9': "Jews shall be gathered in all their lands of promise. Atonement ransoms man from the fall. The bodies shall come forth from the grave and their spirits from hell and from paradise. They shall be judged. Atonement saves from death, hell, the devil, and endless torment. The righteous to be saved in the Kingdom of God. Penalties for sins set forth. The Holy One of Israel is the keeper of the gate."

'Chapter 10': "And now, I, Jacob, speak unto you again, my beloved brethren that Jews shall crucify their God. They shall be scattered until they begin to believe in him. America shall be a land of liberty where no king shall rule. Be reconciled to God and gain salvation through his grace."

'Chapter 12': "Isaiah (The son of Amos) sees the latter-day temple, gathering of Israel, and millennial judgement and peace. The proud and wicked shall be brought low at the Second Coming."

'Chapter 15': "The Lord's wineyard (Israel) shall become desolate and his people shall be scattered."

'Chapter 16': "Isaiah sees the Lord. Isaiah's sins are forgiven. He is called to prophesy. He prophesies of the rejection by the Jews of Christ's teachings."

'Chapter 17': "Ephraim and Syria wage war against Jadah. Christ shall be born of a virgin."

'Chapter 19': "Isaiah speaks messianically. The people in the darkness to see a great light. Unto us a child is born."

'Chapter 20': "Destruction of Assyria is a type of destruction of wicked at the Second Coming. Few people shall be left after the Lord comes again."

'Chapter 21': "Stem of Jesse (Christ) shall judge in righteousness. The knowledge of God shall cover the earth in the millennium. The Lord shall raise an ensign and gather Israel."

Well, all that is beautiful and enlightening but very, very powerful. I empathise with my grandfather but I wonder how he might have carried this load since, as I am, I believe he was a believer but a

Chapter 21

scientific, medical man too, doing whatever he was supposed to do, from deliveries to autopsies, trying to heal people at the best, still remaining as a true believer and an objective man of this life and death game? This is why I am quite curious about his adventures. We all see. Now, I am hungry and willing to eat something.

* * *

The evening meeting at the chapel was short but a nice one. All concerned, that means I and Mr. Gleem from the administration and five fellows, George K., Smith L., Clarke M., Gregor S. and Yani Z., and the building-keeper on the grounds Mr. Chevalier, were present. We walked around and objectively tried to figure out what was needed. Pere Pierre was on night prayers so he could not attend. A few time-beaten doors and windows needed to be repaired and painted, so did the hall. The small room that was situated at the end of the corridor that was going to be used eventually as a 'spare room' for the candidates 1st, 2nd and 3rd degree of examinations, and also presently for storing the necessary clothing, the decorations and bric-a-brac, this and that, could also be placed there. One or two closets and a couple of book cases would suffice for now. Needless to say, the little bathroom also had to be revived and renewed in many ways.

So, we decided these things will be taken care of immediately, and upon hearing the clearance of the candidates and completion of the building, after some public advertisements through Big Screen, we shall make an opening. Everybody involved was in a genuine cheery mood. We said "good-night" to each other and no mishaps or unwarranted mysterious threats, like being followed by strange, dark shadows, some puzzling signs and write-ups that you usually read in mystery books and watch in movies, occurred. Those kind of covered things don't and can't happen in New Atlantis. Indeed can't? We shall wait and see.

Today is Friday. In the morning, we had our usual cabinet meeting with members, but there was nothing unusual to cite. The outcome

Chapter 22

of the newcomers' evaluations had begun to crystalise, principally with regard to manpower, the living headquarters and immediate extra needs that were invisible before; the chapel's repair of course' again the programme of the Summer Literary Festival; the review of the energy resources; and stocks in hands and alike. However, it took longer than I had thought and I missed the 'namaz' portion of my visit to the mosque. To my surprise, there was a massive crowd who dared to listen to my historical speech.

"Wessalamun aleykum" (God's greetings for you!), I greeted them, and got the classical reply, in chorus: "Aleykum salam!" (For you too!)

"I am continuing of speaking upon the religion before Mohammed and his *Koran* in Arabic. As we said last week, this is necessary to understand the birth and the development of Islam.

"The religion of the Arabs before Mohammed, which they call the State of ignorance, as opposed to the knowledge of God's true worship revealed to them by their prophet, was chiefly gross idolatry. The Sabian religion had almost overrun the whole nation, though there were also great numbers of Christians, Jews, and Magians (old Persian priests), among them. The Sabians did not believe one God but produced many strong arguments for his unity; though they also paid adoration to the stars, or the angels and intelligences which they supposed reside in them, and governed the world under the supreme deity. They endeavoured to perfect themselves in the four intellectual virtues and believed the souls of wicked men would be punished for 9,000 ages, but would afterwards be received to mercy. They were obliged to pray three times a day: the first, half an hour or less before

Chapter 21

sun-rise, ordering it so that they may, just as the sun rises, finish eight adorations, each containing three prostrations; the second prayer they ended at noon when the sun begins to decline, in saying which they perform five such adorations as the former; and they did the same the third time, ending just as the sun sets. They fasted three times a year, the first time thirty days, the next nine days, and the last, seven. They offered many sacrifices but ate no part of them, burning them all. They abstained from beans, garlic and some other pulses and vegetables. As to Sabian Kebla, (the part to which they turn their faces during prayer) authors greatly differ; one will have it to be to the north, another to the south, a third to Mecca and the fourth the star to which they paid their devotions. They did go to the pilgrimage to a place near the city of Harran in Mesopotamia, where great numbers of them dwelled, and they also had a great respect for the temple at Mecca and the pyramids of Egypt, fancying these last to be sepulchres of Seth, and of Enoch and Sabi, his two sons, whom they looked on as the first propagators of their religion. At these structures they sacrificed a cock and a black calf and offered up incense. Besides the *Book of Psalms*, the only true scripture they read, they had other books which they esteemed equally sacred, particularly one in the Caldee tongue which they called *The Book of Seth* and was full of moral discourses. This sect said they have taken the name Sabians from the previously-mentioned Sabi, though it seems rather to be derived from Saba or 'the host of heaven' which they did worship. Travellers commonly called them 'christians of St. Joon the Baptist', whose disciples they also pretended to be, using a kind of baptism, which is the greatest mark they bear of Christianity. This is one of the religions the practice of which Mohammed tolerated in that expression of the *Koran*, those to whom the scriptures have been given, or literally, the people of the book.

"The idolatry of the Arabs then, as Sabians, chiefly consisted in worshiping the fixed stars and planets, and the angels and their images, which they honoured as 'inferior deities', and whose intercession they begged, as their mediators with God. For the Arabs acknowledged one supreme God, the creator and lord of the universe whom they call Allah Taala, the most high God, and their other deities, who were subordinate to him, they called simply al Ilahat; i.e. the goddesses. The Grecians did not understand these words and it being their constant custom to resolve the religion of every other nation into their own, and find out gods of theirs to match the others, they pretended that the Arabs worshipped only two deities: Orotalt and Alilat, as those names are corruptly written, whom they would have to be the same as Bacchus and Urania, pitching the former as one of the greatest of their own gods, and educated in Arabia, and the other, because of the veneration shown by the Arabs to the stars.

"The worship of the stars, the Arabs might easily be led into, from their observing the changes of weather which happen at the rising or setting of certain of them, which, after a long course of experience, induced them to ascribe a divine power to those stars, and to think themselves indebted to them for their rains, a very great benefit and refreshment to their parched country.

"The ancient Arabians and Indians, between which two nations was a great conformity of religions, had seven celebrated temples, dedicated to seven planets. One in particular, called Beit Ghomdan, was built in Sanaa, the metropolis of Yaman, by Dahc, to the honour of al Zooarah or the planet Venus, and was demolished by the Khalif Othman (Osman) by whose murder was fulfilled the prophetical inscription set, as it was reported, over his temple: **'Ghomdan, he who destroyeth thee, shall be slain!'** The temple of Mecca is also said to have been consecrated to Zuhal or Saturn.

"Though these deities were generally reverenced by the whole nation, yet each tribe chose someone as the more popular object of their worship.

"Thus, as to stars and planets, the tribe of Hamyar chiefly worshipped the sun; Misam, al Dabaran or the bull's eye; Olakhm and Jodam, al Moshtari, or Jupiter; Tay, Sohail or Canopus; Kais, Sirius, or the dog star; and Asad, Otared or Mercury.

"Of the angels or intelligences which they worshipped, the *Koran* makes mention only of three, which were worshipped under female names: Allat, al Uzza, and Manah. These were by them called goddesses and daughters of God; an appellation they gave not only to the angels but also to their images, which they either believed to be inspired with life by God, or else to become the tabernacles of the angels, and to be animated by them.

"Allat was the idol of the tribe of Thakif who dwelt at Tayef and had a temple consecrated to her in a place, called Nakhlah. Mohammed, in the ninth year of Hejra (emmigration to Medina), sending Abu Sofian to destroy this idol, to the great dismay of the tribal women especially. There is a question whether 'Allat' comes from the same origin of 'Allah'; that may also be a feminine significance, signifying

Chapter 22

the goddess.

"Al Uzza was the idol of the tribes of Koreish and Kenanah and part of the tribe Salim. A chapel called Boss, built and consecrated by one Dhalem, from the tribe of Ghatfgan, where also there was an Egyptian thorn, or Acacia, was destroyed by Kahled Ebu Walid, also sent by Mohammed, in the eight year of Hejra. Some said Dhalem himself was killed by one Zohair, because he consecrated this chapel with the design to draw the pilgrims from Mecca and lessen the reputation of the Kaaba. The name of the deity is derived from the root 'Azza', signifying 'the most mighty'.

"Manah was the object of worship of the tribes of Hodhail and Khozaah, who dwelt between Mecca and Medina. Some say Aws-Khazraj-Thaklif also worshipped the same. This idol was a large stone, destroyed in the eighth year of the Hejra, by one Saad. The name seems to be derived from the flowing of the blood of the victims sacrificed to the deity.

"There are also important but nonetheless secondary idols that we would like to outline in summary forms. The *Koran* mentions all of them by name: Wadd, Sava, Yaghuth, Yauk and Nasr. These are said to have been antediluvian (anti-flood, anti-nature disasters) idols, which Noah preached against, and were afterwards taken by the Arabs for gods, having been men of great merit and piety in their time, whose statutes they revered at first with a civil honour only, which, in the process of time, became heightened to a divine worship.

"**Wadd** was supposed to be the 'heaven' and was worshipped in the form of a man by the tribe of Calb in Daumat al Jandal.

"**Sawa** was adored under the shape of 'woman', by the tribe of Hamadan, or Hodhail in Rabat. This idol, lying under water for some time after the deluge, was at length, it is said, discovered by the devil, and was worshipped by those of Hodhail, who instituted pilgrimages to it.

"**Yaghuth** was an idol in the shape of a 'lion', and was a deity of the tribe of Madhaj and others who dwelt in Yaman. Its name seems to be derived from 'gatha', which signifies to help.

"**Yauk** was worshipped by the tribe of Morad in Hamadan, under the figure of a 'horse'. It is said he was a man of great piety, and his death much regretted; whereupon the devil appeared to his friends in a human form, and undertaking to represent him to the life, persuaded them, by way of comfort, to place his effigies to their temples, that they might have it in view when at their devotion. This was done, and seven others of extraordinary merit had the same honours shown them, till at length their posterity made idols of them in earnest. The name Yauk probably comes from the verb 'aka', to 'prevent' or 'avert'.

"**Nasr** was a deity adored by the tribe of Hamyar, or at Duh'l Kalaah in their territories, under the image of an 'eagle', which the name signifies.

"There were two idols, **Asaf,** the image of a man, and, **Nayelah**, the image of a woman, which were imported from Syria and placed on Mount Safa and Mount Merwa, respectively. Asaf was the son of Amru, and Nayelah the daughter of Sahal, both of the tribe of Jorham, who committing whoredom together in the Caaba were, by God, converted into stone and afterwards worshipped by the Koreish, and so much reverenced by them, that though this superstition was condemned by Mohammed, he was forced to allow them to visit these mountains as monuments of divine justice.

"Some of the pagan Arabs believed neither in a past creation nor a resurrection to come, attributing the origin of things to nature, and their dissolution to age. Others believed both; among whom were those, who when they died had their camel tied by their sepulchre, and so left without meat or drink to perish, and accompany them to the other world, lest they should be obliged, at the resurrection, to go on foot, which was reckoned to be very scandalous. Some believed a metempsychosis, and that of the blood near the dead person's brain, was formed a bird named Hamah, which once in a hundred years visited the sepulchre; though others say, this bird is animated by the soul of him that is unjustly slain, and continually cries 'Oscuni, Oscuni,' that is, 'Give me to drink', meaning of the murderer's blood till the death be revenged; and then it flies away. This was also forbidden by Mohammed.

"Among the idolatrous Arabs, there also were some who had embraced more rational religions.

"The Persians had, by their vicinity and frequent intercourse with the Arabians, introduced **Magian** religion among some of their tribes, particularly that of the Tamin, a long time before Mohammed.

"The Jews, who fled in great numbers into Arabia from the fearful destruction of their country by the Romans, made proselytes (converts) of several tribes – those of Kenanah, al Hareth Ebn Cabaa, and Kendah in particular – and in time became very powerful and possessed several towns and fortresses there. But the Jewish religion was not unknown to the Arabs, at least a century before. Abu Carb

Asad, taken notice of in the *Koran*, was king of Yaman, about 700 years before Mohammed, and is said to have introduced Judaism among the idolatrous Hamyarites. Some of his successors also embraced the same religion, one of whom, Yusef, surnamed Dhu Novas, was remarkable for his zeal and terrible persecution of all who would not turn into Jews, putting them to death by various tortures, the most common of which was throwing them into a glowing pit of fire, from whence he had of opprobrious appellation of the 'Lord of the pit'. This persecution is also mentioned in the *Koran*.

"Christianity had likewise made very great progress among this nation before Mohammed. Whether St. Paul preached in any part of Arabia, properly so called, is uncertain; but the persecutions and disorders which happened in the eastern church, soon after the beginning of the third century, obliged great numbers of Christians to seek shelter in that country of liberty; who being for the most part Jacobite communion, that sect generally prevailed among the Arabs. The principal tribes that embraced Christianity were Hamyar, Ghassan, Rabia, Taghlab, Bara, Tonuch, parts of the tribes Tay and Kodaa, the inhabitants of Najran, and the Arabs of Hira. The Jews of Hamyar challenged some neighbouring Christians to a public disputation which was held *sub dio* (bishop's office)) for three days before the king and his nobility, and all the people. The disputants were Gregentius, bishop of Tephra, for the Christians, and Herbanus for the Jews. On the third day, Herbanus, to end the dispute, demanded that Jesus of Nazareth, if he were really living, and in heaven, and could hear the prayers of the worshippers, should appear from heaven in their sight and they would then believe him; the Jews cried out with one voice 'Show us your Christ, alas, and we will be Christians'. Whereupon, after a terrible storm of thunder and lightning, Jesus Christ appeared in the air, surrounded with rays of glory, walking on a purple cloud, having a sword over the heads of assembly: 'Behold I appear to you in your sight, I, who was crucified by your fathers.' After which the cloud received him from their sight. The Christians cried out 'Kyrie eleeson', that is, 'Lord have mercy upon us!' but the Jews were struck blind and recovered not till they were all baptised.

"The Christians at Hira received a great accession by several tribes, who fled thither for refuge from the persecution of Dhu Novas. Al Nooman, surnamed Abu Kabus, king of Hira, who was slain a few months before Mohammed's birth, professed himself a Christian on the following occasion. This prince, in a drunken fit, ordered two of his intimate companions, who overcome with liquor had fallen asleep, to be buried alive. When he came to himself, he was extremely concerned at what he had done and to expiate his crime, not only raised a monument to the memory of his friends but set apart two days, one of which he called the 'unfortunate' and the other the 'fortunate' day; making it a perpetual rule to himself that whoever met him on the former day should be slain and his blood sprinkled on the monument, but he that met him on the other day should be dismissed in safety with magnificent gifts.

"On one of the unfortunate days, there came before him accidentally an Arab, of the tribe of Tay, who had once entertained the king when fatigued with hunting and separated from his attendants. The king, who could neither discharge him, contrary to the order of the day, nor put him to death, against the laws of hospitality, which the Arabians religiously observe, proposed, as an expedient to give the unhappy man a year's respite and to send him home with rich gifts for the support of the family, on condition that he found a surety for his returning at the year's end to suffer death. One of the prince's court, out of compassion, offered himself as his surety and the Arab was discharged. When the last day of the term came and there was no news on the Arab, the king, not at all displeased to save his host's life, ordered the surety to prepare himself to die. Those who were there represented to the king that the day was not yet expired and therefore he ought to have patience till the evening; but in the middle of their discourse, the Arab appeared. The king, admiring the man's generosity in offering himself to certain death, which he might have avoided by letting his surety suffer, asked him what was his motive for so doing? To which he answered, that he had been taught to act in that manner, by religion he professed; and when Nooman demanded what religion that was, he replied 'Christian'. Whereupon the king, desiring to have the doctrines of Christianity explained to him, was baptised, he and his subjects; and not only pardoned the man and his surety but abolished his barbarous custom. This prince, however, was not the first king of Hira who embraced Christianity; al Mondar, his grandfather, also professed the same faith and built large churches in his capital.

"Since Christianity had made so great a progress in Arabia, we may consequently suppose they had bishops in several parts, for the more orderly governing of the churches. A bishop of Dhafar has been already named, and that Najran was also a bishop's see. The Jacobites

Chapter 22

(of which sect we have observed the Arabs generally were) had two bishops of the Arabs subject to their Mafrian, or metropolitan of the east; one was called the bishop of the Arabs absolutely, whose seat was for the most part at Akula (or Cufa), the others a different town near Baghdad. The other had the title of the Bishop of the Scenite Arabs, of the tribe of Thaalab in Hira (or, Hirta), as the Dyrians call it, whose seat was in that city. The Nestorians had put one bishop, who presided over both these dioceses, of Hira and Akula, and was immediately subject to their patriarch.

"These were the principal religions which obtained among the ancient Arabs; but as freedom of thought was the natural consequence of their political liberty and independence, some of them fell into other different opinions. The Koreish, in particular, were infected with **Zendicism**, an error supposed to have a very near affinity with that of the Sadducees (Descendants of Zadok, believing only the written laws but nothing else like soul, angels, resurrection and alike) among the Jews, and perhaps, not greatly different from 'deism'(Believing in the Creator but not recognising the other religious beliefs); for there were several of that tribe, even before the time of Mohammed, who worshipped one God and were free from idolatry and yet embraced some of the other religions of the country.

"What about the social life of Arabs before Mohammed?

"The Arabians before Mohammed were divided into two sorts; one, those who dwelt in cities and towns, and two, those who dwelt in tents. The former lived by tillage, the cultivation of palm trees, breeding and feeding of cattle, and the exercise of all sorts of trades, particularly merchandising, wherein they were very eminent, even in the time of Jacob. The tribe of Koreish were much more addicted to commerce and Mohammed, in his younger years, was brought up to the same business, it being customary for the Arabians to exercise the same trade that their parents did. The Arabs who dwelt in tents employed themselves in pasturage and sometimes in pillaging passengers; they lived chiefly on the milk and flesh of camels. They often changed habitations, as the convenience of water and of pasture of their cattle invited them, staying in a place no longer than they lasted and then moving in search of new water and pasture. They generally wintered in Irak and the confines of Syria.

"The Arabic language is undoubtedly one of the most ancient in the world and arose soon after, if not at, the confusion of Babel. There were several dialects of it, very different from each other; the most remarkable were that spoken by the tribes of Hamyar and the other genuine Arabs, and that of the Koreish. The Hamyaritic seems to have approached nearer to the purity of the Syriac than the dialect of any other tribe, for the Arabs acknowledge their father Yarab to have been the first whose tongue deviated from Syriac (which was his mother tongue, and is almost generally acknowledged by the Asiatics to be the most ancient) to the Arabic. The dialect of the Koreish is usually termed the pure Arabic or, as the *Koran*, which is written in this dialect, calls it, the perspicuous and clear Arabic; perhaps because Ismael, their father, brought the Arabic he had learned of the Jorhamites nearer to the original Hebrew.

"But the politeness and elegance of the dialect of the Koreish is rather attributed to their having the custody of the Caaba and dwelling in Mecca, the centre of Arabia; as well more remote from intercourse with foreigners, who might corrupt the language, as frequented by the Arabs from the country all around, not only on a religious account, but also for the composing of their differences, from whose discourse and verses they took whatever words or phrases they judged more pure and elegant; by which means the beauties of the whole tongue became transfused into this dialect.

"The Arabians are full of the commendations of their language and not altogether without reason; for it claims the preference of most others in many respects, as being very harmonious and expressive, and withal so copious, that they say no man, without inspiration, can be perfect master of it to its utmost extent; and yet they tell us, at the same time, that the greatest part of it has been lost; which will not be thought strange if we consider how late the art of writing was prescribed among them. For though it was known to Job, their countryman, and also to the Hamyarites (who used a perplexed character called al Mosnad, wherein the letters were not distinctly separate, and which was neither publicly taught nor suffered to be used without permission first obtained) many centuries before Mohammed, as appears from some ancient monuments said to be remaining in their character. Yet the other Arabs, and those of Mecca in particular, were, for many ages, perfectly ignorant of it, unless some of them as were Jews and Christians.

"Moramer Ebn Morra of Anbar, a city of Irak, who lived not many years before Mohammed, was the inventor of the Arabic character, which Bashar the Kendian is said to have learned from those of Anbar and to have introduced at Mecca but a little while before the

Chapter 22

institution of Mohammedism. These letters of Moramer were different from the Hamyaritic; and though they were very rude, being either the same with or very much like the Cufie, which character is still found in inscriptions and some ancient books, yet they were those which the Arabs used for many years, the *Koran* itself being at first written therein; for the beautiful character they now use was first formed from the Cufic by Ebn Moklahi Wazir (or Visir) to the Khalife al Moktader, al Kaher, and al Radi, who lived about 500 years after Mohammed, and was brought to great perfection by Ali Ebn Bowab who flourished in the following century and whose name is famous among them on that account. Yet it is said the person who completed it, and reduced it to the present form, was Yakut al Mostasemi, secretary to al Mostasem, the last of the Khalifs of the family of Abbas, for which reason he was surnamed al Khattat, or 'the scribe'.

"Thus, we could summarise the accomplishments of Arabs as follows:

"The accomplishments the Arabs valued themselves chiefly were: 1. Eloquence and a perfect skill in their own tongue; 2. Expertness in the use of arms and horsemanship; and, 3. Hospitality. The first, they exercised themselves by composing orations and poems. Their orations were of two sorts, metrical or prosaic, the one being compared to 'pearls strung' and the other to 'loose' ones. They endeavoured to excel in both, and whoever was able, in an assembly, to persuade the people to a great enterprise or dissuade them from a dangerous one, or gave them other wholesome advice, was honoured with the title of Khateb or orator, which is now given to the Mohammedan preachers. They pursued a method very different from that of the Greek and Roman orators, their sentences being like loose gems and the acuteness of the proverbial sayings; and so persuaded were they of their excelling in this way, that they would not allow any nation to understand the art of speaking in public except themselves and the Persians, which last were reckoned to be much inferior in that respect to the Arabians.

"Thus, the poetry was in so great esteem among them, that it was a great accomplishment and proof of ingenious extraction to be able to express one's self in verse with ease and elegance on any extraordinary occurrence – and even in their common discourse they made frequent applications of celebrated passages of their famous poets. In their poems were preserved the distinction of descents, the rights of tribes, the memory of great actions, and the propriety of their language; for which reasons an excellent poet reflected an honour on his tribe, so that as soon as any one began to be admired for the performances of this kind in a tribe, the other tribes sent publicly to congratulate them on the occasion, and themselves made entertainment, at which the women assisted, dressed in their nuptial ornaments, singing to the sound of timbrells the happiness of their tribe, who now had one to protect their honour, to preserve their genealogics and the purity of their language, and to transmit their actions to posterity.

"Common discourse upon poetry was never made cheap, they never did it but on one of three these occasions, which were reckoned great points of felicity, i.e. on the birth of a boy, the rise of a poet and the fall of a foal of generous breed. To keep up as an emulation among their poets, the tribes had, once a year, a general assembly at Ocadh, a place famous on this account and where they kept a weekly mart or fair, which was held on our Sunday (Friday). This annual meeting lasted a whole month, during which time they employed themselves, not only in trading, but in repeating their poetical compositions, contending and vying with each other for the prize; the poems that were judged to to excel were laid up in their king's treasuries, as were the seven celebrated poems hung up on the Cabaa, which honour they also had by public order, being written on Egyptian silk, and in letters of gold; for which reason they had also the name of *al Modhahabat*, or the 'golden verses'.

"The fair and assembly at Ocadh were suppressed by Mohammed, in whose time, and for some years after, poetry seems to have been to some degree neglected by the Arabs, who were then employed in their conquests; after their being completed, all sorts of learning were encouraged. This interruption, however, occasioned the loss of most of their ancient pieces of poetry, which were then chiefly preserved by memory, the use of writing being rare among them in their time of ignorance. Though the Arabs were so early acquainted with poetry, they did not at first use to write poems of a just length, but only expressed themselves in verse occasionally; nor was their prosody digested into rules till some time after Mohammed.

"The exercise of arms and horsemanship they were in a manner obliged to practice and encourage, by reason of independence of their tribes, whose frequent conflicts made wars almost continual. They chiefly ended their disputes in field battles, it being a usual saying among them that God had bestowed four peculiar things on the Arabs – that they should have turbans instead of diadems, tents instead of walls and houses, their sword instead of entrenchments, and their poems instead of written laws.

"Hospitality was habitual to them, and so much esteemed that the examples of this kind among them exceed whatever can be produced from other nations. Hatem of the tribe of Tay and Hasn of Fezarah were particularly famous on this account.

"The sciences the Arabians chiefly cultivated before Mohammedism were three; that of their genealogies and history, such a knowledge of the stars as to foretell the changes of weather, and the interpretation of dreams. The Arabians, as the Indians also did, chiefly applied themselves to observe the fixed stars, contrary to other nations whose observations were almost confined to the planets; and they foretold their effects from their influences, not their nature. Hence, as has been said, arose the differences of the idolatry of the Greeks and Chaldeans, who chiefly worshipped the planets, and that of the Indians who worshipped the fixed stars. The stars or asterisms they most usually foretold the weather by were those they call 'anwa', or 'the houses of the moon'. These are twenty-eight in number and divide the zodiac into as many parts, though one of which the moon possess every night, as some of them set in the morning, others rise opposite to them, which happens every thirteenth night – and from their rising and setting, the Arabs, by long experience, observed what changes happened to the air and at length, as has been said, came to ascribe divine power to them, saying, their rain was from such and such a star. Mohammed condemned such expression and absolutely forbade them to use it in the old sense, unless they meant no more by it than God had so ordered the seasons, that when the moon was in such or such a mansion or house, or at the rising or setting of such and such a star, it should rain or be windy, hot or cold.

"Now, I would like to talk a little bit about the State of the Christianity of the Eastern churches and Judaism at the time of appearance of Mohammed; the methods taken by him for the establishing his religion.

"From the beginning of the A. C. third century on, quite contrary to several historians and clergymen who wanted to glorify the newly-born Christianity and consequently changing the niceties of it into controversy, and dividing and subdividing it into endless schisms and contentions, so destroying that peace and love and charity from among them, which the gospel was given to promote. Instead, they continually provoked each other to that malice, rancour and every evil work that they lost the whole substance of their religion, while they thus eagerly contented for their own imagination concerning it; and in a manner quite drove Christianity out of the world by those very controversies in which they disputed with each other. In these dark ages it was that most of these superstitions and corruptions, which we now justly abhor in the church of Rome, were not only broached, but established, which gave great advantages to the propagation of Mohammedism. The worship of saints and images, in particular, was then at such a scandalous pitch that it even surpassed what is now practiced among the Romanists.

"After the Nicene Council, the Eastern church was engaged in perpetual controversies and torn to pieces by the disputes of the Arians, Sabellians, Nestorians, and Eutychians; the heresies of the two last of which have been shown to have consisted more of the words and form of expression than in the doctrine themselves and were rather the pretences than real motives of those frequent councils, to and from which the contentious prelates were continually riding past, that they might bring everything in their own will and pleasure. And to support themselves by dependants and bribery, the clergy, in any credit at court, undertook the protection of some office in the army, under the colour of which justice was publicly sold, and all corruption encouraged.

"In the Western church, Damasus and Ursicinus carried their contest at Rome for the episcopal seat so high that they came to open violence and murder, which Viventius the governor was not able to suppress and so retired into the country, leaving them to themselves till Damasus prevailed. It is said that on this occasion, in the church of Sicininus, there were no less than 137 found killed in one day. And no wonder they were so fond of these seats, when they became by that means enriched by the presents of matrons and went abroad in their chariots and sedans in great State, feasting sumptuously even beyond the luxury of princes, quite contrary to the way of living of the country prelates, who alone seemed to have some temperance and modesty left.

"These dimensions were greatly owing to the emperors, and particularly to Constantius who, confounding the pure and simple Christian religion with anile superstition, and perplexing it with intricate questions, instead of reconciling different opinions, excited many disputes, which he fomented as they proceeded with infinite altercations. This grew worse in the time of Justinian who, not to be behind the bishops of the fifth and sixth centuries in zeal, thought it no crime to condemn to death a man of a different persuasion from his own.

"The corruption of the doctrine and the morals of the princes and clergy was necessarily followed by a general depravity of the people, those of all conditions making it their sole business to get money by any means and to squander it away, when they had got it, in luxury and debauchery.

"The Roman empire declined steadily after Constantine, whose successors were generally remarkable for their ill qualities, especially cowardice and cruelty. By Mohammed's time, the Western half of the empire was overrun by the Goths and the Eastern was so reduced by the Huns on the one side and the Persians on the other that it did not have the capacity to stem the violence of a powerful invasion. The emperor Maurice paid tribute to the Khagan or king of the Huns; and after Phocas had murdered his master, there was such lamentable havoc among the soldiers that when Heraclius came, not above seven years after, to muster the army, there were only two soldiers left alive out of all those who had borne arms when Phocas first usurped the empire. And though Heraclius was a prince of admirable courage and conduct and had done what possibly could be done to restore the discipline of the army – and had had great success against the Persians so as to drive them not only out of his dominions but even out of part of their own – still the very vitals of the empire seemed to be mortally wounded; that there could no time have happened more fatal to the empire; or more favourable to the enterprises of the Arabs; who seem to have been raised up on purpose by God, to be a scourge to the Christian church, for not living answerably to that most holy religion which they have received.

"The Persians had also been in a declining condition for some time before Mohammed, occasioned chiefly by their intestine broils and dissensions, a great part of which arose from the devilish doctrines of Manes and Mazdak. The opinions of the former are tolerably well known; the latter lived in the reign of Khosru Kobad who pretended to be a prophet sent from God to preach a community of women and possessions, since all men were brothers and descended from the same common parents. This he imagined would put an end to all feuds and quarrels among men, which generally arose on the account of one of the two. Kobad himself embraced the impressions of this imposter, to whom he gave leave, according to his new doctrine, to lie with the queen his wife; which permission Anushirwab his son, with much difficulty, prevailed on Mazdak not to make use of. These sects would certainly have been the immediate ruin of the Persian empire had not Anushirwan, as soon as he succeeded his father, put Mazdak to death with all his followers and the Manicheans also restored the ancient Magian religion.

"In the reign of this prince, deservedly surnamed the 'just', Mohammed was born. He was the last king of Persia who deserved the throne, which after him was almost perpetually contended for, still subverted by the Arabs. His son Hermuz lost the love of his subjects by his excessive cruelty; having had his eyes put out by his wife's brothers, he was obliged to resign the crown to his son Khorsu Parviz who, at the instigation of Bahram Chubin, had rebelled against him and was afterwards strangled. Parviz was soon obliged to quit the throne in favour of Bahram. But obtaining succours of the Greek emperor Maurice, he recovered the crown; yet towards the latter end of a long reign, he grew so tyrannical and hateful to his subjects that they held a private correspondence with the Arabs and he was at length deposed, imprisoned and slain by his son Shiruyeh. After Parwiz, no less than six princes possessed the throne in less than six years.

"These domestic broils effectually brought ruin upon the Persians – for though they did, rather by the weakness of the Greeks than their own force, ravage Syria and sack Jerusalem and Damascus under Khosru Parviz; and while the Arabs were divided and independent, had some power in the province of Yaman, where they set up the four last kings before Mohammed – when attacked by the Greeks under Heraclius, they not only lost their conquest but part of their own dominions, and no sooner were the Arabia, united by Mohammedism, than they beat them in every battle, and in a few years totally subdued them.

"As these empires were weak and declining, so Arabia, set up by Mohammed, was strong and flourishing, having been peopled at the expense of the Grecian empire, whence the violent proceedings of the domineering sects forced many to seek refuge in a free country, as Arabia then was, where they who could not enjoy tranquillity and their conscience at home found a secure retreat. The Arabians were not only a populous nation but were unacquainted with the luxury and delicacies of the Greeks and Persians, and inured to hardships of all sorts; living in a most parsimonious manner, seldom eating any flesh, drinking no wine, and sitting on the ground. Their political government also favoured the designs of Mohammed; for the division and independency of their tribes were so necessary to the first propagation of his religion and the foundation of his power that it would have been scarce possible for him to have effected either had the Arabs been united in one society. But when they had embraced the religion, the consequent union of their tribes was no less necessary and conducive to their future conquests and grandeur.

"**Mohammed** came into the world with some disadvantages, which he soon surmounted. His father Abd'allah was a younger son of Abd'almotalleb, and dying very young and in his father's lifetime, left his widow and infant son in mean circumstances; his whole substance consisting of just five camels and one Ethiopian she-slave. Abd'almotalleb was therefore obliged to take care of his grandchild Mohammed, which he not only did during his life, but at his death enjoined his eldest son Abu Taleb, who was brother to Abd'allah by the same mother, to provide for him for the future – which he very affectionately did, and instructed him in the business of a merchant, which he followed. To that end, he took him with him into Syria when he was just thirteen and afterwards recommended him to Kadjah, a noble and rich widow, for her factor, in whose service he behaved so well, that by making him her husband she soon raised him to equality with the richest in Mecca.

"After he began by this advantageous match to live at his ease, it was that he formed the scheme of establishing a new religion or, as he expressed it, of replanting the only true and ancient one, professed by Adam, Noah, Abraham, Moses, Jesus, and all the prophets, by destroying the gross idolatry into which the generality of his countrymen had fallen, and weeding out the corruption and superstitions which the latter Jews and Christians had, as he thought, introduced into their religion, and reducing it in its original purity, which consisted chiefly in the worship of only one God.

"Whether this was the effect of enthusiasm, or only a design to raise himself to the supreme government of his country, or as some say, particularly Christian writers, the ambition and desire to satisfy his sensuality, his original design of bringing the pagan Arabs to the knowledge of the true God was certainly noble and to be highly commended. Mohammed was no doubt fully satisfied in his conscience of the truth of the grand point, the unity of God, which was what he chiefly attended to – all his other doctrines and institutions being rather accidental and unavoidable rather than premeditated and designed.

"Since then Mohammed was certainly himself persuaded of his

grand article of faith, which in his opinion was violated by all the rest of the world; not only by the idolaters but by the Christians, as well as those who rightly worshipped Jesus as God, as those who superstitiously adored the Virgin Mary, saints, and images, and also by the Jews, who are accused in the *Koran* of taking Ezra for the son of God. It is easy to conceive that he might think in a meritorious work to rescue the world from such ignorance and superstition and by degrees, with the help of a warm imagination, which an Arab seldom wants for, to suppose himself destined by providence to effect that great reformation. And this fancy of his might take still deeper root in his mind during the solitude he thereupon affected, usually retiring for a month in the year to a cave in Mount Hara near Mecca. One thing which may be probably urged against the enthusiasm of this prophet of the Arabs is the wise conduct and great prudence he all along showed in pursuing his design, which seem inconsistent with the wild notions of a hot-brained religionist. But though all enthusiasts or madmen do not behave with the same gravity and circumspection that he did, yet he will not be the first instance, by several, of a person who has been out of the way only *quad hoc* (unique, quite special – *Latin*) and in all other respects acted with the greatest decency and precaution.

"Well, good people, thank you very much for listening to my long, long speech but I thought if we shall be fair about 'what was fair', knowing the truths and sequences of historical events, seeing the religion as not only a 'very personal belief' but also as a cultural heritage, growth and social and self-refinement of mankind throughout human history, then 'living religiously' – whatever belief system one might belong to – shall become so natural a way of 'living humanly'.

"God bless you all. See you some weeks later, after our Summer Literary Festival and other thrilling founding experiences are over. So long!"

Today is very important to me: Rabbi Braun is going to talk about **Kabalah** exclusively that I do not want to miss. Among all, Kabalah, for some reason or other, means a lot to me. As you know, my ancestors

Chapter 23

came from a Muslim background and my father and I have been Unitarian, since the birthplace of my grandfather was Thessalonika, Greece, I wonder whether there was Jewish blood somewhere between, for the Jewish faith had interested me a lot; like the stories and movies about the concentration camps of World War II were used to bring tears to my eyes all the time, *Fiddler on the Roof* was the best musical that the entire family had cherished for the past century and the most celebrated painter to the entire family genealogy is that of Marc Chagall, a Russian-born Jewish artist.

Anyway, full of joy, I rushed to Jewish synagogue and caught Rabbis David and

Braun just in time. "Without you, we already could not start Mr. President," commented Rabbi Braun with a kind of pride and in his quiet, comforting voice he started to preach.

"Kabalah, also written as Cabalah, in Hebrew means 'a traditional teaching, a learning that had been transmitting from generations to generations'. It comes from 'Kibel – KBL', meaning 'to receive it'. That refers to 'receiving the secret doctrine of old Jewish religion, orally!'

"The beginnings of Jewish mysticism could be found in ancient times in the first establishments in Palestine and later on Babylonia. The following apocalyptic literature appeared in the writings of the Essenes and in the Talmud. They call this the Gaonic period, lasting between A.C. 7th and 19th centuries. The significant works were done by Otiot de R. Akiva and Sefer Yetzirah. With an eclectic work in the following A.C. 10th to 12th centuries and through the contributions by Sefer Raziel, Sefer Hasidim and Rokeah, and a principal man, a

Sefer Ha-Bahir's philosophical contributions, Kabalah officially shaped up and spread considerably through Spain, Germany and mid-Europe. Then, in the A.C. 17th century, those teachings and mysticism reached Palestine; and, there, in the city of Safed, a Rabbi Isaac Luria created a new Jewish system of mysticism.

"The principal teachings of the Kabalah are, as follows:

1) God did not create the world, directly. God is above all, eternal, and the *En sof* ('Endless'). Higher and lower forms of life and conduct emanate, proceeding God, from the more spiritual to a lesser one. The Ten Spheres (*Sefirot*) emanated and sprung in the following order: Crown, Wisdom, Intelligence, Greatness, Strength, Beauty, Firmness, Splendor (*Zooar*), Foundation, and Kingdom. The Kingdom, which is the last sphere, created the physical world. Through these spheres, God rules the world, and all his activities are performed this way.
2) Everything that exists is a part of Deity; and only man through acts of piety and moral conduct can achieve union with God. Through the observance of the commandments, every Jew can influence the Spheres, and through which can influence God, on behalf of mankind. The Jewish people were chosen by God to preserve the world by the strict observance of the law.
3) Man is judged by his soul. This is the most important thing of his being. During creation, all souls were created at the same time; the soul is in contract with the body and stays pure while alive, whereas after death, it becomes a part of the world, ruled by the Ten Spheres. The contaminated-impure souls, after death, re-inhabit and migrate from body to body, until they are purified.
4) Evil does not exist in itself but is the result of the negation of good. It could be overcome through praying, repentance, self-afflicting and absolute observance of the law.
5) The text of the *Bible* is full of hidden messages and meanings. In spite of the fact that is written in man's language, the words contain plenty of concepts of a divine and mysterious nature. Man, by any means, should endeavour to uncover them. This could be achieved through different techniques that are applied by Kabbalists.

"The Kabalah is both a philosophical and theosophical system which endeavours to be able to find some answers on subjects like God, creation, the universe, faith and mankind. Through it, the significance of human life and its relatedness to the universal laws is demonstrated

Chapter 23

and expressed through some numerical correspondence.

"If we can review, in Kabalah, the principal theme is understanding, absorbing and re-using mental-psychic or para-psychological powers. Thus, the interpretation and expressing of the outer life in terms of our inner creative powers.

"The *Book of Genesis* opens with 'In the beginning God created the heaven and the earth!'. However, this was not in reality, just in potentiality. Plato, in his book *Timaeus*, describes the 'creation of the universe' as, '.... God was the all-perfect ruler of the spiritual world, brought it down and endowed it with life, soul and intelligence. He also created, as lesser gods, Dyonisoen gods: Zeus, Apollo, Athene; then created birds, animals and the rest..'

"God said, 'Let there be light, and there was.' That was the first day of creation. On the 2nd day, 'water' and the 'vegetable world' were established. On the 3rd day, 'the firmament of earth was settled!' From then on, everything did co-exist simultaneously and manifested itself under the light that was God himself. Thus, the world was completed within six days, and on the seventh, which falls on the Sabbath, 'rest' was ordered.

"According to old Kabbalists, the first five chapters of *Genesis* were written in 'code' with Hebrew letters. As we shall see a while later in much more detail, each letter has a specific meaning which also corresponds to a certain number, however with no mathematical significance. Each letter and the corresponding number are simply an ideogram or symbol of a cosmic force. There is also an ongoing cosmic energy interaction in the universe and the man.

"Pythagoras also talked about 'Nature Geometrizeses', referring to the same kind of interaction. Psychiatrist Carl Gustave Jung – believing a 'mutual-cosmic unconsciousness = collective unconscious in all human beings – had thought that the material of the collective unconscious resides in the depth of the subconscious (unconscious), and related numbers to these materials, in the form of "arche-types", did pre-exist even before birth. The term 'Law of Synchronicity' was also coined by him, meaning that 'two meaningful events connected with each other, also with numbers, did exist in the pre-conscious'. A number is a symbol and conveys an idea. In a way, it is also a language, conveying communication.

"Kabalah intends to make people believe that God created the universe by means of the Hebrew alphabet. In that alphabet, there are twenty-two letters and they represent twenty-two types of different

A.C. 2084

States of consciousness.

"If we divide these letters into three further groups, we find:

1) Three 'mothers', also called 'trinity':
   "**Aleph** is the essence of 'air', also giving birth to 'spirit'. In humans, it forms the 'chest'. In day-to-day living, it is the cause of 'temperate weather'.
   "**Mem** is the essence of 'fire', and 'heavens' are created from it. In humans, it forms the 'head'; it causes the 'hot' season; it interplays with 'Shin' to create the opposite forces.
   "Shin is the essence for 'water'; 'earth' is created from it. In humans, it forms the 'belly'. It creates the 'cold' season.
2) Seven 'doubles':
   "**Beth,** representing 'wisdom' and 'folly',
   "**Gimel,** representing 'grace' and 'indignation',
   "**Daleth,** representing 'fertility' and 'solitude',
   "**Caph,** representing 'life' and 'death',
   "**Pe,** representing 'power' and 'servitude',
   "**Resh,** representing 'peace' and 'war',
   "**Tu,** representing 'riches' and 'poverty'.
3) Twelve 'simples':
   "**He** – sight,
   "**Vau** – hearing,
   "**Zayin** – smell,
   "**Cheth** – speech,
   "**Teth** – taste,
   "**Yod** – sexual love,
   "**Lamed** – work,
   "**Nun** – movement,
   "**Samekh**- anger,
   "**Ayin** – mirth,
   "**Tzaddi** – imagination,
   "**Qoph** – sleep.
   "We also should not forget that, the twelve (simple) letters mentioned here, are also:
   "12 months of the year,
   "12 months of the Zodiac,
   "12 organs of man : 2 hands, 2 feet, 2 kidneys, 1 spleen, 1 liver, 1 gall-bladder; sexual organs, stomach, intestines.

Chapter 23

"Well, this was the opening class. Pretty soon, for the newcomers, I would like to spare some time during the weekday evenings for some Kabalah teachings and practices that we have been doing for some time. We will get together, choosing the most available times. For that purpose, I am stopping here and promising what kind of subjects we are going to go into, as follows:

"Kavvanah in meditation; elements of Kabalistic ritual (identification with nature and purification with holy oil; life tree; Avatar; *Siddur*: the vehicle of Kabalah; course of the tides; the cosmic egg, Zahar, etc.

"Now, before closing off, I would like to give brief answers to two questions which were put to me before the ceremonies were started:

"What is Kaddish? One newcomer from another faith asked me.

"Kaddish is an important portion of the daily liturgy in the synagogue. It had been used for many centuries as a mourning prayer. Originally it was a prayer, written in Aramaic, meaning 'sanctification'. When used as prayer, it is recited by the mourner at the graveside of parents or close relatives and during the three daily prayers in the synagogue, for the first eleven months, following the death event. Strangely enough, the Kaddish has no direct reference to the dead or to mourning; essentially it is a doxology, praising God and praying for the speedy establishment of God's kingdom on earth. It is only the special burial Kaddish incorporates a prayer for the resurrection of the dead. In the reform liturgy, the Kaddish is recited only as a mourning prayer.

"The second question, rather request was that of 'would you please outline the Ten Commandments?'

"The Ten Commandments, which are also known as 'Decalogue', are the fundamental law of the Jewish people known in Hebrew as 'Aseret ha-Dihro't, which according to the *Bible* were revealed to Moses and the people at Mount Sınai.

"A shortened form of the 'Decalogue' could be summarised as follows:

1) I am the Lord, thy God, who brought thee out of the land of Egypt, out of the house of bondage.
2) Thou shalt have no other God before Me.
3) Thou shalt not take the name of the Lord thy God in vain.
4) Remember the Sabbath day to keep it holy.
5) Honour thy father and thy mother.
6) Thou shall not murder.

A.C. 2084

7) Thou shall not commit adultery.
8) Thou shall not steal.
9) Thou shall not bear false witness against thy neighbour.
10) Thou shall not covet anything that belongs to thy neighbour.

"Those Ten Commandments are regarded by both Jews and non-Jews as the basic social ethics for every civilised society. They are commonly represented symbolically in the form of two tablets, called the 'Tablets of the Law', used as a sacred design in the synagogue; also as ornaments on different objects and articles."

"Thus ended Saturday, this very holy Sabbath day activities and teachings. Hallelujah!"

Today is Sunday. I told my wife how much I love her, who, smart cookie that she is, immediately told me that "I got the message, on this beautiful day, you would like to stay home, not going outdoors, and read something! Isn't that it?" I told Jada, who, I never lied to in

Chapter 24

my life-time, that she was very correct and I had in my mind very important 'must' things to be done. She could choose whatever she could but I must be forgiven. Even though we share everything in the book, of course she does not know anything about this Mormon business, or the other big secrets of the Statehood if and when they occur, and, when I was in practice, the personal secrets and problems of my psychiatric patients. Not to talk anyone does not disturb me since those things are private properties, right or wrong, I cannot judge. But the basic principle is that "I cannot share some secret knowledge, without the permission or presence of the people involved", which is ninety-nine percent impossible anyway.

So, my lovely Jada took her pastel, crayons and whatever she was using for her painting hobby that I have not even any simple knowledge of and began to sketch and colour – I do not know but maybe for the one thousandth time – our cats' eyes, noses, ears, tails, you name it. And I rushed to my study room and opened my grandfather's diary in the place that I had left it the other day.

January 6, 1969
Code Island

It had been a week that I have been married to Francis. We just returned from a week's honeymoon trip. For sure, there was a visible 'change' in the house and our lifestyle. On the plus side, it is nice to have a young lady at home who cares for you. Even though I am not a social butterfly, going to parties, dances and so on — although I love dancing. When I was young I had taught dance to youngsters to earn some money for school. As I had mentioned before, she was a nurse and working at a municipal hospital nearby in the operation room. That, I am sure, is quite a tiring business. She was not on night duties so it gave us some chance to have a relatively regular home life as far eating and sleeping was concerned. She is a mediocre cook that is good enough for us due to the fact that I followed a single life for quite a while; besides opening cans and utilising the microwave, I myself used to do some simple cooking, like rice pilaf, frying squash and egg-plants, making green pepper dolmas (leaves stuffed with rice and chopped onions), macaroni and alike. As many newly married say, "There is a reason to come home!" now, in spite of the fact that I had always come home due to my son Souhi anyway, but, this was different.

By the same token, concerts, movies and shopping had also been more regular, meaningful and more fun, from both togetherness with an adult who you have a love relation and sharing from the responsibilities point of view. Our Sunday noon lunch commitments at Francis' home with her family naturally go (seem to go) on unchanged, as they had been this noon. Mr. Normand's sure qualities and undeniable paternity seems to be continuing perhaps forever. No complaints (yet).

At the minus side, I am afraid the pan of the scale weighs heavier to that direction than the other. First of all, there is no real 'sparkling' love between the two of us, but I do not blame neither she or me, because of the way that we had chosen each other. There was a 'like', a kind of 'admiration' for general politeness, sense of appreciation and family-orientated social behaviour, general culture and adaptation to social life and likeness on both sides for each other, but again, it is as if something is lacking. To bring two good people together does not guarantee a good marriage though it is too early to make an evaluation of this subject. Francis, in spite of her being in her mid-twenties, had never been in love with anyone. That did not surprise me, as a psychiatrist I know well that if any girl is so much in admiration of and under the domination of her father, she can never relinquish that attachment to the father figure which we call *Oedipal*; if this is true, nonetheless having a baby would perhaps moderate and might nullify the degree of that binding, at least. On that subject, too, we have to wait and see.

Naturally, there is an intimate physical side of any love story. From an untouched girl I wouldn't expect stormy, hell-burning love scenes, but

Chapter 24

nonetheless, we analysts believe the corporal pleasure of the sex also depends upon the natural development of the psychic aspects of growth and human relations. If you don't give a chance to the fantasy because it is sin, or not permissible, and then when one day you are given a legitimate license to do it, one is expectedly a little bit afraid, a little bit surprised and a little bit dissatisfied. "Oh, was that all?", and a little bit satisfied "Thank God, it is over!" Even anticipation of that relation visibly created some anxiety in her, I see. But I am a patient person, it is fair for such a noble girl to be given enough chance, therefore a little bit more time. But one thing did really bother me – that I wouldn't pass without detailing a little bit – and scared me. Here is the story.

You know we had married just before Christmas and at the day of the church wedding, as I had left my nine-year-old son with my next neighbour as usual, my best friend, an Uban doctor and his wife with two children of almost similar ages. Unfortunately, I could not invite them to the church because they were black and this was against Mormon tradition and beliefs. We, in my car, the very same afternoon began to ride towards Nadian shores and wanted to either stay on Two Thousand Islands – from where I have made my first notes after marriage last week, written above – and/or to go up to Réal and stay a few days in that magnificent city. While driving smoothly and after having a relatively simple early dinner at one of the roadside restaurants, when we were on the drive again, I observed some visible anxiety on Francis' face and asked: "Is there anything matter, honey?" "Nothing, nothing!" denied Francis at first but as I insisted she finally broke out:

"Ismailov, I don't know whether we did right or wrong; but I sincerely feel that, before it is too late (namely, we have not been intimate yet!), we may return back!" Surprised and a little bit mad, I screamed:

"Don't be silly! It is ridiculous. Are you aware what you're saying?"

"Yes, I know!", she also angrily responded, "as a matter of fact, I want to punch you right in the face!"

I pulled the car to the side of the road and put the blinkers on. What was my sin for which my lovely (?) bride was going to punch me right on the nose? I gave her a few minutes to think, cool off, and told her in a calm voice that if she insisted, by all means, I would drive her back and close this book even before opening it. She thought for a while. I did not know what was passing from her mind but it was not too difficult to be easily read by almost anyone. She was married to a man with a nine-year-old child. From one hierarchy, she was going to move onto another; but this was going to require a lot of responsibilities, house, child care and sex that she was not used to exercising. On the other hand, should we return back, what was the church — and the most importantly her father — going to say?

I told her that I respected and accepted her mixed feelings about this or any marriage, but I would not understand and could not accept that undue aggression in the form of a punch or any form. What was it? I could not know the details, since I did not observe any visible aggression at their home (However it was too short time to make a logical observation!). I interpreted this a "repressed-pushed down to unconscious kind of aggression" since a woman's status in that religion was just an eternal submission to men but nothing else. So, I was greeting King Oedipus, that supreme power, once again.

After just a few minutes' thinking, Francis, subdued and with a pale face, apologised from me for saying so and said "Let's continue!" Both of us were thoughtful and I began to drive the car forward but the initial joy had gone away. Plus the fact that for my part my hidden anxiety that occasionally used to show itself as a phobia had come to the surface. It used to come from time to time as "heights" or "bridge" phobia. As we approached the bridge that connects the highway to the Two Thousand Islands, I began to shake, and a kind of heaviness filled my chest and a fear of the unknown began to pump my heart. As I stopped the car, Francis asked anxiously:

"What happened now, Ismailov? Is anything the matter?"

"My phobia. It has arisen again!"

"What phobia?"

"Bridges or heights... It sometimes stops me flying too. It comes out when I am unduly anxious or facing some problems. Are you mad at me?"

"No, but I am rather surprised. A psychiatrist with your qualifications... Strange. But I understand, I too have some; I can fly but I cannot take trains or buses. I have the driver's license but because of that anxiety, I don't drive. However, if you wish, if you cannot pass this bridge, I can do it temporarily for you. I see the car is automatic, isn't it?"

"Yes it is, but let us drink some coffee at the roadside restaurant again... And, I shall take some minor tranquilisers!"

After having a kind of breakfast, combined with a few milligrams of benzodiazepines, with my heart in my mouth, we passed the bridge which was one kilometre long. At the top, it was as if the bridge was falling off and I pushed the gas pedal to the speediest. I finally made it. Both of us were silent throughout. We found a place to stay overnight that came first to our sight. With the effect of the pill, I almost immediately went to sleep, saving, or rather deferring, my bride's "first night anxiety" to the next day. Fortunately, in spite of the winter, the nature was beautiful around us. Long

Chapter 24

trees appeared dressed all in white, brilliantly reflecting the Christmas mood. During the time we spent there, three days, we went to see an historical chateau that was built four hundred years ago for his "lovely wife". We both sketched and signed some heart shapes on the damp walls of the building, piercing it through with an arrow, like teen-agers. Being in isolation and with the holiday season's music and tranquillity, we both believed that we might have done something good in marrying each other. Who knows, maybe we did.

On our way back home, especially passing the bridge back, appeared relatively easier than before. On the Islands and on the way back, we bought some small gifts and presents: coloured albums, old Indian crafts, sweaters and alike, and returned home much more settled.

January 13, 1969
Code Island

Business as usual but the marriage began to show more pores in its psycho-biological structure. My wife was still on her yearly vacation which gave us much more time for daily togetherness. One strange thing kept going on, and my wife did not show any willpower to correct or change it: Each morning, after my son went to the school bus at the corner of the street, Francis took her own bus and went to her home at Sea-Chief to change her dress. She, indeed, to my sudden recollection, had brought almost nothing from her native home, nothing but nothing. We did not need any furniture and/or bedroom or dining room sets or something like that, or a refrigerator, washer-dryer or microwave oven. As far as personal belongings were concerned, she had come with only two suitcases, naturally raising the question "Well, lady, are you married, or are you going somewhere for a vacation for a short while?" More surprising was why her well-to-do parents, in spite of my generosity which is another issue, have not suggested, warned her or pointed out this thing? Why did they not ask what is the reason that she is changing at home and not encourage her to reverse it? Was she still showing her loyalty to mother and father? After a few days I raised my voice and asked her whether we were on a trial marriage or not. Weren't we "celestially" married in a Mormon church? She gave me very vague answers, like "I don't know, I guess I am just getting used to it! This way is easier," etc. I finally brought the subject privately and gently to her mother's attention. She very softly replied: "Please be understanding, my daughter is a very delicate person. I understand you have some phobias, she has these kind of phobias too. It will take some time, I guess, to adjust." It was very hard for me to comprehend the relation between my occasional phobias and her strange, unaccustomed style of changing clothing.

This very afternoon, when we were alone with my father-in-law for a while, he very quietly but authoritatively asked me: "Doctor, now I found a chance to ask you. Just before you married, we had found some birth control pills in our daughter's handbag. Would you answer me man-to-man; did you have any sexual relations before you married my daughter?"

"I, for sure, was not ready for this kind of questioning and was greatly surprised and perhaps a little angry too; but I kept my cool and replied: "You should know your daughter better than I could. Right after initial meeting, perhaps due to emotions, her menses had been irregular, so we both decided that she should take pills for a few months until they shall be regulated. That's all."

He took a deep breath, so did I. Something was more than strange in this family members' interrelatedness. Should I have replied to him, saying "Why you don't ask your daughter? Are you checking your older daughter too what they are doing in their marriage, say sex; does she also change her clothing at home and alike?"

One more thing began to bother me too. In the mornings, when my son was going to the street corner to get on the bus, Francis' face was getting somewhat sullen for some time. I finally asked her: "Francis, is there anything that bothers you, as I observe your face gets sullen when Souhi goes to the stand? Is it anything the matter?"

With some hesitation she finally spoke up: "Well, first, he is a big boy, why every morning do you have to go with him and wait for the bus?"

"Francis, you surprise me. Why shouldn't I go? He is just nine, besides, whether this is a sort of duty or not, this is a pleasure too. We grew up together. Do you know what this boy has been through throughout the years, being alone with his father, away from a mother's love, care and tenderness? If one day we shall have a child and he or she will grow up and there shall come the school time, shall I not go to the corner for him too? What is the matter with you?"

Instead of answering my questions, she added another pearl to my troubled mind: "Well, I have another worry in my mind. I constantly worry that if we shall have a child whether he shall be a coloured one? Since, you know where you come from!"

"Hey Francis, are you mad or stupid? Don't you see I am white, and he is also white. Who told you that someone with my background, the country of origin so on so forth, suddenly brings out chocolate babies? Suppose such a miracle happens, if he is ours, isn't he sacred too, aren't we going to love

Chapter 24

him? Incidentally, we are having very little relations, besides, you are on pills. I guess it will take quite some time for your readiness for having babies."

Francis bowed her head down, and murmured: "I want to have a baby so much... I have not been taking pills... I was supposed to see my menses last week but they did not happen. I really, if I am pregnant, would like to stay home this week along, namely here, with my mother. Then, I shall make my mind up accordingly!"

"Francis, what you are talking about? My goodness." But she quietly went away. I was alone for a while. Then her mother came along, with some teary eyes. She said Francis was feeling a little bit nervous and depressed. It was much better for us to be apart for a little while. I, however, should come to visit them next Sunday for dinner and also attend the church.

Tons and tons of bricks had fallen on the top of my head. I took my son and left, without saying goodbye.

January 20, 1969
Code Island

Well, our week passed quietly and without any problem. My son went to his school, I went to my job. Between, I never called Francis from her home asking how she was doing. Whether she could have started her work or not, I do not know. I began to think what was going on? Less than a month's marriage? This was ridiculous. We couldn't have known each other by any means. What about the possibility of pregnancy? God forbid, if she is pregnant what are we going to do? Did she marry me because she wanted to have a baby? Just like that? And here, in this country, should divorce occur, should newly-born babies go with the mother? Of course he will go with mother and I shall support him the rest of my life even without having the pleasure of fatherhood, meaning playing at home with him, going together to baseball, basketball, movies, travelling, camping and travelling abroad, as I have been doing with my lovely son Souhi? I don't want to be a 'weekend father!' What about the baby's rights? What is my destiny? Oh, mighty God, why did you not give any signal to warn me before this togetherness? Well, I am sure no one knows the correct answers to those lamentations. We shall live and see.

My son appears on the surfacenot to be affected by this early separation. He is usually quite a talker but a little bit secretive in this subject. I am sure there had not been a serious attachment to Francis yet, no more than with a baby-sitter who he used to be with for years. But this was a different kind of promise. As a child psychiatrist, I know he might have had a fantasy that one day, maybe, his natural mother was going to be with us, in spite of the fact that he never had consciously spoken out about that. Perhaps subconsciously he could have been glad too that this marriage had not lasted long, I do not know. Nonetheless, I was exposing him to another separation from a promised paradise.

* * *

Time-out! Time-out for a coffee break and maybe a cone of chocolate ice-cream. First I need to visit the W.C., stretch my arms and legs, look out of the window and figure out what strange things are going on in this strange world. If we did not have these sort of problems, was life worth living? Maybe, maybe not. We seem to forget the things and our sufferings; one does not erase them from the mind completely but I guess time erases the emotional attachment to the events. Memories are becoming detached from our body-soul fusion and pass through our minds as if we are seeing a movie that we have seen before: Each time with a little bit less enthusiasm and outpouring of feelings. The people who have some writing skills put these feelings into some other forms of expression, like writing novels, poems or plays. Then, you have different feelings; even though you may be talking about suffering, you have a feeling of triumph, even an ecstasy that you have mastered the underlying sad feelings and made others happy and made some other people applaud you too! I told you, this is a very strange world. Hey, time is up. Let's go to work. We have some business to finish.

January 27, 1969
Midnight, Code Island

A big storm broke today and I am still shaky. How things go this fast, like a heavy truck going downhill with no brakes on, I don't understand. There had been many things today that I just cannot understand *how* they may happen and of course another question with no answer is: *why?*

Let us start with the church which is the main issue on my mind. I dressed up nicely and, in spite of some hesitation that I had at the beginning, had my son with me too, since we were going to be at father-in-law Mr. Normand's house for Sunday dinner after the church services. One could say honestly, they were very kind and gentle, very accepting toward my child throughout. I felt a little estrangement though, particularly when we were going to face each other with Francis; what kind of feeling was it going to be? Had she made her mind up about coming home, or extending her visit, or staying there permanently? Was she pregnant? Off, let us go. I drove first

Chapter 24

to Mr. Normand's house and dropped Souhi there without getting out of the car, just waving my fingers to my mother-in-law who opened the door.

The church seemed to be more crowded than ever. People were talking in the hall before the start, that today some very special and precious speakers were going to talk about a very important subject: *Angel Moroni, Book of Moroni* and *Moroni Plates*. I only know about Moroni, his being a kind of founder angel, a messenger to Prophet Smith from God, that's all. Why this programme was not told to us before, I don't know. I only come to the church from Sunday to Sunday. Maybe some more senior people knew more about the forthcoming incident. There was also a rumour that "some very precious, historical and biblical documents about the gospel were going to be held in our church for a while, since there was a move in the headquarters of the Mormon church and until it was completed, they were going to be held in one of the most trustable churches in the nation, like ours here. They might even be demonstrated too." Well, all this is good, however, they it is just news to me.

Before the ceremonies started, Mr. Normand, my father-in-law, who as I had said before was deacon and the 1st councillor at the church, greeted me with a smile, as if nothing had happened between Francis and I, and murmured to me: "'I am glad you came. This is one of the most important days of our church. Sit close to me!" I took this as a good sign, the man still having good feelings about me in spite of the fact that the things were not that good between his daughter and I.

Anyway, finally the ceremonies started. A holy Most Reverend Christian Whitmer the 4th, in his solemn and very respectable appearance, began to give the history of *The Plates of Nephi*, of two kinds large and small; about the ministry and teachings of the prophets from the time of Mosiah; *The Plates of Mormon*, the *Large Plates of Nephi*, a brief history by Mormon and his son Moroni; *The Plates of Ether*, summarising the history of the Jaredites; and, forth, *the Plates of Brass* that are brought by the people of Lehi from Jerusalem in B.C. 600, containing 'the five books of Moses... and also a record of the Jews from the beginning.' This divine man, reportedly, was the fourth generation of the first witness to Prophet Smith's ordainment as prophet.

"And," Reverend Witmer continued, "in or about the year A.C. 421, Moroni, the last of the Nephite prophet-historians, sealed the sacred record and hid it unto the Lord, to be brought forth in the latter days, as predicted by the voice of God through his ancient prophets. In A.C. 1823, this same Moroni, then a resurrected personage, visited the Prophet Smith and subsequently delivered engraved plates to him. No one had seen them, as historian say, but we, in the sacred hearts of us, in spite of pressures, assassinations and bloody wars, have been able to keep them somewhere. However, the exact whereabouts are not known to anyone. Fortunately, our Prophet Smith, after translating them into English in summarised form, re-wrote those sacred tablets that we had been holding as very precious treasures entrusted to our Mormon church headquarters for safe-keeping. Since there is a renovation that shall be going for a long time there, I proudly brought those treasures and gave to the President of this church, Very Reverend Arthur, for another safe-keeping until due time."

Everybody was smiling and I am sure was very proud of this high honour. I myself, too, felt a kind of joy, being a new and small part of this holy church. Then, almost simultaneously with the time that Very Reverend Witmer completed his opening speech, suddenly fire alarms went off. Besides, some smell of smoke filled the air and men rushing into the hall created a sudden commotion. "Fire, fire, let us empty the hall!"

Mr. Normand told me hastily: "Follow me!" and I began to run after him. Everybody was rushing towards somewhere, most, naturally, to outdoors, but obviously on the way there was a big fire too. Then of course a panic started – where to go? People were charging here and there, opening and closing doors one after the other, hoping to find some hole to get out. Then, we did not know the details yet, but it was as if the fire had started from several points at the same time, possibly, even probably, being set intentionally by someone or some people for the flames were coming strongly from every corner. My father-in-law murmured to me, "let us go to my holy office and get some valuables out. I did not bring my car, I need yours. Come on!"

So, we rushed to the unknown parts – of course to me – of the church building. He finally stopped at a door, short of breath, and then opened it. We entered a prosperously designed and furnished room. He opened some drawers, unlocked a few safes in a hurry, brought out several small packages all carefully wrapped, files and holy books, pulled several certificates and framed pictures off the walls and made a small pile in the middle of the room. First, he loaded me with as many of them as possible and then with himself embracing the rest, gave me the order "Follow me!" As we were rushing out, the smoke and some reddish, hot stuff were entering the room. We turned to the left and from the back corridor, Mr. Normand opened a – perhaps hidden – door and, thank God, we were outdoors on the grass in the backyard. Together we rushed to the parking lot. This time he was following me. After putting the staff into my luggage and on the back seat of the car, Mr. Normand looked around and said: "It doesn't seem fire would reach here. Let us go back and help the others!" So, we went back to the church which was still in turmoil.

Chapter 24

Within an hour's time, everybody was taken out safe and sound, apart from a few bruises and burns here and there. Of course the fire department and police were immediately contacted and soon we heard plenty of sirens. A couple of people, just in case, were referred to the hospital for smoke inhalation and a few scratches, burnt fingers and alike. Religious leaders had gathered in the middle of the road that leads to the church and in their solemnly State, were praying silently. The leaders consoled everybody and ensured they went home safely. For those who couldn't drive, few taxis were called and other people offered a ride. Fortunately, no one was seriously hurt. I have never seen a disaster handled so masterfully, in an orderly and caring fashion. While these things were going on, the President and other big leaders, who were also among the guests, had a short meeting among themselves, on their feet. I assumed they made some future plans about what to do next. Then, they scattered in small groups. At the end, after almost everyone had gone away, like a captain being the last to leave his ship, my father-in-law came near me and said: "Well, let us go home. It is getting late. I may come back later on, after the fire has been put out!"

On the way back I kept silent, in respect to this very dedicated man. Since we had witnessed the tragedy that had occurred abruptly, there was nothing to talk about really unless he was going to initiate something. I put the radio on; the news obviously had gotten to the media and they were giving the details and raising some doubts, thoughts about the possibility that the occurrence of the fire was unusual. I shut the radio off; at home, the ladies who most probably had already heard the story, were gallantly going to question and display plenty of emotions anyway.

Home, as expected, was full of emotions. However, as we two men, quietly, maturely and in an orderly fashion handled the situation quite well, those high emotions did not reach a hysterical level. Some fire had broken out, there was a lot of commotion but no one was hurt. The reason or reasons are unknown, and we are home, safe. That was it. I helped Mr. Normand, taking the material out of the car that we had brought out from the church for safety, carrying it to the second floor of their house that I had never been to before.

He thanked me and said he was going to place them somewhere later on. I went down immediately. He also came down, although a few minutes afterwards.

Francis said "Hello!" to me and I replied the same, after kissing her cheeks gently. Probably, this undesirable accident had broken the pre-existing icy atmosphere and I felt a kind of soft air around, although I was still tense inside. I hugged my son who had watched T.V. a little bit, then played with puzzles. Mother rushed to set the table for dinner and Francis helped her out. A few minutes later, Mr. Normand, too, came down, a little bit serious and thoughtful, but quiet and as nice as possible. We ate to a mediocre degree since our emotions had really taken us one way and another. The local T.V. also announced the event and the gallant efforts of both fire officials and the church people. We completed lunch in a mournful manner.

After dinner, Mr. Normand went back to the church, understandably. That left both of us in a much freer face-to-face contact situation. Mother also found a job for herself at home, so did Souhi. Thus, Francis and I, had an inescapable situation in which there was no choice but to talk to each other. So, here she was, as serious as at all times, however in a much more depressive tone, she asked me how Souhi and I were doing. I thanked her and asked her the same question. The answer was much the same, of course.

"What do you think about coming home, Francis?" I asked directly taking the bull by the horns.

"That's what I wanted to talk to you," replied Francis. "I have been thinking a lot and trying to evaluate the marriage. Whether this is you or I, or both, frankly, I did not find what I was looking for in marriage. You are a nice man, a good man, but I guess I was looking for something different. Your son is a very nice boy too, no problem, but I still feel quite a stranger to him too."

"Yes, then? Weren't you expecting that somehow? We all are experiencing a transitional episode, some estrangement, but some joy too. That was a challenge for both of us. Didn't you advance even one single inch from the beginning?"

"Frankly, no, and there does not seem to be any."

"And, then?"

"Well, one pregnancy test showed positive. However, the doctor says we have to repeat it at least once more!"

"Well, next to the prophets' miracles, that strikes me as the most interesting. How many times did we have relations during this first month? I can count with my finger-tips. Plus the fact that you did not use the pills. That was not fair to me, as a matter of fact to both of us. How were you getting excited about a baby while you were afraid of having a black baby from me? I just can't understand that."

At that point Francis got a little bit upset, probably angry due to the fact that I was a little bit offensive, or she felt that way.

"You take care of your own thoughts, I'll take care of mine. Here is my final decision: I shall wait the result of that test; if I am pregnant, I shall

Chapter 24

stay at home and proceed with the divorce since, according to our church rules, the separation is easily permissible during the first year, afterwards it becomes almost impossible. If I am not, then I may return home, to you."

This time I got mad: "It is too difficult to understand you. Let me repeat, if you are not pregnant, you'll come home. For what? To use me for breeding only? For heaven's sake. I am not Apis! That does not go along with a woman's integrity and sense of family, at least in my book!"

After this last sentence, Francis got up angrily and left the room in tears. There is an old saying in Turkish, "Kiss your grandfather's beard!". I was burning inside.

I stayed in the room alone, with mixed different feelings and quite angry with myself. No doubt, this idea of marriage for me was a compensation for the 'loss' case with Mary, though even if that was so, why should I not have tried a nuptial agreement rather than plunging abruptly into unknown oceans. Then Mrs. Normand appeared, visibly anxious if not with tears at her eyes. So far, I had neither called her by her first name nor 'Ma' or something like that since I don't think she was ten years older than I anyway.

"What happened dear Dr. Ismailov?" she moaned. "Francis is in very bad shape. What did you fight about?"

Well, there comes my grandfather's beard again. She is so unadulterated and far away from any ability at problem-solving. She was asking just for the sake of asking, helplessly.

"No, we were not fighting over any particular subject. I asked for an evaluation from her. I think this is my right, whether she may be willing to return home, to be pregnant or not, a possible separation and alike. I am upset, too, but I did not offend her for any particular reason, I am sorry. Most importantly, a young, newly married lady, of her class, why should she be willing to stay with her mother if she is pregnant but return to her husband if not pregnant. Do you have any ideas about it?"

"I really don't know. This is her idea. She may be feeling much more secure here with us."

"Why she should not feel secure with a man of my calibre, within the boundaries of a safe marriage and clean-cut life?"

"This is true, but personal feelings might be more important than the realities of life."

"I am afraid, there lies your responsibility. In spite of how wisely you might have brought her up, obviously you missed certain points in preparing her in reference to marriage and family life."

There Mrs. Normand visibly got mad, got up quickly and, from the corner of her mouth said: "I am afraid you crossed the lines a little bit more than you should. I am going to call Ray (Mr. Normand), he should come home. I can not deal with this.'" And, she left all in tears.

Another forty minutes or so, I kept suffering. I got out of the room, going into the other room where Souhi was watching 'Bugs Bunny!' I sat near him and enjoyed just being there, with him. One does not need verse from Beaudlaire or watch Puccini's *Butterfly* to be in ecstasy; we may need those fine moments too, but the most essential love, to me, is just to be there with someone who you love to share life, regardless of whatever is happening around you. Just being there, that is the secret formula of happiness. Human beings should have known better, but they did not know, and shall not know that simple truth. "Because, we are in this world just to suffer and be ready for the other world!" say most religions...

Mr. Normand came in all steamed up. He had not finished his work at the church but had to come home sooner because his wife, as we know, called him home for the situation. He came directly to the room where I was staying and, trying to keep his cool, asked what was going on. I said, at this age and stage of my life, I don't like the idea of being questioned by the parents as if I was not doing right, or, I was doing wrong. As his wife had mainly complained to him that, as I had said, "They were not able to bring up their daughter up to par for a marriage!" that had bothered him the most. I told him that I was not going into the polemics of "what I said, what I should have said" and alike, the matter was "why a young bride was changing her clothes still daily in her mother's home and for what reason she was taking time off, first one week, then another week, to decide about the outcome of the marriage. Shouldn't I too have something to say about the situation? What kind of game was going on and I couldn't stand that," I reiterated.

"Until I shall speak to my lawyers, you may stay away from this house," Mr. Normand gently warned me. I replied "Gladly!" and called my son to go home.

"No," roared Mr. Normand, "he shall stay here too."

"Nonsense," I objected, "who is having whose child under custody. Who do you think you are?"

"You can see who I am, just try!"

I am a polite and civilised man, I did my military service long ago, I don't fight with another man or woman, unless one threatens my life. I walked out of the house, even closed the door gently so as not to give them any excuses that they should hold against me, I went into my car and from the wireless phone, I called the State police headquarters.

"Lieutenant Upright? Oh, good afternoon chief. This is Prof. Dr. Ismailov,

Chapter 24

the Mental Hygiene Commissioner of the State. I hope I am not bothering you!"

"No bother at all, no bother at all. Big surprise, Sir, what can I do for you?"

"Sir, this is rather a strange personal business. A family affair. My son is being held hostage. Oh, no, no bandits, just by a reliable, respectable business and churchman. Ya,. ya. Here is the address. I shall be waiting for you with your men... No, I am outdoors and am safe. See you Tom. Thanks a lot."

In a few minutes two State police cars silently parked in front of the Normand residence. I summarised the business to the chief who very politely and patiently listened to. Then asked me: "Doctor, I am sure you are not hiding anything, excuse me, are you? Are any firearms or verbal threats involved?"

"No chief, the man is very respectable person. I don't know him, but I do not carry a gun. Never use it. We did not have any aggression nor violence or threat between us. A divorce process from his daughter may be on the way. I just want my son who is underage and is under my sole custody. He is ten and he is being kept in, against my consent."

"Strange." The chief twisted his lips and walked to the door and rang the bell.

Mr. Normand opened the door and greeted the police chief who had received the fire call that afternoon and knew what was going at the church. He politely asked my father-in-law: "Mr. Normand, this gentleman, the State's Commissioner of Mental Health, as I understand is your son-in-law, correct?"

"Correct, Sir."

"And, he has one ten-year-old son, name..."

"Souhi!"

"Yes, Souhi, and, he is inside the house."

"O.K., so far so good. Do you have custody of the child, or do you know who has the custody of the child?"

"Father, Dr. Ismailov has the custody."

"Is that child from your daughter, namely, is in any way related to you legally or not?"

"Not Sir, he is from the doctor's previous marriage. We do not have any legal rights upon him."

"I am glad you realise that, Mr. Normand. Now, is there any serious threat or any legal complaint that you would like to file against the doctor?"

"No, Sir."

"This is fine too. Now, would you have any objection to the child coming out to join his own father?"

"No, Sir." And he yelled at inside: "Souhi, your father is here. You go home, come..."

We went home. Oh, I was not aware that now was after midnight. I don't need to say how tired and exhausted I was. We shall wait and see what shall develop.

Needless to say, I am equally tired and overwhelmed by my grandfather's unbelievable life story. I still could not come close to why he is going into that much detail and how one connects all these to Sanskrit talk, threat and some plates. However, I have a feeling that we are coming close to the final chapters of this mystery. I am sure there are clues somewhere, in the latter parts of the memoirs.

In the old country, people used to say towards the end of the week "Thank God, it is Friday!" That was to say, people in the new continent worked hard enough all through the weekdays and Friday was the beginning of a long weekend. Since the actual work had been limited

Chapter 25

for some time to five days a week, eight hours a day, one hour lunch and two fifteen-minute coffee breaks, people did believe that they were working hard. Instead of monthly payments as they were accustomed to, pay cheques were paid on Friday nights, so almost everyone after 5 p.m. rushed to 'Happy Hours' which meant 'one and a half dollar cocktails between five and seven', cheap enough to make any youngster come there with his girlfriend, be happy, imbibe himself with some ethyl-alcohol whatever its commercial name would be, and then go home on time, clean. Friday nights felt the most lonesome night of the week, regardless of whether one was married or not. If anyone did not give a clean account about his or her whereabouts on Friday nights, one indeed had to be suspicious about that. Saturdays you went to sporting events, concerts, steak restaurants and alike common places; Sundays were 'family' days, again church, concerts, baseball or football events. You were in the eye-sight of everybody. But Friday nights? Special luncheons, long weekend trips or escapades, country music and dancing in one of the neighbouring State's barns with your secret lover. So, watch yourself then.

Here, in this land, everyone works however long they wish to. Mondays are still the time to get on your horse, so to speak, and get rejuvenated and organised for a very busy, rewarding week; unfinished ones, new ones, you name it. Think free, feel free and act free. Freedom of thinking, especially, is very refreshing. As if one has no limits, like skies. So let me say, 'Thank God, it is a Monday'.

Now, you also know my unfinished business, especially in this Mormon thing. So, let us plan together: I have to read more from *The Book of Mormon* and grandfather's diary; then, some night get together with the prospective founders of the Freemasonry Lodge; and here

A.C. 2084

and there, get some news about the Summer Literary Festival. See, like a botanic garden, pick up any flower you want to. Of course you need to have a certain type of discipline to shape yourself this way, to be ready almost all the time for all occurrences, old and new, yet be flexible enough to shift the programmes and yourself and keep smiling at everybody. Oscar Wilde can afford to say, "I like men of principle but like more the men who aren't!" But I just cannot say "I ain't!" I do what I am supposed to do and wish everyone should have a share in it. Amen.

Therefore, after dawdling around just a little bit, that is to say looking over the newspaper with a quick glance, then answering a few business calls, I plunged again into *The Book of Mormon*. To understand my grandfather's diary and interpret his mode of behaviour, thoughts and alike, I guess I need to know more about Mormonism and then evaluate how it may have effected his behaviour, escapes and alike, if there is a truth in it.

The Book of Mormon – Continuation from the *Second Book from Nephi*:
'Chapter 24': "Israel shall be gathered and shall envoy millennial rest. Lucifer cast out of heaven for rebellion. Israel shall triumph over Babylon."
'Chapter 25': "Nephi glories in plainness. Isaiah's prophecies shall be understood in the last days. The Jews shall return from Babylon, crucify the Messiah, and be scattered and scourged."
'Chapter 26': "Christ shall minister to the Nephites. Nephi foresees the destruction of his people. They shall speak from the dust. The gentiles shall build up false churches and secret combinations The Lord forbids men to practice priestcraft."
'Chapter 27': "Darkness and apostasy shall cover the earth in the last days. *The Book of Mormon* shall come forth. Three witnesses shall testify of the book. The learned man cannot read sealed book. The Lord shall do a marvellous work and a wonder."
'Chapter 29': "Many gentiles shall reject *The Book of Mormon*. They shall say: We need no more *Bible*. The Lord speaks to many nations. He will judge the world out of the books thus written."
'Chapter 31': "Nephi tells why Christ was baptised. Men must follow Christ, be baptised, receive the Holy Ghost, and endure to the end to be saved. Repentance and baptism are the gate to the strait and narrow path. Eternal life comes to those who keep the commandments after baptism."

Chapter 25

The Book of Jacob – The Brother of Nephi:
 'Chapter 1': "Jacob and Joseph seek to persuade men to believe in Christ and keep his commandments. Nephi dies. Wickedness prevails among the Nephites."
 "Chapter 2': "Jacob denounces the love of riches, pride and unchastity. Men should seek riches to help their fellow men. Jacob condemns the unauthorised practice of plural marriage. The Lord delights in the chastity of women."
 'Chapter 3': "The pure in heart receive the pleasing word of God. Lamanite righteousness exceeds that of Nephites. Jacob warns against fornication, lasciviousness, and every sin."
 'Chapter 6': "The Lord shall recover Israel in the last days. Then the world shall be burned with fire. Men must follow Christ to avoid the lake of fire and brimstone."

The Book of Enos: "Enos prays mightily and gains a remission of his sins. The voice of the Lord comes into his mind promising salvation for the Lamanites in a future day. Nephites sought to reclaim the Lamanites in their day. Enos rejoices in his Redeemer."

The Book of Omni: "Omni, Amaron, Chemish, Abinadom and Amaleki, each in turn, keep the records. Mosiah discovers the people of Zarahemla who came from Jerusalem in the days of Zedekiah. He is made king over them. The Mulekites had discovered Coriantumr, the last of Jaredites. King Benjamin succeeds Mosiah. Men should offer their souls as an offering to Christ."

The Book of Mosiah: "King Benjamin teaches his sons the language and prophecies of their fathers. Their religion and civilisation have been preserved because of the records kept on the various plates. Mosiah is chosen as king and is given custody of the records and other things."
 'Chapter 5': "The saints become his sons and daughters of Christ through faith. They are then called by the name of Christ. King Benjamin exhorts them to be steadfast and immovable in good works."
 'Chapter 7': "Ammon finds the land of Lehi-Nephi where Limhi is king. Limhi's people are in bondage to the Lamanites. Limhi recounts their history. A prophet (Abinadi) had testified that Christ is the God and Father of all things. Those who saw filthiness reap the whirlwind,

217

A.C. 2084

and those who put their trust in the Lord shall be delivered."

'Chapter 8': "Ammon teaches the people of Limhi. He learns of the twenty-four Jaredite plates. Ancient records can be translated by seers. The gift of seership exceeds all others."

"Chapter 10': "King Laman dies. His people are wild and ferocious and believe in false traditions. Zeniff and his people prevail against them."

'Chapter 11': "King Noah rules in wickedness. He revels in riotous living with his wives and concubines. Abinadi prophesies that the people will be taken into bondage. His life is sought by King Noah."

'Chapter 12': "Abinadi is imprisoned for prophesising the destruction of the people and the death of King Noah The false priests quote the scriptures and pretend to keep the law of Moses. Abinadi begins to teach them the Ten Commandments."

'Chapter 20': "Lamanite daughters are abducted by the priests of Noah. The Lamanites wage war upon Limhi and his people. They are repulsed and pacified."

'Chapter 29': "Mosiah proposes that the judges be chosen in place of a king. Unrighteous kings lead their people into sin. Alma the younger is chosen chief judge by the voice of the people. He is also the high priest over the Church. Alma the elder and Mosiah die."

The Book of Alma: "The account of Alma, who was the son of Alma, the first and chief judge over the people of Nephi."

'Chapter 4': "Alma babtises thousands of converts. Iniquity enters the church and the church's progress is hindered. Nephihah is appointed chief judge. Alma, as high priest, devotes himself to the ministry."

'Chapter 9': "Alma commands the people of Ammonihah to repent. The Lord will be merciful to the Lamanites in the last days. If the Nephites forsake the light, they shall be destroyed by the Lamanites. The Son of God soon cometh. He shall redeem those who repent and are baptised and take faith in his name."

'Chapter 16': "The Lamanites destroy the people of Ammonihah. Zoram leads the Nephites to victory over the Lamanites. Alma and Amulek and many others preach the word. They teach that after his resurrection Christ will appear to the Nephites."

'Chapter 17': "The sons of Mosiah have the spirit of prophecy and of revelation. They go their several ways to declare the word to the Lamanites. Ammon goes to the land of Ishmael and becomes the servant of King Lamoni. Ammon saves the king's flocks and slays his enemies at the waters of Sebus."

'Chapter 28': "The Lamanites are defeated in a tremendous battle. Tens of thousands are slain. The wicked are consigned in a State of endless woe; the righteous attain a never-ending happiness."

'Chapter 37': "The plates of brass and other scriptures are preserved to bring souls to salvation. The Jeredites were destroyed because of their wickedness. Their secret oaths and covenants must be kept from the people."

'Chapter 43': "Alma and his sons preach the word. The Zoramites and other Nephite dissenters become Lamanites. The Lamanites now against the Nephites in war. Moroni arms the Nephites with defensive armour. The Lord reveals to Alma the strategy of Lamanites. The Nephites defend their homes, liberties, families, and religion. The armies of Moroni and Lehi surround the Lamanites."

'Chapter 46': "Amalickiah conspires to be king. Moroni raises the title of liberty. He rallies the people to defend their religion. True believers are called Christians."

'Chapter 54': "Ammoron and Moroni negotiate for the exchange of prisoners. Moroni demands that the Lamanites withdraw and cease their murderous attacks. Ammoron demands that the Nephites lay down their arms and become subject to the Lamanites."

'Chapter 55': "Moroni refuses to exchange prisoners. The Lamanite guards are enticed to become drunk and the Nephite prisoners are freed. The city of Gid is taken without bloodshed."

'Chapter 56': "Helaman sends an epistle to Moroni recounting the State of war with the Lamanites. Antipus and Helaman gain a great victory over the Lamanites. Helaman's two thousand stripling sons fight with miraculous power and none of them are slain."

'Chapter 58': "Helaman, Gid and Teomner take the city of Manti by a stratagem. The Lamanites withdraw. The sons of the people of Ammon are preserved as they stand fast in defence of their liberty and faith."

'Chapter 59': "Moroni asks Pahoran to strenghten the forces of Helaman. The Lamanites take the city of Nephihah – Moroni is angry with the government."

'Chapter 60': "Moroni complains to Pahoran of the government's neglect of the armies. The Lord suffers the righteous to be slain. The Nephites use all of their power and means to deliver themselves from their enemies. Moroni threatens to fight against the government unless help is supplied to his armies."

A.C. 2084

'Chapter 63': "Shiblon and later Helaman take possession of the sacred records. Many Nephites travel to the land northward. Hagoth builds ships, which sail forth in the west sea. Moronihah defeats the Lamanites in battle."

The Book of Helaman: An account of the Nephites. Their wars and contentions, and their dissensions. And also the prophecies of many holy prophets, before the coming of Christ, according to the records of Helaman, who was the son of Helaman, and also according to the records of his sons, even down to the coming of Christ."

The Book of Third Nephi: "And Helaman was the son of Helaman, who was the son of Alma, who was the son of Alma, being a descendant of Nephi who was the son of Lehi, who came out of Jerusalem in the first year of the reign of Sedekiah, the king of Jadah."
'Chapter 2': "Wickedness and abominations increase among the people. The Nephites and Lamanites unite to defend themselves against the Gadianton robbers. Converted Lamanites become white and are called Nephites."
'Chapter 7': "The chief judge is murdered, the government is overthrown, and the people divide into tribes. Jacob, an antichrist, becomes king of a league of tribes. Nephi preaches repentance and faith in Christ. Angels minister to him daily and he raises his brother from the dead. Many repent and are baptised."
'Chapter 8': "Tempests, earthquakes, fires, whirlwinds, and physical upheavals attest the crucification of Christ. Many people are destroyed. Darkness covers the land for three days. Those who remain bemoan their fate."
'Chapter 9': "In the darkness the voice of Christ proclaims the destruction of many people and cites for their wickedness. He also proclaims his divinity, announces that the law of Moses is fulfilled, and invites men to come into him and be saved."
'Chapter 12': "Jesus calls and commissions the Twelve. He delivers to the Nephites a discourse similar to the Sermon on the Mount. His teachings transcend and take precedence over the law of Moses. Men are commended to be perfect even as he and his Father are perfect."
'Chapter 20': "Jesus provides bread and wine miraculously and again administers unto them. The remnant of Jacob shall come to the knowledge of the Lord their God and shall inherit the Americas. Jesus is the prophet like unto Moses, and the Nephites are children of the

prophets."

'Chapter 24': "The Lord's messenger shall prepare the way for the Second Coming. Christ shall sit in judgment."

'Chapter 29': "The coming forth of *The Book of Mormon* is a sign that the Lord has commenced to gather Israel and fulfil his covenants. Those who reject his latter-day revelations and gifts shall be cursed."

The Book of Mormon: "Ammaron instructs Mormon concerning the sacred records. War commences between the Nephites and the Lamanites."

'Chapter 6': "The Nephites gather to the land of Cumorah for the final battles. Mormon hides the sacred records in the hill Cumorah. The Lamanites are victorious and the Nephite nation is destroyed."

'Chapter 7': "Mormon invites the Lamanites of the latter days to believe in Christ, accept his gospel, and be saved. All who believe the *Bible* will also believe *The Book of Mormon*."

The Book of Ether: "The record of the Jeradites, taken from the twenty-four plates found by the people of Limhi in the days of king Mosiah."

The Book of Moroni:

'Chapter 1': "Moroni writes for the benefit of the Lamanites. The Nephites who will not deny Christ are put to death."

'Chapter 2': "Jesus gave the Nephite apostles power to confer the gift of the Holy Ghost."

'Chapter 4': "How the elders and priests administer the sacramental bread."

'Chapter 6': "Repentant persons are baptised and fellowshipped. Church members who repent are forgiven. Meetings are conducted by the power of the Holy Ghost."

'Chapter 8': "Infant baptism is an evil abomination. Little children are alive in Christ because of the atonement."

'Chapter 9': "The second epistle of Mormon to his son Moroni."

'Chapter 10': "A testimony of *The Book of Mormon* comes by the power of the Holy Ghost. The gifts of the Spirit are dispensed to the faithful. Spiritual gifts always accompany faith. Moroni's words speak from the dust. Come unto Christ, be perfected in him and sanctify your souls."

* * *

Well, quite heavy stuff but fulfilling and lightening for your heart. A brave history of a brave people but frankly very little enlightenment upon the specifics of the Moroni Plates and again once more, my grandfather's involvement with them. I guess we have to follow the diary, as I started. Since it was sometimes after sundown, I called Keith and requested from him that we, cabinet members, plus Brian Ahern, should meet tomorrow late afternoon, say at 4 or 5 p.m., to discuss the forthcoming festival's details in the Rectangular Room. It was quite a tiring day and it was time again to listen to Vivaldi's violin concertos.

The Cabinet Members gathered at 5 p.m. in my office. Needless to repeat, we people know each other well and love and respect each other honestly. Consequently, we greeted each other in a very friendly

Chapter 26

manner, full of affection. I also offered them some orange juice and grapefruit, along with crackers and cheese, as we sat around the rectangular table and, without losing any time, began to talk about our programme.

I started first, as usual. "Dear friends, as you know well, this festival is our pride and a kind of national heritage. Of course I have some thoughts, some plans on my mind, but I would rather leave it up to Edith and Brian first to reveal the general planning and rough headlines of the programme. So, either of you, may you start, please? Oh, incidentally, Timothy, Atilla and Jack, since we have not met for some time, and especially you Atilla, who were willing to talk and bring out new energy projects in details – would all you all and the heads of technical departments be kind enough to get together tomorrow evening, here, say at 7.30 p.m.? OK? Thank you! Nice guys! I am sorry; Edith? Brian?"

Edith took off: "That's OK, Sir. Well, as we do this festival as a two-day event at the weekend, I thought, on Saturday. As our President had suggested, the choice of place, we should start to gather randomly at the Mega Forest Picnic Field by noon time. I am sure some music and refreshments shall be provided. Brian has been talking to some people from Mr. Gleem's and Mr. Weakball's departments to ensure some personnel provide food and drinks; communication systems, electrical set-ups and Big Screen; double the electrical train services for the public; the stands, poetry books and some novels, magazines, etc. I assume that around 2 p.m., I shall make a brief opening speech and then invite you for a live, personal appearance."

"Edith, I am sure you will not forget also to provide the duplicating machines that instantly could multiply the poems and short stories that are going to be read there; because, you know, the jury that you compose shall declare the finalists but the winners will be chosen by the public, so the literary pieces as well as the voting machines should be immediately available to them."

"Yes sir, it is on my mind. Until last year, we first listened to all the entries publicly, then the jury elected the finalists and they read the pieces again. That procedure was taking too much time – particularly short stories' being read again was somewhat boring and causing people to lose some interest. So, this year, at Brian's suggestion, we have changed the procedure just a little bit. Starting tomorrow morning, we are going to advertise on Big Screen that anyone who would like to participate in the 'Annual Poetry' and 'Short Story' competitions should e-mail or wire their works to us one way or other by Friday night. Then, that night and early Saturday morning, the jury members should have all the materials in their hands and on the field, only the finalists' works should be presented. Any objection, Sir?"

"No, it sounds good to me; does anyone want to add something to it? (I looked around, all affirming!) Fine, proceed, please."

"As you also suggested, while the finalists read their creative works, between, some celebrities, with their live appearances and natural voices, should read some poems, maybe some short stories too, to enrich the presentations. I assume, you have some specific things to tell us."

"Yes, Edith. Thank you so far. Naturally almost all the participants shall be from the young generation and, I am sure, they shall present very charming, interesting works. But we should not forget our mature and old generations who still carry the taste of old, good days, the classical literature and well established versus from big poets and writers from the past. That's why I have suggested 'some oldies should present some goodies, like me!' (Some sincere smiles around the table.) Our narcissisms, too, ought to be satisfied. So, here are some poems that I have chosen. I would like to read two of them myself and distribute the others to, say, the leaders of the church, the senior writers for our newspaper, even you, at the university at the Old-Classic Literature Department. Incidentally, short stories may annoy some of the public, so these decorative readings should be rather short and confined only to poems. Here are two poems that I have chosen for myself, see how you find them.

"The first one is from our compatriot Thomas Moore, our predecessor and previous proprietor of this beautiful land. It shall be a salute to him.

BELIEVE ME IF ALL THOSE ENDEARING YOUNG CHARMS

Believe me, if all those endearing young charms,
Which I gaze on so fondly today,
Were to change by tomorrow, and fleet in my arms,
Like fairy-gifts fading away,
Thou wouldst still be adored, at this moment thou art,
Let thy loveliness fade as if will,
And around the dear ruin each wish of my heart
Would entwine itself verdantly still.

It is not while beauty and youth are thine own,
And thy cheeks unprofaned by a tear,
That the fervour and faith of a soul may be known,
To which time but will make thee more dear!
No, the heart that has truly loved never forgets,
But as truly love on to the close,
As the sunflower turns to her god when he sets
The same look which she turned away when he rose!

Thomas Moore

"Beautiful." "Great!" "I am hearing for the first time" "Superb!" and alike sounds.

"Well, this second one is written by some 'unknown' person for whom I have utmost respect. When we display ourselves either through speech, writings, paintings, as actors on the stage and alike, whether we consciously think or not, we derive a kind of pleasure, recognition and sense of belonging, I would say. As art critics say 'artists create to become immortal'. We analysts believe in that too. But these 'unknowns', like the soldiers who sacrificed themselves for their countries and sleep in their eternal tombs as 'unknown', are of different class. They emanate love and respect and some mystery and mystic flavour about their original personalities. To me, as the great Shakespeare said, 'they are made of stuff that dreams are!' Here is the poem:

WILL YOU LOVE ME WHEN I'M OLD?

I would ask of you, my darling,
A question soft and low,

A.C. 2084

    That gives me many a heartache
    As the moments come and go.

    Your love I know is truthful,
    But the truest love grows cold;
    It is this that I would ask you:
    Will you love me when I'm old?

    Life's morn will soon be waning,
    And its evening bells be tolled,
    But my heart shall know no sadness,
    If you'll love me when I'm old.

    Down the stream of life together
    We are sailing side by side,
    Hoping some bright day to anchor
    Safe beyond the surging tide.

    Today our sky is cloudless,
    But the night may clouds unfold;
    But, though storms may gather round us,
    Will you love me when I'm old?

    When my hair shall shade the snowdrift,
    And mine eyes shall dimmer grow,
    I would lean upon some loved one,
    Through the valley as I go.
    I would claim of you a promise,
    Worth to me world of gold;
    It is only this, my darling,
    That you'll love me when I'm old.

Unknown

A series of voices and utterings of appreciation from my friends.

"The third one is Lord Byron's *She Walks In Beauty*, an old-time classic; and I assume, Edith, you, yourself fit better than anyone else to read this in the festival. Here it is:

Chapter 26

SHE WALKS IN BEAUTY

She walks in beauty like the night
Of cloudless climes and starry skies;
And all that's best of dark and bright
Meets in her aspect and her eyes:
Thus mellow'd to that tender light
Which heaven to gaudy day denies.

One shade the more, one ray the less,
Had half impair'd the nameless grace
Which waves in every raven tress,
Or softly lightens o'er her face -
Where thoughts serenely sweet express
How pure, how dear their dwelling-place.

And on that cheek, and o'er that brow,
So soft, so calm, yet eloquent,
The smiles that win, the tints that glow,
But tell of days in goodness spent,
A mind at peace with all below,
A heart whose love is innocent.

Lord Byron

"Oh, Sir, I remember it well from my college years, how did you know it was my best choice? It is so inspiring!" cried Edith.
"I don't know but I just feel. What do you think you gentlemen?"
"Sir, we don't need to express our appreciation. Just marvellous. Beautiful."
"Thank you. Those were my 'must' choices. I have chosen more, for instance, this *Home, Sweet Home!* is also one of the classics. It belongs to John Howard Paine. Even though it shall create a little bit of hardship for the newcomers, I think it shall be quite timely. You decide Edith, who is going to read it. Please now, you read it! And Edith, here in the meeting, started to read:

HOME, SWEET HOME

'mid pleasures and palaces though we may roam,
Be it ever so humble, there's no place like home;

A.C. 2084

> A charm from the sky seems to hallow us there,
> Which seek through the world, is ne'er met with elsewhere.
> Home, home, sweet, sweet home!
> There's no place like home, oh, there's no place like home!
>
> An exile from home, splendour dazzles in vain;
> Oh, give me my lovely thatched cottage again!
> The birds singing gaily, that came at my call -
> Give me them -and the peace of mind, dearer than all!
> Home, home, sweet, sweet home!
> There's no place like home, oh, there's no place like home!
>
> I gaze on the moon as I tread the drear wild,
> And feel that my mother now thinks of her child,
> As she looks on that moon from our own cottage door
> Thro' the woodbine, those fragrance shall cheer me no more.
> Home, home, sweet, sweet home!
> There's no place like home, oh, there's no place like home!
>
> How sweet 'tis 'neath a fond father's smile,
> And the caress of a mother to soothe and beguile!
> Let others delight 'mid new pleasure to roam,
> But give me, oh, give me, the pleasures of home,
> Home, home, sweet, sweet home!
> There's no place like home, oh, there's no place like home!
>
> To thee I'll return, over burdened with care;
> The heart's dearest solace will smile on me there;
> No more from that cottage again will I roam;
> Be it ever be humble, there's no place like home.
> Home, home, sweet, sweet home!
> There's no place like home, oh, there's no place like home!

John Howard Paine

"Bravo, bravo Edith. You read quite from the very bottom of your heart."

"Now, ladies and gentlemen, you know, I am a rather 'believer and faithful man' other than being strictly a religious person. From God to humans, from humans to God; here, we offer anything we can. In my notes I found this poem that is obviously religious as far as the category is concerned but gives us the summary of the development and establishment of monotheism among we, mortal human beings. Again, it is written by one of the 'unknown'. I shall it read to you. First you decide whether it should be read and if yes, by whom it should be read? Rabbi David or Braun? Or Pere Pierre? Now, here we go:

OLD TESTAMENT CONTENTS

In Genesis, the world was made;
In Exodus, the march is told;
Leviticus contains the Law;
In Numbers are the tribes enrolled.

In Deuteronomy again,
We're urged to keep God's law alone;
And these five Books of Moses make
The oldest holy writing known.

Brave Joshua to Canaan leads;
In Judges, off the Jews rebel;
We read of David's name in Ruth
And First and Second Samuel.

In First and Second Kings we read
How the Hebrew State became;
In First and Second Chronicles
Another history of the same.

In Ezra, captive Jews return,
And Nehemiah builds the wall;
Queen Esther saves her race from death,
These books "Historical" we call.

In Job we read the patient faith;
In Psalms are David's songs of praise;
The Proverbs are to make us wise;
Ecclesiastes next portrays.
How fleeting earthly pleasures are;
The Song of Solomon is all
About true love, like Christ's; and these
Five books "Devotional" we call.

A.C. 2084

Isaiah tells of Christ to come,
While Jeremiah tells of woe,
And his Lamentations mourns
The Holy City's overthrow.

Ezekiel speaks of mysteries
And Daniel foretells kings of old;
Hosea over Israel grieves;
In Joel blessings are foretold.

In Amos, too, are Israel's woes;
And Obadiah's sent to warn;
While Jonah shows that Christ should die
And Micah where he should be born.

In Nahum Nineveh is seen;
Habakkuk tells of Chaldea's guilt;
In Zephaniah are Jadah's sins;
In Haggai the Temple's built.

Then Zecchariah speaks of Christ,
And Malachi of John, his sign;
The Prophets number seventeen,
And all the books are thirty-nine.

Matthew, Mark, Luke and John
Tell what Christ did in every place;
The Acts tell what the Apostles did,
And Romans how we're saved by grace.

Corinthians instruct the Church;
Galatians shows us faith alone;
Ephesians, true love, and in
Philippians God's grace is shown.

Colossians tell us more of Christ,
And Thessalonians of the end;
In Thimothy and Titus both
Are rules for pastors to attend.

Philemon, Christian friendship shows.
, Then Hebrews clearly tell how all
The Jewish law prefigured Christ;
And these Epistles by Paul.

James shows that faith by works must live,
And Peter urges steadfastness;
While John exhorts to Christian love,
For those who have it God will bless.

Jude shows the end of evil men,
And Revelation tells of Heaven.
This ends the whole New Testament
And all the books are twenty-seven.

Unknown

"Very good, Sir. It is good, very good," said Edith, "We can decide about it later on."

"OK, I am sorry that I am domineering too much. I have another poem under my hand, I will not read it but I will give it to you, *Life's A Game*, again written by an 'unknown'. About it too, you decide.

LIFE'S A GAME

The life is but a game of cards,
Which everyone must learn;
Each shuffles, cuts, and deals the deck,
And then a trump does turn;
Some show up a high card,
While others make it low,
And many turn no cards at all -
In fact, they cannot show.

When hearts are up we play for love,
And pleasure rules the hour;
Each day goes pleasantly alone,
In sunshine's rosy bower.

A.C. 2084

> When diamonds chance to crown the pack,
> That's when they stake their gold,
> And thousands then are lost and won,
>
> By gamblers, young and old.
> When clubs are trump look out for war,
> On ocean and on land,
> For bloody deeds are often done
> When clubs are held in hand.
> At last turns up the darkened spade,
> Held by the toiling slave,
> And a spade will turn up trump at last,
> And dig each player's grave.

Unknown

"My other suggestions," I added, "are that Saturday, the 'Poetry' and 'Short Story' finals should be all read, and people should have fun; also having time to go to the Animal World, if they choose to. On Sunday, only the final winners and runner-ups should be presented, of course with honour plaquettes. Are they ready?"

"Yes, they are; after the winners are known, their names shall be written and signed by you, Mr. President", replied Brian.

"Good. The other thing we were going to talk was that, since on Sunday we shall have plenty of time between, some amateur groups should play some sketches, plays, demonstrate some sort of modern dance or jazz that I guess are going to be next year's main themes."

"Yes, sir. One of the Brian's students is in charge of it. I am sure a few pleasantries shall be displayed."

"OK, I am mighty happy. More juice or crackers? Debra, you did not eat anything? You three musketeers, kept only to yourself tonight?"

They just smiled, we all know that I did not give any chance to them since the things that we talked about were out of their lines.

"You Lady Debra and other gentlemen, after this Summer Festival business is over, within a few weeks time, we should get together and prepare the basic programme for the Fall Science Festival?"

"OK, Sir, say you don't take any vacation, or something like that?"

"You know, life is a vacation itself, how can I waste my time somewhere else, or for something else? Goodnight ladies and gentlemen, be good!"

Chapter 26

"Goodnight Sir!"
In the morning, the first call I received and talked about on Big Screen was from Mrs.Abel Storm, the head of the retirement-elderly Homes. A very active, direct and stormy lady, she outlined her problem immediately: "We are short of personnel in the kitchen and dormitory

Chapter 27

since within the past months or so, 118 people, ages between 97 and 118, entered the retirement homes while 18 people retired and 9 persons died among the staff," she cited.

"Mrs. Storm, your message is well-taken. I am calling Keith's office right now. I am sure he might have just finished the job force plans concerning newcomers. You'll hear from him pretty soon. Thank you for the good job that you have been delivering."

"Thank you, Mr. President!" And, she ended the conversation very quietly and contentedly. I could see her face was gleaming on the Big Screen.

Then, I naturally contacted Mr. Gleem.

"Keith, good morning!"

"Good morning, Sir. As usual, you are one step ahead of me. All clearances came up, negative. You know I mean the men for the Freemasonry Lodge."

"Good, please called them up, I guess only Mr. Smith will be sufficient enough. If they are ready, we can gather this Thursday evening, namely tomorrow evening at 8.00 p.m. for an opening. Also get in touch with Atilla's department, please give them every kind of chance to advertise this event, say every other hour or so from Big Screen. I want a large crowd there. You have done a good job in the shortest time as far as the building is concerned."

"Thank you Sir. Is there anything else that I would do for you?"

"Yes, Keith, our 'green beret lady chevalier' Mrs. Abel Storm called, and you know, in her nice but stormy way asked for help in the elderly and retirement homes. Please be in touch with her and give priority among the newcomers' job placements."

Chapter 28

"Aye, aye, Sir, right away. See you, thank you."

"Thank you Keith, see you."

That was an accomplishment I guess. If you have a sense of fairness, also having a structured brain to organise the things around and you are holding power, giving service is just child's play. Especially with our technology, you don't have any excuse either, as all these conversations are automatically recorded; then sorted out by the secretaries and, at the beginning of the next week, with just a touch of the button, the summaries of the previous week's planning, jobs either done or undone – if undone, with the reasons why – shall all be laid before your eyes. How could one be unsuccessful?

Now, unless some emergency comes up, no one can take me away from my grandfather's diary. I have free-time until the 7.30 p.m. cabinet meeting. So where are we on the diary business? We have all the basic knowledge, the beginnings and mid-way through, but for the finishing touch, I am afraid we have to know there may be a few more secrets.

January 28, 1969
Monday night, Code Island

As I sat at my table at the administration building of the State offices in order to prepare an administrative meeting in a short while, the telephone rang:

"Allo?"

"A Mr. Normand would like to speak to you," said my secretary Muriel, "says it is urgent!"

"OK, please connect!"

"Yes, Mr. Normand?"

"I am sorry to bother you, but it is rather important, as a matter of fact, very important."

"Anything to do with Francis?"

"No, no, Dr. Ismailow. It is with the church!"

"Oh. It is indeed good recovery wishes of mine to everyone. Has there been big damage? Any human suffering?"

"No, no, Thank God. We are still searching why this happened. This is another matter that we should not talk about on the telephone anyway. The matter is... You know, you helped us during the fire and carried many things into my house, yesterday afternoon."

"Yes, Sir, we did."

"But.. but.. there appears to be, among the valuables that we carried, something missing..."

"Sir, you and I, as you know well, in a true rush, piled certain things into the car and brought them to your home and emptied it. Only you know what they are, I wouldn't know even if my son's picture was there."

"That's true. That's true. No, I am not blaming or anything like that. I already cannot tell what it might be, but, as we checked with the other church leaders as they had also gathered some valuables, a well-wrapped, rather heavier flat block seems to be missing."

"I am sorry for that, Sir, what can I do for you? Your church is also my church and I would like to do whatever I can."

"Thank you, I am sure of it. Well, I would like to come right away and, if you permit, search your car together, just in case if anything might have been out of your sight. Did you take anything out of your car last night after you went home?"

"No, not at all!"

"Can I come right now?"

"I suggest you come noon time, I am entering a conference now, ithat I cannot miss. 12 noon, OK?"

"OK. See you then." So unwilling he was, the same applied to me too.

Well, I wouldn't touch anybody's treasures. What could they be? Some church registrations, gifts, silvery historical material, frankly I don't care. However my curiosity little by little began to turn to a growing anger. He held my child hostage due to a family argument. That was an unlawful act and he knew better. Then, as if nothing had happened, he calls me for the valuables, whatever they might be – I do not care – and plus, he wants to come and search the car together. It sounds as if he does not trust me. Does he, doesn't he? I really don't know and something in my stomach says 'No', 'N. O.'. Is there something there or not that I could keep 'hostage' until the family matters are cleared up. Is Francis pregnant? I hope she is not but if she is, then I shall be at their mercy; again the divorce procedures, courts, lawyers, alimony and child support, Sunday father job, guilt, ifs and buts... and, what shall be my defence? No, I should have something in my hand to negotiate with, at least.

Anyway, with these mixed feelings I jumped up, told Muriel that I was going downtown to my son's school for a few minutes and might be a little bit late for the meeting. I rushed to the parking lot of the hospital and opened my MD 177 Mercedes-Benz' luggage department. I am a neat man, but for my little boy I always keep in there a badminton set, a basketball, two or three frisbees, a shopping cart, a small handbag for us containing some clothing just in case for over-night or weekend travelling needs and alike, a car emergency kit, emergency health kit, you name it. When I sorted out these things from the deeper part of the storage place, I suddenly touched a metallic sounding package, wrapped up with heavy, brown covers, with a kind of decorated colourful strings. Yes I found it, now again, what I am going to do with it? Trials and tribulations.

I also thought just a little bit at the wheel. No, that was my final decision, no. I was not going to give it to them, regardless of how valuable or invaluable it might have been. Somebody or something should be at my side. In spite of my goodwill, why was I the one who was almost always losing? I could not take it to my house where, with or without a court order, it could be easily found. I did not have an office yet since I was just licensed by the State, had bought a house and was trying to establish my residence first. I wouldn't keep it at my State job either. Come on psychiatrist, you are the one who is resolving everybody's problems, why can't you help yourself?

It did not take too long, I guess, to make a wise decision: I dashed downtown to the 2nd National Bank of Code Island and rented a large safe box in which I placed the steel case. I also visited my son's school and asked him whether he needed his gym shoes. Souhi was a little bit surprised by this unprecedented visit but simply said 'no' and I returned to my job, with a little bit of heartbeat, however with a smooth mind. Muriel said Mr. Normand had called again. She said I had gone temporarily. What did he want? Was he checking on me? Was a power game going to start? Wait and see.

The conference with the staff finished uneventfully, as usual. At exactly twelve, Mr. Normand came to meet me.

"Sir, the secretary said you called, was there anything the matter?"

"Well, the President of the church has asked for a meeting tonight. I was going to ask whether you may come to it for that shall be a very important meeting. Then, of course, I did not need to come this noon. But your secretary said you have an engagement tonight for a community mental health meeting, so here I am."

I felt a kind of guilt inside, and, silently okayed his sayings. Maybe he was better willed than I had first thought. Anyway, as we two of us went to the parking lot, I slowly opened the luggage door and carefully moved the stuff that I had mentioned earlier; then I opened the front doors and checked the floor, corners, everywhere. There was nothing. Mr. Normand's eyebrows were obviously frowning.

"Sir, of course I respect the secrecy of the Church, but the material you are searching for, is it irreplaceable, too invaluable?"

A.C. 2084

"A sort of...", Mr. Normand replied in a thoughtful gaze, "I am sorry again I am asking, you are sure you did not take anything out of here at home."

"No Sir, if you wish, we can run home together now and have a quick glance around. I promise I shall look around tonight, after the meeting. But you know, I have a very simple and very organised life, we are just two people. My little one and I, that's all. There are no other persons who could misplace the things, and this thing had happened just yesterday. As you know, I do not keep any permanent help at home either. We have two keys, one with my son and one with me. My life is so simple."

"Fine, I know, I know. Say, I am sorry for the little fellow incident yesterday afternoon. I was so upset. You know I love my daughter and that worries me too much."

"Sir, of course we cannot talk this matter here, on our feet, but I can assure you that you have a very noble daughter, there is nothing seriously wrong between us, but I am afraid she was not ready I guess to quit a very secure family home atmosphere, emotionally I mean. It's that simple. Let her think for a while."

"You might be right. I do not know, let us wait and since we both love and respect her, let us wait for her to decide."

A little bit unwillingly, I responded: "Yes. We don't have anything else in our hands."

And, after shaking my hands in a little bit strong, squeezy way, Mr. Normand left. I took a deep breath, but frankly, I was doing something that I had never done in my lifetime. I don't want that 'curiosity should kill the cat' but I guess it was my right to defend myself. Defend against what? Well, I don't know, I do not want to be a Don Quixote and declare war against the giants, churches, angels, etc. Angels, hey, wait a minute, no, it can't be, it just can't be. You may understand what dropped into my mind: Angel Moroni's Plates. No, it just can't be. No, it could be, no, no, it just can't be. I am not responsible if I do not know anything about it. I'd better meditate!

February 3, 1969
Code Island

Summers are very hot in Code Island and the winters are very cold, covering everything with ice in spite of the fact that the small province in essence is not a real island but a peninsular – the ocean licks it and passes by. There is only one small Gansett river that crosses the entire territory. She is not highly populated either; it is a kind of city State-administered territory with a lot of natural beauty, long, almost isolated beaches and famous people's completely isolated huge summer places, large wooden

Chapter 27

houses and horse farms. In winter, indeed, you feel almost imprisoned in the small boundaries of the territory. There is one good State Philharmonic Orchestra where my son and I are subscribed for every Saturday evening. Sunday mornings, going to church is a 'must' in this primarily Catholic State. In the afternoons, bowling, movies and random shopping is the usual life. In the summer, international tennis tournaments are held here that add a kind of colour to the present quiet, motionless life here. Since there is also a navy base there, lonely sailors march in twos and threes, looking for young, untouched college students.

So, on such a sunny but icy cold winter day, one week after that fire incidence, I went to church alone. My son preferred – so did I – to stay home and play 'Atari' until I returned. Needless to say, the curiosity, anxiety and emotions were easily readable in the air. I hope I am not developing a paranoia; it appeared to me that the people looked a little bit cold towards me, their eyes were kind of questioning. Were they? Nothing publicly was announced other than "Good recovery to all of us... God was with us... Almost all valuables were taken care of... We repaired the damage and took the necessary precautions. The electrical system is all renewed!" Those were quite calming statements but I am sure almost everyone felt that such a multi-facet fire might simply not have started from any electric outlet alone. Anyway, I am sure they shall keep investigating and if and when they shall resolve the problem, one day we shall hear about it. Mr. Normand, solemnly and seriously greeted me, and after ceremonies while I was on my way out, he quietly and gently asked: "Is there any news?" I replied "No, Sir, there isn't!" and walked away with fast steps.

During the week, nothing important happened. I did not call Francis to learn the result of the new pregnancy test. I know she has started to work. Incidentally, I suddenly recalled that during our very brief acquaintance, engagement and marriage (?) period, she never invited me to her hospital. Isn't it strange, a nurse and doctor marry and the doctor has never visited his wife's working place that is a hospital within, say, a ten-mile distance. Perhaps I should have asked too – I accept my responsibility – but it is still strange. That also indicates how she is involved with her own existence only and was not ready to open up to the world, to show that she had a husband, etc., etc., etc. What and why am I talking about this now? What use is it? Isn't it a little bit too late?

The other important point was that of my son Souhi had decided to "give an interval" to his piano lessons due to his heavy winter schedule at home and his serious involvement in electronic machines, like other youngsters. Mrs. K. accepted this very graciously. Incidentally, I had never blamed this

A.C. 2084

nice lady who, in goodwill, wanted to conjoin two lonely people and caused a marriage that did not last too long. I am sure she also feels bad about this situation, but I cannot help.

February 17, 1969
Code Island

Too many important things are happening in my life. During these two weeks that I have not written my notes, let me see, what happened?

Yes, first, and quite importantly I heard from Francis: she is pregnant for sure. She said she was feeling sorry for the marriage but was feeling quite happy as a prospective mother. I congratulated (?) her on her forthcoming motherhood, whatever it might mean. Obviously, whatever and whoever one can call under the name of 'marriage', she had succeeded in getting what she wanted in life: to get impregnated and carry an infant... and be loyal to him (and the father) the rest of her life. I do not believe she could ever marry someone else, the rest of her life. I am not a gambler, but I can bet all my treasures on that, because my 'uncle' Freud says so.

Upon this, I began to search for a 'divorce lawyer'. Principally, the ladies who would like to get a divorce go to the lawyers and poor men defend themselves from their attacks, afterwards. For me, things go a little bit strange. In my first divorce, as I had detailed in my "Memoirs – First Marriage", after my wife had returned to our native land, from here I have written to the Bar Association at home requesting a lawyer to represent me. Now, I have to hunt one, before being hunted badly.

Souhi's best friend Mark, a Jewish fellow, one day had mentioned about his 'lawyer father' while playing ping-pong downstairs in the cellar. Thus, one evening I asked Souhi whether it was proper to request Mark's father as a lawyer in our family affairs. He said he did not have any reason why not, provided that Mark's father was going to accept. I have met Mark's parents at one of the school family meetings and they appeared to be a bright, outgoing, social, perhaps normal, couple. He might have been successful in his business for his son was going to a private school like mine. Secondly, in a Catholic State where divorce is almost nil, if he did survive, that meant he was a good lawyer. Anyway, Souhi called Mark, found out the office telephone number of his father, Samuel Archibald, and I got in touch with him. He knew me better than I thought; met me in his office, treated me very respectfully, talked quite highly about my son and declared his admiration for me both as a father who brings his child up and as a very successful professional at the State's mental hygiene director level.

Chapter 27

Mr. Archibald assured me that Mr. Normand had his own reputation, being a very reliable man. Since the pregnancy was established, we could not go ahead with divorce procedures. The State law required we wait until the birth process was observed, "a live child-birth" be seen first and whatever circumstances there might be with that event". Until then, namely about nine months, I was going to sit tight and do nothing. Once, Francis had mentioned to me: "Should we get a divorce, I am not going to demand any alimony from you, you must know that!" Noble girl, knows her mistake. "I cannot know about child support but I shall only request a guarantee for my child's education!" Good, but this is not as simple as it appears to be. At least twelve years' education, plus, probably college too, would cost me a few hundred thousand dollars. I am still paying the mortgage for my one and half storey little house and do not have anything other than our good health, a well-paid job, three-to-four thousand dollars in the bank, good credit, an almost completely paid for used Mercedes-Benz, and no bad habits like smoking or drinking, gambling, etc. But obviously I was going to open an office to make money and be prepared to pay for an unknown baby's support. "God, do you hear me about this fair business?" I gave the lawyer my father-in-law's home and business numbers and requested that he should get in touch with him and notify my lawyer should any legal questions come up. Mr. Archibald appreciated my comments and also requested that, similarly, should there be any legal demand, question or negotiation, I should not be involved and should call his office immediately. D' accord!

The other, and quite important, matter was that of my job. As I repeatedly mentioned, my job record was excellent, nearly spotless. But for some time, the Governor's office was talking about new organisation in the Social Welfare Department that I am under and taking the Mental Hygiene Department, of which I am the director, apart from it and making a separate Department of Mental Health, as the State Health Department. Naturally, I appeared to be the most suitable candidate for this cabinet level post for during my reign I had done a lot for the State: establishing four community mental health clinics and a Marathon Hosue for drug addicts, running State-wide educational seminars and symposiums and alike. On the other hand, I am a foreigner and the choice belonged to the Governor who was a political authority. Plus, I was in a kind of uneasy State due to the most recent events in my life. Maybe that was affecting my performance more than I was aware of. Even though it was a personal affair, still "instant marriage and instant divorce" might have raised a lot of questions in many people's minds but no one had dared to ask any question about it. The life train was going on as before. Secondly, this church's valuable package. No one, including me,

A.C. 2084

knew what that precious thing was but nonetheless, something that did not originally belong to me, was willingly in my custody, regardless of how I would justify that. A voice in me was telling me that some problems were on the way. Simply to return it could not happen, as easy a job as it might look like on the surface, for what I was going to say Mr. Normand? Still, I was going to hold onto my gun, the arrow was thrown, and one day, after the birth incident and divorce were fairly and squarely dissolved, I was going to find a way to deliver it, maybe through some casual way, like a little baby being left at the church door. Well, then, after getting it, would they have killed me? Now, at least they would not dare to kill me because they don't know its whereabouts. Oh, my bones chill!

March 3, 1969
Code Island

Difficult days. More and more it becomes apparent that I may leave State Services. Silent rumours murmur that the job may go to someone who is a native citizen of Code Island who is presently employed out of State but is planning to come home. Fine with me. The other day, one of the ministers that really admires me said: "The Governor says 'I can't live either with, or am not able to live without, Dr. Ismailov!'" Is someone putting a stick in the beehive? During this two-week period, on two or three occasions, almost at midnight, the telephone rang at home but there was no one on the other end of the line. Coincidence? Maybe, maybe not. I go almost nowhere that could be termed undesirable or would be dangerous. I am a family man; unless there is an official meeting or cultural activity that I or we go to and come back timely, I am almost always home. I did not feel that I was followed either. Wasn't I?

One strange thing happened, however, that I would like to State. One evening, two State police officers came home for a visit. When I asked the reason, they said they would like to see my car. To see my car? We went to the home garage that is already for one car. They asked when I had used the car last. I said about an hour ago, as I was coming back from work. On the way, I had gone to Ears to buy couple of cassettes for a possible recording tonight on my V.C.R.; consequently, my motor was somewhat warm. As I insisted on asking what was behind this, they said "There had been a car fire at one of the downtown plazas and someone had noted a dark-blue Mercedes was passing by from there... and they wondered..." Well, Ears, was no way nearby that plaza. They touched the hood of the car and noted that it was somewhat warm. What does that prove? I showed them the shopping slip from Ears and that somewhat satisfied them; they greeted me politely and left.

No news – which does not mean that is good news – from the Francis side. Strange, two people, just about two months ago, wanted to follow a dream, with goodwill in their hearts, but soon, they become strangers again.

Souhi, under the circumstances, is doing very well. Of course he does not know what is going on, it is not right to load him unnecessarily with some stress that we don't know the facts about anyway. The only solid thing is, we entered in a match that did not go more than two rounds and the boxers abandoned it. What else I would say. Do I miss Francis? Frankly, no. There had not been a love story but eventually there could have been. The fact remains, she is carrying a baby/foetus from me, from my blood, who, if everything is going to be alright, by this Fall shall be on this earth. God help him (or her!).

Considering a possible move, I began to prepare myself for medical exams or a reciprocal exchange with the neighbouring State, Chusetts. The papers are on the way. I also checked with my lawyer, Mr. Archibald, whether there was a legal obstacle should I make a final decision in that respect. He was rather surprised by my way of thinking, but, as long as we were going to notify the courts about my whereabouts, there was no problem. In order probably to support the prospective baby, I had to earn more money. That was the only thing the courts could have been concerned with. That was all.

It is about 5.30 p.m. Fortunately, nobody bothered me. I gave an interval to my readings and made a call to my lively wife.

"Honey, am I permitted to come? Since I have a cabinet meeting to night at 7.30 p.m., can we have a little bite of something?"

"No, you are not permitted; of course, with honours," replied my Jada. "Give me fifteen minutes to set up the table, say thirty minutes if you can stand our little ones all around me."

"You bet! Love you!"

"Love you too!"

So, within the destined time, I was with my wife. She is such a smart cookie. If my mind is too busy – that is almost always so – she does not bother to talk about wishy washy things. She keeps quiet and we only talk about the highlights, whatever the subjects. Just the same happened this evening, too. However, I was a little bit generous to her and gave her some highlights about the forthcoming festival.

Otherwise, generally, I wouldn't speak about governmental affairs, particularly at the dinner table. Oh, I didn't tell you before; Jada does volunteer work involving arts and crafts, colouring and painting with the elderly. So, she spoke a little bit what she had done this noon recess. We kissed each other and said "bye!".

I might be a giant, as some people say, in some ideational things, planning, analysis and alike, but I am a dwarf if the matters are of a mechanical nature. I do not have any skills, even any understanding of the way of working of any simple machinery. That's why I listen to my ministers of energy, communication, transformation, repair and alike with utmost attention and curiosity, hoping that besides learning something I may conceptualise something and add and integrate that into my judgment system. *Helas!* It never happened and shall never happen.

Thus, the three ministers of Agriculture, Industry and Mining, headed by Timothy Allstar; Energy, Transportation and Communication, headed by Atilla Weakball; and, Engineering, Construction and Repair Department, headed by Jack Depare, as I have introduced to you before as the three musketeers, came altogether on time, and sat around comfortably. Before anyone started, Jack commented:

"Sir, I have nothing to report tonight, so, please relax."

"Oh, good," I sighed, "I did not have time this evening to look over some terminology and names from encyclopaedias before the meeting. Thank you again!"

They all laughed. They all know that, prior to meetings, as usual, indeed, in order to understand a little bit more, I used to juggle with the previous minutes' recordings and plunge into some technical matters in encyclopaedias, to no avail.

Atilla took over, due to the fact that my being quite busy at the festival preparations, truly, or to give me a break, said: "Timothy also forgot his home work at home, he says. So, I, *Paradisea apoda*, namely the 'bird of paradise' shall be the only bird to sing tonight."

Since the esprit was so great and timely, we all applauded.

Then, Atilla began to give some details of his department's work.

"Well, we are a modern republic, but only sixty years old. We are well-advanced in many technical areas, but as we know, due to certain commercial policies and living principals, we are not up to date in many areas. There is not any emergency or misdeed, or degradation of any services to our citizens by any means. But, I would like to summarise to you our three basic energy systems, as

Chapter 27

you already know, and would like to make some suggestions for near future.

"The first: **Solar System**. The whole world has been using this for some time. Except for some summer places, no nation in this world could produce enough electricity solely from this system to manage their country. We do not intend either.

"You know, the physical essence in that is 'Photovoltaic Cells and Modules'. This is nothing new. In this, the 'solar nodule' (or 'photovoltaic component of the system') is the heart of everything. It transforms the rays of the sun into electric energy to be used.

"From a technical point of view, the 'solar nodule' (or the panel) contains several 'photovoltaic cells', connected in series, or parallel with some metallic material. In the past, this material was iron, at the beginning, then, it became steel. Nowadays, the most modern countries have begun to use cadmium, which we do not have. This is the problem. They are easily corroded and some energy escapes. Anyway, the energy that is produced by a solar module is influenced primarily by the number of cells within a module and how these cells are arranged within the module. When the cells are connected in series, the total voltage is approximately the sum of the voltages that come from each individual cell.

"When the cells are connected in parallel, the total content is the sum of the currents from the individual cells and the output total voltage is exactly the same as that produced from a single cell. Each cell in a module typically produces anywhere from 2 to 5 amperes and approximately 0.5 volts – that is about the same amount as produced from an ordinary flashlight battery. By multiplying the output current, one can calculate the total electricity produced. Typically, cells are arranged in a module to produce voltages in increments to most modules in the marketplace – 12V, 24V, even 36V.

"Like photovoltaic cells, solar modules also can be arranged to produce any voltage required.

Monocrystalline cells' efficiency rays are about 14-16percent;
Polycrystalline cells' efficiency rays are about 13-15percent; and
High efficiency monocrystalline cells (BP Solar Saturn Cells) are about 16.5 percent

"Almost the whole world now is using BP Solar Cells. We have to find some ways to obtain those. OK Sir?"

"OK, Atilla, what about the other systems?"

"OK. The second: **Wind System**. Well, the system has changed just a little bit since the middle ages.

"The essence in it is that a 'wind turbine' converts the kinetic energy that the wind induces to electrical energy. To start with, the wind blows on the blades in the turbine and makes them turn. Those blades turn a shaft that extends inside the box at the top of the turbine, called the 'nacelle'. That shaft goes into a gearbox and increases the speed of the generator which uses magnetic fields to convert the rotational energy into electric energy, similar to normal power stations. Then the power output goes to a transformer which converts 700 volts of electricity that comes out the generator to the high voltage distribution system of about 33,000 volts. The final phase is, of course, the grid system that transmits the power throughout.

"These are all good. The old system still works very well. Our difficulty is with measuring the wind speed. Lately, we began to observe that the tornadoes, storms and gales that form regularly in the ocean around us had begun to raise their intensity. Consequently, some very strong vibrations had begun to create some transmission problems, particularly in the nucelle, resulting in fluctuations in electrical frequencies and voltages. Remember? You yourself had noticed some interruption or power failure last week. Maybe this was the problem, I don't know."

"Perhaps, but don't you record the speed and all other changes on computers too?"

"Yes Sir, we do, rather machines do automatically, and at the control room, the man can watch and take necessary precautions on time..."

"Like what?"

"Like turning the turbine completely off and using the secondary depot electricity."

"So, Atilla, I see the problem, what is missing or rather, what do you suggest we do?"

"I follow the world literature, nothing new came. Along with solar energy, since they are so natural, wind energy supplies about 65percent of our electrical needs. I wish it could be higher. So, that bring us to the third, namely, to **Bioenergy** and **Biomass,** which, with the increase in our population, obviously we shall have more waste material to work with.

"Bioenergy provides very critical economic, environmental and security benefits. One of the most advantageous characteristics of it is that it's renewable. That adds additional value to farming, forestry and other industries. Consequently, it reduces waste streams. Bioenergy also reduces the emission of greenhouses gases and other pollutants by displacing fossil fuel use. Of course its biggest advantage is the chance that it gives us all domestically available sources."

"What is biomass?"

"Biomass is any organic matter, particularly cellulosic or lingo-cellulosic matter, which is available as renewable or recurring matter, including trees, plants and associated residues, plant fibre, poultry litter and other animal wastes, industrial waste and the paper component of municipal solid waste."

"Swell, where does the problem lie?"

"Sir, the problem is collecting, depositing, transporting and re-using the material. At that level, manpower is almost unnoticeable, but when it comes to recycling, we are short of qualified workers. Our refining machines, I am afraid, should also be replaced in the near future."

"OK, Atilla, if you also agree, let us do this:

1) Get in touch with Keith. I understand he just is finishing up labour force assignments. See whether he could do anything about this last chapter;
2) Get in touch with the President of the New Atlantis University, then with his permission with the Dean of Faculty of Engineering, to see whether this could be a research project there at any level. A few months ago, Dr. Lowell, the dean, at a dinner meeting was talking about burning the debris with 'methane gas' and obtaining some energy. I guess, before we had also spoken among ourselves too. At any rate, see they had come anything out of it. Give my regards to him.
3) If possible, please get in touch with the ABA, the American Bioenergy Association, that is the main source in this anyway, isn't it?"

"Yes sir, but it is amazing you say – and we believe you – that you don't have any technical knowledge in these matters but... indeed amazing..."

"Still I don't know Atilla, but if you are the President of this republic, you have to know at least who you should be asking when you need something. Anything more to say? You gentlemen? No? OK. I cordially thank all of you for your patriotism and dedication to your country, and fellow citizens. God bless all of you! See you!"

"Goodnight Sir... Goodnight... Goodnight Sir!"

A.C. 2084

This is Wednesday night. The big event is the opening of the Freemasonry Lodge. We gathered at the small chapel which was brim full. Keith and his department, plus Jack Depare, and his renovation team, had really done a wonderful job. All lit, painted and decorated,

Chapter 28

with the light blue colour paint giving a very comforting, refreshing air to all. All the governmental officials, starting from me, ministers, surprisingly some church leaders and some people -expectedly – from the Mormon group, were all were present. George K. of both the Mormon church and of the prospective Freemasonry Lodge, kept smiling at me. You know, I have heard his name first on my unauthorised wire line, then talked to him vis-à-vis at the Mormon church. I have quite mixed feelings about him. No question he is a smart, sparkling fellow but he gives me some strange vibes that are sometimes hard to understand. Nonetheless, he is very eager as a newcomer who would obviously like to have a very active citizenship role in our Republic.

The first job was my brief, official speech, to declare the establishment of the New Atlantis Freemasonry Lodge and sign the necessary papers openly, sitting around the table, and shake hands with all the applicants: Smith L., George K., M. Clarke, Gregor S., and Yani Z. Mr. Smith L., who was obviously chosen, as expected, to be The Most Worshipful Grand Master of the Lodge, thanked all for the opportunity and help they had received in an unbelievably short term. Then he introduced the staff, much the same as we had planned, with the duty distributions being George K. as Very Worshipful Grand Secretary; Clarke M. as The Worshipful Junior Grand Deacon, Gregor S. as the Right Worshipful Junior Warden, and Yani Z. as Worshipful Sword Bearer of the Lodge.

The second part of the meeting involved the Most Worshipful Grand Master giving the listeners and prospective people who eventually were going to be candidates details of the membership procedures and a rather long but very illuminative lecture about the meaning and the development of this very important brotherhood society, as follows.

"Freemasonry, the Order of the Free and Accepted Masons, is one of the largest worldwide 'secret' societies, officially established in England, in 1717, as 'The First Grand Lodge'. A few years after, in 1723, a book which compiled the 'old laws' in masonry work had been published – *Anderson Laws* – by the same Lodge.

"Freemasonry, contrary to the beliefs of many, is not a Christian organisation; however it comprises many of the elements of a religion, morality, charity, brotherhood and obedience to the laws of the land. In modern times, for admission, the applicant is required to be an adult male, essentially believing in the existence of a 'Supreme Being' and the 'Immortality of the Soul'. Freemasonry had been banned in many of the world's countries, including the Soviet Republics, Hungary, Poland, Syria, China, Portugal, The United Arab Republic and Indonesia. There are estimated to be more than 6 millions freemasons on the earth, with 4 million of them living in the U.S.A. and over 1 million on British soil. Even though there is no prejudice against any creed or race, in principle, U.S. Lodges reject the legitimacy of Negro Mason and The Prince Hall Lodges. A healthy and reputable middle-class Protestant Christian white male who is able to maintain qualified work is a classic candidate for freemasonry.

"It is basically a kind of 'men's club'; however, there are organisations connected with freemasonry which give a chance for families and children to join. By this token, females, that is to say freemason's wives, are unified under the names of 'The Order of the Eastern Star', the sons, 'The Order of DeMoley' and 'The Order of the Builders', and the daughters, 'The Order of Job's Daughters' and, the most recognised, 'The Order of Rainbow'. These associate organisations organise several fruitful social activities, strengthening the interpersonal relations, sisterhood and brotherhood, humanity and alike. Principally in the U.S.A. and other countries, there are also allied organisations, however secondary, which count themselves as 'allied organisations with those of freemasons', like the 'Ancient Arabic Order of the Nobles of the Mystic Shrine – Shriners', 'The Grotto', formerly 'The **Mystic** Order of the Veiled Prophets of the Enchanted Realm', and 'The Tall Cedars of Lebanon'. In almost all organisations, freemasons are divided into three major degrees: 1st: Entered apprentice; 2nd: Fellow of the craft; and the 3rd: Master mason. Most accept a degree system up to 33rd degree while some go as high as thousands. As a basic rule, or unwritten law, custom is the final arbitrator of all disputes.

Chapter 28

"I just couldn't pass without mentioning a striking period in the evolution and development of masonry: that of the *Count Cagliastro* story, particularly in reference to women being admitted to Masonic Lodges. This could also be looked upon as an endeavour to put a claim over ever-growing power and the universality of the jurisdiction of freemasonry, but a quite serious one.

"Count Alessandro Cagliastro, whether originally George or Guiseppe Balsamo of Sicily and a great charlatan or not, by his prophetic claims, nonetheless was invited to the Convention of Paris for the purpose of explaining his miracles. He passed as the disciple of an alchemist named Althotas, who some scientists have identified with the theosophist Schröder of Germany; and convinced the people that he had received at the Pyramids of Egypt a complete initiation into the 'Mysteries of the veritable Great Orient'. He could make gold and silver and he could renew youth. Using his hermetic medicinal skills, he could make wonders in physical appearances. He could evoke appearances of the dead people since he had lived some two thousand years. He knew all natural and divine secrets, being full of wisdom. He was made a 'mason' in London and visited various British Lodges. He believed, and made the people also believe, that he had the Egyptian rite which he either invented or possessed – it did not make too much difference then, at the midst of the eighteenth century confusion when there was doubt about almost everything, perhaps as a last resistance to overpoweringly flourishing scientific views and achievements at large. He had gained a tremendous recognition around Bordeaux, Strasbourg and Lyons. However, his greatest ambition was to create, rather to inaugurate, a 'Mother Lodge' in Paris, quite contrary to Masonic principles. That is why he proclaimed himself 'Bearer of the mysteries of Isis (in Egyptian mythology, the God of Dead: Osiris' sister and wife at the same time; the Goddess of Nature) and Anubis (jackal-headed god, son of Osiris and Nephtys, a sister of Isis; Presiding God over tombs, also showing the passage to the souls their abode in the unknown world) from the Far East.

"The Roman Inquisition has made public its testimonies against him, however his genius and tremendous ability to demonstrate some of the 'miracles', i.e. reading the future in a carafe of water, selling the 'elixir of long-life', in spite of being an impostor, most of the time made him a magnificent charlatan. He had found very strong admirers, like one cardinal, even King Louis XVI who had declared that 'any one who molested Cagliastro be held guilty by the reason of treason'. He married a Roman beauty, Lorenza Feliciani, infamous then as Sarafina, and in the year when American independence was declared, namely A.C. 1776, in London they appeared as 'Count and Countess Cagliastro'.

"Over the Egyptian freemasonry, Cagliastro was serious and insistent. In Paris, at the 'Rude de la Soudiere' residence, he established a private 'Temple of Isis' and announced himself as the high priest. In the year A.C. 1785, he declared that, following the precedent of the 'initiated priestesses of Egyptian temples', women might be admitted to the 'mysteries of the Masonic science of the Pyramids'. The first woman, a Madame de Lamballe, and some other noble (?) ladies were received as 'First Mason Ladies' at the Vernal Equinox (Spring equinox that is observed on March 21, when the day and night are of equal length), with some Oriental rituals and manifestations. At the end, however, all those perished or were imprisoned for good in the Inquisition's prison. First, he was seriously involved with the 'Affair of the Diamond Necklace' with Cardinal de Rohan in a scandal, in the years A.C. 1785 and 86; he spent nine and a half months in the Bastille before escaping to Italy where he tried to organise 'women freemasonry'. In French Revolution year, namely A.C. 1789, strangely enough, due to his wife Sarafina's backstabbing and denouncing him to the Inquisition, he was sentenced to death; however this decision was later commuted to a life sentence as imprisonment in the fortress of San Leo in the Apennines ended his life story. However, a few spooky movies and some legendary novels carried his intrigues and reputation throughout new generations.

"However, in the history of freemasonry there are far more honourable, world famous, learned men, famous masons like Goethe and Sir Isaac Newton, and many others. Let us see what Goethe said about a Mason, his goal and God.

> Erfüll davon dein Herz, so gross es ist,
> Un wenn du ganz in dem Gefühle selig bist,
> Nenn'es dan wie du willst,
> Nenn's Glück! Herz! Liebe! Gott!
> Ich habe keinen Namen
> Dafür! Gefühl ist alles;
> Name ist Schall und Rauch,
> Umnebelnd Himmelsglut.

"Fulfil your heart, regardless how big it might be – with that

Chapter 28

invisible subjects – And when your heart is fully blissful (with those feelings) – say whatever would like say: Happiness! Heart! Love! God! – I don't have any name to give you – For that, the feeling is everything – The name is only a noise and smoke – that hides the splendour of the skies from us."

"As, A. Pike had written just the same: 'Freemasonry is not a property of any time in human existence, it is the property of all times. Since it does not belong to any religion, it finds its existence in all of the religions. Freemasonry does not eliminate any belief in any belief-systems that pronounce 'I believe!' On the other hand, if this 'I believe' lowers the deep love that one feels toward God to his inner passions and denies the highest fate of mankind, and assaults the goodness and benevolence of mighty God and wrecks the freemasonry's great columns of belief, hope and love, then that 'I believe!' is out of our existence.'

"Even though masonry Lodges had officially been established by A.C. 18th century, the beginnings of it go back to the early stages of civilisation, long before Jesus Christ. As we all know, there were some secretive, hidden, political societies in old Greek and Egyptian times, like Hetaireia and Dyonysien. As early as in Roman times, there were some qualified workers, especially some carpenters and masons artisans associations, which were called 'Collegia', and very specifically, 'Tigari', as is officially known, an establishment by King Numa, B.C. 715. When it is said to be 'secret', that does not mean that those kind of professional organisations had some secret missions, like Crusaders or Illuminati. Old timers used to look upon work – as it is also mentioned in the *Koran* – as 'a kind worship to God, a sacred thing!' The qualified masons had a private home where they used to gather together, under the leadership of the *magister coenae*. Their work, it was believed, was protected by certain gods, and to celebrate those, as it became customary in other sects of human societies, as time went by, some rituals became established to keep the secrets of the profession. By this token, there was a *Velabre Collegia* that was established long before Jesus Christ, and the members of the collegia used to call each other '*brotheren* (brothers). Julius Caesar's legions, besides being military men, were also carpenters and stonemasons and builders.

"After the Roma effect declined in Europe, the collegias appeared to somewhat vanish in France but continued in Eastern Rome territories, including some Byzantine connected lands like Raverna, Venedik and the Rome area. In the Middle Ages, the names of the collegia changes to the *Scholae*. When the Lombardians invaded Italy, they unified almost all professional organisations, principally masons, under the famous name of "ministeria". Among those, the most famous was that of *Magistri Comacini*, namely 'The Masters of Como' (Como, in old Latin means 'to make tidy, beautiful, to arrange, adorn, especially about the hair' – Lucretius). They were invited to build the famous Saint-Apotres Church in Rouen, France, as early as A.C. 530. Due to the development of feodality and seeing the threat of being destroyed, these kind of organisations, in order to secure their surety and even existence, joined the newly-developing monasteries which were already in charge of building churches and monasteries which were also were joining the cornerstones of science and developing fine arts. Thus, the working-class qualified masons' freedom and professional posterity were guaranteed by such monasteries, through establishing 'monastery societies' under their leadership. The divinity of their work, no doubt, was also heightened by this protection. By the same token, the bishops who came from the collegia tradition and had become the administrators of several famous places, like Leon and Grégoire of Tours, Ferréol of Limoges, Rodez of Rodez, Agricola of Chalons-sur-Saone and Fructuoso from Spain, were the real architects of church-building art in their times.

"Parallel to those, there also were developing some '*Guilds*-Gildes', 'artisans' unities' that most probably were derived from old Germans 'convivium', as Tacitus had pointed out 'abundantly eating and drinking, and abundantly talking at the dinner table', in about A.C. 7th century. As time went by, these 'societies' and 'guilds' became more organised and legally recognised so that in France, in A.C. 1268, engineered by Etienne Boileau, the *Book of Crafts*, which was the declaration of the classification and the qualifications of the sworn and chartered craftsmen and their art, was published. In England, in A.C. 1376, the 'London Stonemason Company' and in A.C. 1472, the 'Stonemasons Brotherhood Organisation' were established. In Germany, around the same time, there was a 'Stone Sculptures Brotherhood Society (*Stein-metzer Brüderschaft*) on the scene.

"Needless to say, besides and beyond these good-willed masons, there were established *tariqas* right at the heart of the churches or religious organisations which were also doing a big job as far as buildings were concerned but of course, some of them had more obvious political goals. One example was the Templiers which during the Crusades built towers, churches, roads and bridges to protect Jerusalem, the sacred city. They had their establishment certificate issued from Saint-Bernard, the priest who established and owned Clairvaux, and were quite spread out all over the Europe. In every branch of the *tariqa*, there was a *magister carpentarius* who was indeed an architect. As history records, in the A.C. twelfth century, one third of the city of Paris belonged to them. But as they obtained that much power and consequently created a kind of danger, their existence was abolished by the king in A.C. 1312 and their money and belongings, all rights and privileges, were transferred to the 'Tariqa of Saint-Jean to help the patients in Jerusalem' in A.C. 2 May 1312. Sometime later, in A.C. 1530 to be exact, those rights and privileges were all transferred to the Knights of Malta. The members of the union spread all over the Europe, particularly to Flandre and Scotia, and received a tremendous welcome and honour. As the Tariqa's rights and privileges were protected, in connection with that, the rights of the craftsmen were also secured.

"As we mentioned previously, the first official Lodge was opened in England in A.C. June 24 1717, and Anthony Sayer was elected the Grand Master (*Ustad-ı Azam*). *The Book of Laws* had been published in A.C. 1723. The said book, in its first chapter, about the religion and God cites, as follows:

"A mason has to obey the moral rules due to his responsibilities that he carries. He, any time, cannot be a dull man, an atheist who does not recognise a religion or God. In the past, even though men carried and believed in different religions and belief systems, now he ought to save his personal opinions to himself and has to be an honourable, straight and God-loving, virtuous person who also loves to help others, thus establishing a union point of intimate communication and therefore helping to get people close to each other with an inner desire more than ever.

"In spite of goodwill, the London Great Lodge, which from the very beginning was divided into four groups, soon became divided as 'Old' and 'New'. Old was under the jurisdiction of 'York Lodge' which was much more religious and conservative. Its most effective head was Lawrence Dermont of Ireland. In A.C. 1756, he declared the basic principles of Old Grand Lodge of London in a booklet named *Ahiman Rezon* (Ahiman: brothers, in Hebrew; and Ratson: Law), quite similar to *Anderson's Law* of A.C. 1738. Thus, the Grand Lodge was divided. And this division lasted until A.C. 1813 when the two parties

A.C. 2084

demanded a peace and unified again.

* * *

"In general, it seems to be that masonry is described as 'a peculiar system of morality, veiled in allegory and illustrated by symbols'. The morality belongs to the building, that is to say Solomon's Temple, and symbols that are common to the art (*Ars Magna Latamorum*) and its tools. The craft masonry incorporated three distinct elements, interlinked curiously under the device of symbolical architecture. Such interlinking is artificial yet it arises logically, from the relations of ideas point of view; first, from the candidate's own work 'to build up his personal architecture'. The matter of instruction is practical but in a true sense it is a subject matter of a secret order. Second is the 'building myth' and 'the manner' in which it is put in a kind of the dramatic pageant intimately demanded by – and attached to – the master builder of masonry. Thirdly, a Masonic quest, connected with the 'Secret Word' that is given at the Third Master Degree, however going beyond that.

"In the craft system, there are three distinct degrees that are accepted universally among all grand Lodges of free and accepted masonry. Before entering the first; Entered Apprentice Degree, the candidate comes to the precincts of the Lodge as "worthy and well-recommended" as he is comprehended within himself, to be adaptable to a specific purpose. He first has to be described as a 'properly prepared person'. His fitness has been made not through his personal appearance but his deep personality, commitment to life and living style and other observable social-human-spiritual values. Then he is recommended by the sponsor brothers. Thus, 'preparation', as the name implies, is not an initiation but a declaration of readiness by the person's own concurrence for that experience. During this period, the candidate learns that 'he has not received the light that is communicated emblematically in freemasonry, but learned somehow the significance of a halooing darkness of the brotherhood'. That is somewhat anxiety-provoking and bewildering, however a promise for a new venture, to enter a new order and ultimately a new life.

"Then there comes the attaining of the **First Degree**. In this, the candidate opens his eyes to a new world, represented by the Lodge, a word of symbols. This world extends itself to four quarters, heights above and depth beneath. It may seem that the 'ordinary light may have been taken out of his path and then restored again'. As if the light is given to him in another, new place 'to start his real life' 'as if being born again like a baby, to a new life'. The imputed darkness experienced seems to be reminiscent of his intra-uterine life in his mother's womb, a new light being indicative of re-birth, however this time in a Masonic Lodge that is illuminated by the same light.

"The same light, of course, illustrates many things – from the past – which have to retire and be put aside. This also is, in the actuality of symbolism, indicative of the person's acceptance of a new environment; a new body of experience, intentions, communications and duties connected with those. There appears to be the start of a new vocation in the world. Whole brand new standards and values are about to start that are not the candidate's own but old tokens that belong to all humanity.

"The **Second Degree** is the fellow craft ceremonies that are the confirmation of the mastering of the instructions by the candidate through his own efforts to build up an edifice, leading to a new life. Little by little he learns and adopts in his life somehow the hidden mysteries of nature, science and art through the leadership and supervision that are provided by his instructor.

"The sublime **Third Degree**, master masonry, makes the candidate hear and then realise the direct relations between he and his great creator, the Supreme Being. He is also brought to 'The Mystery of Death' and whatever his going to happen thereafter: The Great Mystery of Raising. As the candidate passes through these experiences successfully, the Most Worshipfull Grand-Master declares: 'Entered, Passed and Raised.' Thus, as Bacon said, 'to wear a new body of intention, desire and purpose,' 'learned how to illustrate in his own personality that new birth in time'; the candidate had: (1) undertaken to acquire the symbolical and spiritual art of building a house of another life; (2) has reached therein a certain point of proficiency; (3) had attained the whole mystery. He had done all of these in a different manner and under the influence of a strange symbolism. Thus, the candidate becomes incorporated in a vital organism, the 'living house'.

"Of course, these ceremonies appear to stem from the very heart of Christian theosophy, in full light of the Mystical City and the Eternal Kingdom. Namely, the three ceremonies seem to symbolise, within their own measures, birth, life, death and the resurrection of Christ, in just the same manner as the story of the master builder should be re-lived through a master mason's experiences and lives thereafter. It does not matter, of course, that this analogy was present or not on the minds of those who gave us the ceremonies of Emblematic Freemasonry.

"As to the officers and titles:

"I am taking the United Grand Lodge of England, as a classical example of a full-blown Grand Lodge that could be anywhere in the world, to line up the rank in succession, as follows:

(1) The Most Worshipful of Grand Master.
(2) The Most Worshipful Pro Grand Master.
(3) The Right Worshipful Deputy Grand Master.
(4) The Right Worshipful Senior Grand Warden.
(5) The Right Worshipful Junior Grand Warden.
(6) The Very Worshipful Grand Chaplin.
(7) The Very Worshipful Grand Treasurer.
(8) The Very Worshipful Grand Registrar.
(9) The Very Worshipful Deputy Grand Treasurer.
(10) The Very Worshipful President of the Board of General Purposes.
(11) The Very Worshipful Grand Secretary.
(12) The Very Worshipful President of Board of Benevolence.
(13) The Very Worshipful Junior Grand Director of Ceremonies.
(14) The Worshipful Senior Grand Deacons.
(15) The Worshipful Junior Grand Deacons'
(16) The Worshipful Assistant Grand Chaplins,
(22) The Worshipful Grand sword Bearers
(31) The Worshipful Grand Stewards.

"I want to talk a little bit about those mysterious Masonic symbols," added Mr. Smith L., The Most Worshipful Grand Master.

"The Universal-Grand symbols which characterise Emblematic Freemasonry are: the Pentalpha, or Pentagram, the hexagonal Seal of Solomon, also called the Shield of David, All-Seeing Eye, the Point with a Circle, the Cubic Stone, the Sun and Moon. The Drawn particular symbols from the Operative Art of Masonry are the 'Rough and Perfect Ashlar', usual Working Tools, and 'the Blazing Star'.

"**Blazing Star**: There had always been an unnatural mix-up between Pentalpha and Blazing Star. It may be due to the fact that Blazing Star is distinguished by five wavering rays and Pentalpha by five points. The Blazing Star is a Masonic variant of the Pentagram, and was already regarded as a star by ancients.

"The order was adopted by the Order in circa A.C. 1735. It signifies: (a) the Star of the Magi, (2) the Glory of Divine Presence, (3) Divine Providence, (4) a Symbol of Beauty, (5) a light from God directing in the Way of Truth, (6) the Sign of a True Mason, (7) an emblem of the Sacred Name of God, in other words, of God Himself, (8) the Sun as the Grand Luminary of Nature, (9) the Dog Star – Star of Anubis, and, (10) a volatile spirit, animated by the Universal Spirit in Nature.

"**The Pentalpha**: In Masonic handbooks, this magnificent and antique symbol had been described as: (1) 'A geometrical figure formed by five lines (don't forget, the Divine Being is the grand geometrician of the universe!) crossing each other, terminating in five points at equal distances from the centre, and equally distant one from the other all around the centre'; (2) 'A triple triangle'; (3) 'a figure containing five double triangles, with five acute angles within and five obtuse angles without. This figure of five points also contains a Pentagram within it, and many other mysteries as detailed by Cornelius Agrippa. Great archaeologist Dr. Thomas Inman confessed that the Pentagram was the only mystery figure that he could not exactly interpret. Eliphas Lévy says: (1) the Pentagram is the sign of microcosm; (2) it represents what Kabbalists of the Zohar term as *Microprosopus*; (3) it's comprehension could be the key to the two worlds; (4) it is absolute natural philosophy and natural science; (5) it expresses the mind's domination over the elements of nature; (6) it is the Star of the Magi, the Blazing Star of the Gnostic Schools; the representative of intellectual omnipotence and autocracy. In the occult philosophy (*philosophia occulta*), it is the symbol of Christhood and perhaps the symbol of the over-ruling power of the grace of God in the soul.

"**Hexagram**: 'The double triangle of Solomon' is the sign of *Macrocosmos*, namely the great world. It has several meanings in the lesser and greater mysteries: It is the Three who carry a recording Heaven and the Three who give testimony on the earth; it is also the sign of the Eternal Creator, namely the Grand Architect; it is of the triune (trinity) man, perfect in the archetypal world as a proto-typical image in the Divine Mind, and reflected into manifestation here below, as will, desire and mind. It also signifies the Hermetic doctrine of correspondences in Zohar doctrine. According to Magus Lévy, the conception of infinite and the absolute. According to Ragon, the hexagram was a sign of: (1) 'generation'; (2) 'the divine fruitfulness'; (3) 'creative energy' by the reason that the number '6' was consecrated of old to Venus. In the palmary sense of its symbolism, the Hexagram, or Star and Seal of Solomon, is macrocosm, while the Pentagram is the sign of microcosm.

"**Sun and Moon**: The sun, in our workbooks is 'an alarm clock' that calls us to 'labour'; that is balanced by the complementary conception of 'repose', and the two may unify in the idea of 'refreshments'. It is also indicative of the 'progress' of human life from infancy on, passing through manhood, up to old age, and the coming of a better day. As to the moon, it fortifies the ordinary theological doctrine that 'the highest saints of earth and heaven, and the most glorious angels, only reflect the light of the Sun of Righteousness'. We all know that, the lunar phases are among the first celestial phenomenon that invited philosophical minds.

"As we turn to the Secret Tradition, we see that the Sun and Moon are lit with spiritual meanings. They are symbols of God and His Shekinah, 'Pneuma' and 'Psyche', the highest understanding of the logical mind. The 'Solar emblem' signifies also 'the light of God' in the soul, while the Moon, which is the feminine side of nature, emanates the love-aspect in deity. In Kaballistic theosophy, Shekinah is divine womanhood and, in a pregnant sentence' it is said: 'God and His Shekinah are One'.

"The medieval occult philosophy recognised a solar and lunar principle in every natural compound and this metaphysical Sun and Moon are joined in a solemn, sacramental union. In classical legends, the moon is sometimes represented as a receptacle and sometimes as a source of souls. The Initiates of Eleusis were called 'Regenerated Children of Moon'; so were the 'Mysteries of Ceres', the souls which were said to be born out of the grotto of initiation and were regarded as regenerated from a door in the side of the moon or born in the 'Lunar Ship', which was one of the names of the titles of the moon, floating along in the serulean sea of heaven. Eliphas Lévy had said: 'Heaven is a mirror of the human soul and when we are thinking that we are reading in the stars is in ourselves we read,' that also refers to why the deep study of the starry heavens is regarded as an advancement in our mystical knowledge. This is a true journey of the mind in God (*itinerarium mentis in Deum*).

"**Points and Circle**: These typify the 'individual brother' by means of 'the point' and the limits of his duty to God and man by means of 'circumference'. Just adding two perpendicular parallel lines, there comes the representation of the patron saints of the Masonic Order, St. John the Baptist and St. John the Evangelist. According to 'The Eternal

Kingdom Symbolism', 'a point is that which has no parts and which has no significance'. In the Metaphysical Doctrine of the Absolute, this geometrical postulate is the only possible representative type of the 'Ineffable God', in other words, the 'God of Mystical Theology'.

"The point 'without parts or magnitude' is the Metaphysical Sign of the Infinite, due to the fact that metaphysical infinity does not connote any extension; and, of the Eternal, because eternity is not time continued henceforward for ever; in a word, of the Unconditioned, which is in such a transcension as regards conditional existence of a verbal subtlety; it is outside the pairs of opposites. The relation between this 'point' and that 'circle' of which it is the centre in the sacramentalism of God, in definition, the limits being place upon the ineffable for the purpose of realisation within the measures of our logical understanding.

"The 'Point within a Circle' has, of course, other important meanings too: it is the Divine Spirit indwelling creation and abiding in the nature of the man; it is the Christhood centred in the church; it is the secret church within that which is official; it's the Real Presence in the Eucharist.

Other Masonic symbols:

"The **Pillars J and B** are the symbols typifying the Wisdom, Strength and Beauty being reflected directly from the 'Tree of Life' in Kabbalism.

"There is a **Cubical Altar** in Masonry, which represents here below the Altar of Incense that is above, whereon Michael the great angel sacrifices the souls of the just, and they ascend as an eternal fragrance to the Lord God in the Highest.

"The **Tracing Boards** are of course symbolical, and so is the **Checkered Carpet** on which all masons trade.

"The **Working Tools** which are many, because the Degrees are many, and accessories of this kind, taken over from the Operative Art, are essential symbols of the art which is called emblematic, and their meanings are ever with us, though the eye is not satisfied with seeing them, nor the ear filled with hearing their expounded moralities.

"**The Keystones – The Cubic Stone**, in grades outside the craft is a great and speaking symbol, for we know who is head of the corner in the great experience which is called the Christian Mastery.

"**The Red Cross** is an emblem of life to come, while the rose placed thereon signifies the interblended joys and sorrows, pleasures and pains of man's terrestrial lot.

A.C. 2084

"Well, here I am coming close to this very long, at times tiring, speech. I hope it gave you some basic information concerning a very sincere fellowship, a sharing brotherhood, in essence the non-secular enlightenment of human development and refinement. Thank you again and goodnight."

It was indeed a pleasure and treasure to listen to. We embraced Mr. Smith L. Whole-heartedly.

Well, this is Friday night. Everyone is getting ready for the festival but I am quite determined to resolve this Mormon business. I want to clear up an account that innocently had raised a lot of questions about my ancestors and more importantly, deprived some real believers of their natural rights. So, I hope I shall finish up reading my grandfather's

Chapter 29

concerned notes tonight and if God wills, after the weekend, I shall come to a peaceful end.
Here are the final parts of 'Sindbad's Adventures', I would say.

March 17, 1969
Code Island

I think I am moving... When Souhi finishes his classes at the end of May, I definitely am going to go. Midnight telephone calls keep coming with no one at the other end. A few times I felt I was being followed but I have no proof of it. Are these scaring tactics or my paranoia? The State job is still in the air but the Governor's man arrived from Sylvania and got established at Arwick. Probably they shall announce the new Director of Mental Health, as a new cabinet member. I, in spite of all my revolutionary work and dedication to the State, I wouldn't say that they are denied but not rewarded properly. I possibly shall remain one of the little Indian chiefs, shall see respect but will be taking orders instead of giving them. Though everyone says I am "too gentle" to give orders, as I always say "thank you" and even write the same 'thanks' on the patients' charts right after daily medication orders that are routine, and mostly repetitions of the previous day. One day the chief nurse asked me: "Doctor, you're the one only one I know who writes 'thank you' after each order, tirelessly, day after day, why?" replied to her: "You are the ones who are taking care of the patients more than I do; I only may request or thank afterwards!" I am such a strange guy anyway.

Since the nearby State is too close, almost forty-five minutes to an hour to drive, it is a real pleasure to go by car at the weekend, naturally with

A.C. 2084

Souhi, to attend a baseball game at Way Park or a B.N.A. basketball game at the Ton Garden. The apartments are too high-priced in the town; old English Tudors are attractive but very expensive too. Will see.

I go to church almost every other weekend but I do not visit Mr. Normand's house. It is not my 'home' anymore. Once in a great while I call home in the evenings, and just to be polite, ask how Lady Francis is feeling and do some exchanges "fine... good... be good... have a good day..." and alike. Obviously the pregnancy is advancing eventless. She seems to be quite satisfied about that but, poor girl, she shall eventually have to learn how to be a mother without a father (of course, her father shall always be around for everyone) especially when the child realises and will ask where the father is and asks why did you get divorce, why this, why that? What kind of stories shall be made behind me I don't know, but I can easily guess since I am listening to them every day. That part does not bother me that much, because I have my beloved one with me, and you are the witness, I have not done anything wrong in this marriage. In the marriage, yes, what about the church? What church? "Not Presbyterian church, Mormon church?" Oh, those things, invaluables, tablets or plates, whatever they might be. I still keep them in the box at the bank. No direct demand or serious question had arisen from the church but I am sure I am always in their minds. I hope I am mistaken. Let us wait and see.

March 31, 1969
Code Island

Expected news broke out: Dr. Goodboy had been announced as the "first and new Mental Health Director of the State of Code Island". There was a cocktails and get together party at the State House for this purpose. I forced myself to attend. I was jealous, I guess, just a little bit, but in reality I was heartbroken. I attended the party of course and as usual I drank orange juice and kept smiling. The man is tall, thin and had a warm smile with a red face. Obviously he is quite a drinker and has some allergic spots on his skin. He was from the State originally but was gone for a number of years to work for the Government. Now, after having a lot of experience, he wished to come back. Then, upon the invitation of his classmate, a well-known political figure in the State, he "readily and proudly accepted the offer!" and came here, to coil in my nest. They expected him to bring a lot of 'research money'. Who was going to run those projects? Of course, me.

Chapter 29

Really? No way!

Meeting the new director forced me to make a final decision: Please let me go. A very authoritative appearing man, he gave some strict 'obedience' rules as if I was at a dog training school. He thanked all the chiefs for "the wonderful jobs done" and "we were going to do better and there was more to come". To be able to afford to give the necessary time to new programmes, I was ordered to stop the entire in-service education programmes that were run at the State Mental Hospital, State prisons and boys' training school, community mental health centres, home visiting nurses association, yearly State-wide education seminars, community civic organisations visits and alike. We were going to report to him at our weekly staff conferences. For the first time in a long run, I felt that I was a "foreigner"!

Things were alright with Souhi who did not seem to be affected by this new move either. As a matter of fact, quite the contrary, he appeared to be enjoying this more sophisticated State, with a lot of museums, places to see and plenty of sporting events. Even though neither of us liked toughness and being physical, we started to go to some boxing matches on the large screen, world championships of the celebrities, including a woman's wrestling match in mud that was a real fun. I guess I never knew how to live in the society before. I did not know where and how to get fun, but I seem to be learning now.

One piece of news, a rather 'bad' piece I would say, had come from Francis: She had to stay in her hospital for a two-day observation for bleeding. A threat of a miscarriage. I had mixed feelings about the event; I did not know whether I should pray for a possible loss that could have made my life easier, however causing me to feel quite guilty; or, she should recover soon. Fortunately, I would say, with bed rest and some supportive medicine, she recovered. I still did not go to visit her. During this separation period she hadn't called even once and asked how Souhi was doing. Why should I have called and asked her how she and her glorious – unborn – baby were doing? She had her own family to take care of her. We did not have anyone to take care of us, except God.

Hunting for a house is continuing very intensely. We are about to come to an end. I will let you know. Bye!

April 21, 1969
Code Island

So many things are happening, one after each other. However, as you know, I myself have been preparing the things all along and now the results

A.C. 2084

are beginning to be picked up.

First. I put my resignation on the director's desk. He is like a politician (correction please, not "like a..", but precisely "he is a..."). He knows he could not do well without me but he cannot make any compromise when a real challenge comes true. He, with his famous smile, said: "I give you twenty-four hours to make your final decision. You know, you are invaluable to us but, in this job, everyone is affordable. I know you have been a little bit unhappy with new organisation, but this is life!" Naturally I did not take my resignation back. It was going to be effective May 31, 1969, coinciding with Souhi's school vacation. I had worked in that position for more than four years but let history make the real evaluation about the situation.

Secondly, I have a rented a beautiful place, a sea captain's house, all wood with a fireplace and floor covered with fine sandstone in the lobby and the kitchen, close to the ocean. Though a little bit rocky, you could salute the sun early in the morning while having your bath in the sea. The other weekend, Souhi, our cat and I visited for the day and enjoyed it very much. I partially began to move. My heaviest part is my books. It is like a public library but I owe them a lot: They made me whoever I am. They are the world for me.

Here, in my "new land", so-to-speak, I shall feel quite free and away from all the personal concerns of the most recent past. I shall walk along to the refreshing sounds and cries of the seagulls, read a lot and be a close friend to nature again. I am so inpatient about moving. I feel like pushing the days forward. As far as the job is concerned, I am somewhat reluctant to open an office for private practice since I am not known in the area; much better to work in a clinic for a while and to indulge in it. By chance, at a nearby community mental health clinic, a full-time psychiatric vacancy was available and I jumped in. Due to my professional background and reputation, I did not have any difficulty in being accepted. I was not too happy but at relative ease. At least I had a new future, if I choose my line quite straight, not to get involved in many things at the top, I could stay like a bachelor prince.

June 5th, 1969
Scottwille, Chusetts

So we moved at the beginning of June, as I had also started to work on the same date. At work I was an Indian again. Regardless of how humble and modest I am, indeed it is difficult to be assigned and asked questions, taking orders for routine work, though strictly professional and fair, after working at commissioner and director level for years. Besides, this, too, was a State job and the stipend was nearly ridiculous. Thus, I discussed the money situation with the clinical director who was a nice Jewish fellow anyway. He sincerely suggested I should open a private clinic right away and I left the work before being emotionally attached to the place and the people. It was a short-lived but realistic venture.

Thus, I opened my office in Alden, a middle-class community with plenty of psycho-social problems and a lot of State-supported psychiatric services were in mode, in a three-storey concrete building which harboured one young psychiatrist and two psychologists, besides the other sort of professionals. They accepted me in quite friendly way and helped to show me the procedures around the paper work. A low key but busy practice that I needed for a while, anyway. It was about ten miles away from my sea castle which was another pleasure in the evenings to shop around, follow the shore road, full of lights, and observe poor but happy-go-lucky people enjoying their lives one way or the other.

June 19, 1969
Scottwille, Chusetts

For the past three days a tempest has been shaking us with a very powerful wind and leaving plenty of raindrops. I had never lived on the sea-shore before, observing the merciless challenge between angry skies and non-submittal waves that were endlessly making smacking sounds. My son Souhi, my cat Tekir and I are watching this repetitious triumphant sea play from inside the house that at times gives us a kind of funny chill. Suddenly, a few sparks from the inside wall dazzled my eyes. That created a kind of scare in me. Just coincidence? The landlord who had rented the house to me had assured me that the whole electrical system was newly-renovated. The tiles on the roof had also recently been overhauled so there shouldn't be any problem of any sort. Nonetheless, I wanted to be sure and in the morning I called up the town office for a check-up. The men came promptly and were surprised to see such worn-out electric switches that required some immediate repair. Even though the telephone had been installed just for the past fortnight or so, at least three strange telephone calls had come up, and upon my saying "hello" there was no answer from the other side, other then a soft clicking sound of the receiver shutting off. Also strange was that the landlord insisted the switches were in no need of repair. I, however, took the financial responsibility and had them replaced.

After the bad days were over, we began to roll along the seashore in the evenings. And, on the third try, when we returned home, our loyal Tekir, who never left the house even one single inch without our company, was not there. We searched through all the surroundings to no avail. You can't imagine my son's tears and agony. I tried to console him, saying that the cats miss their old homes, travel miles and miles, and one day, like a new moon, they appear again. We are still waiting.

June 30, 1969
Scottswille, Chusetts

There is a beautiful sea restaurant at the curve of the harbour. This past Sunday, my son and I wanted to go and eat swordfish which is their specialty. Even though it looks a modest place from outside, at the entrance, my son who was just ten years old you know, since he was not wearing a neck-tie in this summer time, was not permitted to enter unless he was going to wear a bow-tie that was going to be provided by the restaurant. Surprised and bewildered, I asked my son's opinion; he had a few choices: To reject and go somewhere else, or, go back home, wear a tie and come back, or accept the restaurant's bow-tie offer. The smart boy, being practical, chose the last offer and with a comfortable smile, we entered, sat beside the seashore and ate a very delicious fish dinner. Since a few, regardless how small, mishaps were checking us, I asked Souhi how he was feeling living in this town. He, with a somewhat bitter smile, said:

"Dad, after my Tekir is gone, I don't have any feelings for this town. It is as if something is spooky here. No one bothered us openly but I have a kind of anxiety inside of me as if something bad is going to happen. How do you feel yourself?"

"My dear, almost the same as you do. If you wish, let us give ourselves a chance for a week or two, see how the things will come along? Alright?"

"Alright dad. The swordfish was indeed very delicious. Can I have an apple pie?"

"Of course, my love, I shall have too. The skies are too shiny. Isn't it beautiful?"

"Yes, they are dad... They are too shiny!" And he kept smiling devilishly.

Since the restaurant was in walking distance, we strolled along the shore and arrived at our door by foot. We did not know that a big surprise was waiting for us: The door was unlocked. We advanced slowly, reaching the electric switch took longer than usual. Yes, we had watched similar scenes

Chapter 29

on the movies but as a live experience this was going to happen for the first time in my life. As I turned the light, nothing blew out or anything like that. The things in the large saloon were a little bit deranged, but there was something strange, unaccustomed. First of all the air was heavy, mixed with some cigarette fumes that we never use. Oh, the large T.V. seemed to have disappeared, also the princess telephone receiver, V.C.R., a few antique wooden frames, Rembrandt's *Aristoteles in front of Homer's Bust* portrait (a copy of course) were absent. I dashed to kitchen – a few silver sets had gone, also the toaster, an antique RCA radio and the microwave oven. In the bedroom, a newly-bought zoom camera and a small colour T.V. weren't in their usual places. The drawers were turned inside out, perhaps in the search for money or drugs. The wardrobe was upside down too, but it was impossible for me to detect what was missing among the clothing. Perhaps nothing. Souhi's room was untouched, as a matter of fact appeared to be, if this was not an allusion, swept and cleaned up. I don't drink, so it can not be an alcoholic hallucination, namely the D.T.'s or something like that. Even Souhi confirmed that. My blue Mercedes, which was outdoors, also appeared to be untouched.

Well, I am a quick decision-maker. First I called the police right away and, until they came, I got in touch with the administrator of my office building at Alden. In the building where I am practicing, there was a two-room suite for rent. I had my waiting room area too. Then, I called up my moving company that had done a good job – as I had paid them quite generously – and requested that tomorrow morning they should appear at my door to move to Alden. They were a little bit hesitant for they had somewhere else to go. However, when I said I shall pay 'double' under the emergency circumstances, the answer was certain: "We shall be there at 7.00 a.m.". Souhi, a little bit surprised but still maintaining himself remarkably balanced, asked me what was going on? I said I do not know, I was sure something was going on, but what and why, I did not know. I had decided to end living in single houses, all alone, anymore.

In half-an-hour's time two police officers arrived. They were quiet and gentle. One of them, like in a slow motion movie, asked several questions that he wrote all of the answers to in a book, carefully. The other one made tours inside the house. I requested him to check the car too, just in case. He silently agreed and asked for the keys. I asked the officer: "Sir, wouldn't you take finger prints?"

"Not necessarily," the big, tall guy with a very comfortable voice answered. "I am sure we will not find anything. These kind of events are quite usual here, especially for houses that are left empty during the daytime and there are no lights on. Since you obviously moved here very recently, of course the neighbours, too, may not distinguish who comes and who goes. They are too professional; they don't come in disguise, playing their radios openly, talking in high pitches, as if they themselves are the part of the household. Thus, the neighbours do not suspect. Yes, please, would you sign your Statement here?"

No comments. I signed, thanked them for their 'prompt' service (?), and they quit as silently as they had come. I looked up to the skies, with the hope that maybe the stars would break their silence and say something as witnesses. No, they were still shiny but mute.

We put our pyjamas on and opened the windows wide. My son asked me whether he could sleep in my bed too and I gladly agreed. He was the most precious thing in my life. I needed his silent love at this point more than anything else. Soon, we were asleep. We had a lot to do in the morning.

July 2, 1969
Alden, Chusetts

I guess I am getting used to monster movies. I do not know whether I am in a daze, a kind of schizophrenic process that I am going through. Recently, strange and unexpected, unbelievable things had been happening around me, Thank God, nothing happens to us; I am rather a silent participant, however obliged to make quick decisions and protect myself, otherwise the situation might have been disastrous. If anyone does not believe what I am going to say now, I swear on the *Bible*. You can look in local and general newspapers and read there too about the event – that I am going to mention – which took place. Sit tight at the moment.

As I wrote two days ago, what happened, as planned, the movers came early in the morning and packed the things in relative ease, partly because many big packages, including the records and heavy books, were unopened. Two moving tracks of ten-wheelers swept the house within two hours and here we were in Alden, in my office building by noon. I felt really safe and very comfortable. I guess a sea captain's small chateau was going to reign in my fantasies for a long time to come but in reality, an anti-social person like me, no smoker no drinker, having no real close friends to chum with, a home body who cooks and cleans all by himself, would rather belong to this kind of housing: Still isolated at your choice but within reach, if wanted. Go to shopping plazas in walking distance, movies, book/record stores, etc. But something was gnawing me from inside: What was going on? All these were coincidental and could happen to almost anyone else but was I having

Chapter 29

my silent fair share? Or? Oh, I even don't want to think anymore. Maybe I need a new life plan, considering the headlines like: How would I behave, how would I act, what should I should extinguish from my way of thinking? I cannot change my profession, I am born for and into it. No problem there. I changed the "wives" or "companies" sufficiently so far. Maybe I should go into analysis again. During the training years that had coincided with the first divorce, the analysis that I had been through for two straight years had helped me a lot. Perhaps I was somewhat desolate, angry, upset and depressed because I was facing a loss and entering a new phase of my life, all alone. However, the situation appears to be somewhat different now. First, I am kind of settled, much more equipped and adjusted to the social environment, I guess. Am I?

But, considering I had not had any vacation for the past two years, also taking into the consideration that Souhi, my son, was also on his school vacation, I guess the best thing would be to go for a vacation. And I decided to take my son right in front of me, and talk with him 'man-to-man' Oh, gee. I forgot to tell you what the last disaster was. Listen to me.

After moving yesterday, early this evening I wanted to go to Scottsville for the last time, first to check whether there was something left out, then, secondly, and more importantly, whether we could see any trace of Tekir, our beloved cat. I took my son with me too, naturally.

As we approached to the sea coast where the house was located, an unbelievable scene struck our eyes: The house was burnt down to ashes, bricks and stones. What was still standing was like an archaic Roman treasure. The smoke was still in the air. In great surprise, I asked the neighbours what had happened. The elderly lady next door, who I had asked about our lost cat last week, in a quite relaxed manner said no one knew how but a sudden fire broke out in my "ex" house last night. It had burnt down at a tremendous speed. Naturally, the police and fire departments were called in but with little hope. Even a fireman had died during the fire fighting. The elderly lady showed me the local newspaper about the event and added: "We were wondering where you might be. The police officers asked us whether we have seen you; we told them you moved out early in the morning. Of course, we did not know your exact whereabouts. Did they get in touch with you?"

"Oh, no!" I replied. "If they wanted to, they could have gotten in touch with me in my office building, all day." Fortunately I could have proven where I was all night: establishing in my new home almost all night along. Perhaps that's why they did not even bother to investigate or simply ask me. Shouldn't they? I should learn not to ask any questions any more.

So, I thanked the lady for the information and said should the police ask, they can find me in Alden. "What about our cat, Tekir, was he ever been seen around?"

"No," replied the graceful old lady, "no, I haven't seen him either. Goodbye and good luck doctor!" and shut the door.

I am not going to make any interpretation. Whatever you may say, E.S.P. or intuition, our lives were saved 'by chance'. Were they? And, without loosing more time, I am coming to my talk with my son.

So, I took my ten-year old youngster in front of me, and said: "Look my love. Lately, so many things have been happening, and at times, especially me, escaped from life threatening events narrowly, by the skin-of-the-teeth. Of course, willingly or unwillingly, you also are following my destiny. Are you scared or something?"

"Not really, maybe because I trust you fully. You are smart and mostly you seem to know what to do. You take care of things immediately, one way or the other. However, if one can look back, say within the past year or so, it is as if the equilibrium is not there. Some bad things are happening and we are constantly moving. Sometimes I am thinking 'why?' but I cannot find any answers. Of course, you know better and I am sure you will find some plausible answers. I trust and love you and don't have any complaints."

"Thank you very much, son, for your trust. I never did and never shall betray you in my power, as long as I am alive. That's for sure. Well, what about having a vacation, we both seem to be badly in need of? All our furniture and things are here now, under one shelter, and it is summer time. What do you say?"

"Of course I would say 'yes'. It could be good for both of us, going away for a while could be a good idea. What is on your mind dad?"

"Well, we have a lot of choices and as you know me well, I usually leave many things up to you. However due to certain special things, I have much more sophisticated travel plans on my mind. Let me tell you first, then if you have objections or some extra plans, we can moderate accordingly. You know in these issues I am quite fair and square."

"You are, dad, you don't need to remind me!"

"OK. I am planning a European trip, including my old home that I have been away from for thirteen years. I am not too nostalgic about it but I guess one visit couldn't hurt, especially at a time when I am re-considering the direction of my life. A lot of relatives have been wondering about you, too. However, the other important thing is this. You know, I am not strictly following my original religion's principles but if you don't have any objection, being born to a Muslim mother and father, I think I ought to ask you

Chapter 29

whether you may have any objection to a 'Sunna', our religious ritual, being performed on you or not. In our old home, we do that between the ages four to eight or nine. You are ten and this summer is almost our last chance. What do you say to the idea?"

"I principally do not care one way or the other. We have both been going to the Unitarian Church in which I like the liberty, freedom of speech and expression, brotherhood and citizenship development beyond the belief systems that are so great. No, that's OK. I think they say circumcision is sanitary too."

"Yes, Souhi, the Jewish people do it at birth, maybe the easiest and cheapest way, and without elaborate public ceremonies. My objection had always been Sunna's being done at the Oedipal stage when, as you know, the child is aware of having a penis and comparing it with that of his parents, friends, etc. Then, one day, you put a specially-decorated cap on his head, some shawl around the body, with a special dress on and a baton in hand, make city tours, as if to say, 'Hey, I have something and I am going to have something done to it, then, similar to an initiation of primitive tribes, I can prove that I am a grown-up boy, then I am going to be a male to perform something!' or something like that.

"So, assume that we shall have it done, let us go to New York, then with a big boat, namely transatlantic, have a delightful ocean voyage to Southampton, England; we can stay in London for about a week, going to palaces, Trafalgar Square, the famous London Bridge, observe the Changing of the Guards, museums and alike, then go to Paris, perhaps that is optional if we still have enough money remaining in our hands, and the most glorious, with the Orient Express go home. There, staying one week or ten days and performing the Sunna, either by air or some way we can come here, to our real home. Or, we can choose a South American tour, or go to the Caribbean or Hawaii. What do you say?"

"Dad, you offer me a dream. Thanks a lot. The other exotic places, too, are very attractive but since I am having French too, I really prefer a European tour, of course, if we can afford it."

"We shall have to afford. You know I work hard and you and I do our housework, cleaning, cooking, everything. We have not been anywhere for the past two years. So, we really should go. Starting right after the July 4 holiday, I shall be on my pedals.

"Furthermore, Souhi, since you are a great kid, an intelligent and quite responsible guy, I have to charge you with some new responsibilities that you should bear since we are all alone. Now, in a few days, before starting the voyage that may take one week or ten days, depending upon the arrangements, you and I shall go to the Second National Bank in Code

A.C. 2084

Island. In the bank, I have one steel case deposited. In it, there is a secret package even I did not open. I will not give it to you now; it carries quite important documents from old times. I did not see them but I am quite sure they are some copies of religious tablets, I gather. I did not steal it from anywhere. They came into my hands, under some special circumstances during this latest Mormon marriage of mine. I cannot say for sure that a kind of omen that we seemed to be followed by is the direct outcome of it or not. As long as I am alive, you don't need to touch it; after I die, or, we do not know the circumstances I could be on the other side of the world, whatever it might be, since I want to keep it on this continent, you shall be in charge of it. Time will give you an indication and show the way, when the right time comes. Make then whatever you deem to be the right decision; that shall be "the" decision. It shall be completely up to you. Beside it, there is also an envelope, a will. You know what a will is, dont' you?"

"Yes, dad, I know, it leaves some instructions to a wife or children after one passes away."

"Precisely so. Then, take it and give it to Mr. Archibald, your friend's lawyer father, and if he is not around for some reason or other, take to any reliable lawyer. Let him take over what had to be done legally. When we shall go there, I will show it to you and give you the second key of the case. I trust you immensely and the only thing in this world I am charging you to do is this job. D' accord."

"Not pleasant things, dad, you are talking about... I mean... You know... (poor kid, nearly crying. It was maybe more than he could carry, but did I have other choice?) Of course I'll do it. I am your son... You were my partner all along in our lives, why couldn't I carry out such a duty? (with a smile) Especially after having Sunna done, shall I not be a growing-up man?"

"Thank you millions, son. You are really great! "Then I gave him a bear hug and said: You are free now. You can walk around six-feet tall and can put our voyage story on air. Start to make your plans. Now, let me meditate!"

Now, the things are as clear as air. I don't need to read and repeat to you any further. That is how my granddad gave to his son the treasures as a will, leaving it up to him. Just for the curiosity of my readers, I know my grandfather, after having a wonderful dream trip to abroad, returned back and lived many years on the continent, left the valuables to his son when he died – by then his son was already married. My dad, that is to say Souhi, remained a number of years on the continent with his beloved wife and had only me as a son. Then, however, one day after his wife (namely, my mother) died in an

Chapter 29

accident and the world map began to get complicated, humans began to shoot themselves in their own legs, dignity turned to indignity, life turned to death, and wisdom turned to taking advantage of others, my father, having some very significant geological events happen in A.C. 2024, in A.C. 2034, when I was exactly ten-years-old, he, the secret steel case, plentiful books and I, came to this beautiful land... You know the rest of the story.

You must be as tired as I am. Let us have a good night's sleep. We have, you know, the literary festival tomorrow. See you there.

Today is Saturday and here is the Annual Literary Festival. The weather is beautiful, the people are full of joy, charmingly chirping, talking and singing like birds. All trains run to the Mega Forest Picnic Field. With light clothes and straw hats on, sandals on the feet, ladies carrying technicolour umbrellas as if they are going to play in the *Madame*

Chapter 30

Butterfly opera, some young people with their write-ups under their armpits, rehearsing like Cicero, all marching silently and happily. The Communication Department had really done a wonderful job erecting some tents, displaying all pieces that are presented and some other extras; next, a lot of refreshment spots under large umbrellas where fresh fruit and fruit juices are continually supplied. From the skies somewhere Wagner's *Weisendong Songs* and *The Chorus of the Sailors* are blowing, then I am sure it will turn to Edward Grieg's *Lyric Pieces* and *Per Gynt Overture*, then Antonin Dvorjak's *Mazyrek, Songs My Mother Taught Me*, ending with the *Violin Concerto op.53 in a*.

Finally, at near noon time, the State Department of Education chief Prof. Edith Plump, flanked by her assistant Brian Ahern and assistant's assistants, all showed up as a group, and, Edith, in her very charming, flowing voice welcomed the hundreds of participants and thousands of listeners to this State fair. Then, I was invited as State chief to the podium to greet the lovely people of the republic and besides welcoming the people to this magnificent event, also promised to read a couple of poems. Then, some celebrities, starting with Edith, began to read some poems that I had already reported to you in our cabinet meeting. Several intellectuals, literate men and women began to read poems, beginning with Chaucer's *From the Prologue to the Canterbury Tales*, Sir Philip Sidney's *My True Love Hath My Heart* and Christopher Marlowe's *The Passionate Shepherd to His Love*. I love his verses, citing:

> Come with me, and be my love,
> And we will all the pleasures prove
> That hills and valleys, dales and fields,

Chapter 30

> And all the craggy mountains yields.
> The shepherd swains shall dance and sing
> For thy delight each May-morning;
> If these delights thy mind may move,
> Then live with me, and be my love.

There, the entire literary faculty students repeated: "Then he live with me, and be my love!".

And, then, from the real master, William Shakespeare, *Now the Hungry Lion Roars*, *Sigh No More, Ladies*, *Under the Greenwood Tree*, *Fear No More* and *Come unto These Yellow Sands*; by John Donne, *The Good-Marrow*; by John Ford, *Oh, No More, No More* (Love is dead; let lowers' eyes – Locked in endless dreams); by Alexander Pope, *Ode on Solitude*; Henry Fielding's *A-Hunting We Will Go*; and William Blake's *A Cradle Song* and *The Divine Image* (To Mercy, Pity, Peace, and Love – All pray in their distress – And to these virtues of delight – Return their thankfulness.) etc., etc.

Of course, I read my two that brought out a lot of enthusiasm and charm. But the real McCoy was the youth itself. They brought out a lot of beauties, free verses and feelings from the very bottom of their hearts. Here are some of the finalists among them:

MY TIRED EYES

> Countless kingdoms
> of glories and defeats of mankind
> had been through
> my tired eyes.
>
> Your inspiring beauty,
> his enticing speech,
> her serpent hair,
> our tested wisdom,
> their life-long accomplishments,
> and,
> my tired eyes,
> could all instantly be placed in an ash-box.
>
> Should life had been eternal,
> drinking love endlessly

A.C. 2084

from the Mountain of Youth;
caressing your silky, bird-feathered hair
playing the rhapsody of ecstasy on our sour lips, and,
squirming our bodies,
becoming "one" in you.
Would have been "To be".
This is the story of Earth Living.

Now, look up to the skies,
and, see that
silent mood and flirty white clouds
seem to be playing the same
touch-and-go, hide-and-seek games endlessly,
in the boundless blues of the Universe,
with the witnesses of the nude bathing Neptune girls
in open seas,
yet to appear to my tired eyes.

Stars: Mythical inhabitants of the galaxy,
some sparkling, some mute,
some telling stories to each other
of Moses, Jesus and Mohammed,
about the inevitable exodus of mankind,
I mean, "Not to be".

This is the story of Sky Living.
Thus at the final countdown,
"To be" equals to "Not to be".
at the unreachable horizons
of the Kingdoms of the Earth and the Skies,
and,
nothing matters anymore
to my tired eyes.
Read by: **Martin Kudal**
L I F E   S T O R Y

The Earth, The Air,
The Fire, The Water,
That was the beginning.

Chapter 30

Love, share and care
Sorrow, grief and worry
Sunrise and sunset
Was the story between.

Now it is about the end of the journey
Faith is more mute and oblivious,
Feelings and memories are frozen
In the dark shadows of
colourless existence.

Thus, the end of the beginning
And, the beginning of the end
All remains to be:
The Earth, The Air,
The Fire and The Water.
Read by: **Liz Walker**

FLYING HIGH

You serpent haired
Ukranian beauty,
always seem to be
flying high in the sky,
you may be reaching the sun.

It was yesterday.

When I touch you,
I feel you, then,
I am happy, sunny, green and warm,
life is so beautiful.

It was yesterday.
When I don't touch you,
The day is rainy, cold, dark,
and gray, like my hair.

What happened to yesterday?

A.C. 2084

I woke up this morning,
and was still alive until
sun came up, and
surrounded me with its warm
and enticing arms, like yours,
in a purple nightgown.

But now,
sun is going down
and the memories
have no meaning.
I'll just lay down,
And die!
Read by: **Philip Jordan**

SORROW

We are driven
to be ordained to love
as the Bible says so.

Yet, my sorrowing heart
does not warm up
with mornings' young light.
The ashes of my ancestors
who had passed through the scented doors,
and seven layers of Heaven
don't appeal to my eyes anymore.

All hours of sadness greet me
I feel more and more sorrow
and desolation in me that depletes
my calm fortitude.
I wake up to my silent screams
suppressed with grief
from my distempered dreams.

As I try to endure
the pains of evil destiny,
life only appears to be perfect

Chapter 30

to the blind.
I am at the end,
where I'd begun.

What happened
to the serenity of cosy solitude,
eloquent sunsets, and
my mother's transcendental beauty?
Promised paradise that
from childhood's hour on
seems to be frozen in time.

We are driven
as everything says so,
to be ordained to die.
Read by: **Susan Calice**

S U R F

Standing over the cliff,
watching the surf,
that pounds against the shore,
mercilessly.

This is the symphony of the seas,
that had been playing the same melodies
for me, for you, for all beings
over and over again,
endlessly.

Now, the tide is moving
out,
and, the past is going with it,
slowly.
But I know it well,
that the tide shall return,
repetitiously,
moon after moon.

Will the past?

A.C. 2084

Read by: **Maurine Soft**

Today is Sunday and here come the finals!

At the honour table, I, Edith and staff, the Honour Certificates were ready, and we called the first runner-up in the Poetry Competition:

"Bobbie Lace, with *Moonchild*".

A young lady in her mid-twenties walked along and climbed to the

Chapter 31

top of the podium and read her masterpiece:

MOONCHILD

Moon Child
I have seen you
Making music for the Gods
I am
Earth Mother.
Of the mysteries,
Knowing much
I have felt you
In flight
Planets dark and distant
We have met
In other eons
Galaxies are but
Small distances for us
We have touched
In dreams of the strange ones
That visit those who wait
We have loved...
Though your search is
Not ended
I am here
We shall meet again
When the Old Gods

A.C. 2084

>Deem us ready.
>Moon Child
>I know you
>I am
>Earth
>My soul aches with waiting
>To touch you
>In this lifetime.

Hundreds of thousands of claps, kisses and hugs and a 'Silver Certificate'. No doubt, she has a good future as a writer and a poet.

Now, the king of the competition, the first prize in the Poetry Section:

"Eshmael Hakkı, with *I'm Lonely!*"

A man in his late thirties, already well-known for his verses, a loner and man of silence, came to the podium and read with his ocean deep, tired voice:

I'M LONELY

>In life's ceaseless ocean
>I am a stowaway
>in an unnamed, rain-soaked ship.

>There is no reason to abandon craft;
>if healer's hands did yield some hope, and,
>my beingness was reserved for something rare
>that I would have outrun death.

>Oh, I wish my mom were here,
>for just a day or two
>until my soul regains its serenity
>of sunny childhood of yesteryears.

>Remembrance of cooking smells,
>long apron strings drawn tight
>of nestling in the rocking chair
>sunlit mornings, crisp white dresses.

>Oh, I wish my mom were here,

Chapter 31

> Just for a day or two
> to grace my days
> to calm my fears
> in wind-blown lightning nights.

Again, hugs, kisses and a 'Golden Certificate' for his achievement.

Now, it is the turn of the first runner-up of the Short Story competition:

"Here is Dorothy Petti, with her *Rainstorm*, as first runner-up."

A young lady in her early thirties, walked in gracefully and read with a deep, enticing voice:

THE RAINSTORM

Professor Isambert hated rainstorms, he hated lightning and thunder. Ever since he was a little boy he had always hated the rain, because he could never go out and play when it rained. Thinking of the rain, he always felt a mysterious fear overwhelm him. But nobody was aware of this fact.

Everybody respected Professor Isambert; few loved him. A man of few words, he hardly ever spoke to anyone, hardly even smiled, not even when his little daughter Isa was in his arms. Maybe the reason was his great love of books, serious books. He poured over dictionaries and philosophic treatises until his eyes were bleary and tired. Then he would shut the blinds and silently sit in the dark, for long periods of time, until ready to face the light again.

All through this past night the rain had splashed against the window panes. The wind had been unusually strong and the large elm that shaded the small house had been almost upr0oted — so violent was the storm. Professor Isambert did not remember a similar storm in all his life, or at least for the past twenty years he had lived in this house. Since his marriage.

His first years of marriage had been relatively happy. They had not brought any change to his way of life because he really lived mostly with himself. His wife, a most gentle soul, accepted him as he was, never complained. And he seemed to find a certain State of happiness when Isa, their daughter, was born to fill the house with shrill baby laughter. And now, Professor Isambert, and the tragedy that had come upon him, suddenly like the rainstorm.

All night he had slept fitfully. Maybe it was the storm, or the rankling thought that Isa lay there in the cold ground because of him. He wondered whether it was good to love one's children. He thought of Isa, had always considered her the dearest thing in his life, but then what had he done for her? They had been like strangers, he had never found time for her, feeling that Isa was well taken care of by Marta. He loved her in his own silent way and was utterly upset when he found out she had fallen in love with Alessio, the stable boy. But he showed no emotion, he was dedicated to his studies, and ran to them when his soul moved him. All his life, he never remembered ever having wept for anybody, not even his mother or his wife, when they died.

Professor Isambert had scrupulously kept his eyes upon whenever a young man brought her home from school or visited her too often. But Alessio just never crossed his mind. He wondered now, why he had been so naive about his daughter. He really should have known better. Had his wife been alive all this would not happened. She would have known...

But he was in his study most of the time, always alone with his books. He was so absorbed all the time, that he never heard or wondered what went on in his house. Whenever he concentrated in his work, nothing else existed. He seemed to forget his daughter completely. He never asked her what she did with herself all day. He knew she was not alone, for she was with Marta, the housekeeper, and Alessio, Marta's son, who did all the heavy chores about the house.

That day, almost six months before, when Isa had come to talk to him, he had simply laughed at her pleadings. "You want to marry Alessio?" he had scoffed, cruelly. Isa's head was lowered, almost in shame. "I love him, father, more than I can say."

"Forget about him. The quicker the better!" Professor Isambert walked up and down the room, his blood rushing to his temples; but wanting to appear calm, he tried to be casual about it. "You don't know what love is, my dear! At twenty, one is in love with love! Forget him and get down to study... You have exams coming up next week and they are more important!"

The next day Alessio and his mother packed their belongings and left; they had been asked to leave as soon as possible. A new maid was engaged to come the following week. Professor Isambert never realised that Isa loved Marta even more than she loved Alessio. Marta had been the first woman to hold her in her arms when she was born. Marta became part of the house when Isa's mother died. She was more than a mother, all affection.

But Professor Isambert, always deeply absorbed in his work, was not aware of what happened outside his room. Marta took care of Isa night and day. She played with the child and entertained her every moment. She made

Chapter 31

up stories for her, since she did not know how to read. She told her some of the fairy tales her own mother had told her way back, expanding them, adding new details every time she repeated one of them. Isa never tired of listening to Marta's stories. The two would sit by the fireplace until the coals died out and the windows showed black shadows. Then Isa would softly tiptoe to her father's study and bid him goodnight, as a matter of ritual, just as she knelt by her bed and said her "Ave Maria", not being able to sleep if she ever forgot her prayers.

When the new maid, Edvige, arrived, the professor found her very efficient. Dinner was always on time, the house spotless. But the atmosphere became heavy, and the silence, at times, oppressive. Isa would withdraw to her room and pass the long hours with her books and correspondence.

Professor Isambert felt that now the problem had been solved. He had not wasted one hour of his time with his daughter. Father and daughter were like two strangers living in the same house; each in his own room, meeting only at the dinner table. The subject of Alessio and Marta was never mentioned. For Professor Isambert, Alessio was something he wanted to forget; for Isa, something she could not forget, no matter how much she tried.

Professor Isambert continued with his calculations and speculations, and soon found himself completely engulfed in a world that was not his daughter's. He never noticed that Isa was pale and sad, growing thinner every day. He was only concerned about her school marks, and since they were good, he really had nothing to worry about.

The shock came when the new maid, Edvige, went to Isa's room to announce that a young man, Alfonso, had come with his buggy to drive her to the village school house. Professor Isambert could still hear the screams ringing in his ears. Edvige was a cool-tempered person at all-times, screaming was so foreign to her character that it aroused him out of his morning stupor. Edvige was the type of woman who wouldn't scream if a lion walked into the house. But she screamed when she saw Isa prostrate on the bed, face green, eyes wide open, staring at the ceiling.

"*Professore! Professore! La signorina e morta!.. Correte... Correte.. (*).*" Edvige ran from room to room. Screaming.

Professor Isambert and the young man at the door rushed to Isa's bedroom, to stand aghast at the spectacle. Professor Isambert would never forget the way his daughter looked at the moment; her long white nightgown on one side of the bed, her hands limp and lifeless. An end of her rosary

---

(*) Professor, Professor; the young girl is dead... Run... Run...

beats peeped from under the pillow... the little silver cross gleaming like a star. He picked up her hand but dropped it quickly, for it gave him a chill. He shuddered in silence, stunned, unable to think or talk, not knowing what to say or do.

Alfonso picked up an envelope which stood against the lamp on Isa's night table and handed it to him, saying brokenly, *"Professore, vado. I'll send you a doctor".* (*)"

By the time the professor finished reading the note he knew that Alessio was back in the picture again. In her note Isa wrote that she "could not go on living without Alessio and his mother". She was lonely and was sorry to take the easiest way out.

When the doctor arrived, it was almost noon. He examined the girl, and signed the death certificate indicating her death by poison, self-administered.

"But how did she ever get the poison?" Professor Isambert asked the doctor, baffled. "There is no poison in this house, and the druggist would have never sold her any, I'm sure!"

"Look!" The doctor picked up a glass from Isa's night table, smelled it, and handed it to the professor. It contained a handful of large wooden kitchen matches, their red heads all washed away. Isa had soaked them in hot water and drunk the liquid.

Professor Isambert wondered at the cunning of some people. If they want poison they can find it even in a simple kitchen match. He was sad, however, and deeply hurt, that his only daughter should be so selfish as to destroy herself and not care about him. He walked slowly to his room and shut the door. He sat there until late, and dark. He was unable to distinguish the contour of Edvige's face when she came into the room.

"Professor," she said meekly, "they are taking the body to the cemetery for the night. She cannot be brought to church!" And Edvige left the room in a hurry to hide her tears. It was the town's custom to keep a dead body overnight in the little chapel of the cemetery, since they did not practice embalming. The body usually remained at the foot of the altar through the night and the following morning, until taken to the cemetery, followed by members of the family and people of the village.

Professor Isambert was well known in the town. He had lived there all his life and was one of its most respected citizens. He was terribly hurt because the parish priest refused to accept the body of his daughter, a suicide. He felt the church should make some sort of exception and this

---

(*) Professor, I am going.

bothered Professor Isambert. It irked and irritated him that the priest could be so firm in his decision! What does a young girl know about the soul when her mind is in turmoil?

When the house was quiet again, Professor Isambert went to bed. No one else was in the house, not even Edvige. He did not undress, but threw himself down on the bedspread in such a stupor that he must have done it almost unconsciously. During the night, the rainstorm came up with such vehemence that it wakened him. The rain and wind made the window panes tremble and it seemed as if they would cave in any moment. He did not know if he was awake or dreaming, but he thought he heard Isa's voice calling: *"Papa!... Papa!... Apri... Apri... Apri la porta!"* And then again *"Papa! – Papa!"* (*)... It seemed so real he went to the window to peer out. The rain was falling mercilessly and the trees were swinging in the wind. He could bear the steady downpour and then a big splash as if someone were throwing bucketfuls of water from the window above.

He could hear the shutters banging, and that terrible moaning over and over. He could hear her voice calling: *"Papa! Papa!"* What a weird night it was. He wandered through the house, going to the housekeeper's room, and to Isa's room, but of course no one was there, the house was empty. He went back to bed. This time he undressed in a hurry and began to feel better when he was under the covers. He did not put a light on because the lightning was coming in with sudden flashes so that even the darkest corner of the room became bright.

In his mind he still heard Isa's voice outside the window; but he knew he must have been dreaming. He decided to remove all thought of Isa from his mind, thinking of other things. Soon he fell asleep.

It was ten after seven when he woke up. Dawn was clear; no clouds in the sky – they must have all emptied out during the night. He got up and began to dress, searching his closet for his black Sunday suit, the formal one he always wore on special occasions. Today they were to bury Isa and all the people from the nearby villages would be there since they all loved Isa. He wondered how long the funeral would be. He felt a great urge to see things in their normal State again. He wanted to get back to his work and forget all these terrible happenings.

Suddenly he heard Edvige's voice from the street below. Again she was screaming: *"Professore! Professore! Correte!"* Wondering what could have happened now, he made quickly for the door. Edvige was on the ground, weeping and sobbing aloud and pulling her hair in wisps. Beside her, with

---

(*) (Dad!... Dad!... Open... Open... Open the door!..... Dad! Dad!)

her gown in shreds and smeared with caked dirt, her hair tangled about her face, was the body of Isa.

Professor Isambert could not at first understand what had happened. He remembered the sound of Isa's voice crying in the night; a sound he thought was the product of his overwrought, imagination. But it had not been so, evidently. Isa had not been dead, but in a coma; and during the night had awakened, and had made her way back home. She had called repeatedly, trying to gain admittance, but in vain. No one had answered her calls.

Professor Isambert felt a sharp pain in his stomach. He could not breathe and was beginning to choke. Feeling he would fall any minute, he sat down on the doorstep. Now why did these things have to happen to him, he wondered.

Professor Isambert was a law-abiding man, a scholar, a hard worker, he never gave anyone any trouble. He was happy and satisfied in his world of books and numbers. He was methodical, never late for dinner, never missed Mass, never kept anyone waiting.

And yet, here he was, the cause of his daughter's death. Twice he had killed her: The first time when he did not believe in the sincerity of her love; the second, when he did not answer her cries.

He bent down beside the body and brushed her hair from her face. Her hair was filled with raindrops and her face had a peaceful look, but her hands were clenched together as if holding something. He opened one of the hands and found a broken piece of rosary which he took from her and put in his pocket. It would be something for him to pray with, the last thing she had touched before she died. He would keep it as a sort of talisman. He fixed her wet garment as best he could; realizing how clumsy he was with women's clothes. Suddenly he heard voices coming up the winding mountain road.

The people of the village were arriving in readiness for the funeral. At the head of the procession was Father Adolfo, the parish priest. He had come to take Isa's body to the church, since she was not considered a suicide any longer. He would see to it that she had a fine burial, like her mother's.

Edvige helped Father Adolfo pick up the wasted remains of the poor young girl. They carried her inside and laid her on her bed. They folded her hands across her breast. Edvige combed her hair, dividing it neatly in the centre, and then made two plaits, one on each side, and brought them forward and crossed the ends on her bosom.

Edvige had to stop to wipe tears of perspiration from her face. Then she straightened out the body, fastening the feet together. She wanted to make poor Isa look as pretty as she could. The funeral would be a solemn Mass

Chapter 31

and the entire village would attend.

Professor Isambert went into the living room and sat down in one of the deep easy chairs. People came quietly to express their sympathy, as was the custom. The men uncovered their heads and the women wept. Everything resumed a normal air, just like all funerals. In a week, or a month, it would all be forgotten. Work would be resumed and everybody would be busy again. Isa would become a legend, and all the mothers would be able to warn their children, if ever they were to fall in love.

Professor Isambert got up and walked over to the window. He saw the clouds beginning to gather and the sky getting dark again. He prayed to God it would not rain. He felt dizzy and his stomach was empty. He had to go to church and listen to the litanies.

All that he could tolerate, but not the rain. He had never hated the rain as much as now. After the funeral, Professor Isambert went to his room, undressed and got into bed. He could hear voices in the street; the sounds seemed to hush as they came nearer the house. Were they talking about him? He turned over and buried his face in his pillow. What must I do, he asked himself. "I don't think I can go on this way. Why did all this have to happen to me?"

Soon the voices died away. He heard a wind come in from the trees outside his window. He got up to open the window and feel the cool air on his face, then returned to bed and again buried his face in the pillow. He stopped thinking about his daughter. Slowly he fell asleep.

During the night he heard the trees again, moaning, but went back to sleep. In the morning the wind was still blowing and he lay awake a long time, before he remembered that his daughter was dead. He stood by the window thinking of Isa. He could not forget her image, her cries, he thought of himself and his grief. He saw the sun slowly appear behind the distant houses of the village. He walked over to the mirror and looked at himself, seeing a haggard face, eyes bleary from lack of sleep. He wanted to break down and cry, but he hated to do that. It seemed too puerile to cry. He wanted to face life as it appeared and keep calm all the time.

That was the reason he must go back to his work and bury himself in it. Nor to think, not to weep, nor to go mad he must do that. It was the only way he could forget Isa, forget the sound of her voice ringing in his ear over and over. "Yes," he said to himself. "I must get down to work." He picked up a book, opened it at the centre and sat by the window. He read avidly, but did not understand what he was reading. Then the sun streamed in through the window, golden and strong. He felt surprised, as he said to himself. "It will not rain today... I know..."

A.C. 2084

Applause, shaking hands, hugs, kisses and the 'Silver Certificate' in the Short Story Competition.

Then, the final came, the biggest and the most prestigious:
The winner of the Short Story Competition:
"Soliman Mert, with *The Quest for Pork Chop Hill.*"
A young man in his mid-thirties walked solemnly and took his place on the podium:

THE QUEST FOR PORK CHOP HILL

> ... *the killing of the enemy with whatever accompanying ritual, is performed to consolidate and reaffirm the existing social order.*
> Robert J. Lifton

My name is Walter... Walter M. Gattell to be precise... I was born and raised in Chelsea, Massachusetts, on the hills that face the Navy Shipyard with a silent serenity, feeling the salty water of deep oceans on my lips all the time. The Great Bridge always sounded to me like a rainbow, a big one, emerging from one infinity and running into another. My birthdate is A.C. October 11, 1928; that means, now, I am now quite over forty years old, balding, and possessing a whitish halo. That gives me a rather distinct, professional look that I like. I am the only child of my Mom and Dad. I never knew why my parents did not want to have more children, particularly in those days. It was a matter of pride to have a family, meaning a lot of *bambinos* and *bambinas*. I believe my mother might have felt her forthcoming fate; or my father, who had suffered a back injury in his construction job, might have developed an impotency, or something like that. I shall never know.

By virtue of my birth date, I am a Libra, and as my gypsy fortune-teller once had interpreted to me, I am supposed to be a determined, well-balanced and just person. I am jesting when I am saying 'Gypsy' about her. She is a well-trained astrologer from Cambridge, Massachusetts. Since the exact hour of my birth is not known, my zodiac sign either reads "wisdom – discovery of deeper elements after intellectual knowledge wearies," and, "a perpetual growth through awareness of basic meanings of existence," or, "representing a dwelling above and beyond the normal stress of existence. Superlative mental vision. Quiet inner strengths..."

Chapter 31

Well, after all, I am supposed to live up to the expectations of my seventh southern sign, at least to symbolise the equilibrium between the psychic zone and materialistic universe. Peh, all good stuff, but let us read now of the evolution and the outcome of my individual life story. Then, you draw your own conclusions.

I do not know my parents' astrological signs or their exact birthdates, yet in my home, during my childhood, everything was quiet. As a matter of fact, too quiet. Even arguments between the two grown-ups were low-pitched, even-tempered, unemotional. My darling cat, Tiger Baron, never did learn how to meow. I hardly heard him purring. Oh, one thing was interesting; we did not have a time clock at home either. My mother was the time clock. Sunrise, school time, lunch, sunset – you name it – were arranged with her accurate intuition. I don't think she ever needed to be repaired.

Helas! The faith proved that I was wrong. One day our time clock stopped, I mean, eternally. I was nine years old. One afternoon, as I returned from school, I noticed all the neighbours crowding in our small, shadowy kitchen. Through and between their legs I noticed my mother's half-naked body lying straight, and motionless. The oven was half-open, and there was a strange, garlic-like odour in the air. My father, with a long, tired face and deep, frozen blue eyes, cried out, "Oh, Walter! Mom is gone. Heart attack!"

The memories of those silent, bloody moments remained indelibly etched in my mind throughout my life. "My Mom is gone... She is dead..." I remember burying my face in my dad's chest, sobbing and succumbing into our home's usual silence. I do not remember observing any wake or burial. God is my witness, I do not. I am sure she had merged into heaven, instantly. Perhaps through the Great Bridge. Could she?

The growing-up years of my youth had the same vagueness, fuzziness, and lack of clarity. I am positive I attended school, regularly. I made friends, went to church and Sunday school, definitely observed Thanksgiving Day, Christmas, birthdays and other important events. But I can swear to Saint Thérèse of Lisieux that I do not have any clear vision or emotional remembrance of any particular event or happening. And believe me, I am not an absent-minded person either, otherwise how could I have entered Boston University?

The only absolute remembrance, I recall, however, was that my dad, who had chronic emphysema and a number of heart attacks, still kept smoking heavily in spite of the doctors' warnings. A few days before collapsing while climbing the stairs, in his final moments, he silently murmured to me: "Son, you are grown now, so you can take it better. Your mother did not die of a heart attack. She committed suicide – with gas."

Then I was mad like a bull. I was angry at my father who kept the secret away from me all the time. I was mad at my mother too: How could do this to me? Didn't she love me? How could she leave me behind without a time-clock, if she had a choice? What about God? A door opening to heaven or hell? Willpower or wickedness? A choice or a faith? Is there anyone there to hear me? God, you narcissistic God, mute God, wait for me. One day when I reach you, I shall challenge you for a debate on this subject.

From that point on, I felt, my personality changed. A scary-cat became an aggressive, lion-hearted person. Come on, let us fight. Reason? Just look around. You will not find any difficulty to justify it. It is a mad, mad world. There are enough subhuman politicians who could push enough brand-new ideologies. Dreams to surface the inherent aggression of mankind, pardon me, animalkind, and there shall be bloodshed. Let us kill. The more you kill, the more your nation will be proud of you. Who is the referee in this roller-ball? God? Here we go again! When He blows His whistle, we go – one way or the other.

That is how I got involved in the Korean War. Year A.C. 1950, I left my college education behind and became a patriot by joining the marines. What glory! Hallelujah! I had my basic training in Tennessee, two months in a boot camp and I think I performed miracles. Before flying over to Korea, I finished an infantry course in Japan in just six weeks instead of a regular ten-week schedule. I was specifically trained as a map sergeant. That dissatisfied me somehow for I had a thirst for blood – for active combat. Nevertheless, I was going to be in the front line. That counts. Watch me.

I was one of the one thousand and two hundred men comprising the First Battalion's Seventh Rifle Division. We were approximately one-third of the 32nd Infantry Division that comprised about three thousand marines. Our rifle division was composed of four companies, two hundred and fifty to three hundred men in each. The four subdivisions were 'Able', 'Baker', and 'Charlie' – those three fighting groups were equipped with light 105 mortars – and 'Dog Cop' Supportive Group which I belonged to.

My primary job was to take a logistically-designed map of the area, along with a small group of marines, to infiltrate behind the enemy lines, sometimes in daylight, supported by an air attack but mostly after dark. We were to advance ahead as far as possible, then sit unobstructively in a cave or at the top of a tree until sunrise. We would get out our shell like a turtle, look around, and try to locate some strategically important areas: Ammunition depots, supply and manpower locations, even noting mine fields. It was important to observe whether there were anti-personnel or anti-tank, M6, M12, or M15 mines. If you are lucky enough you will identify them, otherwise you may be trapped and – boom!

Chapter 31

I recorded my observations on the map immediately, as if we were in a hurry to get back, scribbling afterwards. I had no need of any sophisticated instruments, for many of the maps were made by aerial photography and the logistics division of the Korean army, if there was one around. Nonetheless, I had to carry a pair of powerful night binoculars, a compass, crayons, and a metallic ruler that could give approximate distance of an object form afar if handled skilfully.

Our headquarters, not a secret anymore, were about ten miles west of Port Hungnam and a few miles away from Kimpo Airfield. It is obvious that whoever controlled the airfield could also control the strategic roads for supplies and manpower alike. This is why in a few square miles, those hills named 347; 2,000, Old Belly, Bloody Ridge and Pork Chop Hill were named after their heights or the way they looked from the air.

All those have been, at some time or other, a stage of bloody, savage fights that had succumbed to history silently — as my mother's death — as thousands and thousands of men from both sides rained their blood, whether red or yellow, into the soil. The outcome? Let history be witness by some other intellects, in their warm, fire-placed colonials while on sabbatical leave, playing with their spoiled kids. Let us go into action!

I would like to add another important aspect of our military structure. Our division, at times, was composed of Ethiopian and Turkish troops, and that was a great relief. Emperor Haile Selassie had sent over very talented, well-trained combat troops of his own Royal Guard as well as having brilliantly and gallantly trained young Turkish soldiers and officers with us. Even the Chinese knew that. When those friendly foreigners were with us (it is funny to say 'foreigners,' as we say in the United States, for we all were foreigners in this jungle), it is very rare that they would attack. Many times I had witnessed perhaps twenty or twenty-five Turkish soldiers storming into the Chinese lines of one hundred and fifty or two hundred men, bayonets pointing up the sky, shouting, "Allah, Allah!" (Muslim name for God). They would return quickly with a few prisoners, laughing uproariously, and with no casualties. War was a game for them — a pleasant one.

I had never seen a Turkish soldier. As a matter of fact, I had never seen a Turk, but I had heard the myth about them. A splendid amalgamation of ferocious fighter and soft-hearted comrade, a close friend to be trusted. They would share their last ounce of tobacco with you, never complain about the shortcomings of everyday needs such as hunger, thirst, or tiredness. Most importantly, in a combat situation they would never turn their backs to the enemy. In short, they were our security blanket.

I had the opportunity to be very close to one of the Turkish sergeants during my last mission to Pork Chop Hill that I will detail. His name was Omar. He was educated in Robert's College in Istanbul City, therefore he spoke English fluently. One day I asked him all the questions that had been accumulating in my mind regarding their heritage and attitude about the war. As usual, he released a very comfortable smile from his cigarette-burnt lips, and said:

"Kardash," (brother) I don't have to repeat the historical facts, primarily based upon the geographical importance of Asia Minor. Thorndike and others document it well. Since the Darius the Great (I) of old Persia, all great commanders of ancient times crossed the Bosphorus from one side to the other, as Alexander the Great of Macedonia came to the famous Gordian knot (blind knot), to prove his mystic power as he cut it with his sword. Xerxes of Persia also tried to do his best. That was the last attempt from the East. As you know, the Romans took over for centuries, and the Ottoman Turks reached eastern Anatolia by A.C.1071 and established the Ottoman Empire in A.C. 1453 by Mohammed the IInd, conquering Constantinople (Istanbul city) from the Byzantines.

"Then we had it for a little more than the last five and one half centuries. Winston Churchill, in A.C. 1915, as a navy lieutenant in the British Navy, tried to pierce through the Dardanelles with no success. So it is a land of history and culture, and, as anyone else may feel the same way about his homeland, we love it. We are ready for any invasion, any time. We have that survival instinct, perhaps. Thus, fighting when and if necessary had been a way of life." Needless to say he was giving me a history lesson, unprepared and unmolested.

"According to Muslim religion," he proudly added after puffing from his cigarette three times, "if one dies in war, he goes to heaven. So, one has no fear of dying. No man returns home wounded, hit by a bullet from behind. Otherwise, cowardice or similar condemnation shall be carried on from generation to generation, and you cannot live like that in my home. If you look at the trenches, in and out, you cannot see one single Turkish body out of soul, unless they are hit in the forehead or chest.

"In addition, whatever strength we have in our family structure, namely, respect for our elders, or father, or whoever has the position, is carried through the military, blindly. In other words, your commanding officer, or any high-ranking comrade, is your father figure. Authority and obedience are delegated to him automatically, with no question or qualms in your mind. If the commander dies, then the second oldest in command takes over the post, like the oldest son in the family. If things are in confusion, and there is a disaster or blast, the leadership is lost. Then, one just looks around, out of

Chapter 31

the corner of his eye, and someone who is a natural leader, would emerge and say "Let's go!" That's all it takes. He is a new commander. Very simple, isn't it?" He smiled again.

Then, his brown eyes gazed into the depths of Pork Chop Hill, where the approaching sundown was laying its shades, inch by inch, over the dark, green terrain like a silky, grey, tiny veil, mesmerising our senses first, then thickening and darkening constantly into a black mask, impregnating us to the bloody games. Hello, gladiators, jungle rule is starting again. From now on you may live on your last chance. And believe me, you can count on any single breath you take and any single pulse you tick. Good luck.

* * *

"OK, Walter, Omar, Dick and Bill," whispered Lieutenant Clark, our unit commander, "get ready for tonight's mission. You have twenty minutes to move out. Bill is in charge. You know how much they cost us. I expect you guys back, at the latest, half an hour after sunrise. Yellow Dog."

'Yellow Dog' was our motto for good luck. So far, on this spot, we had had seven missions to get Pork Chop Hill back, but those damn mortars. So, this one was a big undertaking, maybe the last chance. I never understood why General Troudeau, who was in charge of local operations, had never utilised jointly the 25th Infantry Division and other supplementary forces to sweep up that bloody hill; perhaps General Almond, commander-in-chief, wanted to keep the 17th Regiment intact for other future plans, but you know in war you don't ask any questions, you only try to do the job which you are assigned to. So, we got ready. That included darkening our faces with dirt and charcoal, putting leaves and parts of branches randomly all over our bodies. Sometimes I wondered if we, a bunch of imported Indians, were playing hide-and-seek games with funny feathers on our heads and toy guns in our hands. I wish we were.

As I described earlier, I did not have any heavy equipment with me, other than simple tools. In war, each mission is a new experience and everyone involved mostly functions by intuition rather than knowledge. Sometimes you may combine the two. For example, suppose you see enemy fire and you hear the sound. You count the seconds between the two, and, if you multiply the result with three hundred and forty, it would give you the approximate distance between you and the origin of fire. Sound travels three hundred and forty meters per second, slower of course than the light speed; if you multiply by a thousand, the distance is that many feet.

Just the same, if you do not know how high you are climbing, the inclination of your toes in your boots as a certain degree could give you an approximate altitude. Sometimes you develop expertise from your pulse rate or deep breathing. To use a flashlight, even a masked one, is an absolute no-no. Previous troops had suffered many unnecessary casualties simply due to sparkling flashes from cigarettes lit in the dark of the night. The Chinese mercilessly gunned those fireflies.

Team leader Bill gave us the last instructions, like a referee in a boxing match gives to two competitors who appear to listen but do not hear because their minds are preoccupied. We were rather preconditioned from what we had learned or had experienced before, tinged with new emotions, a kind of fear of the unknown.

Bill was a funny guy. It was coincidental that he, too, came from the Bay State although we did not know each other before. When he was fourteen, his parents had left him on the streets of Everett and moved to Philadelphia, so he had learned all the tricks of street fighting and gangs, everything right from the street school. He was as smart as a fox and as cool as reptile. He always wore a serious, but funny-looking smile on his face, joked a lot, and finished his speech saying "OK clowns, let's go!"

Clowns, though, were his special hobby; in his free time, whatever it meant in our situation, he used to make clown dolls either from newspapers or a cloth's remnants, whatever was available. His masterpiece was that of a Chinese Clown. That, he said, when he was going home, he could hang at the entrance of his bedroom to sleep better. He always hoped to rejoin his wife who had deserted him due to his drinking, and his small boy who maybe a marine too, one day, like his daddy, he hoped.

Dick was a farm boy from Tennessee whom I had met in basic training. I do not recall that he would initiate any conversation, but he was an easy-going guy, an amazing person and as straight as a spear. You could talk to him and confide in him; he would listen to you endlessly, and at the end he would just pat your back, that was all. That meant you were OK in his eyes. His answer to the problem of war was his Thompson submachine gun, with which he was a real expert. He was the best sharpshooter I had ever met. Just the same for Omar. He also could use his automatic rifle as easy as a slingshot. How many times had I felt like hiding behind his rocky body when I had really been scared. Fortunately this had not occurred too often.

In the chill of that silent night, our little team began to move. When you start to walk in the dark, you walk with your ears. Any slight noise caused by a falling leaf, the hissing of a snake, a smooth-blowing breeze, or the chirping of a bird could be interpreted as an ambush. It is very easy to become paranoid, especially if and when such occurrences in the jungle are repetitious or if they are interrelated. And when one loses his cool, then

Chapter 31

one is the victim of his own fear and becomes more susceptible to making mistakes, not only for himself but the entire team. So, be careful.

Our walking tactic, in structure, was that of a diamond shape. Bill was at the far front, Omar at the right flank, Dick at the left; myself at the hind, six yards apart. At the start, we took three steps forward, then stopped; one more step and stop again, and start all over again the same. A silent observer might believe that we were chocolate soldiers playing a war ballet with no background music than of Korean jungles that were mute and blind inhabitants of nature.

With that very monotonous and nerve-wrecking strategy, we advanced almost twenty or twenty-five minutes distance. Then, the first alarm signal came out the sarcastic moon with a broken face, smeared behind the clouds for a moment or two. In the jungle, as a rule, we do not like to see the moon and would rather choose moonless nights for an expedition. We also do not like it if a road suddenly widens or narrows too much without trees or rocks around, to be able to use them if and when necessary, just in case. Sensing a kind of danger approaching, Bill signalled us by raising his right hand straight up twice, changing walking tactics to caution: Two steps forward and stop, one step forward and stop, then start all over again, with a slower pace. It still felt like a ballet.

As we followed a tortuous path for about seven or eight minutes – you know how minutes are hour-long in those situations – we approached a corner with heavy trees hanging on the right and a small, square hill at the left. This, to my recollection, was not recorded on the map. Bill turned his head and, reading the same question on my face through pure intuition, he raised his left arm straight in the air. This meant extreme caution: Stop, no walking anymore until further signalling.

I began to feel my nose, ears and eyes as if were on the same line: the human antenna system is trying to pierce through and read the darkness. I also felt my heart beating in my mouth. Strange enough, I smelt the same funny odour that I had felt before, when my mother was lying on the kitchen floor, and listening to my surroundings now was much the same as listening to her heartbeat.

And then, in a split second the expected happened: That rock opened up with a barrage of mortar fire that knocked Bill instantly flat on his face, without giving him a chance to say his prayers. They suddenly flooded Dick with deadly bullets as he screeched with an unearthly sigh and fell. While falling, his Thompson vommited two scattered, aimless shots at the ever sarcastic moon and some scared starts behind the clouds. That was it. I was stunned and ready to turn back and run. I suddenly felt Omar, gently touching my shoulder and whispering "Kneel down and don't move!"

I did what he said, but I thought my heart was in my mouth and not working for me anymore. After two minutes that seemed like two centuries – what a murderous waiting – two small figures who I was sure were our assailants, cautiously began to move out from the 'rock' that was their hideout, a disguised tank or jeep took a few steps forward. Then I heard Omar's whisper again: "Walter, throw your hat and equipment, whatever is handy to your left as far as possible – now!"

As I followed his order automatically and things touched the ground, two little guys opened another round over those objects. At the same time, Omar's automatic rifle responded with a series of bullets, like a chorus line over those more visible targets. They both fell instantly like sacks of potatoes. We had exchanged thus far two for two, and there were four dead bodies in the middle and four souls wherever they might be.

After another two-century wait, I again felt Omar's soft hand on my shoulders and calm voice, however with a little bit higher pitch: "Are you alright Walter? Come on, let's get up!" With very cautious steps we approached the 'big rock' from two different angles and it turned out to be a disguised jeep. After searching the inside carefully, Omar asked me to help him carry the dead corps of the two Chinese soldiers' to the back seat of the jeep.

While doing these things like a somnambulist, I observed his face; his peaceful smile was still there, looking as if nothing had happened. While sitting in the driver's seat, Omar advised "Let's wait a little bit more until the things are settled." What answer could I give? He was the commanding officer. I silently agreed. And, when the moon with its ugly shape escaped – perhaps ashamed – behind the clouds, Omar murmured "Let's go!"

I took a deep breath for we finally were going back to our lines to share our sorrow, accept defeat or misfortune, and look for another venture, but why were we leaving our comrades' dead bodies behind and carrying the Chinese? Oh, no, Omar was driving the jeep toward the Chinese lines. Sensing my feelings, he added with a soothing smile: "Our mission is just starting, Walter. Don't talk, just take it easy." He obviously was taking chances but at the same time playing the most courageous guerrilla tactic that I had ever seen. Now we were in a Chinese patrol jeep, two mannequin bodies sitting behind, thus not needing to be spotted and ambushed as spies.

I wish I knew what was in his mind at that moment and what possible adventures we might encounter. Nothing really exciting happened. We drove for about fifteen to twenty minutes, circling around the hill up to a point that appeared to be a good hideout for us: a small flat area, behind the

Chapter 31

trees, facing the valley. After camouflaging the vehicle somewhat, Omar whispered: "Come on Walter, let's take a nap. We have quite a bit to do in the morning" and, without expecting an answer from me, he shrank to his corner, covered his face with his hat, falling asleep in less than five minutes. I swear, my eyes remained open without a blink until the first warning of the Sun God when Omar opened his eyes and smiled: "Good morning. Come on Walter, let's us start to work. I'll cover you!"

I did not believe that I had any adrenalin left in my body. So, I acted very cool and did my job. Checking through the horizons one hundred and eighty degrees, I spotted very important conglomerations, overly covered unnatural terrain that I noted carefully on my map. Surprise! My adrenalin was flowing again, and I was in a kind of ecstatic State like that of a schoolboy who was doing an excellent home assignment and enjoying it.

As I gave a "that's all" signal to Omar, he began to drive the jeep back, however with a much more serious face; his automatic rifle resting on his knees, watching with eagle eyes almost three hundred and sixty degrees around. At times we slowed down, other times we moved faster; at one point, at about fifty or sixty yard away, we saw three Chinese soldiers gazing at us, perhaps trying to identify the vehicle. Then Omar raised his hand and gave a friendly finger wave in the air as if we were returning from a promenade. We had one sad but another patriotic duty when we came to our last night's massacre place where we exchanged the dead Chinese bodies from our back seat, replacing them with those of our comrades. God bless them.

As we were approaching our headquarters, I felt my heart, beating in its right place. We were immediately surrounded with friendly faces. Sergeant Omar gave a standing salute and a brief message to overtly anxious Lieutenant Clark: "Sir; mission is completed with success. I am sorry, we gave two casualties. Bodies are in the jeep. Walter will give his report to you directly, Sir!" He turned around with solid steps and went to the group of marines who were having their typical breakfasts of canned soup, crackers and coffee.

After I gave my report and necessary documents to Lieutenant Clark, I also came back and sat next to Omar. He was sharing his meal with our comrades, however in a solemn silence. His noble features were frozen, his sweet smile gone, as he sipped his coffee slowly. I wondered whether his mind was replaying the events of the night before, however this time in its silent movie version. A light rain had already begun to fall. A few drops seemed to crystallise at the corners of Omar's eyes, but I could not distinguish whether they were sprung from his heart or dropped from the sky.

A.C. 2084

I was able to put the pieces together and give an accurate logistics report to my commanding officer who immediately wired it back to our artillery. Within an hour's time another bloody attack had started, yet this time with almost no resistance, we secured Pork Chop Hill. Almost all enemy resources and supplies were destroyed by our mortars, combined with a very aggressive air support, as if General Troudeau had bet his life on that hill. However, another unanswered mystery of the Korean War had been on my mind that, after we captured the legendary Hill, the general gave the orders for our complete withdrawal with its total destruction. We did flatten it down to the ground, making it no man's land. Why? We shall never know.

After that mission, I never saw Omar again. Strange, no one talked about him either. I assumed he had asked for a transfer, since I do not believe that heroic man would die in a war.

The ordeal lasted six more months before the peace agreement was reached and I returned home. Among many, one of the most significant memories of mine were of that mission and one precious gift: the Chinese clown, Bill's masterpiece. It hangs at the entrance of my bedroom; every morning and night he smiles at me, as if he wants to tell me how ignorant we are about the relativity of our lives: The meaningfulness and meaninglessness of our existence. It makes me feel ashamed also that not only I am a part but also a hero of this destructive so-called human society."

Again long applause, a standing ovation, congratulations and the 'Golden Certificate' for the Short Story Competition.

So, that was the end of a glorious, long, long day. So long.

After those facts, I decided what to do. Everything shall be resolved in the way that it should be and should have been throughout the human history: In peace and brotherhood. *Cae'sar's right should belong to Caius Julius Cae'sar*. No cardinal or bishop killings, no shaming the Pope or the church, blood-shedding, international intrigues, 17-miles-a-minute speedy flights and codes that be dissolved at the expense of

Chapter 32

Finale

human dignity and sorrow.

Thus, I called President Arthur, the head of the Latter-day Saints Church, and gave the good news. I had felt that something was going to be done otherwise I should not have made this decision soon; maybe tonight may be tomorrow, something terrible might have happened or not, I don't know.

"Reverend Arthur, this is Ismailov, the President. How are your Sir?"

"Thank you. This indeed is an honour your majesty. (He always called me in these terms. A very polite, courteous and kind man!) I don't need to congratulate a Statesman like you for the job that you always do wonderfully. The literary competition, I mean. What can I do for you or for our State?"

"I am going to give you delightful news. News that shall break the hearts from joy and tears that will spill over the ashes of the millions of people's ash-boxes to glorify the truth and human dignity. A celestial union between your souls and the forgotten magic spell of ..."

"You mean... You mean..."

"Yes, I mean the Moroni Plates. God make you believe that I did not know it was in my possession throughout my life, amongst the belongings of my late dad. I have been sensing something for some time. I finally broke my own code – I opened my father's belongings, the steel briefcase and found the gift. Still unwrapped though. It will be another Virgin Birth for you! What glory it is. It is yours but also belongs to all god men and women in the world to share God's glory, infinity and eternal love. Your church is its eternal place. So, if you are available tomorrow evening, that is to say Monday, if we are making history, October the 11th, 2084, my birthday coincidentally, I would like to present it to you, with honours."

"Excellency, I am in ecstasy and astonished by your great humanity and astral existence. I am crying, I am crying from the bottom of my heart; my tears spill from the depths of great oceans. Oh, glory, glory to God. Well, tomorrow evening we were gathering from our four Stakes. We had two 'Calling Marriage' ceremonies and a 'Baptism of the Dead' ritual scheduled. Hmmm. If we start at 6 p.m., I believe we shall be ready at about 9 p.m. for that glorious moment. I am immediately informing our councillors, naturally the presiding bishop and whoever I can gather from the First Council of Seventy. By the way, I know that you love music very much and it has to exist around everything beautiful, and since after the ceremonies we cannot play our religious music, what would you like, what music should play in the background for that glorious moment?"

"Sir, if you do not have any objection, I could make about a three-to-five minute speech that is good enough for me and the rest belongs to you and your people. When I start to talk, I propose either Beethoven's *9th Symphony* and the finale of *Fidelio*; or maybe Tchaikovsky's *1812 Overture* or Verdi's *Nabuccho's The Chorus of Slaves*.

"I would have preferred the *9th Symphony* due to its extravagancy, more than that of in *Eroica*, the movements containing the genius' most beautiful, human and graceful movements and orchestral strains.

"Listen to the Chorus: Prestissimi – in D Major:

> Seid emsehlungen, Milionen & o.
> (O ye millions, I embrace ye.)

"The military instruments' very noisy beats. And, toward the close, with the abrupt introduction of 4 bars, maestoso's return, and a mighty finish from the mighty chorus:

> Tochter aus Elisium
> Freude, schöner Götterfunken!
> Götterfunken!
> (Daughter of the starry realm
> Sing we of the Heaven-descended!
> Heaven-descended!)

Chapter 32

"I would have preferred *Fidelio*, due to its perfect purity, Florestan and Leonara (no longer as Fidelio) joining in a duet:

> O namenlose Freude
> (O nameless Joy)

That is the very ecstasy of happiness, joining together, as you and the Moroni are doing.

"I would have preferred Tchaikovsky's *1812 Overture, Op.49*, due to it's glorifying celebration, though a slow, melancholic start, perhaps mourning for the death, then mounting to a strong sense of existence, with raptures of enthusiasm, exuberance, excitation if not ecstasy.

"There is also a sentimental memory part of it too. Souhi, Sr., the father of my grand-father, in Old Rica at the time of the 200th celebration of that republic was in Boston. He had cited to his father, as my grandfather writes in his memoirs, as follows:

"It was downtown Boston. A city of intellectuality, music and grace. We met at the Public Garden first, then walked along Boylston St., then Memorial Drive to gather at the open field, at the side of the Charles River. The river which we had other memories of too, living at the other end of it, our house was just beside it in the town of Winchester. Our backyard directly opened to the river that was almost a small pond, and in good weather with a pedal-boat, I and my dear dad Souhi used to sail on it. The fish used to swim almost at the shore. One day, being a beginner, I was trying to fish, a line in my hand, with no result of course. My father seeing my sullen face and hours of exacerbation, came with a bucket in his hands and plunged it in the waters of the river and brought out three or four fish, fluttering in and out, forwarded them to me: 'Son, here are your fish!', smiled and went away. Anyway, Arthur Fiedler, who had conducted the Boston Pops Orchestra for 50 years, was going to give a 'farewell concert' on the night of A.C. July 4, 1976, just six years prior to Orwell's world. The entire orchestra was on a small ship, full of lights and ornaments, flowers. The colourful explosions of the sky-rockets were creating a scenery of a real paradise. About 500,000 people, hand-in hand, tears in their eyes, were watching and listening to beautiful melodies that were spilling into the waters, right under Longfellow Bridge.

"Fiedler, with snow white hair and still very dignified body, in his eighties, in his black formal-ware, baton in his hand and with an angel-like smile, first

A.C. 2084

played the famous "*March*" from Sousa that was his favourite at his historical theatre building where he used to mesmerise the people, all the time. As the ship began to take off, inch-by-inch, from the harbour, there came the "*1812 Overture*" with its celebrating battle-field tarrakas and cannon fires, embedded with, here and there, some callings from the '*Marseillaise*':

"Allons, enfants de la Patrie,
Le jour de gloire est arrivé!"
"The children of the Country, let's go,
The day of the glory has just come!"

ending with triumphant bells and a mixture of sounds that conveyed us to an ecstasy.
"It was an unforgettable scene and Fiedler, just prior to his departure from this world, had written history."

"Well, last but not the least, I would highly have preferred Verdi's *Nabukko*, and particularly *The Chorus of Slaves*, sung by the Jewish prisoners of war, along the Euphrates River, circling around the fire, and singing the song of yearning, longing for their mother-land. I had never heard in my life such low-pitched sound bouquets, with a Wagnerian depth and supernatural spirit, wishing and praying, particularly in the form of the chorus, symbolising centuries-long human suffering, wish and hope, embracing me from the bottom of my soul and vibrating so vividly up to my tears. It may carry a particular importance, especially for you, since the opera takes place in your original ascendance place: Jerusalem and Babil, 568 years before Jesus Christ, depicting the enslavement of the Jews by the Babylonians with its own patriotic uneasiness; converting an oppression into the embracing of Judaic monotheism. And, pandemonium broke lose when the celebrated chorus declared:

"Va, pensiero sull'ali dorate"
(You, thought, that flies with the gilded wings!)

"This Moroni plate, just the same, will give you a sort of new independence, a sense of belonging, freedom, a celestial union, rather a recognition, as *The Chorus of Slaves* had sung at the famous – newly restored – Scala Theatre, soon after the Second World War and the Declaration of the Republic in Italy, on A.C. December 26, 1946. That should have been the last cry, the last begging and praying for freedom from all unnecessary passions, killings, envies, submissions but love for God, love for each other. Plus the fact that, at the end of the Act IV, the Jewish head priest, Zaccaria, blesses the King Nabukko who saved all the slaves all of whom, including his own daughter Fenena, were about to be executed at the temple, wishing a prosperous and eternal life. Anyway, the final choice of music is yours. Those were my mere suggestions.

"Well, my dear friends, God bless all of us, and I wish you an eternal togetherness too.

See you tomorrow at the temple."

Vox populi vox Dei!
(The voice of people, the voice of God!)